Mirror Bound

BOOKS BY RHIANNON HELD

THE SILVER SERIES
Silver
Tarnished
Reflected
Wolfsbane
Death-Touched

STAND ALONE
Hound and Key

Mirror Bound

Rhiannon Held

To Grandad
J. Kenneth Sanderson
January 2, 1919–September 21, 2016
For he was a storyteller too

1

When Verity and Dakota approached the small park, Verity spotted three mantas immediately. To Verity's eyes, as a creature of the mirror realm herself, the mantas looked like spun glass, shimmering like liquid in the middle and refracting into rainbows at the edges. One manta spotted them and left the floating group to bank in their direction. It swerved off at the last moment, the tips of its long, flat wings rippling in a way that evoked the ocean-going animal it had been nicknamed for.

"Three," Verity called after Dakota as the woman jogged for the edge of the park where lawn met sidewalk along the road. They'd found a good location for this hunt: a patch of tall, urban forest abutted the park on two sides, and the back of a library formed the third, leaving only the sidewalk for Dakota to block off with an illusion.

The lazy orange cast to the sunlight, this late in the day, made Dakota look especially golden. It wasn't just the tint of her hair, but the confidence of her movements as she lifted one hand in acknowledgment of Verity's count. She paced along the concrete, dragging the glow of an illusion spell behind her. It would show caution tape, or something similar, Verity assumed, to keep people out as well as hiding the coming light show.

Verity planted herself on the lawn near the library and did a quick scan for innocent bystanders as Dakota worked. No one so far, after the library's closing time and in the middle of the dinner hour on a chill fall day. Good. Mantas could kill a human, in theory, if they caught one sufficiently unaware. The mantas who made it through to this realm tended to only bumble around, disoriented, and Dakota was paid to hunt them mostly to prevent panic from people encountering invisible monsters, but it never hurt to be careful.

The group of three mantas roiled as three more zipped in from the trees to join them. Six? There couldn't possibly be that many. In the mirror realm, the mantas traveled in flocks of up to ten, but only a few could slip through the boundary between realms at any time. Before tonight, the most Dakota had ever fought at once had been three. The anxious movement of the flock kept increasing until one broke free and buzzed right for Dakota's head as she returned from setting the illusion.

Her reactions were good enough that she sensed something was wrong and ducked what was to her an invisible presence before Verity finished shouting her warning. Dakota jerked out her modified paintball pistol as the manta swerved off. She settled into a looser stance, paintball pistol up, ready to burst into motion at the right moment.

When the manta curved back around toward her, she shot, missing it by only a narrow margin. The creature's dodge dipped it into a beam of the day's last sunlight that lanced between the shadows of two great evergreens. The light caught the manta, refracting into a flash visible even to human eyes. Dakota nailed the creature with a blue splotch square on the centerline of its body. The electricity spell bound to the paintball exploded with an audible pop and a singed smell. The manta dropped. One down.

Verity tucked her hands into the pockets of her hand-me-down fleece jacket and returned to her regular hunt role, keeping half an eye on the mantas, and another half out for approaching bystanders. Maybe she could convince Dakota to let her teleport them home after this hunt. It would save time, after all. None of the new team members Dakota had been accumulating lately could offer anything like it, either.

And the binding spell that kept her human, kept her under Dakota's control—however reluctant that control was—would shred just a tiny bit more in the act of teleporting. Verity glanced sideways at the library building. With the sun so low, one of the windows might provide the flawless reflection she needed.

She shouldn't let herself get distracted, though. Verity refocused on the mantas, which were twisting in an even tighter knot. Not only were there too many, but they were behaving strangely. They should have been floating in lazy arcs, senses disrupted by being outside the mirror realm. They'd adjust eventually, but the process took days for less intelligent monsters. These ones seemed riled up. Frightened?

Dakota brought an explosion spell into being in her hand. She tossed it up, and the bodies of the three closest mantas exploded briefly with bluish light, like shining a bright beam into a faceted crystal. Dakota squeezed off shots as fast as she could, trying to tag each one with paint even if she couldn't get the electricity burst central enough to drop them. Three went down in succession, and Verity called out to confirm the kills.

Shimmering movement in the trees caught Verity's attention. She shifted her position to try to get a better angle on it. Had she lost track of one of the mantas? No, four on the ground, two in the air. But there *was* something there.

Verity broke into a run toward the trees. A jogging path revealed itself fully between two bushes as she approached it straight on. A woman, dressed in the blinding colors of fashionable athletic-wear, folded silently to the ground. A manta was spread across her face and upper body, another at her side, fouling whatever instinctive defense she might have attempted with her arms.

"No—" Verity wasn't sure why she shouted. The human couldn't hear her. The woman's brain was dark, the manta having eaten her living electricity even if she could have come back from the suffocation. But that wasn't *right*. In the mirror realm, mantas were a danger to those of her people who slept outdoors without precautions, but if one attacked you while you were aware, you could generally fight it off.

Then again, attacked by an invisible monster she didn't know existed, the human wouldn't have been very aware, Verity realized with a sick feeling.

Dakota whirled when Verity yelled and arrived a few steps behind her. The manta on the human's side took to the air, but Dakota shot the manta on the woman's face before it could rise off its prey, twice, three times. She fell to her knees and hauled the limp corpse off, pounded the woman's chest in a motion Verity vaguely recognized from television. Something to do with the heart, but of course the heart wasn't the problem. "Dakota, she's dead, you have to—"

Dakota gasped something inarticulately negative. Verity hauled at Dakota's shoulder, but the woman was apparently too much in shock to hear her. She kept pounding.

Verity fumbled out her own paintball gun from the back of her jeans and pointed it at the roiling flock as a whole. If only she wasn't such a terrible shot, hadn't relied on Dakota so much. She whistled a keep-away call, as she would have done at home. Rather than scattering them, it only seemed to rile the mantas more. They swerved away, gathered themselves, then bore down on her and Dakota.

Verity tried to steady her breathing, failed, and aimed as best she could. One, two, three shots in close succession and none of them hit. She didn't have enough time to aim, she didn't have enough paintballs to not aim. She could do this. She'd practiced with Dakota before, for the hell of it. Another shot—there, a wing. And then the mantas were on top of her and she had no more time.

Forget breathing. She emptied the rest of the clip, two for each manta. She aimed, hoped against hope at least one of the two paintballs had hit, and aimed at the next. And the three mantas fell and she realized she'd been holding her breath only when her next inhalation made it mostly possible to think again.

Verity stomped each manta several times to make sure they didn't move. Silvery blood from her bootprints on the fragile wings oozed out into liquid-metallic pools between grass blades still wet from the day's earlier drizzle. If only she hadn't been bound human, she'd have consumed their lifeforce to make sure they were fully gone. But who knew what the electricity that powered a creature's neurons would taste like after being zapped, anyway.

A car door slammed in the library parking lot. A man and a woman were wrangling their luggage beside a taxi. Verity checked Dakota to find her searching for the dead woman's pulse as if it would have spontaneously reappeared in the last few minutes. All right. Up to her, then. She shoved her gun away, made sure the hem of her fleece hid it, pulled out her cheap phone, and switched it to video camera mode for their backup cover story. If only her damn binding didn't prevent her from lying along with everything else, this would have been so much easier. *Oh, sorry, did we scare you? It's our college film project, weren't those special effects great?*

But if she tried to say that, the binding would stop her, and she'd be left stuttering or silent, looking even more suspicious as she tried to find something she *could* say. The only solution she'd found was to think up something misleading but true ahead of time, and she had little enough time for that now. Verity practiced lines in her head as she jogged across the wet lawn to meet the newcomers. *Think of the hits it would get if I were to upload this footage…*

"Hello?" the woman called out as the taxi pulled away. The man followed her to the sidewalk along the edge of the park, where they left their wheeled suitcases before continuing toward Verity. They both had pale skin and red hair too orange in tone to be fashionable, so Verity presumed it was natural. Siblings? Related, almost certainly.

Verity set her teeth and tried an insincere smile. Her binding didn't prevent that, at least. "Can I help you guys?"

The woman, the younger of the two, held out a hand soothingly. A rain jacket disguised her shape, but her hair was short, in a cut that managed to look sharp and confident, rather than cutesy, with her delicate features. "Don't worry. Power is knowledge. We're looking for Dakota. Archivist Khare sent us. And the young woman who answered the phone at the house said we should come straight here in case you needed help?"

Her voice trailed upward at the last minute and she peered past Verity.

Mages, then, if they knew the passphrase. Verity wished there was a way to distinguish mages from regular humans simply by looking. Though the mention of an Archivist was a giveaway as well. The mages of the Archives might have kept their titles from when they were merely information collectors, but they'd been using that information to act as a de facto governing body for centuries. "Dakota's kind of busy at the moment—"

To say the least. Verity had no idea why these mages were here, but someone needed to get rid of them, and Dakota clearly wasn't currently up to the job. At least they didn't seem to know who she was—when mages realized she wasn't human, they almost always lapsed into a type of covert stare she'd become intimately familiar with.

Verity focused on Dakota herself, gauging if the situation was obvious from this distance. The dead woman's running pants and shoes were clear, but why Dakota knelt with head bowed over her was less so. Verity supposed Dakota would have to come clean to the Archivists soon enough about what had happened, as they were her bosses, but it was no business of random mages.

Running interference for Dakota was way beyond her job description, though. Especially since that job description was "bound against her will, and helping out the woman holding the leash for lack of anything better to do." Because at least Dakota treated her like a person, when almost no one else did.

And of course Verity was also helping because, in an abstract sense, if regular humans discovered they were in danger from invisible mirror realm monsters and panicked, that was good for neither the mages, nor Verity now she was living with them.

Though that situation was suddenly much less abstract.

"Look, now's a terrible time," she said, refocusing on the strangers. "Can you come back later?" She strode back to Dakota, and of course they followed. She ignored them.

"Dakota." Verity dragged the woman bodily to her feet, turned her to face her. "We've got to deal with the dead mantas before anyone else shows up."

The new woman gasped, maybe when the jogger's unnatural stillness dawned on her. She pointed to the shapes probably vaguely visible to her as silvery blood, crushed grass, and paintball spatters. "God, were those...phantoms?"

"Mirror realm creatures. Or just monsters, if you prefer. Phantoms are from the mirror realm, but they're something else," Verity snapped. Something like her. She should be used to mistakes like that by now, she supposed. Except for the most powerful Archivists who formed the Quorum and their researchers and hunters, a lot of mages didn't have any contact with mirror realm creatures.

Dakota shook herself, some sense coming back into her face. "We need to call...an ambulance or something..."

"There would be nothing they could do." Verity supposed she sounded cold. It wasn't that she didn't care about human lives, but she'd been a lot closer to deaths from mirror realm creatures than Dakota had ever been. Creatures' victims couldn't be saved. "We need to get out of here, let someone else find her, and let them determine it was natural. Right?" She appealed to the strangers. They said they'd come under orders from an Archivist, maybe they knew the Quorum's policy for dealing with situations like this.

"She's right." The man spoke for the first time, and Verity felt Dakota metaphorically sit up and take notice. Verity supposed he was fairly attractive. If Dakota had a type, Verity had never been able to determine it, unless it was "passionate and generally lacks basic judgment."

His cheekbones were as delicate as his—sister's?—but his jaw was plenty strong, even clean-shaven. Out of habit, Verity searched for his asymmetries. She found one corner of his mouth that tucked a bit higher in irony when he noticed her attention and a long-healed-over piercing disrupting the outer edge of one brow. Both ears were pierced, without anything in them.

Dakota drew in a deep, shuddering breath, and some of the poise she'd begun the fight with came back. She took out her phone and started texting. "Lucy says the others have taken care of the second group of monsters—they had only two, apparently—and Gabe's on the way back with the car to pick us up." She slotted her phone away. "I'll put up an illusion to hide…the body now, so it will fade once we're gone."

"And we'll take these along to burn later so no one stumbles over invisible corpses," Verity explained for the newcomers. She grabbed a manta by the wingtip to start dragging it to the sidewalk by the parking lot, then stopped. She didn't want to leave drag-trails in the grass around the dead woman. The strangers seemed to come to the same conclusion. The woman helped her lift the manta while the man bent over another and felt out its shape before settling it over his shoulder.

Gabe arrived as Verity was turning away from her second load, so she stayed to meet him when he slammed the door to his Prius and sprinted over. "We took care of all the mantas, but one of them got a jogger before we could stop it," Verity told him.

"Thanks," Gabe said, granting her a brief nod before he kept going for Dakota. Verity was too far to hear their words, but Dakota gestured emphatically, probably an explanation of the fight, before he enfolded her into an embrace. They made a nice picture, the two of them, her golden head—though Verity was well aware that perfect shade had help—on his shoulder. Gabe's skin was deep brown, fading into the gathering night, but his regal curves still stood clear: biceps, skull under his close-cropped hair, and lips. He pulled back to kiss Dakota quickly, then embraced her again.

Verity looked around for a distraction from all the charming reassurance going on. Being useful to Dakota gave her the chance to teleport, and if nothing else it was better than pure imprisonment. But with the numbers of monsters rising, and Dakota accepting others' help on hunts, Verity was starting to wonder how long before Dakota decided Verity was more troublesome than useful. Especially when the alternative included one of the hot guys she was banging on and off.

Verity gritted her teeth. The way to address that was to continue to be noticeably useful. If she popped the car's trunk from inside she could start loading. The strangers forestalled her, though. With all the mantas piled up, the woman approached Verity again, the man following once more. "I'm Siobhan Dubois, this is my brother Davin. I wish we could have met in better circumstances."

Verity was at a loss, briefly. Mages didn't usually introduce themselves to her. But of course they were still treating her as a human. "I'm Verity." She let her hands fall open at her sides, an invitation to examine her that Davin took her up on. Six years bound into human form had introduced asymmetries into her own face, but she knew she still flummoxed people when they tried to place her. With very light brown skin and black hair with just a hint of wave, was she a mixture including Mediterranean? Middle Eastern? Hispanic, Indian? Less African, or more Native American? Around here near the liberal big city, people rarely pushed after "where are you from?" yielded a "Seattle," but she could tell from the length of their stares they wanted to.

Davin cast a speaking glance up to the illusion covering the jogger. "Is this the first time—?"

"Yes." That came out too fast and defensive, so Verity tried again. "Dakota handled the monsters around here on her own easily for years. It's only in the last few months, there've been so many more and she's needed a team. And then this is only the second time we've had to split the team because there were two clumps of monsters spotted at once. We don't know what's causing it—and now they're behaving weird—"

Siobhan's brows rose. "Dakota took all these down on her own?"

"Well, three were my kills this time." Maybe it was a moment of weakness from the sour adrenaline, but Verity let herself bask in Siobhan's impressed expression. She could almost imagine herself meeting these new mages as the person she'd been in her youth, when the grounded realm was somewhere exciting to explore, and her curiosity had drawn her here to interact with humans for the fun of it. When she'd been the phantom most experienced with the grounded realm in her whole town, before that experience had gotten her offered a mission. Before that mission had gotten her discovered. And then bound. "Lucky shots. Plural. Since I needed so many of them."

Siobhan laughed and Verity joined her, knowing the stress had made her punchy and not caring. Dakota looked at them both funny as she and Gabe arrived.

Verity introduced the siblings, pausing over Siobhan's name. "And…Shuh-vahn?" Verity glanced over at the woman and got a nod of confirmation. "The Archivists sent them. And then Lucy sent them here, I presume." She couldn't think of any other young woman who would be answering the house phone.

"Archivist Khare sent us to—" Siobhan began.

Gabe stepped past Verity, offering his hand to Siobhan. "To help? Good. We need it." He shook Davin's hand next. "The number of monsters coming through from the mirror realm has been going off the charts."

Rather than try to break back into the conversation, Verity turned to the car again. Davin's voice stopped her, low enough not to disrupt the parallel conversation among the others. "Are you doing okay?"

She frowned at him. "What?"

"A woman died. I just wanted to make sure you're—"

Apparently Davin hadn't been quiet enough, because Gabe turned away from Siobhan. "But Verity's not human." His tone wasn't accusatory, just surprised that Davin would even consider asking the question. That didn't really make it sting less.

Dakota, predictably, stumbled in with what were presumably the best of intentions. "Well, yes, she's a phantom, but you don't need to worry. She's not—a monster or anything. Phantoms versus monsters like those—" She indicated the pile of mantas. "In the mirror realm, they're like humans versus animals here."

Verity lifted her wrist. An embossed leather cuff bracelet hid the stainless steel chain that held the binding spell, since that was too tight to be fashionable and she didn't like one more odd note about her appearance among regular humans. "Bound up all safe, don't worry." The siblings were apparently too polite to draw back, but she caught Davin's attention sharpening. It wasn't quite the look she'd been expecting, but close enough. Now they'd start to fear or dismiss her.

Just so long as they didn't shoot her in the back.

Rather than listen to any further verbal flailing on Dakota's part, Verity grabbed a manta corpse and dragged it to the car, since she didn't have to worry about marks on the pavement. She'd had longer to enjoy the newcomers assuming she was a person than usual, she supposed. So be it. If it hadn't been Gabe now, Dakota would have clued them in soon enough, out of some kind of misplaced impulse to warn them not to treat Verity any differently. Which was the supreme irony that was Dakota all over.

The manta corpses from the second fight were piled on a tarp inside the trunk. A long, cheap mirror was tucked out of harm's way against the back of the backseat, a placement Verity was glad to see. For her to use them, they had to be flawless and big enough an adult could technically squeeze through, and while the modern age was full of flawless mirrors, it got expensive to buy new ones if people let them get cracked all the time.

The mirror gave her an idea. Rather than wrestle her corpse up, Verity drew the mirror out, averted her gaze so as not to be taunted with a connection to home, and set it reflective side down against the side of the car. At least some small use could come out of tonight, even if Verity would never have chosen to make that trade for a human life. She hurried back to Dakota and jumped into the next pause in the conversation. "We could probably fit everyone into the car, but we could never manage the luggage. I should teleport someone home."

Siobhan winced, embarrassed. "We can call another taxi—"

Dakota waved that away. "No, she's right. I'll go home with her, and that will leave room. Gabe, as the last one out, would you do a sweep to make sure nothing looks weird around here before you leave?" When he nodded, Dakota joined Verity.

"I'll go with you." Davin seemed to startle his sister as much as everyone else with his words. He nodded to their luggage. "So no one gets squished." He twisted his sister's suitcase to roll it over to the car's back door in tandem with his own.

"The screwed-up visual input makes some people feel sick on their first couple times through," Verity warned him, while the others seemed to still be trying to decide if he was serious. She figured he probably wanted to start early with making a favorable impression on the famous Dakota in case he wanted to turn suitor later on.

"I think it's actually kind of exciting, in a roller-coaster kind of way." Dakota grinned and gestured Davin over to the mirror. She flipped it over for them. Verity forced herself to look at the reflection long enough to check for cracks.

She extended an arm toward Davin. "Hand." When he complied and clasped hers, his grip—just a bit too tight—gave the lie to his nonchalance. Verity wasn't sure what he would consider reassuring, or if he'd accept reassurance from the phantom, but she could at least give him an idea of what to expect. "Two steps in a straight line. One in, one out. You can make it on one breath, or even close your eyes if you need to. I'm the one guiding us."

Dakota took Verity's other hand without being directed. Verity kept her gaze on Davin. "Ready?" He dipped his chin in a minimal nod.

"One..." Verity stepped forward. To her eyes, it seemed as if her foot landed on something that moved so quickly, so unpredictably, that it was impossible to see their surroundings as more than a blur. Or maybe they stepped onto the only stable patch in a chaotic, swirling world. The fading-toward-twilight colors of the parking lot, their own reflected faces, darted away so quickly that they stretched into lines, only these were lines that shivered in the peripheral vision, like something was there that couldn't quite be seen. Or a nothing was there that shouldn't be seen.

And it wasn't home. Verity didn't know if she was grateful to not be taunted with glimpses, or if her homesickness could have been assuaged with tiny sips now and then. If she'd been traveling home, the colors would have solidified, settled into a new pattern, more self-contained than the grounded realm where everything was connected to everything else. She'd have left this formless stuff and stepped into her town. But she wasn't traveling home.

Second step. Lucy, with her talent for unusual connections, had said once it was like climbing an escalator. Verity had immediately gone to the mall with that in mind to test it. Lucy had been right. Stepping out of a teleport was like climbing with the escalator and not noticing when you reached the top. You strode out onto nothing and the place you'd left spat you out even farther, and you stumbled. Always.

Verity knew how to roll with it, though. "Two," she said as they emerged into the living room of Dakota's house. She caught her balance in time to pull against the jerk Davin's stumble put on her grip. Dakota caught herself without help and dropped Verity's hand.

After that, she lingered, seeming to have lost her sense of purpose. Verity wondered if she was seeing the dead woman's face in her mind. "You could go update the map," Verity suggested. Dakota started, nodded, then strode away.

Verity had to flex her fingers before Davin let go. Even then, he kept staring at the mirror over the mantel above the absurdly shallow little gas fireplace with the 2-D ceramic logs. She presumed he was wondering why they were standing on the floor rather than clambering down out of the mirror. "Don't be so literal."

That got his attention. He shifted his stare to her, question in his expression. She didn't make him articulate it. "You're wondering why we didn't have to wiggle through the physical frame of the mirror? It's a connection, not a door. A larger mirror is a stronger connection, but we're not actually stepping into *it*, we're stepping into the universe next door." Verity fidgeted with her cuff. The stress on the binding spell always made her feel like the metal chain was cutting into her skin hard enough to bruise. She knew if she looked she wouldn't see anything, though.

She frowned at Davin when he remained silent. "You okay? Bathroom's that way." She pointed down the hall. "First door to the east."

Davin shook his head and some life came back into his expression, though not enough for a smile. "I'm fine. That was... interesting." He focused on her face for a second. "Thanks." Then he did head for the bathroom.

Now Verity found herself lingering without a purpose as well. She supposed that when the others got back, they'd do some kind of debrief—more informal than not, given that Dakota still wasn't used to hunting with anyone else and probably wouldn't think to lead one properly. No one would care about Verity's opinions, but she could at least remind them how useful her teleporting had turned out to be. If this pace of monsters kept up, and she teleported to even half the hunts, her binding would be worn away in no time. And she'd be free.

Verity strode in the direction Dakota had gone. No need to get ahead of herself.

2

Dakota already had their poster-sized, laminated map of the city spread out on the dining table when Verity arrived. Verity glanced over it and munched a handful of marshmallow cereal from the box she'd snagged from the kitchen on the way in. With the debriefing to come, it might be quite a while until dinner.

Thinking of the newcomers who would undoubtedly be joining them soon, Verity scanned the room and found not too much dust. At least the dining room was furnished well, making it more presentable for guests than the rest of the house. The long, light wood table and chairs were expensive, high quality enough to stand heavy use, and with clean enough lines they could watch fashions come and go without causing embarrassment. They'd belonged to Vasily, Dakota's mentor who'd owned the house before her, of course. Dakota, even had she not been perpetually strapped for cash, prioritized comfort. The furniture she'd brought with her for her bedroom, though not actively ugly, sagged in every possible dimension.

Dakota frowned over the map, probably searching for the

park. The map already had a spattering of red dots next to tiny numbers, the time, date, and number of monsters encountered at each location. So far, there was still space to write the information on the map, but it wouldn't be long before the dots got too numerous in some areas for that. Dakota selected a black marker, inscribed an "X" over the park, and then notated it with a "1." One death, Verity presumed. Grant that they wouldn't have to mark more.

"I still don't see any patterns. Maybe Lucy's computer program will spit out something this time, though," Dakota said, heavily.

"They were definitely upset for some reason, when they haven't been before. Make sure Lucy adds that to the data." Verity set the cereal box aside and joined Dakota in front of the map. "As for any other pattern—they do fly. So a map wouldn't really show where they were coming from. And they're so confused when they first arrive, we can't really backtrack based on a hunting pattern." And even their hunting patterns were skewed—they seemed to be able to smell mages' magic and were attracted to it, so while Dakota hunted by going to the general vicinity of reported monsters, once she arrived, they tended to come to investigate her.

Dakota's pocket gave the low hum of a cell phone still on vibrate after the hunt. She pulled it out and Verity saw MARGARET STILES on the screen over her shoulder. Dakota hissed a curse under breath, and Verity vehemently agreed with the sentiment. How had Archivist Stiles found out what happened so damn fast? The Quorum used to only require monthly reports from Dakota, and while they had been calling after each hunt since the monster numbers had started climbing, usually they waited a day or two to demand the debriefing.

Dakota answered and barely got her greeting out before she had to listen intently. Verity's instinct was to edge closer to hear the other side of the conversation, so she made herself edge back instead. She needed to stay as far out of this as possible, and a little physical distance might help remind Dakota of that. Dakota dropped in a few "yes"s and a "that's right," apparently in response to Archivist Stiles' summation of the hunt's events. So the Archivist's information was not only almost impossibly fresh, it seemed it was pretty detailed.

Someone must have called her, after they left the park. Someone like one of the newcomers. Verity would bet money that of the two of them, it had been Davin. Dakota distracted her before she could follow that train of thought any further, though. "No, she was a big help," Dakota said, set her phone on the table, and stabbed the button to switch it to speaker. "She's here too."

Verity shook her head desperately at Dakota, receiving a look that seemed to be begging for help in return. What did Dakota imagine Verity could say to Stiles to defend herself? The Archivist had already made up her mind about the scary phantom, that had been more than clear in past calls. *Was the phantom a hindrance? Do you feel up to the responsibility of being a hunter and watching the phantom at the same time?* Verity wasn't stupid, she could tell Stiles wanted her under the Quorum's direct control.

"The fact remains that an innocent woman was killed, Dakota. If everything went as planned in the hunt, how could that have happened? You and the phantom were the only ones there." Stiles' tone was brisk, somehow worse for holding no audible anger.

"There were too many mantas," Verity said, trying to sound

small and unthreatening. If she had to stay with someone, she wanted it to be Dakota, not Stiles and the Quorum. She couldn't think of anything else to say, especially with her heartbeat rising loudly in her ears. An impassioned defense was hardly likely to convince the Quorum to return to their former benign dismissal of her situation.

"It was my fault." Dakota spoke ostensibly to the phone, but more to the floor at her feet. "I was too focused on the mantas closest to me. Verity was the one who saw the danger first."

Verity silently urged Dakota on. That was why Dakota needed her, because she was familiar with the monsters, could see them so easily...but like so much of Dakota's treatment of her, the defense only went so far and then stopped frustratingly short.

"Ah," Stiles said, after letting Dakota's silence continue a beat too long. "There will be no more deaths, do you understand? Or the Quorum will be forced to take more serious action."

"I understand," Dakota said. Stiles ended the call before Dakota even reached for her own phone.

Verity let out a breath in a rush and turned away to press the heels of her palms to her eyes. She *had* her escape in her grasp, as teleporting wore away the binding spell, but how long would that take? How much time did she have left before the Quorum confiscated her like a dangerous animal? She doubted they'd ask her to hop around even if by some miracle they didn't notice the state of her binding.

And what about the newcomers? Were they just here to watch for her to make a confiscation-worthy mistake and report it back to Stiles, or for some other reason? Maybe to trick her into making that mistake?

Or maybe they were here to solve the problem much more simply, and shoot her in the back. Verity had read that case file, about a hunter in Europe, when Dakota left it lying around her desk. A phantom had escaped to this realm, pursued by mantas, and mysteriously expired in the course of the fight between hunter and monsters. The file said the mantas finished her off before the hunter could help, but it also mentioned the phantom had unspecified "wounds." Mantas had no teeth, no claws, nothing to make wounds *with*. Verity could read between the lines. She didn't doubt the gunshot had been accidental, but that didn't make the phantom less dead. When fighting dangerous monsters, you didn't worry too much about hitting innocent monsters. And when those innocent monsters started looking like a problem, putting them down might well seem like a good solution.

Dakota touched her shoulder from behind, and Verity lowered her hands from her eyes, turned reluctantly to her. "I'm glad you were there," Dakota said, the weight of her seriousness making her shoulders slump.

"You're welcome." Verity summoned something at least smile-adjacent. Dakota wouldn't shoot her. Or let anyone else do it. That was something. That meant Verity only had to worry about Dakota not fighting hard enough to keep her, especially now she was accumulating a shiny new team of humans to help her. And the logistics of more people hunting did mean more opportunities to show the usefulness of teleporting. If nothing else, Verity could focus on racking up as many trips as she could before her situation changed for the worse.

Speaking of the team, Lucy burst into the room. Seeing Verity, she hesitated, but then continued her rush forward to hug Dakota from the other side. "Thank God you're all right! I heard someone got hurt." Her silky black hair fanned over Dakota's shoulder. Next to Dakota she should have looked short, but she moved with a physical confidence that had nothing to do with combat and everything to do with never hesitating because she had places to be and information to gather.

Dakota hugged Lucy back, briefly squeezing her eyes closed, maybe against tears. "Someone got dead. Some—jogger, I don't even know her name…"

Lucy let go and pulled out her phone. "I'll set up an alert for when the news is posted. I'd do that anyway, because the Archivists want to track anything mage-related to make sure nothing's going awry with the cover story. But once they release her name, I'll look her up to see if there's…anything anonymous we can do. To help her family." Her voice wavered, and she looked very young for a moment. Verity tended to forget that she was only twenty-one, to Dakota's twenty-five. Everyone else Dakota had tapped for backup was in their late twenties. But Lucy had dropped out of Archivist training early and moved home, which was why she was available to be tapped.

"I'd have helped her family by saving her. That's my *job*, Lucy. To make sure that the mirror realm monsters don't hurt anyone. The Quorum doesn't pay me the stipend for practicing my target-shooting." Dakota retrieved the marker and darkened the black mark on the map in frustration.

"There were *seven* of them. However much Stiles bitches, I'm sure that's more than any other hunter has had to deal with," Verity said. She wrested the marker from Dakota and capped it.

"You killed seven all alone?" Lucy asked Dakota, even more wide-eyed now.

"I wasn't alone, Verity helped." Dakota offered Verity a weak smile, while Lucy eyed her nervously, as if she couldn't imagine Verity killing monsters without imagining her killing humans as well.

Verity hurried to forestall any more well-intentioned defense from Dakota. "Moral support," she joked, thinly. None of the new team members knew what to do with her, and Lucy was the one who wavered closest to fear. She didn't want to push the young woman, make her go running to the Archivists demanding they do something. She tugged the map down the table a little and acted as if she was absorbed in studying it, to give Lucy an excuse to go back to ignoring her again.

Siobhan peeked into the dining room with the slight diffidence of a guest who didn't know where they were supposed to be, and relaxed when she saw Dakota. Her brother followed silently. He didn't seem to be paying attention to Verity more than anyone else, but Verity couldn't watch him for that attention for long without drawing notice herself. His observant manner did suggest he was here to catch her getting into trouble, not create it himself.

And she wasn't going to get into any trouble. She may have been sent here as a spy, but she didn't consider herself one anymore. She'd accepted the mission knowing it could be a long one, but she hadn't planned on being bound or abandoned by her people. Then her original target had passed her on to Dakota, who had nothing to hide. Davin couldn't catch her spying when she wasn't doing any. She'd still avoid him with extreme prejudice, though.

"Who...?" Lucy asked, seeing the newcomers. Understanding dawned in her expression after a beat. "Oh! You guys are the ones I sent out to help." She twisted back to Dakota. "Was that okay? I wasn't sure, but since you were alone—"

"No, it was fine. They helped clean up." Dakota smiled wan-ly and performed the introductions between Lucy and the siblings. She paused at the end, as if waiting for something. Verity couldn't figure out what until Davin filled it in.

"We're a binding pair. She's the crafter and I'm the sensitive." Davin tipped his head to his sister, then rocked a step closer to Verity. "I'm actually curious about that rather elegant binding spell. May I look at it?" He held out his hand to Verity.

Her heart spun up to a panicked rate, ready for evasive action she couldn't take without looking even more suspicious. A binding mage? That had to be the worst possible person they could have sent. What if he noticed that her binding spell was starting to wear through? Not only would that give him more than enough to report to Stiles, he and his sister could repair the binding even before she was dragged away.

But Dakota had never noticed the wear, and while she was unobservant, she did see Verity every day. What if the wear wasn't obvious, and Verity made Davin suspicious by trying to hide the spell?

Dakota nodded in confusion, but Davin kept looking at Verity's face instead. Did they honestly expect her to agree to this? She didn't know how to react, so she stayed frozen, heart having reached a point where she could barely breathe. After another beat without an objection, he gently lifted her wrist.

Dakota spoke in the background, something about how useful a binding spell pair would be, though she could do simple binding spells on her own. It dawned on Verity that her panic was moot; Davin had had plenty of time to observe the binding at the park. What happened next was out of her hands. That didn't calm her heart, though. In fact, it made it worse. Her muscles ached to *run*, worse than they had since the very beginning, when she *had* run, only to find that she couldn't travel home to the mirror realm or even teleport within the grounded realm without the one who held her binding. And when that person called her back, she had to obey.

This time, Verity didn't run. Focusing on not-running helped a little, draining away the energy that urged her to other stupid actions. She walked a chain of logic back to a state something like calm. If he could see the binding was worn, he would have noticed already. If he'd noticed already, he would have told Stiles when he reported the jogger's death. Stiles hadn't taken control of her, so Davin must not have seen the wear.

"Did you make it?" Davin looked over at Dakota and didn't add any comment about the spell's condition. Verity dared to take a deep breath, then another. So she had a little more time. Grant that it would be enough.

"My mentor, Vasily, crafted it. He's the one who found Verity. Then when he had to go away for a while, he asked me to take care of her." Dakota grimaced.

Relief made Verity punchy, and she snorted when she shouldn't have. "Take care of her," like Verity was his pet cat. Everyone looked at her, and she scrambled to cover it. "He's hiding, you mean. Out in his fortress of solitude."

Davin's brows lifted. "With a truth binding that allows hyperbole and metaphor. Impressive."

"Some truth bindings don't?" Verity took a moment to contemplate a life with one of *those*, and couldn't suppress a flash of nausea.

"The simplest ones are fairly pedantic about their definitions, yes. But nothing about this spell is simple." Davin sketched shapes in the air, presumably something to do with whatever he saw as a sensitive. The same senses that allowed Verity to see all mirror realm creatures let her see spells as well, but only as faint glows. She understood that was how sensitive mages experienced spells outside of the aptitude they'd been trained in, like how Davin would see an illusion spell. "It combines multiple bindings with a *permanent* geas..."

Dakota squinted at Verity's wrist. "What? Geas?" Her gaze flicked to Davin's face, and even without him reacting to, or perhaps even realizing, her ignorance yet, she started playing it off. "Obviously, I can't be an expert in the more detailed spells..."

Lucy stepped in smoothly, apparently recognizing her cue. Lucy's Archives training: obviously designed to make her into Dakota's magic-related smartphone. "The class of binding spells should more properly be known as compulsions. Going from simple to complex, it begins with binding spells, which *prohibit* actions, and moves to geasa, which *force* actions. Bindings are negative, geasa are positive. Abstractly, the progression makes sense, because it takes much more power and finesse to make someone do something they don't want to do than it does to just prevent them from doing something. And then it's nearly impossible to make a permanent geas, even if the Archivists didn't prohibit them without permission."

"So Verity's obedience is a geas," Davin said.

"To Dakota." Verity made sure everyone knew that the instant they found out about the obedience. "Only to Dakota."

"I try not to use it very much. Or at all," Dakota hurried to specify. True enough, Verity supposed. Dakota did try to be a good...caretaker. Master. Whatever the word was. She'd tried to break the binding herself back when she first inherited Verity, but when she couldn't, she'd relapsed into following Vasily's orders and didn't take it any further. Verity figured Dakota could have researched and taught herself to break a binding ten times as complex by now, but Vasily had said not to mess with the spell. To "protect" Verity. Ha.

Davin continued without comment. "And the truth spell is a binding, since it prevents her from telling lies, but doesn't force her to tell the truth."

Siobhan elbowed her brother in the ribs. "Enough about bindings. Have you forgotten who we're talking to?" She beamed at Dakota.

Verity couldn't tell if Siobhan was being ironic, but in case she was serious, she hurried to head off any fawning with obvious irony. "Indeed, she walks among us, the only living mage known to be both a crafter and a sensitive for all specialties." Which was technically true, because very few knew about the other mage of that kind.

Dakota flushed and looked at the table. "Verity, please." Her humility only made people like her more, of course. If Davin wanted to fall in lust with Dakota, he'd have to take a number.

"Does the mage talent rub off?" Siobhan leaned in and touched Dakota's shoulder with a fingertip. She peered around. "Damn. Still not seeing any magic. I'll have to settle for your autograph."

Dakota was starting to look a little hunted, so Siobhan took pity on her. "I'm kidding. Still, it's an honor to work with you."

Speaking of working with Dakota, someone needed to consider the logistical details. Verity would have much rather gotten rid of the siblings entirely, but that was clearly not in the cards. "How long are you guys going to be here for?" Verity asked. "The nearest hotel—"

"No, you should stay here." Dakota gestured widely in invitation, then shrugged apologetically. "Unless you'd prefer not to. We're a little crowded right now, but we could convert Vasily's old workroom back into a bedroom with an air mattress on the floor or something."

"We're here until you don't need us anymore, so we'd appreciate the space." Davin dipped his head in gratitude. Verity resisted the urge to fidget with her cuff or hide it behind her back. Just what she needed, to be on guard every single moment, worrying that her behavior could be interpreted as suspicious, wondering whether he saw the wear in her spell yet.

Heavy footsteps sounded in the hall, and Lance strode in. He was still wearing his pair of long knives over his back, and his long black coat flapped around his ankles with each step. His paleness, against the dark hair flopping into his eyes, seemed almost sickly, but he'd turned what could have been computer nerd skinniness into wiry strength. "Dakota!" He opened his arms to her, and she fell into them. "I heard about what happened. It's not your fault. You can only protect humans so far."

Dakota protested again, low-voiced, but Lance cut off her words with a kiss. He looked ready to hold it indefinitely, but Dakota pulled away when Siobhan shifted uncomfortably and glanced around as if wondering if she should give them the room. Given the kiss with Gabe earlier, she was probably also wondering what Dakota's relationship was with each man.

Verity just wondered if Dakota could ever bring herself to pick one of her suitors. She was dating both, on and off, sleeping with both, on and off…but both of them seemed to hold out hope for an eventual exclusive relationship. Verity preferred Gabe herself, because though he frequently had a stick up his ass when it came to doing things by the book, at least he was polite to her. And Gabe being boring was better than how Lance self-consciously tried to turn brooding into something stylish.

"Who are they?" Lance demanded, finally acknowledging the siblings. He hadn't looked surprised when he entered, so Verity suspected he already knew, he just wanted to force them to justify themselves.

Davin was the one to repeat the introductions this time. Lance snorted. "What kind of Celtic surname is Dubois?" He looked Davin right in the eye, perhaps to emphasize his additional few inches of height.

"The kind that isn't. It's French. From Belgium. Grandparents came from there." Siobhan barged in between the men to shake Lance's hand. "When Davin was born he had this little red puff of hair, though," she gestured, and Davin looked pained, "so they went with the Celtic name. And then they had to follow the pattern with me. But I can do a mean Irish accent." She doffed some kind of imaginary hat, then intoned: "They're after me lucky charms!"

"Across the world, real Irish people are arranging for hitmen," Davin said, clapping a heavy hand on his sister's shoulder. "Should we go see about setting up that air mattress?" He spoke to Dakota and completely ignored Lance. His tone was so similar for both comments, Verity wondered if anyone else realized that the first one had been amused, not annoyed, with his sister. At least, she thought it had.

"They're staying?" Lance gave Dakota an incredulous glance, then crossed his arms. "And helping in hunts too, I suppose? We don't need more people stumbling around, getting in the way."

"Someone died, Lance!" Dakota actually raised her voice. Given how much she usually let Lance get away with, Lucy looked a bit shocked. Lance even more so. "We need as much help as we can get. Even if we can mostly handle the sheer numbers ourselves, we need to get out *ahead* of this. We need to find out *why* there are so many, but we can't do that if we're just running from hunt to hunt."

This discussion was a familiar one, and Verity didn't have anything to contribute even if anyone besides Dakota would have listened to her. Lucy seemed to feel the same way, because she discreetly slipped out. Verity collected her cereal, stepped up beside Dakota, and put her hand on her shoulder. "I'll see about dinner," she said, and turned to go herself, munching a last few marshmallows.

"I could *tell* you why, if anyone would ever listen to me!" Lance jabbed a finger at Verity. "We're swimming in mirror realm creatures, centered around yet another mirror realm creature, and no one is going to make the connection? I will. She's attracting them. Get rid of her."

Verity froze and turned back. She'd thought she'd heard hints of this before in Lance's mutterings, but she'd hoped it was hyperbole born of frustration and exhaustion. At least Lance was so transparent you knew he was simply a dick, not working for the Quorum. She could defend herself without worrying. "Well, you're a jackass, but I don't see any donkeys following you when you walk down the street. What is that supposed to mean, 'attracting them'? How the hell am I attracting them suddenly when I've been stuck in the grounded realm for six years and they've only been showing up all at once in the past couple months?"

Lance sneered at her. "Maybe you only just figured out how to open the way for them."

"See, there's a flaw in your cunning plan of tossing around baseless accusations, and that flaw is a truth spell." Verity faced squarely up to Lance. She'd learned long ago not to protest that she shouldn't have to prove herself over and over again. That only wasted time. Better to repeat simple statements under the truth spell ad nauseam. "I didn't open the way for the monsters, or do anything at all to draw them here. I have no idea why there are suddenly so many more."

She clenched her teeth on anything further, and spoke to Dakota as if no one else was there. "Dinner?"

Dakota, predictably, looked too upset and confused to defend Verity yet. "Uh—yes. You could order..."

"I'll go shopping and cook something." Dakota's stipend from the Quorum wasn't meant to feed this many people period, never mind stretch to takeout every night. Much longer, and Verity presumed Dakota would have to get over her embarrassment at asking guests to contribute to the food budget when they'd all had to quit their jobs to manage a hunt practically every day. Either that, or they'd all die slowly from acute orange powder poisoning from all the macaroni and cheese. Dakota had seemed in real danger of that, the last time she'd miscalculated the stipend before Verity taught herself to cook. Meanwhile, shopping would get Verity out of the house and give her something productive to do, so she wouldn't have to stand around being ignored, accused, or watched.

Dakota nodded gratefully and Verity escaped. Lance wasn't done with her yet, though. She heard footsteps behind her while she was rummaging on the floor of the pantry for the canvas shopping bags.

"I didn't mean you were doing it on purpose," Lance apologized, with little hint of actual apology making it into his tone. She supposed he wanted something from her.

Sure enough, when she raised her brows at him, he pulled out a wad of cash large enough to choke a horse and peeled off a fifty. She hadn't seen that before. Nice of him not to offer to chip in before now. "I'm out of Scotch," he said.

So he wasn't actually chipping in now either, just putting in a special order. Classy. "That's not my problem," Verity said. He kept holding out the money until she snatched it to make him go away. Fine. She'd get him the cheapest bottle she could find and pocket the difference.

After Lance left, Verity took her bags and collected Dakota's car keys. She supposed she should be grateful that Dakota had taught her to drive years ago. Running a few errands, even errands for Lance, was a small price to pay for a feeling that even approached freedom. Driving away into the sunset wouldn't get her any closer to the mirror realm, and would only get her ordered to stay put once Dakota caught up with her, but it was nice to imagine she could.

She would escape, though. She still had time to try. Maybe Dakota would even discover why the monsters were increasing, fix it, ditch the team, and give Verity more time. And in the end, Verity supposed she didn't want to see the humans overrun with monsters any more than Dakota did.

3

When Verity returned with her ingredients, no one bothered her as she unloaded and got set up in the kitchen. Just her, the huge soup pot, and Dakota's aging electric stove. The kitchen was nicely large, and the fridge and microwave were new and brushed-steel gleaming. The range, on the other hand, was from Vasily's period of ownership. Since Dakota didn't use it much and it hadn't failed catastrophically, it hadn't been replaced.

Verity stirred the meat as it browned, thoughts circling endlessly back to the problem of the new binding mages. Could she approach this proactively and try the pity play on them, hope it worked well enough they wouldn't report her? When Dakota's adherence to her mentor's orders had proved her a dead end, Verity had tried the pity play on other mages once or twice in desperation before she'd noticed the effect of teleporting on the spell. She'd presented herself as the sad-eyed, pacing tiger in the crooked zoo. Humans didn't have to think a dangerous creature was safe to suffer the impulse to set it free.

Those previous attempts hadn't been with binding mages, either, so the hypothetical escape had been much more attenuated. Pretty please, convince someone else to set me free! If she could play on Davin or Siobhan's emotions, they could possibly set her free themselves. Dakota said she couldn't break the spell, but while Dakota could create every kind of spell, she could make few with a fine degree of control.

Verity pressed her lips together in a brief line. No. It wasn't worth the risk of Davin examining her spell more closely, and she doubted his loyalty to the Quorum was so easily subverted. Besides, she was no animal, and she didn't need anyone's pity.

Time to dump in the canned ingredients, but Verity could have sworn she was missing one. Footsteps sounded behind her, probably male, and she ignored them as she twisted cans to check their labels. "Kidney beans," she muttered.

"To your right," Davin said.

Verity held out her hands. Now. The physical component of her binding was on her *left* wrist because without it she would have left already. So the other one was right. She belatedly turned that way and caught Davin's bemused look.

"Left hand makes the 'L,'" Davin offered, thumbs and forefingers spread. He stepped up and touched her—actually touched her—without a hint of hesitation. Everyone else besides Dakota, she usually had to talk into even taking her hand for teleportation. Verity was so shocked, she didn't pull away.

He extended his hands to either side of hers, the inside of his upper arms pressed against the outside of hers. The touch felt comfortable, addictive in how it urged her to share it. If she leaned into him, her back would touch his chest and that would be almost like an embrace. That was enough to make comfort turn to a warmer, sharper feeling, banked low in Verity's body. She didn't let herself lean. What a report to the Quorum *that* would make.

"Left, right," he said, and lifted each hand in turn. He wore a thumb ring on his left. Verity focused on it to distract herself. It was the only jewelry he was wearing, despite his pierced ears, and Verity wondered if had some kind of significance. Didn't wedding rings go on a different finger?

"No shit. And a reference to the English alphabet is exactly what's going to be intuitive to me," Verity grumbled. She knew she should pull away from him, but somehow she didn't yet. "I know my directions, it just takes me a second. Why can't you people say north? That doesn't change." Now she was looking in the right place, she spotted the can of beans on the other side of the stove where the bulk of the pot had hidden it before.

Davin laughed and the sound wrapped around her. "You're probably right." He disengaged and retreated to lean on the far side of the counter. "Do they make you clean as well as cook?"

Verity caught herself before she ran fingertips along the outside of her opposite arm as if she could gather up residual warmth. This was getting ridiculous. She was touch-starved, yes, but not enough to turn off her brain. As for his question, matching his humor seemed the best course.

"Cinderelly, Cinderelly," she sang in her best cartoon mouse voice. "Dakota and I had chores divided more or less equally, but all the new houseguests have shot that to hell. I expect that if the hunts continue at this rate, we'll end up living in squalor sooner rather than later. I don't really feel like sitting on my ass and hurrying that process along, though."

"And it gives you some control of your situation," Davin

remarked to the counter. His tone sounded matter-of-fact, not judging.

Verity stumbled in the rhythm of the conversation, let silence fall a little too long. Was he right? Was it about control? She had little enough, but she hadn't thought of housekeeping as part of it.

She didn't want his thoughts heading in that direction, whatever his tone, though. Maybe she could draw him off with Dakota. Everyone was interested in Ms. Unique Mage, presumably even Quorum narcs. "So what do you think, now you've met the famous Dakota? Is she everything you imagined?" She finished opening all the cans in a row, and started dumping them into the pot.

"Certainly not what the wildest tales painted her." Davin settled into a more comfortable lean, like he planned to stay for a while. "What's she like to work with?"

She could reel off an answer to that question without thinking. "She's very committed to her work. She's probably the best monster hunter the Archivists have." Verity took the cans to the sink to rinse them before they went in the recycling bin.

"Now tell me what you really think." Davin held Verity's gaze without flinching when she looked up.

Verity pretended to be very involved in getting the last dot of diced tomato from the bottom of the can. She set her jaw. "You know I can't lie."

"I know that was very carefully phrased to be both true and diplomatic and it sounded like you'd said it at least a hundred times." Davin let silence fall as an invisible pressure.

"She's a terrible leader. She can handle herself, but can't really coordinate anyone else." Verity shrugged, and returned to the soup pot. He'd asked for the truth, so she'd given it to him. A beat later, she wanted to snatch the words back. What if that gave Stiles ammunition?

"So a contrast to working with Vasily?"

That was an unexpected turn to the conversation. And maybe a safer one, since Vasily had nothing to do with her current situation. "I was only with him for around nine months. He was much more experienced than her, sure."

"With magic as well?" Davin was almost *too* casual now. "You know, I've always wondered…did he bind you all by himself, or did he have someone else there to pair with him?"

Verity flexed her fingers on the spoon she'd picked up. This was a restriction she hadn't come up against for a long time. She didn't fight the evasion Vasily's standing order pushed her into. "I thought mages can pick up more than one specialty if they study every waking moment for decades." Which was true.

What was also true was that Vasily was exactly as Dakota was—only older. Where Dakota was jack of all trades and master of none, Verity wondered how many masteries Vasily had managed to carve out. She was missing any real details of his magic—in her months with him she'd been fresh out of the mirror realm, and knew almost nothing about how human magic worked. Anything she'd seen, she'd attached no importance to and forgotten by now.

But hiding even what she didn't know she'd seen had been important enough to Vasily that he'd made a deal with her. She wouldn't visibly fight the prohibition against speaking about his magic and thus make it clear that there was indeed something she was being prevented from saying. In return, he'd allowed her a single lie, nestled deep in the center of the truth spell: if someone asked if she was a spy, she could say "no."

"True enough. Most mages don't have the patience for that kind of study," Davin said, sounding lightly exasperated, and not suspicious. Good.

"Anyway, I probably don't know as much about mages as you think I do," Verity said.

"There are no phantom mages?"

Verity glowered into the soup, but that question was followed by the same waiting silence as earlier. She'd assumed it was rhetorical. "Why are you asking me? Mages have known about phantoms for a couple centuries," she deflected.

Davin huffed a small laugh. "Much we have to show for it. You enter and exit through reflections, and show up even more infrequently than the monsters do—did, I suppose. Now that the monster frequency has changed. You look slightly strange and doll-like. Some claim phantoms also have a visible magical signature you can be trained to see. Mentors usually advise mages to leave them alone, since they don't seem to cause any trouble. They might even simply be tourists. And that's it. All we've got."

Verity turned that over in her mind. She supposed he might not be understating his knowledge. "All right, I guess we're not in the grounded realm that much."

Davin shook his head. "You said that before. 'Grounded realm.' You mean here?"

"Most mages I hear talk about it use the term 'the real world,' but yes. From my perspective." Verity allowed herself an ironic smile. Davin echoed it.

"But what about at home? Aren't there mages there? I thought the mirror realm was full of wild magic."

Verity let the silence stretch this time, as she considered whether she wanted to answer. She'd already said much more than she'd ever have thought she would before he came in here and touched her. Had he done that on purpose, to foster trust?

But mages already knew the basics of the mirror realm, and Vasily had visited and must have told them more. He'd shielded her from anything other than basic questioning about whether she was a spy and if she meant harm, but she assumed that as the leaders of an organization built entirely on information, the Archivists wouldn't have stood for that if they hadn't been getting their answers from somewhere else.

Perhaps if she continued to answer questions, Davin might begin to get a picture of her as a person, rather than as a faceless phantom you'd shoot by mistake. And as a bonus, it was a chance to talk about herself, instead of the legendary Dakota. Which shouldn't have influenced her choices, but it did anyway. "Not really wild magic. It's formless magic. The mirror realm is by nature ungrounded, except where reflections from the grounded realm press it into a shape." Verity gestured that pressure. "Our explorers walk the formless space and find impressions of places that have been destroyed so we can attach them together to make the towns, which are sort of islands of space that humans would perceive as stable. And the explorers help anchor paths between towns."

She could tell from his face that meant nothing to him, so she tried again. "So think of the formless magic like an ocean. It isn't really, but—well, close enough for now. Anyway, think of impressions of grounded realm places as ships. Once the grounded realm ship is destroyed, the corresponding mirror realm ship loses its anchor and goes drifting. Explorers travel the ocean, find the drifting ships, and the rest of us tow them back periodically to lash together to make an island that's fit to live on."

Davin's expression cleared. "And paths between towns are like, what, pontoon bridges?"

Verity considered. That was wrong, but was it more wrong than the metaphor already was, by its nature? She shook her head. "More like stepping stones set beneath the surface. Makes it safer to travel, but you're not really building something." Verity shrugged. "Anyway, even explorers aren't really mages as such. There are no phantom mages; we're all part of the magic, to varying degrees."

Davin was listening intently enough he neglected to prompt her further for several moments. "And are the phantoms who come to the grounded realm actually tourists?"

"More or less. They're mostly young adults, if they're here for any length of time. It's useful for an explorer to be able to bail into the grounded realm if the formless magic pulls them in too far, and sometimes it's faster to travel to another town through the grounded realm. If you don't want to stand out those times, it's easier to learn to pass as human when you're young."

And maybe saying that to anyone who would listen would help kill an invasion rumor or two before they started. Humans would never survive in the mirror realm long-term, something that would be manifestly obvious to any that visited, and the grounded realm was crowded, frequently dirty, and soul-suckingly mundane. She'd never heard of a phantom who settled here permanently. But everyone always eventually worked around to whispering about invasion forces arriving from outside. On both sides.

"You seem a bit older than a young adult," Davin said. "Why did *you* come here?"

"I was younger when I first arrived," Verity said automatically while her thoughts churned. Here it was, after all. He'd been going somewhere with these questions, and it wasn't to get to know her as a person.

"But why would Vasily bind a tourist? That would only make sense if you were spying on him or something."

All her muscles tried to seize up at once. Did the Archivists still have doubts about whether she was a spy? But that made no sense, they'd let her go six years ago and ignored her until recently. Perhaps Davin was trying a few shots in the dark to see what she'd react to.

Anger bubbled up in Verity, collecting into an impulse to hit something. So she was a spy. It didn't *matter*. She longed to shout it in his face: *How do you picture phantoms using any information they gather to hurt humans? To craft an invasion? We aren't going to invade, we're just worried you are.* And she'd found no sign of such plans on the mages' side when she'd been around Vasily.

"I am not a spy. Can I say that more clearly for you?" She yanked open the fridge door to retrieve the rest of the vegetables and slammed them down on a cutting board beside the stove.

"I'm sorry," Davin said. Verity didn't check his face to gauge his sincerity. As long as he didn't say anything to the Quorum, she didn't care what he believed. And she was under a truth spell. If that wasn't enough to convince him, at least he couldn't offer the Archivists any proof.

"By the way, it's not 'doll-like,'" she snapped, to change the topic. With an effort, she smoothed her tone. "It's excess facial symmetry. Near-perfect symmetry is attractive, perfect is impossible. Your brain knows that's not right so it creeps you out."

Davin offered her a subdued smile, as if he hadn't noticed

the snap. "You're not particularly creepy."

Verity ran a handful of carrots under the faucet and collected a peeler. "I've had years to accumulate wrinkles and moles." So now she looked imperfectly average, like any other human. When she'd chosen to wear this look, preparing for the mission, she'd thought aggressively average would blend in. But stuck with Dakota in the Pacific Northwest, the mid-brown skin shade definitely didn't, and while her completely undistinguished features probably did, she missed being beautiful so badly sometimes. Not always. No one wanted to be beautiful always. But it had its place as one of the looks you could choose to wear.

One of the looks she *couldn't* choose to wear, now she was bound human, constrained to one look. She didn't know if mages were aware phantoms could change their faces, but that was one thing she definitely wasn't going to tell them.

"Mm," Davin agreed, breaking his gaze from her face. "Near-perfect. Resulting in attractiveness. True enough."

Verity figured that for some kind of deadpan joke, especially with Dakota around for comparison, so she didn't respond and the conversation lulled. Carrots peeled, she selected a knife. After chopping a few rounds, she rested the hand with the knife on the cutting board for a moment, to give the soup a stir with her other hand, then went back to holding the carrot to chop it.

"You're ambidextrous," Davin commented. His tone was intrigued this time, rather than pushy. Verity didn't know if that was progress, but he didn't appear to be going away, so she supposed she might as well continue to engage.

"I'm not a freak who feels the need to ignore one of two perfectly good hands three-quarters of the time, no." She set the knife down and tapped the spoon off so it wouldn't drip on the floor. She turned to him and pointed it to his ringless hand. "You're probably right-handed, correct?"

Davin lifted that hand. "Correct."

Verity changed the spoon's angle to his left hand. "Why's the ring on that hand, then?" She dipped the spoon back in the pot as an idea occurred to her. "But if you want to put it on with your usable hand..." She tried out the action herself.

"Dominant hand. Off hands aren't *useless*, per se." Davin looked down at his ring and much of the animation left his manner. "It's to keep it out of the way of tasks done with the dominant hand more than anything, I suppose."

Verity prodded the possible sore spot to see what would happen. "What does it mean? Some kind of relationship? Wedding rings go on a different finger, don't they?"

Davin's manner tightened to even greater stillness. "It's a reminder." He cleared his throat. "Rings don't need to have a particular meaning, unless they're on the ring finger." He indicated that one. "They can be worn for any number of reasons, same as other kinds of jewelry. I mean, you wear earrings, I presume." He nodded to her ears.

"I got these done after I was bound." Verity rolled her lobe between her fingertips, finding the tiny empty hole. "That's why they're uneven." One of her first asymmetries, at least that she'd noticed. She'd decided pierced ears would make her stand out less, so she'd done one herself. Only she'd fumbled it with the pain, and Dakota had discovered her trying not to drip blood on her bed. She'd made Verity accompany her to the mall to get the other one done.

Verity's lips thinned. Enough. She'd found some kind of weakness in him, but she would rather he just *go away*. She was tired of playing this game, examining her every word to see if it could be used by the Quorum against her. Maybe if she called him on it, he'd leave her alone, at least for a while. She lifted her wrist to show him the leather cuff. "And this is to cover the ugly-ass chain Vasily chose for the binding. Everything explained to your satisfaction now, or do you have more questions?"

Davin held up his hands calmingly. "I'm sorry. I let curiosity run away with me. Is there anything I can help you with, for dinner?"

"Well, your curiosity can run you off to interrogate Dakota or something. I don't need any help." Verity turned back to her carrots, picked up the knife, then used it to point to the hallway out of the kitchen.

Davin's footsteps moved off without further attempts at apology. Verity was alone again. She chopped a couple carrot rounds with unnecessary force. Was no human ever going to trust her, even bound into complete compliance and truthfulness? If they wouldn't let her go home, couldn't they at least leave her in peace?

When she'd finished up and turned the soup down to simmer, Verity went to return unused ingredients to the fridge. Light shimmered on the floor, revealed by the open fridge door until the source apparently scooted back from the new edge. Verity startled back before she even quite processed what she'd seen. That had looked like the edge-of-glass shimmer that you got from a monster, but what monster could possibly fit under the fridge...

Verity took a deep, calming breath, and knelt to lay her cheek on the floor. Rainbows shimmered at the edge of something under there, yes. Something pretty small, maybe a foot and a half wide. Could it possibly be a *pet*? "Come on out, little mantie," she murmured, then whistled a "come" command.

The pet mantie flung itself at her neck, all edges rippling wildly. The poor thing must be terrified and missing its family. It had to have one, if it had been trained to commands. It flattened its miniature manta ray body against the side of her neck, nose end poked into the corner of her jaw. One wing wrapped over her mouth and she pried it off to whistle a light "no, down" command. No smothering your new owner.

She nudged it down to splay across her chest. She could feel it trembling, but that eased as she stroked it, reveling in the softness of the winter-coat-lining fur nap of its back. "Oh, mantie. You're so scared, aren't you? I'm sorry. I can't get you back to the mirror realm, but I can take care of you. Okay? I promise." As much as she could promise that, when her own situation wasn't exactly stable.

The pet was still damn lucky it had found her. Or maybe that wasn't luck after all. She didn't know how long it had wandered after coming through from the mirror realm before the smell of magic from the mages in the house had attracted it.

If it had been wandering, it must be starving right now. This little guy could probably pull from a rat or something if it had to, but it wouldn't know how to catch it. Otherwise, they ate mushy things, like rotting plant matter, and she'd bet it hadn't been able to find any garbage that wasn't closed off in plastic bags or bins. Verity shifted the pet to lie with wings on either side of her shoulder so it could rest against her skin without her holding it up and went to search the cupboards. She knew what she'd feed it at home. What should she feed it here?

She mentally smacked herself. What was she doing? What if someone else noticed her petting the air? She checked both entrances to the kitchen and stood still for several seconds, listening. No one, but she should have checked the moment she saw the mantie. She kept one ear out as she returned to the stove. At home, usually you boiled the leftover soup for a few extra hours in the evening, and handed the mushed vegetables and broth over to the pets before bed. If she nuked a bowl of this soup to death in the microwave, that should get it at least near to the right consistency.

While she waited for the bowl to heat, Verity whistled a soft, happy tune to the mantie and coaxed it to perch on her arm so she could check it for injuries. Nothing that she could see, though with it being stuck in invisible form in the grounded realm, she couldn't be sure. Rainbows slid along its wing tips as it waved them enough to remain stable on her arm.

Getting the mantie up to her room took a lot of juggling. She got it back onto her shoulder, tucked a plate for it to eat from under her arm, and picked up the bowl, but she still had to avoid being seen carrying all that to her room. She paused around every corner and listened, and made it upstairs having splashed only a few drops on her hands.

Inside her room, she practically dropped the bowl on the floor and hissed. Hot! She sucked off the soup droplets and held the side of her finger against her mouth until the pain had faded. She poured enough soup to cover the center of the plate and waited. The weight didn't move from her shoulder.

"Mantie, are you too scared to be hungry?" Verity craned her neck to try to see the pet. "Come on." She pried it off gently and set it with its nose end at the edge of the plate. It made a distant teakettle noise, which cut off when it must have realized the plate smelled like food. It covered the plate completely, so its mouth was centered over the soup puddle.

Verity petted it and poured in more soup from the side until it had eaten about half the bowl. It floated up to the bed and splatted out contentedly on the blankets. "I've my own dinner to eat, but you'll be safe up here, I promise." She considered the cooling soup, then left it. The mantie might want more tonight, and it wouldn't get unsafe for pet consumption in that time.

She paused in the hall to make doubly sure the door was latched. Maybe it was stupid, but happiness fluttered in the vicinity of her chest. She could make the mantie's life better right now, anyway.

4

After dinner, Lucy started clearing the table and Siobhan jumped up to help. Dakota seemed to have run out of momentum again. She remained at the table, staring morosely at the surface. Gabe dragged his chair closer to take her hand and Lance bristled.

In Verity's opinion, Dakota didn't need more reassurance. She needed something to do. "I think we only have about one hunt's worth of ammo left. We might want to make some while we have some breathing space," Verity said.

Gabe and Lance ignored her, but Dakota's head came up. "That's a good point. Can you get the stuff?"

Verity rose, but Gabe's growl stopped her before she got any farther. "You need to rest, Dakota, not burn more magic. You must be exhausted after the hunt today."

"I need to not run out of ammo in the middle of a hunt." Dakota glared Gabe down, then scrubbed at her eyes. "We have a binding pair now, anyway. We might as well use them. I'll work with them and you, rather than doing the whole spell myself."

And that would have the side benefit of keeping Davin

busy for the evening, so he couldn't watch her as closely. Verity approved. On her way out to the garage for the supplies, she ducked into the kitchen. The dishwasher was shushing away and Siobhan was drying the soup pot while Lucy tried to fit the plastic container of leftovers into the fridge. "They're going to make ammo, so Dakota needs you, Siobhan," Verity told her. She looked the wrong direction and the windows out to the dark back yard threw a reflection at her.

A couple strides took her to the blinds. She should have done that when she came in to cook, but at the stove she'd been at the wrong angle to notice. Siobhan started at the sudden zip of the lowered blind.

Lucy edged closer to Siobhan and spoke in an undertone. "It was the reflection. She screws with all the mirrors, too. Sprays them with cheap cleaner and smears it for maximum streaks."

"I don't like the reflections to catch me by surprise at the corner of my eye," Verity said with as much dignity as she could muster. She swallowed anything more heated. She didn't like staring into a doorway and knowing home was on the other side but she was barred from it.

Everyone was waiting around the table when Verity returned with a dropcloth and large plastic jar of unmodified paintballs. She set the jar down and lightly tossed the cloth's edge in Dakota's direction. She helped spread the cloth out from that end while Verity did the same from hers.

"Why paintballs?" Davin asked, a bit dubiously. He was the soul of politeness compared to Lance's initial reaction: "What are we, children? Give me some fucking bullets."

"Originally, hunters were generally explosion pairs, since the electricity burst is the best way to take monsters out, but packaging the explosions into something anyone can use is an amazing help. And it means I can keep shooting even when I'm out of magical energy as well." Dakota had her own pat answers. Verity supposed she'd known that, but hearing Dakota use one now, edged by her emotional exhaustion, sparked a flicker of sympathy.

Dakota speared Davin with a glare, much less pat. "And I defy you to shoot at an invisible target and not hit anything else. Like, I don't know. Your allies. Joggers. The kid sleeping in the bedroom on the other side of a house's wall." Dakota's voice twisted up with anger and unshed tears, but she pushed on before anyone could jump in. "There's a noticeable lack of abandoned warehouses around here to shoot up like in the movies, so half the time the best I can do is try to draw the monsters toward an empty lot."

Verity was also quite aware that paintballs would have been much less lethal for that poor phantom who'd gotten caught up in a hunt. She kept that thought to herself, and forced her tone to stay light. "Besides, if Dakota only wings one, the paint gives her a target for the next shot. And 'sorry, officer, my friends and I were just playing paintball, what do you mean that's illegal within city limits?' is a *much* easier sell." She smiled, thin. Everyone belatedly seemed to recognize the humor and the air cleared a little.

Verity slipped off again to get the empty clips. When she returned, Dakota had already started on the spells. After tipping out a handful of paintballs, Dakota rolled them one by one across the cloth. Even the great Dakota couldn't create a binding spell beyond the range of her touch. Or any spell, for that matter, though explosion spells looked that way when she tossed them immediately after creation. Dakota made intermittent noises of concentration that never quite coalesced into a hum, and each spell built itself up too quickly to distinguish more than its finished glow.

Davin's brows flew up, probably because he was a sensitive. Siobhan idly lifted a finished paintball and touched her brother's wrist to find his pulse point as was necessary for a pair to share their talents and create a spell together. Or, in this case, for Siobhan simply to get the benefit of his sensitivity. She gasped. "You're—these are layered spells. You're just—churning them out like that? All by yourself?"

Dakota finished her handful and winced. "Not for very long tonight." She gestured for the others to pull their chairs closer. "It's pretty simple as layered spells go. Gabe and I can make the electrical burst, and you two can bind it stable until the paintball bursting triggers it."

"We could add an extra dimension to our spell to specify the trigger conditions more precisely." Having scooted her chair, Siobhan rolled her fingertip around on top of a paintball like a circus performer balancing atop it. "Something about velocity on impact so they don't go off when dropped or stepped on or whatever."

Dakota smiled at her. "Good idea." Siobhan found her brother's pulse again, and Gabe and Dakota did the same. Lance slouched in his chair with studied boredom, but Lucy leaned forward, watching.

And it was worth watching. For all that she lived—used to live—in magic, Verity found human magic fascinating. Now Dakota wasn't working so fast, there was an elegance to the formation of the spells when you concentrated on seeing them properly, like patterns of frost flowers on a window. The magic followed constrained paths, as frost would the shape of a pane, but from there it was almost—what was the word she'd read that she'd thought was perfect for that?—fractal, that was it. When finished, the spell settled into the low-level, mixed-color glow Verity could see in the same way she could see mirror realm creatures in their invisible forms.

She'd always wondered who among the mages had it worse when alone, crafters who could work with magic but not see what they were doing, or sensitives who could look but not touch. She supposed she was more like a sensitive herself, but while sensitives could see spells in much more detail than her, they registered little more than the presence of a spell outside their specialty.

At first, each paintball took nearly five minutes each, what with frowning and spinning out the magic and tucking in the spell's edges and making sure they didn't fray. They got it down to about a minute and stopped visibly concentrating so hard. Lance must have decided they'd be able to converse simultaneously now, because he straightened slightly.

"So, Dubois and Dubois. Do you have any actual training in something useful, like combat or target shooting?"

"Yes," Siobhan said, not bothering to hide her satisfaction at being able to cut off his snideness before it started. "They covered pretty much anything you can think of at the advanced training program I attended in Boston."

"Boston." Verity tried to chase her mage associations with that city down. People talked around her all the time, and while she paid attention a great deal of that time, she couldn't remember everything. "It's set up like a human school, isn't it?"

"Non-magical human," Davin corrected. "Mages *are* humans."

With only his deadpan manner to go by, Verity took that as a joke and countered with one of her own. "You all look so similar to me." That squeaked by her truth binding only by the skin of her teeth, and she had to breathe against a tightness in her chest for a couple beats. Lucy looked vaguely offended.

Siobhan filled the resulting silence. "It's designed to be more like college. The Archivists still match young mages up with nearby mentors in their same specialty, but when they're young adults and a little more mobile, they can join a cohort in Boston or a couple other places, like Taiwan. Once you have the basics in your own specialty, it's easier to get something out of learning things about the other specialties. And you can meet people to pair with."

"And yet you still put up with your brother." Verity pulled over an empty clip and started loading in finished paintballs. "Where'd *you* train?" she asked him.

Davin was focused on the latest spell, though, like he wasn't paying attention to the conversation anymore. Again, Siobhan filled the gap. "Sad to say, we do sometimes think on the same wavelength. I doubt we'll pair for life, though." She leaned over to knock her shoulder into his, and he pretended to come back down to Earth.

"It sounds nice." Dakota pushed her chair back and massaged her temples. "I think that's enough spells for tonight." She cupped her hands into an arc to ferry the rest of the finished paintball pile down the table to Verity. "Is it true they started those programs because of me?"

Everyone froze, awkwardness congealing in the air around them. Even Verity stayed silent, though in her case it was because she had no idea what Dakota was talking about. Siobhan finally managed an, "Uh? What do you mean?"

"Because my powers manifested so early, and then I bounced from mentor to mentor." Dakota grimaced. "To mentor." She dodged a reassuring pat from Gabe and stood. "I'll leave you guys to load the rest into clips, if that's okay."

When Dakota had left, Lucy looked after her with a hint of hero worship in her eyes. "I bet it was hard for her having such a splashy power, too."

"Splashy?" Verity finished a clip and started the next as everyone else grabbed one to at least fidget with. Dakota wasn't particularly splashy. Not like Lance, always showing off how intricate or big he could make his illusions, or even Gabe with his flashy booms. She did do magic outside of the heat of a hunt, certainly, but small quick things, like when she needed an instant illusion to change the car's plates in front of nosy neighbors or something. Verity had always suspected that Dakota had some kind of twisted self-esteem issues surrounding her magic that made her downplay it, but boy did Verity not feel the need to go digging for Dakota's issues. There were enough on the surface to deal with.

No one paid attention to her question, of course. Lance tried out his next jab. "So you two have come here to show off your shiny new training, then?" His wish to get rid of them was starting to get pointed, and Verity suddenly wondered if he was worried about Davin as competition for Dakota's affections. Or maybe he was worried about greater division of the credit for the grand defeat of monsters he'd constructed in his mind. She wished they'd go away just as much, but she knew Lance would never be successful with that kind of strategy.

"No, we're here to have adventures and cruise for chicks," Siobhan said. Her humor had finally given way to sarcasm with an acid bite, but it didn't last long. "It's a good thing we're usually drawing from different pools—and have different types, to be honest—otherwise I'd charm them all away first." She set her clip down and hooked her arm into her brother's. "Anyway, I dragged this guy along because he hates excitement and fun, so it'll be good for him."

"Of course I hate fun. What's it ever done for me?" Davin's delivery was so dry, everyone hesitated. Verity couldn't help herself. She laughed. She didn't trust this guy, was reasonably certain he was working against her, so why did he have to be so *funny*?

"So where'd everyone else train?" Siobhan asked. She didn't look at Lance, but Verity doubted that fooled anyone.

Lance least of all, apparently. He eyed her. "Well, Lucy Liu here dropped out of Archivist training."

Lucy drew in her shoulders. "I've asked you not to call me that."

Lance shrugged and made a smarmy "just kidding" grimace. Gabe also stilled visibly, the closest Verity had ever seen him get to bristling, but he was apparently too polite to call Lance out.

"Yeah, you're saying what, all Asians look identical? She doesn't look anything like Lucy Liu." Siobhan sat straighter, challenging Lance.

Lance deserved that challenge, but Verity knew Lucy was all too aware she'd have to work with Lance on the next hunt. Verity had to agree. Better to defuse the situation, if she could. "Liu's face is narrower than Lucy's. Not longer, but the width at Lucy's cheekbones means that her eyes are a little farther apart and her features look a bit more open."

It was only after she said it that Verity realized how not-human that kind of detail was, and mentally cursed. Too late now, though. And Davin was plenty aware she was a phantom. There was no way he could connect an obsession with facial structure to being able to change her look.

Lance eyed her. "You are so fucking weird." Then he pasted on an insincere smile for Siobhan. "I wasn't thinking of the actress. Just 'loo,' like lookie-loo."

Verity decided she'd better take over the introductions. "We're kind of like the island of misfit toys around here. We've got our explosions crafter without a sensitive." She nodded to Gabe. "And our illusion sensitive who's also a caterpillar Archivist—"

"Caterpillar?" Davin said it dubiously, like he'd spotted the straight line, but couldn't guess where she was going with it.

"Well, you see, caterpillar Archivists get training, and when they're so full of research they're about to burst, they spin it into a chrysalis…"

Lucy rolled her eyes and Lance scoffed, but Davin laughed: a startled, completely natural laugh, and that was totally worth it. It wasn't flashy—no growl or honey or anything lyrical. Just low and warm and wickedly addictive. She felt like she'd taken a hit of something and was using the high to plan how she'd get more. Which wasn't just stupid, it was *dangerous*. She needed to stay away from Davin, and yet she kept talking to him.

"And then our illusions crafter." Verity nodded to Lance. Really, she should have stopped there, but she couldn't resist a jab. "So you and your sister are our first actual spell pair, since Dakota doesn't count," she told Davin.

Lance growled. "We're a pair."

"No, you're a crafter and a sensitive who occasionally create spells together. You're too much of a dick to function in a pair." Verity knew she'd gone too far as soon as she said it, but damned if she'd backpedal in front of Lance.

"You're forgetting the last member of the team, Dakota's mouthy pet." Lance knew he'd scored a hit, too, because he returned to his earlier slouch, pleased.

"Not a pet." Verity stood and retrieved the tub of unaltered paintballs, as if that could hide the fact the insult stung. It shouldn't. *Six years*, she'd been bound, after all. She knew the score.

Jar of paintballs held to her chest, Verity pointedly pushed by Lance. She didn't really need to go through the kitchen to get to the garage to put the jar away, and they were both aware of that. As she passed him, she snapped her teeth at him. He ignored her completely, but she heard Lucy gasp. Grinning, she slipped through the kitchen to the hall.

Davin caught up to her in the garage, leaning his shoulder against the doorway into the house as she rummaged, organizing lawn equipment and spare paintball guns while she was there. The damp cool of being surrounded by unheated walls and a concrete floor was relaxing, at least in this season. That would change soon enough, and she'd hurry back into the warmth and let random possessions stack up haphazardly for another winter.

"Lucy is utterly convinced that you're draining Lance of neural electricity, a spark at a time." Davin's tone wasn't accusatory, but Verity was starting to wonder if it ever was.

She really shouldn't have done that, Verity admitted to herself. She was lucky Davin was giving her a chance to deny it directly. "I'm not, because it's impossible under the binding. She's right phantoms are omnivorous, though. Both food and lifeforce." She pulled a broom away from the wall, decided she wasn't in that much of a cleaning mood tonight, and settled it back again.

"Your binding prohibits you consuming elec—lifeforce?" He waited for her nod that he'd applied the term correctly. "And lying. So why does Lucy believe a lie?"

Verity dusted her hands on her jeans and looked at the floor. Which was the safer path? Further obfuscation, or 'fessing up? "I never lied to her. I...misled her a little, by implication." She lifted her hands, a helpless gesture. "She can't really get more suspicious of me." It was Lance she was pissed at right now, not Lucy, but she didn't have any way to get to Lance, so this felt at least a little like—control? Perhaps. As Davin had said. Damn him.

Silence in response. Davin only spoke up when she tried to slip past him. "Could you do it, if you weren't bound?"

Verity looked him right in the eye, challenging. "The word you're looking for is 'would.' Would I do it? Would you eat someone's finger? Even if you weren't tied to a chair?"

Davin jerked back with the strength of his visceral reaction. Just a half step, but it gave her room to get by. "No!"

"Exactly." And Davin seemed to actually get it, so Verity stopped herself before she was tempted to oversell her point.

A shout reached them indistinctly from the main house. Probably Dakota, though Verity couldn't be sure. The cadence indicated she was summoning them, and presumably everyone else.

It couldn't possibly be *another* hunt. Could it?

5

Verity, Davin not far behind her, found Lucy and Dakota conferring at the foot of the stairs, hunched over Lucy's phone. "Are you sure it's not delayed reports from the monsters we already took care of?" Dakota asked a little desperately.

"Both the Archivists' computers and their human analysts agree that it's more likely something new. The reported behavior is different..." Lucy scrolled something on her screen to show Dakota, but Dakota didn't seem to need it. She hissed a curse and gestured the others in close as they arrived.

Davin and Siobhan hung back while Dakota argued about routes and strategies with the others. Verity wasn't invited, of course, so she edged closer to Siobhan and nodded to Lucy's phone. "The Archivists have a search engine that combs social media—and news reports, but I think that's a bit slower—for reports of weird shit." Better to keep the siblings' attention on the hunts rather than on her. "There's some set of criteria for 'weird shit that's probably invisible monster attacks' they're always refining, but Lucy's hooked into their system, and she gets notices sometimes before they go through the formal process of declaring it a monster and notifying the closest hunter. Though I suppose we're almost at the point where the formal process is useless, with this rate of attacks."

Now would be an excellent opportunity, Verity realized, to suggest that she teleport part of the team to whatever location, near the reports, Dakota had chosen for the showdown. With timing tight, and too many people to fit into one vehicle, it seemed logical enough to her, though she presumed convincing everyone besides Dakota would be more difficult. Who'd have thought she'd ever long for the days of being dragged along with just Dakota on all her hunts.

"I could take some people—" Verity stepped over to Dakota, but Lance spoke right over her.

"The guests will need guns," he told Dakota, hooking a thumb in the siblings' direction.

"We can grab another case on our way out." Dakota hesitated, eyes locked on Lance. "It's sounding like we might be dealing not with mantas this time, but a jaguar-type." Lance's back snapped straight and suppressed emotion burned in his eyes. "If you need to sit this one out—"

"I'm fine." Lance whirled away, long coat slapping against his ankles rather than swirling as it did when he paid attention. He strode away and the door into the garage snapped open and slammed closed.

Dakota let a breath trickle out slowly. "Well. Okay. Gabe, would you grab the weapons and ammo? Thank God we made more. And the lantern, too. Save us some effort on spells." She sought out Lucy next. "Would you be willing to come along and set up the perimeter illusion with Lance, since it will need to be bigger to cover all of us?"

Lucy let her phone drop for a second, expression filling with excitement. Even if Verity hadn't been aware Lucy usually stayed home from hunts, she'd have been able to tell from that look. "Anything I can do to help." She clasped at Dakota's hand.

Dakota pulled her hand away distractedly. "We'll have to take two vehicles." She headed for the garage, Lucy trailing.

And there was Verity's moment, gone. She gritted her teeth, and reminded herself there would be others. Others hopefully when Davin wasn't watching, too, to wonder why exactly she was being so insistent in her offers of teleportation.

Gabe surveyed the three of them remaining and nodded to the siblings. "You can come in my car." Verity fell in with them. Gabe's driving was a pain in the ass, but she definitely didn't feel like riding with Lance in his current mood.

"So what's Lance's deal?" Siobhan asked, when they were settled in Gabe's older Prius, two cases of the paintball guns and clips in the trunk with the specially modified camping lantern they used to light up the monsters to save explosion spells. They started out following Dakota, but Gabe drove as much like a grandmother as ever, so they soon lost her. Hopefully Gabe remembered where they were supposed to meet.

"A jaguar-type monster killed his little brother." Verity figured if she was going to flaunt Gabe's well-known disapproval of gossip, she might as well be brief about it.

"Okay, that's…concise." Siobhan was in the backseat with Verity, which made giving her the side-eye easy. "Let's try this again. *What*?"

"At the Archivists' North American base. Near Toronto." Gabe stopped there, like that additional detail would be sufficient.

Verity took it as permission to tell the story properly. "His parents both worked there. Lance wasn't even there. A jaguar came through and since the Northeast rarely gets monsters, the Archivists had to scramble to find someone to deal with it. The team did their best, but it got away from them and went for Lance's brother, in the residences. He must have been…eleven? Twelve? Anyway, they took the jaguar down while it was feeding, so no one else got hurt. But Lance thinks that if he'd been there to defend him—" Verity made a blah-blah talking motion with one hand. "Never mind that this was years ago, so it wasn't like Lance had had any training in monster hunting either. But now I suppose he's finally got his chance for his own private vengeance."

Said wish for vengeance was why Dakota hadn't left Verity alone with Lance for months after he'd rolled into town and she'd started sleeping with him, about a year or so before she'd been forced to ask for his help in hunting. Verity only knew the details of the story because she'd demanded a reason for Dakota's protectiveness or she'd threatened to flaunt it at every opportunity. It seemed ironic now, since she preferred knowing where she was with Lance, who'd turned out to be all talk, to the unknowns of Stiles and Davin.

Verity shifted toward the middle of the seat to see out the windshield. The roads had dried from the day's earlier drizzle, and without storefronts, she only got a shiver of reflected light from a few house windows as they cut through the residential neighborhood.

They turned into the parking lot of a rec center, wooded on three sides, though the strips of mature trees were narrow enough they probably didn't even hold a walking path. When they pulled up to the building, the sports fields beyond became visible. Even hours past the center's closing, Gabe ignored the clump of handicapped parking spots in front of the dark building and pulled precisely into a spot farther along. Dakota had already pulled haphazardly up to the "fire lane keep clear" curb that abutted the fields.

Siobhan stepped out of the car and squinted off into the darkness to the scattered squares of lit windows in the houses beyond the trees. "All those houses…the monsters won't have killed anyone before we got here, will they?"

Verity went straight to the trunk for her paintball gun. "Probably not. Before today, I'd have said definitely not. Monsters are disoriented when they first find themselves in the grounded realm, and the less intelligent they are, the slower they adjust. So mantas flail around for a few days, knocking things over, before they work up to eating the lifeforce of cats or dogs, never mind humans. They can smell magic, though—maybe it reminds them of home, or maybe they like the taste of mage lifeforce—so if Dakota stands around, they generally home in before too long. So she can pick their battlefield to a certain degree. I assume Dakota wanted the open space, and the contained area they can cover with an illusion." She gestured with her gun to the sports fields, then tucked it into her waistband.

"Mage lifeforce has a taste…you know that from personal experience?" Siobhan was giving Verity That Look. Verity ignored her. She'd done that explanation once today. She wanted to get this hunt over without any more human deaths, maybe teleport someone home if she could talk them into it, and then go to bed.

Davin paused by his sister. "No," he said, hand on her shoulder, and leaned in, presumably to provide more details. Verity supposed she should be grateful to him.

She stepped up onto the sidewalk and followed it to the main building. Lucy and Lance were getting directions from

Dakota. Probably about the illusions, because she pointed to various locations along the chain-link fence that surrounded the farthest reaches of the fields. The regular orange streetlights cast enough light to make that out, but not much more. An impeccably flat grass surface stretched in front of them, the new wood beams and generous skylights and steel and glass walls construction of the rec center behind them. The air was cold enough that Verity transferred her gun to her front coat pocket and zipped up.

The movement must have caught Lance's eye because he paused in his scan of the fence and glowered at her. "What the hell does the phantom have a gun for?" He strode over, trailing Dakota.

"How about so I can defend myself and don't die?" Verity took a quick step back so he couldn't grab for the gun and pressed her arms protectively over the hard lump felt through the coat's fabric.

"Verity always has a gun when she helps me." Dakota put a hand on Lance's arm, sounding confused as to why there was even an issue. "A good thing she did, the last hunt."

Deeper glowering. Lance crossed his arms, throwing off Dakota's touch. "But how do you know she won't—"

"Let her keep it." Gabe detoured to their little knot, hardly paused to speak, then veered back to his original path. "She can't really hurt any of us, and she knows she'll face consequences if she acts up."

For a beat, Verity was grateful Gabe seemed to be on her side, and then the rest of his words penetrated. Was he complimenting her intelligence, saying she knew stepping out of line wasn't worth it? What about the implication there that she *wanted* to act up?

As Dakota pulled Lance out of the way, Verity decided it couldn't have been intentional. Gabe was always so polite to her, and his tone just now had been as distractedly respectful as usual. Though the issue seemed resolved for now, she kept her arms crossed over the gun as she watched the others return to their tasks. Grant that they wouldn't have to have a rematch on this argument next hunt.

Lance, grumbling under his breath, and Lucy set out around the perimeter fence, spooling out the glowing line of their illusion. It always seemed odd to Verity, the way magic glowed, but didn't illuminate anything around it. She could see the fields no better than before they'd started. Gabe and the newcomers joined Dakota and they headed into the middle of the field in a knot. The beam of their lantern scattered here and there on water vapor in the air, but illuminated no monsters.

Now, they waited. And Verity too. She followed the curving sidewalk through the rec center's landscaping until she could back up a few steps and get a good angle on the roofline. A breath, two, then a rainbow-edged head peeked over, ears pricked. Great paws gripped the edge as it sat up straight, and it slid its long prehensile tail to hang down. The plumed tip twitched, thoughtful.

Verity opened her mouth to shout a warning, but didn't voice it when another thought crowded it out. She pressed her lips together, tight. Dakota had never taken on a jaguar before, yes, but there were four of them—five, once Lance finished— out there with guns, and no regular humans in sight. The jaguar was acting normally, as relaxed as could be expected in a strange environment, no sign of excessive fear. Even though it was more intelligent and thus less disoriented, the team would take it down in no time if she pointed it out.

And what if Verity didn't say anything? The others wouldn't notice; most of them were probably still wondering why she was along at all. Where mantas subdued their prey by suffocation before pulling lifeforce, jaguars attacked with teeth and claws to injure prey badly enough it kept still. So if the jaguar could approach without a warning from Verity, maybe it could drop on someone—Lance, if she was especially lucky—and get in a few claw-swipes before the other four shot it. The wounds would probably bleed badly, and need to be teleported immediately to the local healing pair…

So Verity watched the jaguar, and didn't call out. "Grass isn't any greener in this realm, kitty," she murmured under her breath. Not that she would particularly mourn its inevitable death. Jaguars roamed the edge of the phantoms' fields, searching for children they could pick off. They were too smart to attack adults, too smart for anyone's good. Packs of the wolf-type monsters attacked you more quickly and more viciously, but they roamed the formless magic and didn't bother the towns.

Verity pulled out her gun and gripped it tightly, pointed at the ground for the moment. All right, she'd admit it at least to herself. She retained a certain visceral fear of the jaguars. Childhood programming, that was all. Never walk beside a tall tree or isolated building without looking up. Hold your knife up in front of your chest.

The jaguar leaped to a nearby fir, then down to a streetlight. It wrapped its tail down the pole and balanced lightly on three paws, all the flat top of the light could fit. Verity could imagine its thoughts. On one hand, a whole pocket of tasty, tasty mages were just standing there. On the other hand, they were all adults, and out in the open where it couldn't drop down on them. On a third hand—with four paws, Verity figured she could grant it three rhetorical hands—the adults weren't re-acting like phantoms would have, and in fact seemed not to realize the jaguar was even there. What was a lifeforce-thirsty carnivore to do?

Movement at the corner of Verity's eye caught her atten-tion. She froze. Another jaguar leaped from the other side of the center's roof onto a maintenance shed. From there, it leaped to the top of the chain-link fence and paced along it, long tail in constant motion to keep it balanced.

That changed the odds, but still left them in the team's fa-vor. Probably. Verity swallowed, though that only highlighted how dry her mouth had become. She found she'd clutched her gun up where she'd hold a knife, which was useless for aim-ing, except perhaps at the sliver of moon above. She forced her hands down, turned to keep the gun out of the team's sight. This wasn't her fight, she reminded herself. Though Dakota trusted her, the others wouldn't thank her if she helped, as Lance had made abundantly clear.

The streetlight jaguar lifted its tail from the pole to wrap around the light. Light shone through it, but shattered, spar-kling. From his position in the outward-facing knot of people in the field, Gabe pointed. Dakota was the one who shouted, thin tone showing her tension. "There!"

Paintballs struck the jaguar and spattered onto the street-light from four guns. Two hit its body, one its tail, and little webs of charge spat and then died, like miniature lightning. The light bulb made a soft *fzzt* noise and died of its own wounds. The jaguar toppled and fell, boneless.

A few cheers, and the team edged up to the jaguar to make sure it was dead. Even without a shower of sparks worthy of a movie, the dead streetlight created a pool of shadow bigger than Verity would have expected. She took a deep breath. If things continued this smoothly, the team would escape uninjured. They'd dispatched the first jaguar easily enough. Jaguars didn't know about guns.

A chuff like a gust of window buffeting a windowpane sounded, and Verity whirled for the rec center again. Another head appeared, cautious.

Three? *Three* jaguars?

Verity rocked back a step. But wasn't that what she'd hoped for? Difficult enough odds that someone would be sure to be injured?

"Lance! Wait." Lucy's volume jerked upward at the end as Lance apparently didn't listen. Verity spotted her standing anxiously at the edge of the parking lot while Lance dashed into the fields.

"The spell's finished," he threw back at her. Verity could imagine the voiceover: time to avenge his little brother! Without slowing, he shot at each streetlight around the field in turn. Verity could only imagine he thought he was blanketing every possible jaguar perch with fire. While he looked impressive, gun out as he ran, it was too dark to measure the miles by which he'd missed each target. Had there even been a jaguar on any of the poles. Another bulb *fzzt*ted into darkness, though.

The team started shouting at each other, a mass of confusing demands and instructions. Verity's nerve failed. Two at once was too many. She needed to distract the third until they'd finished with the second. She used the cover of the noise to whistle at the third jaguar, the whistle that phantoms used when one was spotted from town, which said "fuck off, or we're eating you for breakfast."

On the roof, the jaguar startled up, side-stepping about

a body-length away from her. There, it stopped, tail grabbing the gutter as it considered. Verity took an exaggerated step forward, herding it back up the roof. If it would just stay there another minute or two…

"It's on the ground!" Siobhan's shout distracted Verity. She'd apparently been quartering the fields with the lantern. The fence jaguar must have jumped down because it flashed with light, running along the grass, straight for the team.

When Verity looked back up at the third jaguar, it had moved. Toward the parking lot, where Lucy had paused in her walk back to the car to watch the fight.

Because Lucy was a mage. Alone, rather than in a defensive group. And jaguars were more than clever enough to do that math.

Verity whistled again, but of course the jaguar ignored her. "Lucy! Watch out!" Verity didn't know if that would help either, so she ran—her legs slammed into something and she collapsed against it, expletives at the pain disappearing into one long hiss. Bike rack. She hadn't even seen it in the darkness.

Shouts came from where everyone was shooting at the fence jaguar, but Verity had to get to Lucy. Her legs didn't want to work at first, when she cleared the bike rack. Then two steps later her foot went off the sidewalk down to the dirt in the adjoining landscaping. She stumbled, kept her feet, but she couldn't find the jaguar. Where was it? "Lucy!"

She focused on the woman, who was staring at her in confusion. The jaguar launched from the rec center roof and landed on Lucy's shoulders.

Its tail whipped around her chest, pinning her arms, before she could even scream. If she'd been raised as a phantom, she would have been carrying a knife. It would have been up, ready to slice herself free as she pulled the jaguar's lifeforce. But Lucy couldn't get to her gun and the jaguar leaned down to bite at the side of her face. Flesh and lifeforce, they liked eating both equally.

The jaguar's teeth scored bleeding arcs over her cheek, and now Lucy did scream. Verity was still running, but she couldn't—couldn't get there in time and she forced herself to stop and aim. Really aim. She had to hit it. *Had* to. She'd practiced this, she wasn't that bad. Brace her feet, her arms, aim—

There. A burst of electricity in the jaguar's shoulder. Verity squeezed again and again. They both started to topple, but was that because she'd killed the jaguar, or because Lucy's legs had given out? Verity sprinted the last few yards, pressed her gun to the underside of the jaguar's chin, exposed by the fall, and painted it with an incongruously green-tinted splatter.

She knelt and started tearing at the tail, getting it off Lucy, but no, that wasn't what she needed to do. She needed to deal with the bleeding. She pressed her hand to Lucy's cheek but the blood just kept pumping out. Human blood was so absurdly colored, like a thousand balls of red paint.

She hadn't wanted to get anyone killed. She'd just thought, what if someone got hurt a little. Like Lance or Gabe, who'd accepted the danger, or Davin if that would get him and his sister to go home. And she hadn't even *done* anything, she'd just stayed quiet too long. She hadn't meant—

"Lucy!" Dakota's voice, behind her. "Oh, God, Lucy! Verity, is she—?"

Siobhan knelt calmly at Lucy's head and sought her gaze while smiling reassuringly. Lucy wasn't making any noise, and her eyes were unfocused, maybe from shock. One of Siobhan's knees squished into the dead jaguar she couldn't see, but she shoved it aside. "She's alive. Facial wounds bleed like fuck. Davin, come here, we'll bind it shut. In Boston, they taught us to do it so you can get someone to a healing pair."

Davin touched Verity's shoulder from behind, gently moved her aside so he could take her place with room to touch his sister as well as lean over Lucy. The blood steadily coursed from her cheek again the moment Verity moved her hand, but as the binding spread its glow, the flow slowed.

Verity stared at her hands. Absolutely smeared, all over, like she'd been finger-painting red, a toddler splatting handprints up the walls. "Thank God you saved her," Dakota was saying.

Verity looked up, remembering there was one jaguar still unaccounted for, but Lance was returning from the field, one corpse over his shoulder, another dragged along by its tail. Dakota strode a couple steps to meet him. "This is your fault! These aren't like mantas, you know that. You shouldn't have left Lucy alone until she was safely back in the car!"

"What the fuck are you—" Lance seemed to see the group on the ground properly for the first time. He frowned at them in the dark, but then his gaze skipped to Verity's hands. His face crumpled, looking so lost that for a moment Verity almost felt sympathy for him.

But who was she to be offering or withholding sympathy in this situation?

"Ready," Davin said, and stood. His hands were as red as Verity's now. "If someone will help me lift her into the car—"

"No, Verity will take her." Dakota and Verity started speaking at the same time, so Verity fell silent and let Dakota explain. "The healing pair we use, they're forewarned, and keep a mirror in their spare room for us. Gabe, call them for us, would you? While we're in transit."

Gabe actually made the bulk of the call while they were preparing, getting Lucy up and standing slumped against Dakota, and Verity placed so she could touch both women as well as take the necessary step forward into the mirror leaning against the SUV's bumper. Verity felt Davin's eyes on her accusingly the whole time, but every time she looked at him, he was watching no more than any of the others were, worried about Lucy. Was the weight of her internal guilt making her imagine things?

Finally they were ready to go. Verity stepped them forward, into the teleport she'd thought she wanted so badly, at the beginning of the night.

6

When she'd teleported Dakota and a healed Lucy home, Verity washed up and ended up sitting on her bed, with no desire to sleep whatsoever. The healing mages had agreed with Siobhan's assessment—the wound had bled badly, but it had been well suited for a healing spell, which accelerated healing, but couldn't accomplish anything the body couldn't have done on its own more slowly. Lucy's cheek had been smooth except for the faintest of white lines, but she'd need to rest and eat and drink to replace lost blood.

Verity poured some cold soup onto a plate for the mantie now gently whistle-snoring atop a pile of Dakota's sweaters, unworn gifts from relatives, stored on a high shelf. It didn't rouse, probably still sated from its meal earlier. Gradually, even the snores died away. She decided to let it keep sleeping the sleep of the just. At least someone was content around here. She poured the soup back into the bowl and tucked it away.

It was a good thing she did, because someone rapped on her door—the one that led to the hall, not the one that led to Dakota's room—and opened it before she said anything. Apparently that was a warning, not a request for permission. Davin leaned in the doorway as he had in the garage. His hair was still wet from a presumable shower, which made it indeterminately dark rather than red. The color made him look more average, which Verity wasn't sure was an improvement.

Despite her attempts to distract herself, Verity's heart rate redlined waiting for him to speak. She was fucked now, wasn't she? Was someone from the Quorum already on the way to pick her up? Davin looked at the room rather than her, though. "Is this—this is a walk-in closet, isn't it? They're having you sleep in a walk-in closet, seriously?"

"It *used* to be a walk-in closet. Vasily didn't need it, I guess, because he or the original owner of the house had it converted." Verity nodded to the door Davin was standing in. "They added that door so it could be used as a bedroom without going through the master suite all the time. I guess they kept the other door so it could continue to share the master bathroom."

She knew babbling wasn't doing more than delaying the inevitable, but Verity couldn't help herself. "When everyone started crashing here at the house between hunts, I volunteered to move in here. Since I don't have all that much stuff to move." She stood and touched the empty shelf built along the same wall as her bed, near the ceiling. "And this way, I get to keep at least some privacy."

She stepped to the other side and ruffled the clothes hanging along half the length of the bar along that wall. She carefully didn't look at the silent mantie on the shelf above. Still sleeping, she hoped. "Though it does feel a little silly. With all the hunts, Dakota hasn't had the chance to move the rest of her clothes out."

"Verity." Davin's word was calm, but Verity shut up instantly anyway. And now the inevitable was here. She backed toward the door into Dakota's room. Running away wouldn't do any good in this situation, but the impulse snatched at her again anyway.

Running away hadn't ever helped her.

"I saw you watching something, on the roof at the rec center. Then you were running for Lucy. Were you chasing that monster toward her?"

"No!" Verity tried to stand tall. It was hard, when guilt felt like it was eating her stomach, making her want to hunch over the emotional pain. She should have said something the moment she spotted the jaguars.

Davin was *infuriatingly* calm, just standing there with his shoulder against the doorframe. "You know Dakota's death wouldn't break the binding."

Anger buoyed her for a moment. "Yes, Vasily told me that in the beginning, and everyone *loved* to remind me thereafter. I wasn't trying to get anyone killed!" Pure truth. She slashed her next gesture. "I'm not stupid, I don't want to be bound to whoever the Quorum happens to choose. Or whoever gets to the loose ends of the spell first."

"What were you doing, then? Why didn't you warn her or the rest of us about the monster you'd seen?"

The guilt washed away her anger and then ate up all Verity's smooth evasions too. All she had left were lies. *I just caught a glimpse, I wasn't sure what I'd seen,* she tried to say. She tried so hard, and her chest tightened, and tightened. She coughed, trying to bring in air, then wheezed, coughed again. She bent over, gasping as she finally gave up on the lie. "I didn't want to say anything."

"Why?"

"I knew you could take care of it—" Truth, yes, but walking the line and her next words would have been lies. New tightness squeezed tears from Verity's eyes and she collapsed back sitting on her bed. She could choose to remain silent, but that would be just as much of an answer. "Because I wanted a minor injury I'd have to teleport to the healers!" She flung it at him— and at the spell, she supposed, like the spell cared—heedless of how much worse she was probably making things for herself.

"Because teleporting frays the binding." Davin pushed off the doorframe and stepped inside, softly shutting the door behind him.

Verity clutched her braceletted wrist to her chest. He'd noticed. Of course he'd noticed. Why had she ever kidded herself otherwise? "You saw."

"Yes, I did." Davin sounded almost…tired? Reluctant? He sat heavily beside Verity and held out his hand for her wrist. She let him take it without a struggle, too much in shock to protest. "Actually, fray is the wrong word, I think. It's like a piece of clothing that gets thinner until it's almost transparent, but there's never an actual hole. Worn away, I suppose."

His hands on her skin were warm and gentle as he examined the spell at close range. Verity broke free of her shock like bursting to the surface of cold water. She was not going to just sit here and let this happen. There had to be something she could do. "What do you want? To not tell Stiles. Have you told Stiles yet? If you haven't, I'll give you anything in my power." And what if he wanted her to reveal phantom secrets? And what secrets did phantoms have, anyway? There'd been enough information leaked back and forth in their contact with mages over the years. The only secret she could think of was changing looks.

"May I?" he asked, fingers hovering above her leather cuff's snap. Verity nodded, jerkily. He must be considering. *Was* there anything she could give someone like him?

He unsnapped the cuff and drew in his breath in a hiss when he'd removed it. "This is far too tight." He pried at the steel chain, trying to get a finger between it and her skin. He only succeeded in rolling it over, one turn of flat side to flat side, up her wrist. The revealed skin showed a perfect chain in negative space, darkening a little as blood seeped back in.

"I move it up or down regularly." What did it *matter*, anyway? "I'm not supposed to be able to get it off, after all." Her laugh came out a little too sharp. Far too sharp.

"If this spell was as elegantly crafted throughout as it is in places, there would be a binding that prevented you from removing it, not simply a binding that prevents the clasp from opening and the chain from breaking." Davin huffed in apparent annoyance. "It doesn't make sense." He smoothed the chain back carefully, then handed her the leather cuff.

Verity held it without replacing it, for something to do with her hands. She ran her thumb over the embossed design. "What do you want?"

"Your promise to participate whole-heartedly in further hunts—no failing to mention monsters you've seen, or things you know about them—and never to try to get anyone hurt in a hunt ever again." Davin closed his hands over her wrists, including over the chain, like a clasp over some kind of formal agreement.

"That's it?" Verity searched his face for mockery, found none. "I promise that and you'll promise to not tell anyone that my binding's worn? Why is it that easy?" Because it was far too easy. She pulled her hands away.

"All right." Davin gave her a thin-lipped smile. "Tell me this, under the truth binding. Is this getting ready to snap tomorrow? This month?"

"No." Months, plural, maybe. If she continued teleporting three times in a day on a regular basis.

"That's what I see in the spell as well. So it's not really my problem, is it?"

Verity shot him a glare. Please, he could at least not insult her intelligence. "Not your problem? Why are you even here, if not to report to Stiles on me?"

Davin's brows rose. "Archivist Stiles? What does she have to do with anything? Siobhan and I are here to help Dakota hunt. Given the increase in monsters I believe you've remarked upon yourself...?"

Verity transferred her glare down to her hands. She couldn't think straight, even now she'd backed up from the most raw edge of panic. Did she believe him? He was perfectly capable of lying, after all.

After waiting for her to respond for a beat, two, Davin shook his head. "I don't see how your binding spell failing sometime in the far future affects Dakota's ability to hunt, so it's thus not my problem. If you'll give me your word—" He broke off, exhaled on a ghost of a laugh. "Do phantoms have their word? Or something else to swear on?"

"I have a truth spell." Verity shot him a smile without warmth. "Which is a stronger guarantee that I mean to keep a promise, since that's the only way I can say it out loud, than anything I have on you."

"Touché." Davin let a breath trickle out in a thinking pause. "I guess you'll have to trust me. I don't gain anything in particular from exposing you. Once the monster problem here is solved properly, I'll be on my way."

"I guess I don't have any choice," Verity admitted. A realization that had been grinding away at the back of her mind finally burst to the surface, and crystallized what bothered her most about all this. "This is a lot to just look the other way from, though. Not giving a shit, I get that, but it would be just as easy to not give a shit and drop a word in Dakota's ear. Are you actually *helping* me, here? Why?"

Was she imagining it, or did Davin look strained? Verity sensed what leaked into his face was all the answer she was going to get, but damned if she could read it. "Look," he said, finally. "I…"

Abruptly, Verity couldn't stand it. She didn't want to hear him say it out loud, so she said it herself first. "No, never mind. Who would think that hard about a phantom's situation, right?" Frustration took over his expression, so she must have been right.

All right. Deep breath. Verity snapped her cuff back on. "I promise not to try to get anyone hurt ever again." That was the easy part, she'd already resolved that on her own. "And I promise to not hold back something that would help the group on a hunt. Good?"

Davin nodded. "I promise not to tell Stiles, or Dakota or anyone here—"

"Including your sister?" Verity doubted Siobhan was reporting to the Quorum if her brother wasn't, but it never hurt to be sure.

"Including my sister, about your worn spell." Davin offered his hand to shake. Verity accepted it and tried to feel relief. She should feel relief, shouldn't she? Instead, the reaction from seeing Lucy get hurt surged back again and she felt shaky.

She pressed her hands to her face. "Christ."

Davin's weight shifted beside her, but he didn't rise, only adjusted a more comfortable distance away. "Are phantoms Christian?"

Physical shakiness transformed into punchy laughter. "Of course not. What am I supposed to use as expletives, then? Frak? Frell? Some other word with a suspiciously familiar arrangement of consonants? Something poetic? By the shattered mirror! By Grabthar's hammer, you shall be avenged!"

She scrubbed her face a last time, then sat up. "No, I picked up the curses wholesale along with the language. Why not?"

"Fair enough. Are most phantoms bilingual?"

Verity groaned. "What is your *deal*, with the questions?"

Davin barked a laugh, and even looked sheepish. "I'm curious. Honestly. If I had the patience for it, maybe I would be research-track with the Archivists. The mirror realm is a whole section of magic that I know very little about. And it's interesting hearing you talk about it."

"Is it?" Verity frowned ahead at a formal dress that she'd never actually seen Dakota wear. She wasn't sure why she'd bought it. Maybe Verity liked the idea of someone even pretending she was interesting. He already had enough information to hang her with, what harm would babbling a little more do? If he went away, she'd just be sitting here alone wallowing about Lucy.

"Most of us are bilingual, yes. Our language is riddled with loan words from various languages for the concepts that came over from the grounded realm anyway." His face lit, subtly, and

Verity found herself continuing to coax that light. If he really was interested for curiosity's sake, she had a guess what he'd ask next. "Today I went to the store," she said in her native language, and continued narrating the shopping trip long enough that she judged he'd gotten a sense of the loan words.

Davin grinned. "That's almost...tonal. Like Mandarin? But with the whistles, it's almost like one of the African languages, with the clicks. Say something else?"

"No." Verity didn't let herself laugh, but did smile. This was getting dangerous again. She knew her longing to keep talking to him was only emotional exhaustion. Now she could feel the relief, dripping into the spaces the adrenaline had left. "Out." She pointed. "Out of my closet. It's late."

"Right." Davin stood. "Night." He nodded with the farewell and let himself out.

Verity smoothed the denim of her jeans over the top of her thighs, then unsnapped her cuff and rolled the chain up, then down. So. On the surface, no farther from home. Unless Davin broke his word, since he didn't have a truth spell.

Verity needed to stick around in the grounded realm long enough to excise some of what she owed Lucy, though. That thought felt settled enough that she hoped she could get some sleep.

7

Verity woke early, hungry, had a bowl of marshmallow cereal, then took up fresh soup for the mantie. She went back to bed to sleep with the mantie splayed across her hip until the hour when the rest of the household staggered out to breakfast. She ate a second bowl of cereal and watched Davin. He wasn't on his phone, and didn't talk to anyone in particular.

Around the time the food was gone, the coffee had hit, and most people had returned from getting dressed, Dakota walked into the dining room, saying final goodbyes on her phone. Or less "goodbye" and more "yes, I understand, right away" so Verity didn't have to see the anxiety on her face to know who she was talking to. Stiles.

She jerked to look at Davin, but he gave a small, minimal shake of his head. He hadn't contacted her, she presumed that meant. That was all very well, if she was supposed to just take his word for it. But Dakota ended the call, and Verity shifted her attention back to her. She wanted to know the worst as soon as possible.

"They want us all to attend a debriefing about the last hunt at the Archives," Dakota announced generally to the air. Verity reminded herself to take a few deep breaths while she figured out if that was bad news or not. Not good, but maybe she was getting too self-centered. Maybe it was only poor Dakota in for a chewing out.

"We're supposed to waste time talking when there could be another monster sighting at any time?" Lance growled.

"It's not like you guys will be taking a plane to Geneva," Verity said. "I'll be teleporting you out, and I can teleport you back just as quickly. More quickly, honestly, than you probably could drive from here to half the locations monsters have shown up before."

"She makes a sound point." Gabe tipped back the last of his mug of tea. "Shall we?"

Verity eyed the bottom of her mug. It was mostly sludge from sugar that hadn't dissolved completely before she started drinking. "I can't take six of you all at once, though." She caught herself almost looking at Davin again. She'd better not make a big deal of the extra work when he knew exactly what her ulterior motive was. "It'll have to be two trips."

Dakota frowned at Lucy. "I guess she did say everyone, but are you sure you should be going?"

Lucy lifted her hand to the side of her face, then changed the movement to smoothing some of the fine hairs that always escaped her ponytail. "I can't do anything strenuous, but it's not like I'm confined to bed."

"I'll avoid turbulence," Verity said solemnly. No one seemed to appreciate her joke. Or maybe Davin was appreciating it silently, but she wasn't allowing herself to look at him, because she absolutely shouldn't care about amusing him.

"What's your upper limit on passengers?" Davin asked. She did have to look at him then. Now she wasn't focused on what Stiles wanted, she noticed his hair was a bit rumpled on one side, so he must have gone to sleep not long after he talked to her with damp hair last night. It was bright red again, giving him character.

"Theoretically, who knows. Practically, three or four, since you all have to be able to both touch me and walk forward without tripping over each other. So I'll do a trip with four and a trip with three." Verity saw the math not adding up on the newcomers' faces. "Dakota has to come along on every trip, or the binding won't let me, remember."

"And two trips in a row—or three, I suppose, with the leg returning here—won't bother you?" Davin didn't seem to be worried about her answer, because he stood and tipped back the last of his coffee as well. "You'd still be able to bring us back if there's another attack?"

"I can go all night." Verity ducked her head to hide her smile when Dakota was surprised into a titter. Lance snorted mockingly.

No matter how many times Verity teleported people from inside a building to inside a building, they always collected their coats when it was chilly outside their starting point. Verity supposed it was part of the psychological exercise of making sure they all had their phones, keys, and other assorted possessions. She waited in the living room, coatless, while everyone organized themselves. She'd closed her eyes because she was facing the mirror, so she let people determine the composition of the two groups themselves.

Someone touched Verity's shoulder. She knew it had be Dakota, because the feeling of teleportation connections and possibilities exploded before her. Verity reluctantly opened her eyes. She grabbed Lance's hand because she wanted him there, not touching her shoulder where she couldn't see him. Gabe took her other hand and Lucy her other shoulder. She stepped into the mirror.

In Geneva, she didn't even pause to look around. She released the men, stepped out from under Lucy's touch, and jumped right back in. The illusion of freedom, for a few steps at least. When she and Dakota arrived back in the house, the newcomers looked a bit glazed, glancing from them to the mirror. Verity wondered what she actually looked like when she teleported. Was it a complete appearance, between one instant of perception and the next, or did she fade in?

"Okay, you two get hands," Verity said. She held them out to the siblings and Dakota's touch squeezed on her shoulder. She waited a beat to see if Dakota had something to say, but apparently she was endorsing Verity's usual explanation. All right then. "It's three steps this time, since we're going around the world. I've heard it's a little more upsetting, since there's that second step where you're going from limbo to limbo. But then the next one you're out."

"You can look, but don't try to focus your eyes," Davin advised his sister, leaning forward around Verity. "You can't, and that's when your stomach turns."

Verity offered him a nod. She'd have to add that to her "so, you've let yourself be talked into teleporting with a phantom" repertoire. "And count in your head. It helps. One step—"

On the other side, Siobhan definitely looked a little green. Verity let her keep her hand while she took deep breaths. Davin looked unaffected, but since he didn't offer to help his sister,

Verity suspected that was half an act.

When Siobhan disengaged herself and Verity looked around, only Lucy was waiting for them in the marble-clad hall. The Archives always made Verity think of a historic bank, both this hall and the outside of the building. She'd only seen that once, when she'd made Dakota take her out to explore the city a little, as long as she was on the other side of the world. It wasn't as sumptuously appointed as a palace, but every metal fitting and length of stone floor shone with polish. Soberly colored new armchairs in historic styles were placed in small groupings along the walls.

An elevator bank and doors to the hallways for the first floor offices and meeting rooms lined the rest of the walls. Huge glass doors with windows above made essentially a glass wall that separated the hall from the comparatively small foyer that fielded any contact with non-magical humans. From this side, it was hard to see through because of the thickness of the constantly renewed illusion spell's glow. Verity recalled that from the other side, the hall looked perpetually nearly empty, with only an occasional person in a business suit passing through for camouflage.

"Where did the boys go?" Dakota peered around, as if there was somewhere they could hide in the two stories soaring to skylights above.

Lucy shrugged. "I don't know. They both had 'something to take care of.'" Her air quotes were emphatic with her annoyance. "I let know Stiles we're here, anyway, and found out where she's meeting us. They swore up and down they'd catch us up there." She named the room, though it didn't mean anything to Verity.

"As will I." Davin squeezed his sister's shoulders. "I promised I'd stop by and see an old friend. It won't take long." He
strode off.

Lucy, glowering, unerringly led the way to the elevators
and down hallways on the correct floor to reach the wing they
wanted. Verity noticed Siobhan didn't gawk. She supposed every mage ended up at the Archives for some reason in their
lives, but Siobhan had apparently been here enough times to
get comfortable with its grandeur. Not often enough to know
her way around, though. Another mark in the column for Davin being the one she really had to worry about.

Their destination was apparently somewhere down a cor-
ridor where the wood framing was no less historic, but could
no longer reach any kind of shine without being completely
refinished because of that age. The hall held classrooms and
meeting rooms rather than a high-ranking Archivist's office,
Verity guessed.

A few steps down the hallway, Dakota snapped out an arm
to block Verity's way. "Shit, I forgot. You can't be down here,
Verity. There are databases and records in this wing as well."

Oh, right. Records stuffed with mage secrets. Verity suppressed any glower before it could make it onto her face. Secrets that would obviously leap off the page and into her eyes if
she was so much as in the room next door. And meanwhile, she
couldn't defend herself at the debriefing. "I don't see what it is
that I shouldn't know. Mages and phantoms have known about
each other for centuries. We even have a treaty."

Lucy gave her a sideways look. "A treaty not to reveal each
other to anyone non-magical, sure. That has nothing to do with
any other knowledge." She nodded back the way they'd come.
"There's a break room. She could hang out there."

"Stay in the break room—" As Dakota spoke, Verity felt the frisson beginning at her throat and settling near her heart that meant the binding was taking this as an order, so she abandoned her next argument, about how she couldn't read secrets if she was under Dakota's eye every minute, and hurried to keep the order from being impossibly confining.

"Or bathroom?" Who knew how long this damn debriefing would take, after all.

"Stay in the break room on this floor, or the nearest bathroom, and no poking around in between, okay?"

Verity snapped a salute before marching off, because joking was the only way to deal with orders. Even trying to keep a lid on resentment, her stomach soured. What if Stiles started in on blaming the phantom again? Would Dakota still defend her? What was Verity supposed to do while she waited, sit around and imagine the worst?

The break room's door was open, making it easy to find. It had a hot drink vending machine, a sink, some relatively comfortable looking couches, and chairs pulled up around a couple of tables. She revised the time before she fretted herself to death upward a little when she found an abandoned magazine, even though it was in German, but then she flipped it open to discover it was some kind of trade journal. The only pictures were graphs.

Maybe it was time to work on becoming trilingual. Verity took the magazine to a table and started searching diligently for cognates, page by page. She was going to *kill* Dakota for this. She couldn't have listened thirty seconds longer before deploying the order?

Or, since she had neither the ability while bound, nor the literal inclination to kill her, maybe she'd start hiding Dakota's possessions. Which should she hide first? Dakota's birth control pills, though very important to her, seemed like they would be as much a punishment for everyone else as for Dakota, if thwarted horniness made her moody. Her credit card? Definitely irritating, but too soon noticed.

The walls had a series of framed ancient maps and drawings, and after several hours had passed—or possibly a little less than one—Verity went and stared at those for a while. The largest depicted the grand sweep of a Middle Eastern building, maybe a palace.

"That's the old Archives." Davin's voice. Verity turned to find him, inevitably, leaning one shoulder against the doorway. "In Damascus. That's where it started, back when it was just a few people collecting knowledge, before everyone started coming to them for advice, and they stumbled into governing. The Archives remained there until the height of colonialism, when they moved it here. People make noises about moving it back somewhere more in keeping with magic's roots every so often, but it's a lot of shit to move, and the political stability here is a plus."

Part of Verity shouted at her to prolong the conversation to distract herself, but the rest of her was suddenly angry. It wasn't like he actually cared if she was anxious, he was just trying to indulge his curiosity some more. "Aren't you supposed to be in the debriefing?" she snapped. She crossed her arms on the table and pretended to read her magazine.

Footsteps approached, Davin sat down across from her, and tugged the magazine away. "That's going to burst into flames if you keep looking at it that way. We just finished. Lucy said she wanted to do some research on jaguar-types, and Archivist Stiles pointedly declared that a good idea, so she and Dakota are off doing that now. If you need something to do while you wait, I was wondering about how you saw those monsters last night. Is there any way you could teach—"

Verity shoved to her feet. "Yes, I could teach you. But do I *want* to? Did you ever think of that? Of course not. Go ask Dakota to order me to do it! If she doesn't mention a time period, it never wears off, so get her to order me once and you're good until she rescinds it." She was so angry she was shaking, and she wasn't entirely sure why. Wasn't she overreacting a little? She stepped to the doorway purposely to feel the clench of the order keeping her from even peering down the hall too long.

"Go!" She strode back and spat the word at Davin. "Go, leave me alone. I am *tired* of questions, I am *tired* of orders and waiting tied to the bike rack outside the coffee shop because they don't allow dogs inside—" To her horror, she felt the sting of tears gathering at the corners of her eyes. She turned to stare at the drawing of the Damascus Archives and grabbed control of herself. This was absurd. She needed to be interrogating Davin about what had been said about her in the debriefing, not breaking down. Scratch that, she just wished he'd leave her *alone.*

"Verity, when did you last eat?" Davin's tone was concerned, which only made her irritation surge again. Was he pitying her? She didn't need pity.

"Breakfast, same as the rest of you." She pulled her phone from her pocket to check the time. It was complaining about being unable to find a network in Switzerland, so it still displayed the original time zone. They hadn't even been here an hour yet. "Teleportation doesn't take any more calories than does an average spell, and that's no worse than, what, ten minutes of working out?" She didn't bother to keep the sneer out of her voice. See? They weren't making her sleep in the ashes of the fire and not go to the ball, and they weren't starving her either.

"Shit." He said it so softly, Verity gave in and turned around to check his lips to see if she'd missed something more. He raised his voice to normal volume. "I'll be back."

"Can't go anywhere!" Verity called after him. She went to slump on the couch. How long was this research going to last? She wasn't tired enough for a nap. She brought a black lock of her hair up to her eyes and started searching for split ends. She needed a trim, now it was nearly below her shoulders, but she hated wasting her savings on something so vain, and hated asking Dakota to cover it even more, even though she knew Dakota would.

Davin returned before she'd made any decision about her hair, two bottles of soda in his hands, and a third under his arm. Though the shape and probably exact volume varied from U.S. soda, they looked vending machine–sized to her. He extended one to her. Verity took it automatically and examined the label. Some kind of citrus flavor, if the pictures of fruits were any indication. "What?"

"Drink that. You'll feel better." Davin flopped onto the couch with the other two bottles.

Verity unscrewed the top and took a sip. Didn't taste too bad. Maybe grapefruit? She couldn't quite tell, since it was so sweet. Davin was still staring at her, so apparently she was supposed to drink all of it, immediately. She was still pissed at him, so she tipped it back and chugged it. He could deal with the inevitable belching.

When she set the empty bottle on the floor, he had the next one open and ready for her. "You're serious?" She eyed him. "My eyeballs will be floating if I drink all that."

"Beats eating sugar by the spoonful." He was apparently serious about that too. Verity couldn't catch even a flicker of his deep humor. He seemed content to let her sip the second bottle though, and didn't bat an eye when her first burp bubbled up. "So they never told you about the side effects of being bound? I assumed you knew, given the snacking on kid's cereal."

Side effects? Verity clamped her soda between her knees so she could pop off her cuff and set it on the arm of the couch. What had he seen in the spell? Had the multiple teleports in a row seriously damaged it? That would be a good thing!

The glow looked the same as it ever had, though. She didn't feel sick, either. Maybe a little less cranky. "These side effects involve sugar?" She sipped the soda. Still rather pleasantly tasty. She supposed she hadn't really tasted the first one to be sick of it yet.

"Shit," Davin said again. For the first time since Verity had met him, he looked *angry*. On her behalf? He couldn't possibly be. "A simple spell pulls caloric energy from the mage, as you were saying. A more complicated spell can be set to draw energy from other sources, like heat or electricity in the environment. A lasting spell needs to keep pulling its energy from the environment long-term. When that spell is a binding on someone, that environment is *you*. Easiest to pull is the quick energy from sugar."

"So the binding's been—" Verity started swigging her soda a bit faster now. Already, the edge was off her anger. She had to stay on her toes to get out of this situation, and wallowing didn't help. Neither did letting anyone see her sulk. "I just—you know. Thought the marshmallow cereal tasted good."

"Well, and the spell wouldn't usually be so stressed." Davin offered her an apologetic smile. "By all the teleporting, and whatever orders are keeping you here. I wouldn't try to fight to shade the truth until you've made it through all of these." He lifted the final bottle, still resting on his lap. "Then you'll be set for all your misleading needs as usual."

At least his humor was back. Verity rewarded him with a lift of her lips, before she caught herself. She didn't trust him enough to joke with him, except some part of her apparently did. No one had showed up like he'd reported on her, and he had noticed and fixed the binding's side effect. But wasn't the latter a cheap enough way to earn credit with her? "What did they say about me at the debriefing, anyway?"

"Nothing. Archivist Stiles did ask—" A frown flickered over his face, quickly gone. "But Dakota told her how you waited on the sidelines and teleported Lucy to help."

"That's good." Another stay of execution. Verity assumed they couldn't continue forever.

Davin let silence settle for a beat, then shifted to face her. "Verity, don't feel obligated to answer, but… What is it you're afraid mages are going to do to you? You clearly don't trust me, or maybe anyone except Dakota. But aside from the binding, no one's mistreated you, have they?"

Verity zipped her thumbnail along the threading at the mouth of the bottle. How did she want to answer that? What *was* she afraid the Quorum would do to her, in the end? Was it all paranoia and fear of the unknown? She didn't think so. Dakota knew her, saw her as a *person*. Without that foundation, she had no guarantees about anyone's treatment of her.

She wondered what it meant about how Davin saw her that he bothered to ask that. Unless they were back to the morality of the tiger in the crooked zoo again. She decided to dodge most of the question. "Dakota's kind enough. She has no idea what to do with a bound monster of her very own. We both of us sort of stumble through keeping our little household running." She shrugged, and finished off her soda.

She reached for the final bottle and Davin let her take it. "And I won't blame her about the sugar thing. You're part of a binding spell pair, no one else around here is. I'm not surprised Dakota didn't know about it."

"True." Davin reached across her and grabbed the leather cuff when she would have snapped it back on, bottle once more between her knees. Verity let him have it, though she had no idea what he wanted it for.

He drew a remarkably similar cuff from his jacket pocket, this one with the leather tinted slightly red. He unrolled both to compare their lengths, then offered the new one. She examined the design, a line of fleur-de-lis, and snapped it on. She hadn't imagined Davin was a fashion plate, but the new one was pretty.

The glow of her binding spell brightened.

Verity sucked in a breath and fumbled at the snap. Was it really—? When she removed the cuff, the binding spell looked the same as always, a little dull from all the wear. Cuff back on, and it looked as good as new. "What is this?"

"A very complex, very tricky little illusion spell. It spins an illusion of a different spell—or a lack of a spell—that covers both itself, and whatever magic is underneath it." Davin grinned, proud. "My old friend is part of a *very good* illusion pair."

"So another binding sensitive would see a whole spell—and an illusion sensitive would see a whole binding spell as well?

No one sees the illusion spell?" Verity clutched the bracelet to her chest. This was exactly what she needed. Her stomach swooped with anticipation. If she could continue to stay out of the Quorum's clutches, she'd be able to wear the binding away unobserved and go *home*.

"That's right." Davin's grin widened.

Reality intruded in a rush. Why the hell was he doing this for her? She was planning ways to make him tell her his real motives this time, when a stranger knocked on the doorframe.

Verity would have mentally accused Davin of arranging the interruption so he wouldn't have to explain anything, but he looked as surprised as she felt. His former grin suddenly seemed as much an illusion as the spell on the bracelet because his expression grew neutral once more, humor hidden as deep as when she'd first met him.

The woman in the door was tall with pale skin just tinged with yellow at her age, and short, straight hair a color that could only be called iron because of the rigid power in her stance and her expression. She seemed to be hovering on the edge of the age at which many humans dwindled from extra weight to frail thinness, but there was no hint of a stoop to her back. Verity looked again and wondered if the woman was younger, and a previous illness had deceived her at first. Was she in her fifties, or her seventies?

"Archivist Stiles," Davin said, rose, and pressed his hands together in front of his chest, formal.

That was Stiles? Verity had only ever heard her voice. Verity barely had time to jerk to her feet before the woman strode over and clasped her hands. "I'm delighted to be able to meet you in person, Verity."

She smiled, and Verity didn't trust it. Wouldn't have, even if she'd never heard of Stiles before in her life. In the gaps where the expression didn't quite cover Stiles' real mood, Verity thought she glimpsed a sneer. "Nice to meet you," Verity managed. That couldn't be farther from the truth, but pat social greetings fell under the same logic as hyperbole when it came to her truth spell.

"Everything's arranged with Dakota, so if you'll just come with me, we'll get you settled." Stiles' grip tightened when Verity tried to jerk her hands away.

No! Just when Verity had dared to imagine actually getting home again, shark woman showed up and snatched that away. She had to believe—*had* to believe, or she'd give in to despair— that everything had *not* been arranged with Dakota. So she had to stall, stall with everything she had, until she could talk to Dakota herself. "Dakota ordered me to stay here. I can't leave until she releases me."

"I'll text her," Davin said, and lowered his head briefly over his phone. "Has the Quorum held a special session over this matter, then? I didn't see it in the last publicly posted minutes."

"Nothing for you to worry about, Dubois." Stiles turned her attention to him briefly, smile sharpening. If that was possible. Then she started pulling Verity toward the door. Verity dug in her heels and found Stiles was surprisingly strong. The order wouldn't kick in until she passed the bathroom, but Stiles didn't know that. And Verity wasn't even sure what the order would do if she was under duress. Would it snap rather than force her to hurt herself?

Stiles' grip slackened and Verity managed to pull her hands free. Verity fled out of reach, and only then realized Davin blocking the doorway was what had made Stiles stop.

Dakota came up behind Davin and frowned in at them. "What's going on?" Her eyes widened with anxiety at seeing Stiles.

Stiles approached Dakota as Davin let her in, perfectly poised as if she hadn't been grappling with Verity only a moment before. "Please release your order holding your phantom. We need her for study. The composition of her magic should provide the insight we need into how the magic of the mirror realm is behaving—"

"Dakota needs me. To teleport people in emergencies." Verity tried to beg Dakota with her eyes. She knew the Quorum intimidated Dakota, but let her stand up to them now, in this.

A little steel seemed to enter Dakota's spine. "That's right. And we have the monster problem under control. There's no need for you to take her."

"She has no *authority* to take her," Davin said, tone painful in its neutrality.

Stiles spread her hands. "Another week, then, for you to pursue your own leads on what's causing the problem." She pressed her hands together, as if to emphasize a removal of options. "Then I'm afraid the Quorum will have to insist. We can't let this situation drag out forever."

"It won't, I promise." Dakota and Stiles seemed caught in stalemate for a few seconds, each waiting for the other to move, then Stiles shot a poisonous look at Davin and swept out.

The moment she was out of sight, Verity wiped the hands Stiles had touched on the sides of her thighs. "Fuck, she's creepy." If she'd needed confirmation that she wanted to stay the hell out of the Quorum's hands, she'd just been provided it in spades.

"I believe that was her playing relatively nice." Davin let irony trickle up into the last word. "Don't judge all Quorum members by her, though." He nodded to Dakota. "The deadline sounds like something she could actually get support for, but if

we can show progress, I'm sure the exact timing can be negotiated. And even if it can't, Verity, you really are important to the
hunts. They can't keep you here."

Davin was certainly talking like he knew the Quorum pretty well. Verity glanced at Dakota for confirmation, and found
the woman nodding slowly, no surprise in her expression. So
perhaps all that was common knowledge among mages.

Whatever else he'd just revealed, however, Verity now knew
Davin was *definitely* not on Stiles' side. Unless they'd staged all
that, but why? If Stiles was trying to get control of her, walking
her out of the break room here and now seemed vastly prefera-
ble to some complicated future plan making Verity trust Davin
might set up.

Verity scrubbed her face. She just wanted to go home, but
at the moment she'd settle for things being quiet and simple
with only her and Dakota again. She'd been a terrible spy when
she first started this mission, and she was still terrible at chart-
ing ulterior motives now. "Is Archivist Stiles a particularly
powerful mage on the Quorum?" She looked straight at Davin,
not even bothering to pretend the question was addressed to
both of them. Whatever his connection was to the Quorum,
she might as well get some use from it.

Davin hesitated a beat, then shook his head. "That's two
questions. I don't think she's as magically powerful as some.
The Quorum's about charisma and administrative talent more
than actual magic."

"Otherwise I'd be Quorum-track," Dakota said, and held up
her arms. "God. I get hives just thinking about it."

Verity did have to laugh at that. Davin looked a bit uncomfortable—probably because he didn't know how to agree without being rude—and then continued. "As for the second part,

you probably wouldn't think of putting 'Archivist Stiles' and 'charisma' in the same sentence, but she gets shit done."

"Anyway." Dakota gestured between Verity and the hall. "Let's get the hell out of here while we still can. I release the order about staying put."

When she looked for it, Verity found marked strain around the edges of Dakota's expression. She assumed the debriefing hadn't been enjoyable for her either. "Amen," she murmured, and preceded Dakota out.

8

As if they needed the extra encouragement to leave, Lucy caught them halfway down the hall. "We have to get back *now.*"

Verity didn't need her to specify the reason. "Jaguars?" The remaining team members, except Lance, were not far behind Lucy, and the two groups coalesced into a rough knot around Lucy and whatever alert she was reading on her phone.

Lucy spoke to Dakota, as if she had been the one who asked the question. "The reports look like mantas to me. And to the computer. It has those pretty dialed in."

Dakota growled under her breath. "Where the hell is Lance?"

"We could leave him here," Gabe said, mildness not entirely disguising the fact that he seemed quite happy to leave his rival stranded across the world, given the chance.

Not that Verity objected to letting Lance cool his heels in Geneva either, but she wanted to get out of here, not stand around arguing. Dakota would definitely not agree to leave him behind. "I'll take him on the second trip. Whoever I drop off at home first can drive out to the site with the weapons and set up the mirror. Then I can take Dakota and Lance straight there. That will give him a little more time here to show up."

Dakota squeezed Verity's shoulder in a gesture of gratitude that caught her a little off-guard, seeing as it was in front of the others, instead of in private. Verity hurried on with logistical details. "Closest mirror is the one in the bathroom." A single, rather than gender-segregated, fortunately. She headed in that direction.

Dakota gestured for Lucy specifically to follow. "You should go in the first group, and then stay at home."

"No argument here," Lucy murmured with a thin smile. Siobhan and Gabe hurried after her. Three steps to the house, a brief pause to pack the car, and three steps back. Verity's jumpiness ratcheted up with each additional minute she was forced to wait with Davin and Dakota in Geneva, but Stiles failed to show a dorsal fin around any corners. Lance strolled down the hall about fifteen minutes after they'd returned, just when Verity thought Dakota might explode from the waiting as well. Dakota's dirty look slid right off him. Verity grabbed for Lance's hand so as to not give them time to start arguing.

Three steps took them out of the mirror propped against Dakota's SUV. Verity had to spend several seconds blinking at the transition from indoor electric light at midnight to the softer afternoon sunlight through clouds. Gabe and Siobhan had placed themselves in a parking lot sandwiched between an empty, low office building and a three-story building of some kind of light industrial warehouse space on the other. In the absence of an illusion, the vehicle was parked to at least block the main entrance.

Dakota shrugged off the transition more quickly, snatching a paintball gun from the case in the back of the SUV and shoving it into her waistband. She splashed through a puddle as she dashed to the secondary entrance, briefly fracturing the wavering blobs of buildings reflected within it. Earlier rain must have stopped a few hours ago, as the pavement was dry between the last few puddles clinging to potholes.

Davin hung back by Verity for a moment. "Got your paint gun?"

Verity lifted the one she'd grabbed for herself, then let it fall back to her side. "I'm not going to use it on any of you," she snapped. Maybe that wasn't what he'd meant, but tension still knotted her muscles from watching for Stiles. "I've promised to only help, remember?" She jogged after the rest of the team and ignored him pointedly.

As Dakota started laying the perimeter illusion, Gabe tossed up a burst of light. He and the others might have gotten a flicker from the nearest manta, but the main flock of around half a dozen was too high for the light to reach.

"Give me half a minute, someone will see the light," Dakota shouted at Gabe.

"You should add some construction chain-link fencing to keep people back as well as hiding what we're doing," he called back.

"I've got it under control." Dakota was much kinder in her tone than Verity would have been. She supposed Gabe was only trying to be helpful, but Dakota was the one who'd been hunting on her own for years. Hunting with Verity, that was. Verity didn't need to help the others in discounting herself.

Illusion glow laid down, Dakota sprinted back to the others, drawing her gun as she ran. "Verity, how many?"

"They're bunched up, but—" Verity took a few slow steps, eyes on the mantas as she searched for a better angle to count. "Five—" She didn't get to refine her estimate because the flock chose that moment to turn straight for them, buzzing low over everyone's heads. Another riled batch. Great.

Verity decided she'd give Davin all the evidence he'd ever wanted of her helping the hunt, and lifted her own gun and got it mostly aimed. She'd never hit a manta on this pass, but if she was ready on the next...

Lance shoved her out of the way as one manta dipped low with a splatter of paint on one wing and crashed into the pavement. Verity caught herself with a few stumbled steps and turned angrily back as Lance fell on the manta, pinning it to the ground with his long, double knives. His long coat settled around his ankles and he twisted his head to flick his dark hair out of his eyes.

Yet another reason why she usually stayed out of the way. They didn't even need her, at one to one odds. Less than that, because she doubted Lance's victim was going to get up. Gabe knelt over it anyway, avoiding the spreading silvery pool of its blood, and shot it right on top of the head. In their ongoing battle for Dakota, Verity supposed Lance hoped to win on style and Gabe on adherence to the book.

Verity tucked her gun away at the back of her waistband and retreated to lean against the car as Dakota called to the others. "Gabe, throw more light, everyone else, get ready to aim, on my mark." Dakota paused a beat, then shouted with admirable authority to her tone. "Mark!"

The explosion spell flashed and the spelled paintballs pattered up into the manta flock, splatting or whiffing past to arc back down and *fzzt* on the pavement beyond. Another manta dipped low enough for Lance's knives.

Davin broke away from the main group, backing up slow-

ly with his gun still aimed up. Verity gritted her teeth as he
neared. He just couldn't leave her alone. "Three." She scanned
the horizon just to be sure. "That's all."

"We could still use you." Davin squeezed off a shot, mostly
blind, and missed by a good foot.

"Not as much as you think." Verity and Dakota had actually
figured this out on their own already. She pointed to one of the
mantas, following it with her finger as it dodged and weaved
above everyone's heads. "Try aiming where I'm pointing."

Davin did try, but lowered his gun in frustration after a few
seconds. Verity lowered her hand too, because her target was
down. The remaining two followed soon after with help from
a light spell from Dakota. "You'll just have to learn to see them
yourself," she said sardonically.

He gave her a dry look, then jogged back to the main group.
Siobhan was laughing and slapping Dakota's back, while Lance
smirked and loaded one of the dead mantas on his shoulder to
bear it stylishly back to the car.

Gabe, of course, picked up two, one for each shoulder. Verity got out of their way, circling vaguely in Dakota's direction.
She wasn't celebrating like Siobhan, but she did look a lot more
like her usual self. Maybe an easy victory was good for her. And
the fact the team wouldn't all fit in the SUV on the way back
was good for Verity. She used the thought of another teleport's
worth of wear to chase away residual tension.

Back at the house, mantas dumped in the backyard to burn
later, Dakota refused to let anyone escape to clean up until she'd
had a chance to talk to everyone. Most of them slouched around
the dining table, chairs at varying angles, but Verity remained
standing with Dakota. She knew what this conversation was

going to be about, and she didn't relish the coming argument she'd have to have with whoever suggested they hand her over to the Quorum immediately.

Dakota surprised her, though. "So we have a week to figure out what's going on before the Archivists take it out of our control." And there she left it. No mention of Verity.

Lance sputtered loud objections, liberally interspersed with obscenities. Dakota's lips curved. "That's pretty much how I felt. We can do this, guys, right?" She caught everyone's eyes, including Davin and Siobhan. Her glance at Verity was more sideways, apologetic. For the Quorum trying to study her? Verity wasn't sure.

Gabe and Lance both immediately expressed baseless confidence, but Lucy looked more worried. Verity watched her, because of any of them, she should have the best idea of what it would take to figure this out. *Could* they make the deadline? "We have a much better chance at succeeding than they do." Lucy grimaced. "Nothing beats direct, on-the-ground data. We didn't exactly find much about jaguars at the Archives, after all."

"Where mantas are focused on lifefor—neural electricity, jaguars like eating flesh too. That's why they're so bitey. Mantas just smother their prey to keep it from getting away." Verity looked at her hands rather than at the humans. She'd promised Davin she wouldn't keep information back, and the need to make the deadline provided another reason to share what she knew. "They're stealth predators and usually hunt alone. They like to drop on their prey from above and immobilize it briefly with their tails, to give them time to injure it properly."

No one said anything. The silence got so heavy Verity couldn't stand it any longer. "Look, none of you ever asked, all right?" She tried not to make it sound sullen, but she probably didn't succeed.

Dakota blinked her way back to speech. "You're right, I didn't. I should have. I mean, you told me about mantas, but that was long enough ago, I didn't think of it..." She coughed, floundering.

"Why were there three last night, then?" Lucy's eagerness held a ghost of what Verity had heard in Davin's tone after he extracted the promise from her. Maybe he'd been telling the truth about his curiosity.

"No clue." Verity shrugged. "What about other recorded jaguar attacks at the Archives? Any with multiples?"

Dakota shook her head. "None. Not that there's a decent sample size." She glanced at Lucy when she said that, so Verity guessed it must have been a constant refrain from the younger woman as they worked. "The hunting strategies others have stumbled onto have ended up being...a bit like ours." Her expression twisted with guilt. "Have one person stand alone beside a high point, while the others shoot up that point."

"I think we should celebrate tonight," Lucy said a bit stridently. Maybe she didn't want another round of concern from everyone. "The jaguars didn't *kill* anyone. And it sounds like you guys kicked ass in this last fight. That's worth something. We'll be kicking jaguar ass soon enough. And when you're trying to solve something, you have to stop thinking about it for a while sometimes. Let your unconscious mind work, making connections."

In the face of a round of agreeable murmurs from everyone, Dakota managed a smile. "I'll order pizza." Dakota paused as if for objections, but Verity shrugged. One night of pizza wouldn't break the budget. Besides, she liked pizza too. "And someone can go out and buy the beer."

"Forget beer, I'll get us bubbly." Lance leaned in to Dakota to whisper something more in her ear. She blushed. Verity wondered briefly if he was offering to pick up something else to help with the not thinking, maybe pot now it was legal. Probably not, though. Since the word had spread that the designer drug Ghost was significantly more addictive to mages than it was to regular humans, she'd noticed Dakota and probably a lot of other mages avoiding all recreational drugs.

Gabe chose that moment to start up a very serious conversation with Dakota about tactics for the next time they encountered jaguars, coincidentally distracting her from Lance. Verity left them to it. She wished she had something to celebrate. The fight had been their win, not hers. Let their unconscious minds work, she'd probably spend this party consciously worrying about what Stiles might try next.

At least there would be pizza.

9

After the first round of pizza had been distributed, and the bubbly had been poured, Dakota stood, holding her wineglass high. "To Kathleen—" Her face crumpled as she apparently couldn't find the rest of the name in her memory. Verity couldn't figure out what Kathleen she meant, either.

"Kathleen Kimmel," Lucy supplied in a soft voice. Her champagne was in a drinking glass instead of a wineglass, as they'd quickly strained Vasily's leftover supply, but she raised it too.

Then Verity got it. The dead woman. "And magic she is once more," she said in her native language, low enough that hopefully no one would hear. And who knew what happened to humans' lifeforce when they died, of course. It wouldn't join the formless magic as it did for phantoms.

Everyone else at least raised their glasses. Dakota drained hers, then sat down and started on her pizza, like she planned to regain a celebratory mood by sheer force of will if necessary.

Everyone's volume got louder as the pizza and, more importantly, the bubbly disappeared. Verity had to admit, Lance had purchased plenty, but that was probably just for the look on Dakota's face when he walked in carrying it all. Davin got quieter and quieter and finally slipped out, while Siobhan claimed a corner of the room to tell a story that required a lot of gesturing, evoking heckling and laughter from her audience. Gabe and Dakota seemed to be giving the story only half their attention, the rest going into staring into each other's eyes across the few feet between chair and couch. Verity knew eye contact was supposed to be intimate in this culture, not challenging, for humans interested in sleeping with each other, but it was still *weird*.

Verity could take or leave champagne, but after her first glass dedicated to the dead woman, she only finished off the dregs from a couple bottles as she transferred them to the kitchen. It was a good thing their recycling bin was big enough to have a lid, because otherwise they would definitely have one of *those* loads this week. Davin stood with his drink on the counter, staring at the window at the twilight.

Verity rinsed out the bottles and eyed him sideways. "If you're a non-drinker, I'm not sure the evening's going to get better. They'll be turning on the music soon, killing more bottles, and telling bullshit stories in the living room until the wee hours."

"I don't not drink," Davin said flatly. He sipped his champagne in illustration, then put it back down on the counter with a thump.

Verity set the bottles in the crate they used to carry recycling out to the bin, and returned to the sink. She followed his gaze out the window. "We don't have a porch, but you could go stand in the backyard. Then you could get miserably wet in the drizzle while you stare up at the stars that are hidden behind the clouds and you couldn't see them even if it was clear because of light pollution."

"Christ." Davin pressed a hand to his face. When he lifted it away, he was laughing, low. "That's a dangerous sense of humor you have there."

"Phantoms are well known to have weaponized it centuries ago." Verity realized suddenly that she felt comfortable back here, swapping dry jokes with Davin. She should want him to leave her alone, should be walking out. Instead, she *wanted* to stay near, draw his laugh out of him again. "What's wrong?"

"Partying isn't my scene." Back to flatness again. "Anymore." The addition had such weight, Verity felt like she'd been trusted with something huge, but she couldn't for the life of her have said what it was.

"Well." That kind of trust prompted her to reciprocate instinctively, but what was she doing, even considering it? But she *wanted* to trust him with something. Wanted—no. Verity spoke quickly to cut short that train of thought. "If you still want to learn how to see mirror realm monsters, I have something you can practice on upstairs." And maybe the pet would help her not think about week-long deadlines too.

"You keep a claw or something as a trophy?" Davin asked as he followed, leaving his drink behind. He immediately frowned. "No, you wouldn't. Lance seems like the trophy type. We're not breaking into his room, are we? I'd rather avoid that kind of awkwardness."

Verity tried out shoving his arm playfully. He didn't flinch at all. "No, we are not. He's only crashing here, anyway. He hasn't moved his stuff in." And hopefully never would. "Hurry up and you'll see." She opened the door to her room slowly, checking for the pet waiting to escape. But she could see the gentle rise and fall of its back among her blankets. As lazy as most pets. Good.

She pushed Davin in and closed the door behind them. Only then, standing so close to him in a relatively dim space— the overhead light really needed the help of the standing lamp she had in the corner—did she realize how this could be mis-interpreted. Or was that interpreted? The moment she became aware of his physical presence, so close, she also became aware of a longing to have him touch her again, like he had when showing her left and right.

Not that she kidded herself that Davin thought of a phan-tom that way. "I swear, there's something here." She hurried out of touching distance and sat down on the bed. She whistled at the mantie and it rippled its wing tips briefly. Still sleeping, go away!

She picked it up anyway and spread the warm, floppy shape across her lap. "Here. Promise not to tell anyone about it, and you can pet it."

Davin leaned down, fingertips extended, expression dubi-ous. "I promise." When he touched the mantie's skin, he jumped his hand back in instinctive surprise. "There *is* something there. It's…furry?" He slumped to a seat next to her on the bed.

"Very short fur. They're a domesticated version of the big mantas. Very friendly." Verity guided his hand around the edge of the mantie, nose to wing tip to tail to wing tip. The mantie, finally fully awake, wriggled in joy and floated onto her other forearm to lip the skin on the inside of it. "I forgot how much that tickles." For a breath, homesickness surged up and brought tears with it. She didn't let them fall.

Davin didn't notice or kindly ignored them. "If he's little, does he eat little bits of electricity, then?"

"It. They don't have sexes until mating season." Even when Verity released his hand, he kept petting, down the mantie's backbone. "It could probably pull lifeforce from animals up to a raccoon, but the hunting instinct was bred out, so if the raccoon ran away, it wouldn't know what to do. We feed them mushy vegetables." She looked for the bowl of soup she'd fed it from that morning and only then noticed that the mantie had knocked it over. The pet had vacuumed off the carpet, but a stain marking where the liquid had soaked in remained. "Bad mantie!" She supposed that would teach her to leave the pet alone with food all day.

"Definitely a pet," Davin said, laughing outright. "Does it have a name?"

"It wouldn't have a name as such, it would have a particular whistle." And Verity hadn't thought so far as coming up with a whistle for it. Doing so now tugged the homesickness still lurking at the edge of her thoughts closer. Maybe since the mantie was trapped with her in the grounded realm, she should come up with a name for it in English.

"Washcloth," Davin suggested, deadpan, then dodged a swat. "Or Zoomer." He squinted at it, hard. "I think I can almost see—kind of a distortion with rainbows—"

"Exactly—" Verity's enthusiasm was interrupted by a knock at the hallway door.

"Davin?" Siobhan's voice. "Lance is down there making it sound like you and Verity are up here fucking. If she hears him—"

Davin practically sprinted to open the door. "If Dakota hears him, she can come up here and see for herself," he said as he opened it to his sister. Verity wouldn't have thought anything of his answer, but Siobhan seemed so surprised to see her. Had Siobhan meant, if Verity heard Lance, she'd know Davin was sneaking around her room? But he'd been in here before, and she credited him with enough intelligence not to imagine she had incriminating secrets hidden under the mattress. No, Siobhan must have meant Dakota would get worried if she heard Lance, like Davin had taken it. Even if he hadn't chosen to make a move on Dakota yet, he probably didn't relish the idea of having her think that about him.

Davin tugged his sister inside. "We were just…" He glanced at Verity and the mantie, expression tight.

Verity appreciated him keeping his promise, but she didn't mind Siobhan, so she released him. "Here, you can meet a real live monster too," she invited Siobhan.

Davin gave Siobhan his seat next to Verity and hovered near the door like he desperately wanted to escape but didn't want to seem suspicious. But then Siobhan was petting the mantie and cooing a bit drunkenly and he probably figured Verity was distracted. "I'll go correct Lance's misapprehension," he said, and slipped out.

"He'll just change it to me and you," Verity grumbled under her breath to Siobhan.

Siobhan scrunched up her face. "Would he? No offense, Verity, I'm not attracted to you sexually—"

"You are very drunk, though." Verity sighed, and since *she* wasn't drunk, she didn't tell Siobhan that the same was true about her own attraction. Siobhan's humor was a bit too brassy for her taste. "Anyway, you'd gross everyone out if they thought you wanted to sleep with me. Lucy would probably consider it bestiality."

"Why are you so protective of her, then?" Siobhan only allowed Verity an inarticulate noise of protest before she continued. "No, you are. I saw how torn up you were when she got hurt."

"It wasn't her specifically. I don't want anyone to get hurt. But she's especially young, inexperienced—stop drooling on me, stupid." She pried the mantie off her arm. She'd spoken without thinking, only wanting to hide the part where Lucy getting hurt was her fault, but the truth spell hadn't even given her a twinge.

"She's only two years younger than me." Siobhan flopped back on the bed, top of her head barely missing the wall. "What are you, as ancient as my brother?"

"Did he tell you to ask me that?" Verity tried to hold onto her earlier lightened mood, rather than getting annoyed.

"No, he can ask his own questions." Siobhan flopped an arm over her eyes. "I suppose I am fairly drunk. It's probably a good thing I'm up here, sobering up a little." She flopped the arm away and rolled her head toward Verity. "Can you get drunk? That's a question of mine. You don't have to answer."

"I'm bound into a body that's pretty well human in every physiological sense at the moment, so yes." She was acting a lot like Davin the non-partier, though, Verity realized. She spread the mantie over Siobhan's stomach and the woman giggled at the sensation. Verity got up and rummaged in the bottom of her dresser for her vodka and shot glass. She poured herself a shot. "You'll welcome to some too, if you'd like. I only have the one glass, though."

Siobhan pushed up on her elbows to peer at the label. "That's some top shelf shit." She lowered herself down. "But I'm sobering up a little, remember? So as not to end tonight hugging the toilet."

"Dakota used to get it for Vasily every birthday. Give the Russian vodka, right? Only he doesn't drink vodka. He accepted it without letting on, and had a whole stash piled up by the time I was around. He gave the whole thing to me." Verity tossed it back. Very nice stuff.

She came back to the bed and lay down in a position echoing Siobhan's. "Not that I drink a lot. Might get maudlin."

"When I went to that training program, it got very college-y very quickly with a bunch of young people in one place. And we were all mages so we didn't have to hold back from making spells for fear of being seen by regular humans. Get too drunk, you don't have the coordination for it, but there's this sweet spot—" Siobhan illustrated a distance between her two palms, "where you can still do magic, but your judgment about what spells would be a good idea goes. Like drunk driving, I imagine. They ended up making us appoint a chaperone like a designated driver, who went around making sure no one sat next to a complementary half of their specialty."

"So you did regular college too?" Verity found herself intrigued to hear about someone with a normal life. A normal mage life, at least. Dakota hadn't had any kind of normalcy anywhere.

"Yeah. Just four years and out. Davin was the one looking at graduate school—" Siobhan twitched, she cut herself off so hard. "But who wants to talk about him."

"Not Davin himself, certainly." Verity frowned at the underside of the shelf above and considered asking Siobhan what was up with Davin's anti-party stance. But she doubted Siobhan would answer. "Hopefully he succeeded in convincing Dakota we weren't doing anything untoward up here."

"I'm sure it's fine." Siobhan flopped a hand over to pat Verity's. "*Can* a phantom even have sex with a human?"

The vodka had warmed her enough that Verity laughed. "Yes, of course we can. Whether we want to..." She stared at the wood grain of the shelf some more. "I think there's something of a species barrier to real pleasure. Or maybe he just sucked. Either way, if there were any phantoms around, I'd be jumping at the opportunity, but since there aren't..."

"Oh, sweetie." Siobhan winced. "I wish I could let you go."

Verity didn't want the conversation veering in that direction. She sat up. "No maudlin, remember?" She hooked one heel on the edge of the bed and looped her arms around her knee. "I'm surprised Davin hasn't been trying harder with Dakota. Given her current options, he compares favorably. Unless he only likes men?"

Siobhan snorted into laugher and trailed off into coughing. She sat up too, to gather her breath. Dislodged, the annoyed mantie floated over to sleep atop its favorite pile of Dakota's sweaters near the ceiling. A scarf that had been stuffed beside them wafted down to catch on the shoulder of a jacket below. "My brother is not gay. And I can assure you personally that Dakota's charms are resistible."

Verity must have still looked dubious because Siobhan pulled out her phone and flipped through photos. She found the one she wanted, zoomed in, and held it out. "Look. His former fiancée. He likes women, trust me." The woman in the picture was fairly pretty, if her hairstyle was unusual. One side of her hair was earlobe-length and the rest was buzzed short.

Verity zoomed the photo back out, because she was nosy. A man had his arm around the woman's shoulder. "Who's that—"

She cut off. Wait. "Davin? He's so different." Much thinner, hair darker. His eyebrow piercing in, wearing a leather jacket. And he was grinning. It was the thinness, Verity realized, that had fooled her. Phantoms changed their look all the time, but never their basic size, except through the same ways a human would change size.

"Yeah, he wouldn't want people seeing that." Siobhan pressed her phone to her chest. "Shit."

"I won't tell. Promise. And you know it's a true promise." It was an easy promise to make, Verity couldn't think of any reason she'd be dying to remark that Davin had gotten more straight-laced in his old age. Not really a shock.

"Well, as long as I'm in for a penny…" Siobhan closed the photograph, then looked back up at Verity. "The fiancée's probably your answer. He's needed some time to get over her. It's been long enough, I suspect when he falls, though, he'll fall hard." Her look sharpened into something Verity couldn't interpret, then she shook her head and put her phone away. "Lance and Gabe aren't exactly subtle, are they?"

"Not particularly." Verity snorted. "You know, I'd be happy if she'd just *pick* one of them, as long as that one is Gabe. But no, she can't decide. And if she does think she might have decided, then the other one does something sooooo sweet—" Verity's impression of Dakota's voice was probably overdone, but she was getting into it. "And they're both in the running again."

Siobhan laughed. "So you're a fan of Gabe?"

Verity shrugged. "Not a fan, per se. But I think he's the better choice. Even if he's not as good in bed. You can teach someone that kind of thing. You can't teach someone not to be an asshole. Actually, Lance already knows how not to be an asshole, he just chooses to be one."

That got an even bigger laugh. "I love it. So Lance is supposed to be good in bed?"

"Apparently." Verity made a face. "If you're into that kind of thing, I guess. When she forgets to shut the door, Dakota seems to like it." She nodded to the wall that adjoined Dakota's room.

Siobhan's eyes narrowed as she apparently got hold of a thought and chased it to ground while handicapped by the alcohol in her system. "Are you telling me Lance was the human you—?"

"For my sins." Verity fidgeted with her hands, rubbing her thumb against the opposite palm. The joke came out on autopilot, but the rest of her braced for Siobhan's real reaction. "He likes to imagine he's edgy, I was curious. And horny. It didn't work out that well."

Siobhan made an encouraging noise, like a conversation with a friend. Verity supposed she'd been missing those too over the last six years and hadn't even realized it. "And my joke earlier about him sucking—not in a good way—aside, I don't think it was all on him. The human body does pleasure differently somehow. When I was bound, I had to relearn my own body even by myself, for Pete's sake."

"And how do phantoms do pleasure?"

Verity examined Siobhan's face. Open, interested. Sympathetic. Like a friend. Which would be a much better way to get her to spill secrets than Davin's pushing, but if humans wanted to know how to please a phantom in bed, more power to them. "It's a…sort of state of body you switch into." Dancing past the fact that it was one state among the many different physical looks a phantom could change among. "Everywhere is sensitive and pleasurable, it's not just pooled into a couple areas."

"Well, if someone's a good partner, they'll pay attention to more than just 'a couple areas.'" Siobhan frowned. "But if it's a difference you found even on your own, that seems legit. I still think it's too bad it didn't go well for you."

Verity sat up. Time to change the subject again, keep running on the thin ice over the pessimism below. "Sometimes I help Gabe out a little. Come on, I'll show you. It's actually pretty funny."

A hand to the back of her head suggested her hair had gotten messy with all the flopping onto the bed, so Verity crossed to the laptop on top of the dresser, opened it, and checked herself in the webcam's mirror feature.

"You really don't like mirrors, do you?" Siobhan was sitting up too now.

Verity smoothed her hair so it framed her face properly, and did some rough finger-combing in the back. "Yeah, the next time you're in exile, you tell me if you like recreationally staring down the road that leads home—worse, *feeling* it there, like a spell." She bit her words off before they could get even sharper. Time to make a joke. "Small ones are fine, but I'm sure you know what it's like doing your hair using a makeup compact."

She smoothed the back of her hair again. She still didn't sound nonchalant enough. "Do you think I need a haircut, or should I grow it out?" Growing out hair as a human took so very long, she usually chopped it off before a year had passed for at least the feeling of some kind of change.

"I think you'd look pretty with long hair." Less drunk, or socially skilled enough to craft a believable compliment even when drunk, Siobhan crossed to the hanging dresses. "Wear it loose with something like this. The intense red would be good with your skin tone, I'd bet."

"Those are Dakota's." Verity pressed the laptop's screen closed and tugged the dress out a little farther. "I do borrow occasionally, but her stuff is all baggy on me because of the difference in our bust size."

"You should have your own clothes." Siobhan frowned and examined Verity minutely. To check for current bagginess, Verity realized. She tugged on the hem of her top to illustrate that it lay properly along her bust. Completely the right size. Just old.

"I do. But shopping is a pain." And not that fun when she was trying to buy things to fit in with the humans, rather than to suit her taste. "Borrowing's easier."

Verity checked that the mantie wasn't poised to escape, then opened the door for Siobhan. There was helping of Gabe to do. And she'd bet it would cheer up Dakota, too.

Downstairs, Siobhan trailing a bit dubiously, Verity found Dakota's phone out on the dining room table. For some reason. She must have been checking something after dinner. She typed out a text to Gabe and showed it to Siobhan before sending.

Want to slip away from the party? Meet me in my room in five minutes and don't let anyone see you!

Siobhan gave her a dubious look. "That's the kind of booty call a fourteen-year-old would send."

"Anything more explicit would embarrass Gabe, trust me." Verity set the phone back and threaded past Siobhan toward the living room. In the archway, she held up a hand for Siobhan to wait so the group didn't open up to welcome Siobhan in. Nobody much paid attention to Verity, so she could discreetly slip up behind Dakota in the conversational circle where Lance was holding forth on tactics.

"Gabe asked me to tell you that he wants to 'talk' to you in your room." Verity kept her voice low enough to be private, but made sure to layer on plenty of annoyance at being forced to play messenger, and irony on the verb, though she couldn't make air quotes without someone seeing.

Dakota had probably the least discreet reaction ever, startling when Verity spoke, looking pleased, then guilty, then guiltily pleased. Her work done, Verity slipped off and collected Siobhan on her way back upstairs to her room.

"Now, we wait," she said. It wasn't even a full five minutes before they heard the door to Dakota's room open and shut. A minute later, it opened and shut again. Verity put her ear to the door to the adjoining bathroom. She couldn't make out words, but there was definitely both a male and a female voice talking on the other side, amplified by the pipes. She turned to Siobhan and took a bow.

Siobhan's expression twisted. "I can't believe that actually worked. That's not a very nice thing to do someone, you know." She opened the door to the hallway. "I'm definitely not going to stay and listen."

"Imprisoning someone isn't very nice either," Verity grumbled. Was it also because part of her knew Siobhan was right? But that was in normal circumstances. What about Verity's circumstances? "I'm not planning to listen! I don't get off on that, trust me."

"You want power over her in return." Siobhan's face suddenly held dawning understanding. She winced. "Sorry. It's none of my business. I'd better get back to the party."

She shut the door politely behind her, though the mantie still hadn't stirred. Verity was left desperately wishing Siobhan hadn't apologized, so she could have dismissed her words wholesale.

10

Verity woke the next morning to a cold stomach, where she'd shoved aside the blankets and the mantie had pushed up the hem of her tank top. The mantie was gone now, long gone, by how cold her skin was. She'd cracked both her door and a window in the hall bathroom, so the pet could go out and do its business, but it hadn't been gone this long before. That she'd noticed. But it had seemed so anxious to stick close to her or here, in safety, when she'd been awake.

She flipped the blankets over herself, but she was fully awake, so she sat up and whistled a come command. No mantie appeared. Was it exploring downstairs? That was worrisome. She pulled on some clothes, left her hair as it was, and slipped out. After last night, things were pretty quiet this morning, everyone sleeping. Except Gabe, who was undoubtedly already up, meditating in his room—unless he was in Dakota's room. Verity glanced at the room's outside door as she padded down the hall. She found she didn't have a prediction for that.

She winced, remembering what Siobhan had said last night. Even if she didn't agree with Siobhan—and she probably didn't?—maybe she wouldn't set up Dakota and Gabe again. She whistled softly. No mantie floated into view. Hopefully it hadn't gotten itself shut into anyone's room. But why would it enter one in the first place? She doubted anyone had mushy food set out in a nice, flat vessel. Maybe it had found something it could knock over.

Downstairs, bits of reflection winked at her from windows as she surveyed each room in turn. Sunrise would be soon, she could tell from the diffuse tint of brightness in the light, rather than lines and points from electric sources outside. No pet.

Verity rubbed her hands as she went back upstairs, whistling softly still. Should she check outside? Or leave the bathroom window open and wait? The thought reminded her that she hadn't checked the bathroom. Her surge of imagined relief didn't last long: just a few steps from the hall into the doorway.

She shivered at the temperature it had sunk to overnight with the steady trickle of outside air through the high, small window. She could see in one glance the mantie wasn't there, but she looked twice anyway, pushing the slasher-flick-bloody shower curtain—a gag gift Dakota had received at some party—first one way, then the other. With so many people sharing one space, every horizontal surface was covered with hair products and bath products and shaving products, and she had a hard enough time moving around herself without knocking something over. She doubted the mantie had done more than loft high, straight to the window.

It was probably outside exploring. It might be stressful, but she needed to wait for it to come back. It had survived long enough for her to find it in the first place, after all. Verity brushed her hair in the streaky mirror, and went to get some breakfast. She shouldn't really be worrying about a pet. The team had six days now, so they needed to make the most of them.

In the kitchen, a subconscious sense of something being off tugged at her while she was getting the milk out of the fridge. She set the jug on the counter, let the fridge door swing shut, and cataloged her impressions of the room. Glasses in the sink, bottles piled in and around the recycling crate, those were new, but hardly worthy of note. No, on the wall, a stain. What had someone spilled last night? And how had they managed to spill it on the *wall*?

Verity left the milk and wandered over. The stain was grayish, shimmering slightly in the changing angles of light as she approached. Almost like—

Mirror realm blood? Verity slapped her hands to either side of the stain and leaned in, trying to verify the shimmer. No, please. When she got so close she was observing the stain at an oblique angle, a vertical line jumped out at her in the center. Like someone had stabbed…a knife…

She was going to *kill* Lance. Verity was already halfway up the stairs before the thought finished forming properly. She used the corner of the wall at the top to turn herself and sprinted to Lance's room. She pounded on the door with the side of her fist, and that wasn't nearly loud enough, so she kicked the door, again, until it thudded in its frame. "You stabbed my pet! Why did you have to stab my pet? It couldn't even physically harm a human! Why did you kill it?" Verity knew she was probably shouting loud enough to wake everyone, not just Lance, but she found she relished the idea.

Gabe arrived first, from his own room. "Verity…?" Lucy appeared from the old office where she had the airbed, next, then the siblings from the room they were sharing.

Verity gave up pounding but kept shouting through the door. "Why are you always such a fucking asshole?"

Dakota arrived last. She reached out a hand to Verity's shoulder, but didn't complete the touch. Then Lance distracted Verity by finally opening his door. His pajama pants were incongruously plaid, given the dyed hair and sullen expression. "What the fuck is wrong with you?"

"You. Killed. My. Pet!" When Lance shook his head, Verity gestured the mantie's dimensions. "Miniature manta, about so big? Don't lie to me, there's blood on the wall downstairs, around a stab mark I bet matches the width of your knife perfectly."

"You never told us you had a pet." Lance folded his arms and looked down his nose at her.

Verity opened her mouth—and stopped. She had no answer to that. She supposed she'd wanted to keep the pet *hers*, at some subconscious level, which explained why she hadn't thought it through enough to figure out how stupid that was. There were too many people in this house not to notice a flying presence, even if it was invisible. She'd have kept it safer by telling everyone. Dakota wouldn't have tried to take it away from her, she was pretty sure.

"Just because she didn't, doesn't mean you have to kill everything that moves, Lance." Dakota gave Verity a sideways almost-hug with her arm over her shoulders. "When did you find it, Verity?"

Verity glimpsed the firmer ground Dakota had handed to her, and she jumped onto it with both feet. It hadn't been that long. "Day before yesterday. Ask Siobhan and Davin, they met it last night." She stood taller. "I was using it to teach Davin how to see mirror realm creatures." That came out too pious, even she was annoyed listening to herself. "They're just *little*. Literally—" She measured a foot and a half in the air with her hands again. "They can't even eat from a bowl without knocking it over..." And that sounded too pathetic. She bit the inside of her cheek to keep from saying anything else. She hadn't even decided on a name for it yet.

And the mantie must have been terrified at the end. Had Lance chased it around, or snuck up on it so its death was mercifully quick? She jerked out of Dakota's grasp. "Can I at least be the one to burn it?"

Dakota nodded, providing an endorsement that was the last thing Verity wanted in the current mood, but she probably needed, which just made it all worse. Lance's look of disgust finally cracked into something that got within spitting distance of guilt. "I don't have it."

Dakota frowned. "What do you mean? You're not telling me you were out at the burn barrel in the wee hours of the morning because you couldn't leave a small, invisible corpse on the patio for a few hours?"

Verity folded her arms to echo Lance's position and sneered at him. "The domesticated pet mantas eat rotting garbage and soup. Were you so scaaaaared of that you had to burn it instantly?"

"Look." Lance focused on Dakota, like the rest of them weren't important enough to justify himself to. "I gave it to a couple of friends, all right? They're mages, and they use dead monsters in their research." He held up his hands to forestall other questions. "That's all I know, all right? They're willing to do pick-ups whenever, so why leave the thing stinking up the place when I don't have to?" He saw Verity's sneer and raised her one that practically magnetized her fist to punch him right in his disgusting, self-righteous mouth. "I didn't realize that it was someone's hamster that needed a fucking Viking funeral."

Verity couldn't find any words. For a frozen beat, she considered growling her wordless rage at Lance, but that wouldn't do anything except make her seem unbalanced. Instead, she whirled and strode for her room, shoving people out of her way without really seeing them. Dakota's voice rose with annoyance as she chewed Lance out behind Verity.

Inside her room, door slammed, she sat on the edge of her bed and stared at the bit of wall visible between Dakota's hanging clothes and her dresser. Stupid. She should have chased the mantie off immediately. Of course a bunch of trigger-happy humans would kill anything even remotely like their usual targets. Maybe it would have been hard for the mantie to survive out in the wider grounded realm, but at least it would have had some chance. Here, it had obviously had none.

Someone tapped on the hallway door, and Verity considered for a moment whether she wanted to tell them to go away. It might be Dakota, arriving to hand out equal chewing-outs to keep the peace. Verity wasn't sure if Dakota had that much grasp of household diplomacy, though. "Come in."

Siobhan opened the door but didn't enter. She shook a box of cereal diffidently. "Want some?"

Verity eyed her for a beat, then held out her hand in acceptance. "Your brother been coaching you?"

"What, on pushing sugar?" Siobhan handed over the cereal and took a seat. Verity wasn't sure she wanted company, but it seemed like only a fair exchange, since Siobhan had brought her food. "No, he didn't say anything. I just thought you'd like some breakfast. Being as it's breakfast time."

Interesting, Verity suddenly realized, that Siobhan had known exactly what she was talking about, even though she claimed her brother hadn't mentioned it. Was it such a well-known fact among binding mages? "Thank you." She stuffed her hand right into the box, heedless of manners. Siobhan didn't seem to mind, and even pulled out her own handful when Verity angled the box in her direction in invitation.

Siobhan broke the munching silence first. "Can you adopt another one? I mean, I'd like to think I'm not a person who'd ask their friend when they plan to get a puppy the day after they had to put their dog of fifteen years down, but you hadn't had it very long."

"I've never seen one in the grounded realm before." As she said it, the strangeness of that—seeing a pet here now, not the lack before—struck her. She was too keyed up to follow the thought to its end, but she pushed it nearby, so it would pop up again soon.

Another knock. Who was it this time, Verity wondered, Davin? But when Verity responded, it was Dakota who opened the door. "Davin's making waffles, if you guys are hungry," she said. She picked with her fingernail at the doorframe like she'd found a splinter there. "I'm sorry, Verity…"

Verity hurried to forestall any "but." She didn't want to hear it, and if she said it first, she didn't have to, in a way. "But I should have warned you guys. How would you know pets were even a thing?" She carefully closed the flap on the cereal box and got up.

"Well, yes, but—" Dakota's expression turned flustered as Verity approached, and she didn't move out of the way yet. "Maybe you can get another one."

"Or I could get a cat or dog," Verity said, shrugging. She couldn't hold up the nonchalance much longer, so she squeezed past Dakota and headed downstairs. She didn't want a stupid grounded realm pet. She wasn't even sure if she would have kept the mantie long-term, or tried to find a way to set it free. It had just been a piece of home, and it had been ripped away before the balance of comfort shifted to pain over a reminder of what she was missing.

The first waffles were coming out of the iron when Verity arrived. Everyone else—minus Lance—made somewhat stilted conversation, but that was pretty par for the course before coffee had hit.

After her third waffle—she was overfull now, but she'd wanted it, so she'd let herself have it—Verity stacked her cutlery on her plate and felt her thoughts finish slotting into place. She looked at Davin. She felt a bit more comfortable telling him this, rather than the others, even though it might be part of the answer they needed for the Quorum. Maybe it was because on the surface it followed the tone of their earlier, curiosity-driven conversations. "I think there must be a hole in the boundary between realms."

And Davin took her seriously, which also helped. "What are the signs of that?" The team gaped like she'd uttered the most egregious of non sequiturs, which she supposed was somewhat fair.

"I don't know if there are signs, per se. At home, it happens plenty in legends, but I can't remember anyone seeing one in modern times. But that was the first pet I've seen in my time here, and while I suppose they could have been coming through and not surviving very long, I'm dubious. At home, pets were bred to be territorial. Not to defend it, but to not leave it. You teach them which house and garden is theirs and then they stay right around that area. Otherwise, they'd wander into the formless magic and get lost."

Verity nudged her cutlery a little around the rim of her plate. "They're not like the other creatures. Those are well-known to look for the thin places between the realms and squeeze and wiggle through in hopes of richer hunting grounds. But with so many more monsters, more often, rarer types of them… there must be a hole. That way, an exploring pet could wander through, and not realize how to get home. It wouldn't take the effort of squeezing through a thin place."

"How long since you realized this?" Gabe's words fell heavily, breaking off Verity's train of thought.

"You hear that? That's why I don't volunteer information," Verity shot at Davin. He winced. At least the truth spell meant when she gave Gabe an answer, he had to accept it. "I had no idea about any of this until people started talking about the possibility of other pets showing up, roughly half an hour ago. I'm as aware as the rest of you of our deadline. If not more." Verity scrubbed at her eyes. "It's only a theory right now, anyway."

"Easy enough to test." Davin stood and started collecting plates, starting with Verity's. When he was next to her, he gave her a nod that might have been meant to be reassuring. She ignored him. "We go out to the scene of a recent fight and check for a hole."

"Which will look like what? A big movie FX glowing oval in the air, with psychedelic swirls on the other side?" Lucy scoffed. Verity imagined she'd been on the receiving end of "go out and look for spell residue" commands before, when there was absolutely nothing left to be seen. She pointed at Verity. "Is the plan to walk around after her, waiting for her to see one?"

"The plan's to walk around after her and me." Davin paused in the kitchen doorway, sounding perfectly reasonable, but Verity thought she could detect his humor. "Presuming the mirror realm magic on the other side of the hole looks anything like the mirror realm creature I learned to see last night.

Verity's right, I think any sensitive can learn how. It's hard with-out an example, but if we do find a hole, I can show both you and Dakota."

"Oh." Lucy's annoyance drained away instantly. "Really? See it? Like seeing a spell?"

"Promise." Davin's arm muscles shifted under his pajama T-shirt like he would have made some gesture to back it up, like crossing his heart, but his hands were full of dishes.

Verity was suddenly oddly jealous. That was her lesson Davin was taking advantage of. Lucy's interest should have be-longed to her. But of course it wouldn't have actually worked that way. Someone needed to convey the knowledge to Lucy since Lucy wouldn't listen to Verity.

"Okay, sensitives and Verity, let's meet back here in half an hour, and then we'll head to that office park," Dakota said.

"Or better yet, the rec center." Verity appealed to Dakota this time. She supposed she shouldn't forget that Dakota was also usually willing to listen to her. "That's the most out-of-charac-ter hunt we've had so far. And jaguars can't fly. I think the hole might be closer."

"Good idea. We'd better hurry before the center opens, though." Dakota plucked at the waistband of her pajama pants, covered in penguins with winter hats. Everyone scattered to get dressed, and Verity stayed at the table, slowly revolving another thought that had just occurred to her.

If pets could wander through a hole, could she wander *back* without tripping the binding's prohibition against traveling?

11

Scattered sun greeted them when they arrived at the rec center and pulled politely and neatly into a spot at the back of the
parking lot. With only four of them, they'd all come in Dakota's
vehicle. Verity hopped out and switched her phone to camera
mode to give a good excuse for peering around in random directions. To cover her truth spell, she found a tipsy pine cone on
the sidewalk and a patch of sunlight staining the edge of a cloud
and saved them in the phone's memory. Now it was true to say
she was taking pictures.

Dakota and Lucy stepped into the unlandscaped strip beyond the curb, feet cushioned by needles, to consult over her
phone. "The initial reports from the jaguars were here, in that
neighborhood where you killed all those the mantas a few hours
before. That's why they were initially hard to tease out. So the
hole might be around there, but we probably still want to track
the jaguars' probable path back from here." Lucy dragged the
presumable map around with a fingertip.

"Along high surfaces, right?" Dakota looked up and smiled
at Verity.

Verity was surprised enough by the acknowledgment she didn't answer for a beat. "Yeah. A path along rooflines."

Davin joined her, phone out to copy her camouflage, so Verity left that area to him and strode closer to the building. If she was going to slip through a hole, she needed to find it before anyone else, without someone hanging over her shoulder. Whatever Davin said, she wasn't entirely sure he'd see a hole on his own, either. Once he was done with the back of the parking lot she'd circle back and do that area herself.

Her steps along the sidewalk took her to where Lucy had fallen. Despite her best intentions, Verity stopped. She sincerely hoped Lucy wouldn't come this way. Was that a suspiciously brown stain on the sidewalk, or just somewhere a leaf had rotted away? Its shape wasn't very leaf-like. Maybe a pile of leaves. She cast a covert glance at Lucy, but she seemed happy to stay in one place and direct matters with lots of gesturing to and from her map. Lucy wasn't stupid. She wouldn't come over here.

Verity aimed her phone at the grass, searching hurriedly for something photographable that wasn't that stupid stain. Nearby on the grass, rougher here than the stuff on the sports fields proper, her eye was caught by—what? A trickle of light, it looked like.

No, magic. A cloud drifted by, cutting off the sunlight in that spot, and the trickle's feeble glow became clear. Verity edged up to it, following the trickle to its source. The magic was even fainter above the ground, but she could make out—yes! A vertical tear, two sides that didn't quite match up.

The moment the thought to step through formed in her mind, pressure imploded across her chest, her shoulders, her jaw, radiating down her back to her legs—for a moment she couldn't even move. She knew better than to fight against the binding but for a moment she did, until every muscle that wasn't seized, quivered. If she could just be *strong* enough, if she could just *break* through, she could get home—

But none of this was about that kind of strength. Verity knew that, intellectually. When pressure turned to sharp pain across her teeth where she'd been clenching them too hard, she stepped back and breathed for a while. So that hadn't worked. On to the next thing. She had a few days left yet. Verity massaged the side of her jaw. How was tooth pain so much worse than almost anything else you could do to yourself without violence?

"Found it," she said, as she walked up behind Davin. He turned, took one look at her, and drew an individual Halloween-sized packet of skittles out of his coat pocket to press into her hand. "Stop that," she said, and tore it open anyway. Then, because her issues weren't actually his problem, she added, "Thanks."

She tipped it up to dump the candies straight into her mouth as she walked back to the hole, leaving Davin to round up the others. They arrived at a jog and Dakota and Lucy managed to peer in almost every direction except the right one. Fortunately, Lucy seemed absorbed enough in the search she didn't notice the sidewalk.

Davin homed in on the right vicinity, but his blankness didn't resolve further after that. Verity flattened the packet to make sure no more candies were hiding at the bottom, folded it, and slid it into her pocket. "Want a hint?" she asked him.

"How will I impress you with my manly sensitivity if you give me hints?" Davin said, deadpan. "I'll admit I'm not seeing much, though."

"That's because there's not much to see." Verity cast a quick glance around to make sure no regular humans were around to watch them, then crouched and touched the trickle of magic, following it with her fingertips to the hole proper. "Psychedelic swirls aside, you'd think there would be a lot of magic to see, with all the formless stuff on the other side—"

She straightened abruptly. Duh. "It's grounding."

Dakota squeezed her eyes closed a couple times, then stared at the spot like she was trying to make a 3-D movie resolve without the glasses. "What the hell are you talking about?"

"Magical energy does do that." Lucy's eyes widened. "And if any coming through from the mirror realm is doing that, there wouldn't be much to see, that's correct…"

Verity paced around the hole, examining it from all sides. "It's probably lit up like a Christmas tree in the mirror realm, with all the formless magic sticking to the edges and trickling through." She stumbled over her next words because her mind was suddenly racing so fast it left them behind. *If we could look at it from the other side…*

She had to play this oh, so carefully, and she had to play it *now,* while it still seemed natural. "If you want to know how it was formed, you'll probably want to look at it from within the mirror realm. And it would be easy—" The truth spell didn't like the strength of that assertion, so she modified it on the fly. "It might be easier to see even for those of you without the trick of it." She nodded to Dakota, since she seemed less likely to take offense than Lucy. "It would give us something *substantial* to report to the Quorum."

"You're saying—we should go into the mirror realm? Really into it, not just teleporting through to another place in the real world?" Dakota pressed her palms together, excitement flickering over her expression. "Now?"

Dakota was hooked, that was one step. Lucy looked shocked, and Davin, Verity couldn't read, but she only had so much attention to spare for him as long as he wasn't actively trying to throw a wrench into the gears. Now she had to start tap-dancing along the truth. "If we go in right here, it'll be into the thickest of the formless magic. The formless magic can be dangerous, and I'm no explorer with experience navigating it. I think we should travel into a town and approach the hole from there, using paths explorers have already anchored." Would a step into the formless magic right here, right now, be that dangerous? Probably not. The biggest dangers were getting lost, losing one's mind, or getting attacked, none of which were likely to happen with a step in, a quick examination, and a step out. But the possibility of danger existed. That was true.

And if she could get to her home town and get someone there to break her binding—she'd told Davin phantoms didn't have mages as such, that was true, but one of the elders might be more familiar with human spells than the others, or someone might have learned some trick of using the formless magic while they were out exploring. Maybe if they couldn't break it, they could hold her there and drive the humans out. It didn't really matter to her. She could talk to her people, her family, for the first time in six years, and they could *help* her.

"And what about the phantoms living there? What would they think of that?" Dakota asked, overlapping Lucy's more heated question.

"What if it's a trap?" Lucy touched her cheek unconsciously, then crossed her arms to stop herself doing it.

"A trap six years in the making. How patient do you think phantoms are?" Verity snapped. No. She needed to be nonchalant. But not too nonchalant. Of course she'd want to visit home, so they'd know something was up if she seemed indifferent. "It's not a trap. I'll state that whatever way necessary so you'll believe the truth spell is enforcing it. The people living there will probably be suspicious, but probably also curious, and I'll be with you."

"It's worth considering." Davin nodded to the SUV. "I suggest we get back to the house and put it to the others as well. There's a chance that Siobhan and I could bind this hole closed, but then we'd have no idea what caused it, and whether more holes will appear. I'm pretty sure the Archivists wouldn't accept that as having solved the problem, when it comes to our deadline. Going to the mirror realm might be a calculated risk we need to take."

"I think it's a *stupid* risk…" Lucy caught her lower lip in her teeth briefly. "We'd really go *into* the mirror realm? See it from the inside? No living human besides Dakota's former mentor has ever done that."

"Think of the bragging rights in Geneva," Davin said with a small smile, and gestured in invitation to the SUV again. This time Dakota and Lucy went.

Davin hung back to talk to her privately. Of course. Verity supposed she should have expected something of the kind.

"How much of this is to help you escape?" he asked, after a beat of silence.

All Verity had left at the moment was gallows humor. "You ask that kind of question of someone under a truth spell and expect an answer?"

Davin didn't laugh. "If Dakota doesn't think of safe-guarding all of us with every order she can come up with before we leave, I'm going to have to suggest it to her. If what keeps us safe keeps you bound, I'm sorry."

He reached out, maybe to clasp her shoulder. She didn't find out because she knocked his hand away. "I fail to see why you feel the need to apologize to me or even justify yourself."

"Guys! Hurry up!" Lucy shouted at them from across the lot. She looked like she was about to continue, but cut herself off at the last minute.

Verity jogged for the vehicle a little ahead of Davin. Dakota spoke over her shoulder as she climbed into the driver's seat. "Lucy got a message about more mantas. Supposedly just a couple, back near that office park. We called the boys, they'll probably get there before us, but we better get going."

Verity and Davin ended up in the backseat. He leaned forward to search for an angle to see something in the rearview mirror even though it was set for the driver. Lucy, Verity realized after a second. "Were you really going to yell about mantas in front of a bunch of non-mages?" He didn't sound accusatory, precisely, but there was no humor there.

"Of course not. And if I had, I'd have added something about a video game tournament." Lucy squirmed in her seat. "All right. Maybe monsters have me kind off-balance right now, okay?" Her next breath came ragged, the one after that she smoothed out. "I'm a good-for-nothing twenty-something anyway. The worst people might figure is that I was high on Ghost."

"What?" Davin's voice deepened for a moment. Verity wondered if it was delayed anger, barely held in check to give Lucy a chance to excuse herself, which she apparently hadn't done well enough. In Verity's opinion, Lucy was right. She deserved a bit of slack, and Verity didn't see the real danger with so many movies and TV shows around. With mantas, for that matter, they could be talking about an off-brand Shark Week.

"You know, the club drug? Popular with the kids these days?" Lucy's voice turned ironic, looping herself and Dakota in one group, older than stupid kids but still cool, and the practically thirty Davin in another. Who knew where Verity fit in that scheme. Probably outside it completely. "Obviously I don't have personal experience, but supposedly it makes some people spout rambling sorts of stories. Like pot makes some people paranoid."

Davin made a choked noise like he was swallowing some kind of stern lecture on the Dangers of Drugs. He must be older than Verity had originally assumed if he'd had that installed already. Dakota concentrated on driving and didn't answer.

In the continuing silence, Verity's mind circled back to Davin's words before they'd reached the SUV. She wasn't planning to escape at the expense of anyone getting hurt, he should know that by now. But having other phantoms break the binding wouldn't hurt anyone. And "don't try to escape" was too vague an order to be enforceable. She still had a chance.

12

There proved to be only two mantas after all, and the others took care of them before the sensitives group even arrived. They all headed back to the house together. Verity stayed silent for most of the ensuing argument there. They assembled in the living room, Verity explained the situation in the most academic tone she could manage, and everyone had their say. Now they'd reached the stage of repeated restatement of fundamentally opposed positions. Verity watched her hands and didn't interfere. She would only do more harm than good. At some point, everyone would wear themselves out and someone would make a decision. Dakota would have been a good candidate for that, but Verity wouldn't count on her having spontaneously grown that much leadership ability.

Verity had picked a chair against the wall with the mirror so she wouldn't have to see it, but that also marked her out from the main group. The matching dark blue couch and loveseat had belonged to Vasily, and were arranged in a pleasant conversational arc facing the gas fireplace. The other armchairs, accreted over time, matched neither the couch nor each other. Verity's current seat was tucked into a corner because there really hadn't been any room left for it otherwise.

Lance had left his seat to pace so he could shout at Gabe more effectively. Gabe, in contrast, looked like wild horses wouldn't drag him standing because he was proving how little he needed to meet Lance's posturing on the same field. Assuming that you didn't realize that his studied calm was as much posturing as Lance's bluster.

"The risk simply isn't worth it. We have monsters coming through to our world, so how is the solution ever—ever!—to blunder into the world crammed full of the damn things? We'll get eaten before we go a hundred feet." Lance twisted back to glare at Gabe. He wasn't wearing his coat indoors—for once— and the movement lacked some of the flair it must have had in his head.

"How can we afford to blunder around *without* the information we'd get by going to the mirror realm?" Gabe spread his hands on his knees. "Forget about the Archivists for a second— as hunters, *we* need know what caused that hole. Maybe the monsters tore the hole, and they're pushing into the real world for some other reason. We have no idea. And if we simply close that hole and walk away with our fingers crossed, we will continue to have no idea right up until the monsters are slaughtering humans left and right. A hunt every day—sometimes two, three in a day—how can we ever sustain that pace before more people are killed?"

"And what about her?" Lance pointed at Verity dramatically. "We're supposed to trust her? Just follow her in, to become jaguar kibble? Or get slaughtered by a bunch of phantoms?"

Davin left his position holding up the wall and came to

stand with one hand on the back of Verity's chair. Verity pointedly shifted position so she was leaning into the opposite arm.
Was this the point where he advised Dakota to start layering on
the orders?

"I don't see that trustworthiness needs to be a problem."
Gabe reached across the gap between loveseat and couch to put
his hand on top of Dakota's on the couch arm. "If you would
simply order her, she'd be an asset. A local, on our side. She
could ask if they know anything about the hole."

"Oh." Dakota glanced at Verity, then away. "I don't like
to—"

Verity was tired of this. This close to home—*so close*—she
only had so much patience. She stood and held her arms wide.
"Just do it, Dakota. Get it over with. We're burning daylight.
Soon it will be five days left." She managed a smile, teeth only a
little bit clenched.

"Verity, tell us immediately if you become aware of any
danger to us in the mirror realm, and don't plan anything to
hurt us with the phantoms." Dakota pressed her lips together when she finished, and gave a short nod. Verity's muscles
squeezed so briefly she would have missed it if she hadn't been
waiting for it.

Lance sneered at her. "You should have told her to make
sure we didn't get hurt."

"That's a bad binding. It would never hold. She can't control everything that might threaten us." Davin stepped around
Verity's chair, ending up between Verity and Lance, almost…
protectively? That was rich, coming from him.

"And it might do something shitty like forcing her to jump
in front of a bullet for one of us. I never want someone doing that for me of their own free will, never mind bound to it."

When Dakota found her position, Verity did have to admit, she was confident in it. Lance didn't physically back down, but he didn't say anything more either.

"And we need to be sure she'll take us home," Gabe added quietly.

"Oh, right. Stay with the group, Verity." Dakota looked around the room. "Well, I for one am going to the mirror realm. Anyone else? The sooner we go, the sooner we can be back, so a bunch of monsters don't have time to show up while we're gone."

Everyone growled or murmured assent. *Stay with the group, Verity.* Fuck. But not the end of the world. She had to remember that. When the binding was broken, no order would matter anymore.

She stood and held out her arms. "I assume you want to do this in one trip? That might take some choreography."

Dakota's face took on a touch of hesitation. Abstract, meet concrete. "Just…like that? We don't need—" She glanced around. "Supplies?"

"It's not the moon. Or faerie. You can eat the food and drink the water." Verity lowered her arms. She wasn't desperate to leave before they changed their minds. She wasn't. No need for sarcasm. Maybe treating it like the trip to Geneva would make them more comfortable. "You could get your coats. The best place to come out will be the edge of the fields, so there might be a few minutes' walk."

"Good idea," Dakota said. Everyone scattered, probably to fill their pockets with granola bars despite what Verity had said. She retrieved her coat from where she'd shrugged it off into the chair on returning from this morning's search and pulled it on. Without anything left to do, the twitching of anticipation through her whole body started to get out of hand. Her heart was racing and she wanted to pace, to wring her hands, bleed off the nervous energy somehow, but she simultaneously wanted to stand as still as possible, to project the appearance of control.

Davin returned wearing his coat first. Predictably. He touched her shoulder and she started, hand raised to push him away out of sheer instinct. "Always with the touching." Her humor came out edged. "Don't you know phantoms steal your soul that way?"

"I'm sorry, I didn't realize you didn't like it. It's—rude? For phantoms?" Davin backed up a step.

"It's not that I don't like it." Verity hugged herself. That didn't look in control, but she didn't make herself stop yet. "It's just that no one except Dakota does, without a reason. You're weirding me out."

He didn't touch her again, but he came to stand so close behind her shoulder he might as well have been. "Verity—"

Then Lance thumped in and the others followed soon after. Verity got more than a little jostled as they sorted themselves out. Finally, she resorted to watching them in the mirror to direct them. Home tugged at her so hard that she had a difficult time breathing normally enough to speak. When she had Gabe and Lance at the length of her hands, Lucy and Siobhan touching near her elbows, and Davin and Dakota more intimately behind her shoulders, she stepped in.

13

One step, this time. One step into home, or at least the formless magic. That stole too much of each footfall to count them. But Verity was such a grounded creature now—forced into such grounding—that the stability of the town called to her like never before. One step into formless magic, uncounted steps to lead the humans out at the edge of the fields. Like that, done. Home.

The formless magic sang to her, or perhaps hummed. Perhaps whistled at the edge of hearing like the wind. Human languages had no words for it. To be fair, neither did her native tongue—some things were too ever-present to need description. Each moment of every phantom's life, it waited at the edges, curled in with questing tendrils of mist that held every color and none at once like white light capriciously licking a prism.

And she'd never realized it had a scent. Maybe that was an artifact of her bound human form, but every breath spoke to Verity of home in a language of frost before sunrise, sharp moisture locking away all else. Beside her feet, the irrigation canal burbled out of the formless magic into the fields and she rocked forward in parallel with its energy and momentum, shedding humans.

With the movement, she broke from the touch of the formless magic, but of course magic touched all here, Verity realized. Some things less, some more, but still she heard it, smelled it, breathed it. Nothing to ground it, drain it away, only a few ties, to lend a town stability from one day to the next. She tilted her face up to the sunlight, gentler here. She'd forgotten that. Or was it her human senses, filtering everything to something different, something new? If she was fully phantom, what would she see?

If she was fully phantom, she probably wouldn't see—wouldn't *notice*—anything. Human or not, she was seeing with new eyes. Seeing home. So tightly, exhilaratingly, incontrovertibly, home. She was crying, but that didn't matter.

"Now what?" Lance said. Verity turned back to his scowl. "We going to stand here and snivel or what?" Formless magic ghosted up his back, burst into breakwater sea foam around his shoulders. At his feet, the scrub grass of the in-between spaces of the fields, outlining the crops, sharpened a little with a certain sense of confidence. Humans were so grounded they brought it with them.

"You can't see—" Davin's voice came out strangled. He stared into the formless magic as if he could trace a source of light within it, if only he triangulated shadows properly. The bright mist had no wish to be triangulated and so twisted back and back upon itself. "Of course you can't. You're a crafter."

"I see fog and wheat or something." Lance shrugged and settled his long coat with a tug at the lapels. "I guess it's a little creepy."

With a tiny frown between her brows, Siobhan grasped her

brother's arm and found the pulse in his wrist. Her curse came out whispered, perhaps a prayer instead. "It's just—everywhere. Like one big spell. No, like we're the odd crafted little spells in a *world* of magic."

"What's that supposed to mean?" Lance twitched a hand toward one of his knives and then crossed his arms.

Davin laughed, sound cracking in the middle which allowed a little magic song to seep in, then slip its melody off again, into the soft background of the world. "Someone sensitive for Lance so he'll shut the fuck up, would you?"

Dakota woke up enough to gather Gabe and Lance both to her, hands on her shoulders to touch the sides of the stronger pulse in her neck. Lucy remained still, hands at her chest balled together for strength more than clasped and lower lip held tight in her teeth. And Lance did shut up.

Verity walked up to the edge of the crops and drew the leaf of the nearest corn stalk through her fingers, tracing the ridge of the underlying central vein. Now was the time to perhaps not feel so keenly, to think. Think like a phantom, and not notice what she took for granted. Think like a human, and protect what phantom secrets she could. Fight her way free of the humans so she could stay here.

"Someone should be out to greet us before long." A few yards along the crops, she realized the humans weren't following. She retraced her steps and surveyed them and tried not to find them muddy. Davin and Siobhan's hair was bright enough, and Gabe's brown skin had a burnished quality. But they none of them shone. None of them belonged here.

A figure approached, tracing the lines between the fields from the direction of the town. Verity mentally stumbled, realizing only when reaching for a gender-neutral pronoun that she still thought in English. The figure moved as quickly as she could, without appearing to run. "I've brought trouble in my wake," Verity called out in their language. She could still speak it at least. Rustily. That greeting was traditional enough, for an explorer returning home, though "no trouble" was the more common form.

"I see that." The phantom assessed the numerous humans with darting glances. She wore white lace fingerless gloves, a feather clipped to her hair to hang before an ear, and a solidly built female look, very dark-skinned with epicanthic folds over green eyes. The odd combination made Verity wince, then again as she realized once she would have known no better than that herself. Humans did have eyes like that, after all. Humans had skin like that.

What Verity should have seen first, she saw second: the unique magical signature beneath the look that differentiated one phantom from another. Thoughts in English were the least of her worries now—her thoughts were proving entirely too *human.*

The phantom frowned at her. "Is that you—" And she said Verity's name.

Verity hadn't expected it to hurt. Why should it hurt? But she'd been Verity so long, her real name seemed almost mocking. What did she have left of that person? "Just call me Verity," she said.

Then she switched to English, and wished she could pretend to herself that she spoke in that language only because the humans were getting restive. The pulse of magic of home had laid her self-delusions bare. "This is—" Hard, to render a phantom name in English. Verity chose the closest approximation of the sounds in the first syllable, and left the rest of the name for those who could actually pronounce it. "Lrehn."

Lrehn's face lit with interest rather than annoyance at the corruption of her name. She was young, though, probably around the age Verity had been when she left, if she calculated correctly. The grounded realm would still seem exciting. "Hello. It is nice to meet you." Her pitch was odd, but the English words were formed distinctly enough.

"We are worried the boundary between the realms has been torn, so the humans have come to investigate." Verity glossed a couple of the more complicated terms for Lrehn as she went, but otherwise stayed carefully in English. She would not have the humans suspect her of some small mischief when it might lead them to the larger. "Maybe the mayor could meet us in the gathering hall? And any explorers visiting who might know something of the current moods of the surrounding magic?" There was one warning she should keep from the humans, however. She hoped they'd take it for another gloss. "Tell everyone to keep to one look as they would in the grounded realm, all right?"

Lrehn dipped her head and headed off at a run this time. Verity lingered rather than following. The news would spread quickly enough, but everyone would need time to gather themselves, decide how to act, what to think of these humans and the phantom who brought them. Who had no real choice but to bring them, but would phantoms understand that?

She looked back at the humans. Crafters had retreated from sensitives, perhaps more comfortable that way, as none of the sensitives looked precisely happy. Buffeted, perhaps. Davin especially stood with feet braced as if the magic was a physical force to be resisted. "Misty fields," Lance muttered, not sufficiently under his breath for everyone not to hear.

Dakota was the first to move after Lrehn, though she stopped beside Verity. "So this is your home? The mirror realm?"

Verity figured a question of such supreme obviousness wasn't meant to be answered, but the very muddy idiocy of it was reassuring in an odd way. She'd changed, yes, seeing home had made her abruptly realize how much, but she hadn't changed into someone she didn't know. She'd changed into someone she knew intimately, someone more human, to survive. "Are you disappointed no one has evil goatees?" She started in Lrehn's wake.

The town boasted a few more residences around the edges, but the core was as Verity remembered, outwardly a blend of storefronts and grand stone or brick administration architecture, smoothed together from any number of eras. The gathering hall had the breadth of its door set in the outward appearance of a barn, probably pulled from the reflection of a stock pond generations ago. Phantoms had renewed the original paint with cheerful white.

Deep breath, time to make an entrance. Verity paused a beat so the humans would clump together behind her and pushed both doors open to stride in as the center point of a "V." A binding had forced her hand, but she would not cower behind those who held her leash.

Half the town seemed to be waiting for them. Where the fields and formless magic had pulled Verity's emotions to grayness with homesickness, the gathering hall buoyed her up, filled her. It held such color and variegation: feathers, hats, chokers, gloves, scarves, bright bootlaces, and short skirts over petticoats. Every shade of skin a canvas for every jewel-tone of fabric or adornment.

"What is this place, a saloon? Which steampunk convention did you guys mug?" Lance asked all too clearly from the back of the group.

"Christ, Lance!" Dakota rounded on him. Verity edged to the side so they made a tableau in the doorway—everyone was craning their necks anyway, might as well save them the muscle strain. "If you do not shut up this minute, I'll have Verity take you home, I swear to God I'm not joking. Did you not notice the part where that phantom spoke perfectly good English?"

Bravo, Dakota. Verity was mildly impressed. Lance pressed his lips together with a scowl—probably because he wanted to have sex again with Dakota ever. Lucy tittered apparently from sheer nervousness, then pressed fingertips to her lips in mortification. "Not steampunk. They don't have any gears. Or goggles." Apparently she judged admitting to the thing punchiness had made seem funny was better than leaving the phantoms to imagine what she was laughing at.

Verity shifted back to the point position of the group and led a path between two of the room's tables. Arranged in several rows, they could seat about a quarter of the town, while leaving space around the outside for the other three-quarters to mingle and chatter. One was formed from a great oak slab, finished by the touch of ages, not varnish. Another was rawer, newer, with a simple but precise pattern of rings cut by lathe onto the heavy, round legs. Phantom work, from scrap wood, she guessed. No two tables matched each other, and few matched their benches, more useful than the original chairs in a group gathering. Bunch together, laughing, intimate, and fit one more, two more people on the end.

When she reached the patch of clear space around the mayor at the head of the room, Verity looked up to see who watched from above. A staircase climbed to a walkway on the second level, lined with doors no one had ever bothered to patch rooms to. Weathered boards and faded wallpaper belonged to the original state of the room, left—perhaps unconsciously—to be a canvas for the bright colors worn by the phantoms who leaned on the railing in their curiosity.

The mayor wore a male look, neatly bearded, which probably suited her height, to human eyes. Verity wondered if perhaps she'd chosen it on purpose. She'd been an explorer, in her younger days, and so probably had seen more of the grounded realm than most here. She might also realize the flavor of unconscious respect a male look brought one there. The mayor examined Verity, but did not speak her name. Perhaps Lrehn had warned her about that. She'd also chosen a dark leather jacket, very sober in this color-boisterous crowd.

"Everyone, this is Mayor Bsayt," Verity said.

"Or Ben, on occasion," she said, dipping her chin in acknowledgment. The correct cadence of her words seemed impressive enough to the humans, but she compounded their apparent surprise by pressing her hands together respectfully in the manner of the mages. "Years ago, now."

Everyone copied the gesture after shaking off that surprise, except for Lance. And Gabe, oddly. He might have missed the original gesture, however, as he seemed to be trying to quarter the whole room with his eyes, like he could take in every single detail if he was methodical enough.

Verity introduced each of the humans in turn, even Lance. "They are hunters, ones I have…aided, for some time. I have brought them here, because they seek the source of the great number of mirror realm creatures that have found their way through to the grounded realm. The hole we discovered was difficult to observe in the grounded realm—"

"Holes," Bsayt corrected matter-of-factly, then waited for her to continue.

"Plural?" Lucy's voice squeaked. "How many?"

"Four." Bsayt crossed her arms. Verity caught a flicker of amusement at the humans' expense in her expression. "That we have observed in this vicinity, at least."

"There can't be any others in other vicinities, or we would have been getting monster reports from all over." Lucy spoke too quickly, as if trying to convince herself of that. She got out her phone, like she'd check for reports right now. She looked up with another nervous laugh when confronted by the lack of signal.

"Can you show them to us?" Dakota spoke a little loudly, probably in an attempt to seem confident and like a leader in comparison to Lucy's scattered worry.

"Certainly. But first, we hoped you might consent to stay and eat a meal with us? We have never had humans visit this town before, and I know I would love a chance to simply speak with you, as might others," Bsayt said. The low-voiced chatter that had been simmering around them all swelled to enthusiastic agreement. She must have read Dakota's reluctance in her face. "I will send people to watch over the holes, so no creatures can reach the grounded realm while you are here."

The humans all looked at Dakota, who looked at Verity for some reason, then down at the ground. "I—guess there's no reason not to, if you guys can guard the holes from this side. I've only met one phantom, too."

For a given value of meet. Verity didn't consider any impression she might have given Dakota to be representative. She gave Bsayt a nod of thanks. It would be much easier to slip away from a party than a beeline to the holes and home again. She summoned a smile for Dakota, falsely wide. "Shall we?" she said, and gestured to the nearest bench.

The humans had to sort themselves out, jostling for places along the bench. Lance and Gabe took positions on either side of Dakota, like bodyguards, and Siobhan sat next to Lucy and leaned in, listening as Lucy entered extensive notes into her phone. Davin sat a little apart, watching Verity, because of course he did. She sat down on the very end of the bench, and tried not to find friends and cousins in the crowd. One more gust of familiarity buffeting her now might be her undoing.

Phantoms crowded up, a few with good English to ask questions, most to listen, as the rest swirled away to bring food, bring speakers for low music which mixed with mere noise to tip it into a more pleasing cascade of cadences like their clothes. Bright and wild on a solid foundation. Verity retreated inside herself and stayed silent. Not yet. She needed to be patient a little longer. None of the phantoms tried to talk to her, perhaps reacting to her body language, perhaps finding her too much of a strange thing they couldn't understand.

The humans nibbled at the small treats offered them, and drank from quickly refilled cups. Verity held herself steady through half an hour, then an hour, until the conversation including the humans had settled into something almost approaching comfort. A number of young phantoms had clustered closest, across the table from Dakota, and now they were trying to teach her how to pronounce their real names interspersed with much laughter. Lucy pointed her phone at each in turn, trying to record over the general roar.

Verity took a deep breath and stopped trying so hard not to see. When she looked, she found what she needed almost immediately. A young phantom named Kjul was working her way steadily in from the edges of the group, a latecomer determined to seize her chance to speak to the humans personally. Verity recognized her as coming from two cohorts after her own, which would put her now at an age to make her own decisions, but also an age that retained a tendency to throw herself into new experiences a bit precipitously. She'd be perfect for providing a distraction while Verity slipped away.

Verity rose and slipped over to Kjul and curved fingers over her elbow. "You wouldn't be interested in learning what kissing a human feels like, would you?" she asked in their native language. Kjul jerked her head to look down at Verity. Verity pushed on before they got entangled in a discussion of how, yes, it really was her, and yes, she'd been in the grounded realm all this time. "I don't know if you still wear that male look, with the skin like this—" She held up her own forearm. "And the very short hair, but it's the sort of look that Dakota there likes."

"It's one of my favorites," Kjul allowed. "Are you serious? She'd kiss me? Would she—"

That was when Verity knew for certain her target was hooked. She laughed. "Slow down. Are you sure *you'd* want to have sex with someone you'd just met?" Kjul pulled a face at her, and Verity slipped her hand away to push Kjul toward the nearest door. "Go change looks where they can't see. Then when you return, come up behind her, touch her shoulder, then offer your hands and invite her to dance to the music. That'll be your in."

Verity drifted over to lean a shoulder against one of the square posts holding up the second level-walkway. Davin's eyes trailed her, and she pretended to be listening to the music. As long as he didn't get up to follow her...

Kjul, when she reappeared with her male look, was even

more perfect for the purpose than Verity had remembered. Tall, square-jawed, she now wore one trailing red scarf tied at her elbow and another deep blue one tied at the opposite wrist.

With all the noise, Verity couldn't hear what was said, but she watched it unfold exactly as she'd coached: Kjul gently touched Dakota's shoulder. She turned and Kjul spoke to her, while holding out her hands and grinning. Dakota's face lit, and she clambered over the bench to join her. At the last minute, Dakota hesitated, but that only made the way her hands eventually settled into Kjul's more elegant, like a bird alighting.

Verity silently urged Lance on. Look at the way that disgusting phantom smiled at Dakota. Look at the way she touched her. His face clouded into a thunderstorm of a scowl while Gabe's expression seemed wiped down to bare clay, utterly lacking in animation.

Kjul swayed with the music and set a hand on Dakota's hip, sliding it soon to the small of her back. Dakota laughed, leaning into the attention, and that was when Lance struck, vaulting to his feet and seizing Kjul's shoulder. He growled something, and Dakota tried to simultaneously pull away from Kjul and lean against her as if that would hide her from Lance, or she could protect one hothead from hurting another if she really tried.

Gabe stood as well and drew closer, setting himself up as a bastion of stability and sense, yet somehow Dakota did not run to him. Verity held her breath. Now was the moment. She couldn't influence the events, couldn't even hear them, but still she threw her will into watching. The building tension might waver, dissolve into simple awkwardness…

Then another young phantom knocked Lance's hand from Kjul's shoulder and Lance twisted with a punch. The second phantom ducked, laughing, and so missed Lance's kick to her legs. Violence exploded around the two of them, expanding outward while simultaneously imploding as a widening circle of people directed their steps and their blows inward toward the humans. Siobhan jerked Lucy out of the knot and toward the edge of the room and Verity seized her opportunity. Now!

She wove between phantoms, arriving to gawk or try to contain the fight, underneath the second-level walkway, and out the nearest door that led into the rooms attached to the back of the gathering hall. She doubted the distraction would last long, so she had to move fast. Reasonable humans technically outnumbered idiots in their party, and mature phantoms outnumbered young hotheads. They'd pull everyone apart soon enough, and with the idiocy and hotheadedness being so manifestly evident, she judged there should be no lasting diplomatic harm from the incident.

Verity had her privacy, however brief it proved to be.

14

She closed the door with one hand on the knob, one pressed against the wood to control its speed, to close it with scarcely more than a click. It probably wasn't necessary with the rising volume of voices in the hall, but she needed to hold tightly to something at the moment. Apparently remaining in the same building counted as staying "with the group," as she'd hoped. Good.

The hallway was from an older style of hotel, as many hallways were in the town. They had many useful doors and quite often held a mirror to reflect down their entire lengths. These doors were painted white, between a lightly textured wallpaper of orange-brown like faded autumn: leaves or gourds, perhaps. Verity knew there were several people she needed to find and not much time to find them in, but she hesitated in the between space of the hallway, between actions herself.

"The mayor said she saw her go—" The door from the gathering hall opened and two people stepped through. They wore similar looks, as such long partners as they were often did: very straight, black hair, like Lucy's, and long, expressive faces like Lance's, though theirs were not usually put to so much scowling as his. Or perhaps they were, now. Verity hadn't seen them for six years.

She didn't know what to say to her parents. It appeared they didn't either, for when they saw her they closed the door, pressed close into each other, side by side, and stared at her wordlessly. After a moment, her carrying parent—she supposed she might as well use the English word in her own mind, human as she was proving to be—her mother murmured her name.

More moments of frozen silence crawled by. Verity scrabbled to pin down her own emotions. Shouldn't she want to run to them, embrace them, weep in relief? But maybe she did want to do those things, fear simply held her frozen. Fear of…what? That wishing too hard for this moment for so long would have soured it, somehow?

"You brought humans here," her father said finally, expression twisting with disappointment. "When you to left to find a way to keep them from coming—"

"No!" Verity brought up her wrist, ripped the leather cuff off so hard the leather dug a painful line into her skin. "They captured me, bound me, I have to follow their orders—I didn't want—" She spat out a breath to get past the tightening around her throat. Truth even here, even now. Tears sprang up from the humiliation of it. "All right, I did want to bring them here, because that's the only way I could get here myself, and I need help to get free—"

"Oh, fleck," Verity's father murmured, mobile emotions as ever the ones to turn first. Fleck: a shortening of reflection, a small thing, a small, dear child. It had been so long since she'd heard that. "You're *alive*. We thought they'd killed you."

She stepped away from Verity's mother to enfold Verity in her arms, and Verity's mother was not far behind.

For some time, none of them said anything of sense, though Verity thought she remembered a steady flow of words from all of them, between tears. She couldn't remember what a single one had been. At the back of her mind, the clock of her time before the humans noticed she was gone ticked down.

She pulled back first. "I need someone to break this binding for me. I can't do it myself. Can you think of anyone—someone who knows spells—?"

Verity's father touched her hair, needlessly tidying, smoothing. "If you have been with the mages all this time, you probably know more of their spells than any other phantom. Certainly more than anyone in this town."

Verity's hope drained away so quickly she almost swayed like it had been blood that left her head instead. Of course phantoms didn't know how to break human bindings. Why had she thought differently?

Her mother cupped her face in her hands, tone sharpening. "But now we know you are alive, where you are, we will send messages to the other towns. We will find someone, send some way to free you."

Verity tipped her head to the side, lifting her chin from her mother's grip. "No, don't risk anyone else. I've been wearing away the spell. I'll be patient. It was foolish to expect a quick, miraculous fix." She sniffed back snot and started scrubbing salt from her drying cheeks.

"We can at least convince the mayor to cease sending all those monsters if you are in danger from them as well," her father said, brow tucking in slightly with the strength of her resolve.

Verity caught her father's wrists. "Phantoms did tear the holes? But *why*?"

"We didn't make them, we found them. The nearest turned up at the head of the irrigation system one day, and we found the rest not far into the formless magic." Verity's father pulled delicately out of Verity's grasp only to clasp Verity's upper arms in turn.

"But the hunters have been chasing the worst monsters they can find into them. It was the mayor's idea. We'll make the humans realize the real perils of the realm they might be thinking of trying to conquer." Verity's mother crossed her arms, proud. "They'll be too afraid to even think of conquering here."

Words piled up at the back of Verity's throat too thick and fast for any of them to escape for a moment. "Or they'll come sooner because they feel threatened! I can't believe you guys wouldn't see—" Her tongue tripped, and she had to spit out a few words to start the angry flow once more. "Why do you think these humans are here? They never would have come, except that they were following a threat back to its source. The mantas didn't kill anyone until you chased them through so they were all frightened and riled when they arrived. You've brought humans here faster. What if they decide that they should simply nuke the whole realm to stop the lethal monsters coming out of it? That's not outside the realm of possibilities!"

"If they don't respect our realm as more powerful than theirs, they'll think they can simply walk in and take it over," Verity's mother reiterated, though at least a hint of confusion had entered her expression.

Verity opened her mouth, but she didn't have any easy answer to that. How did you weigh the two risks, the humans' fear against the humans' disdain? Should the phantoms posture as a threat, or as the absence of one? Her human-forged instincts surged to the surface, and she spoke without thinking, to capture them. "We need them to treat us as other humans. That doesn't guarantee anything, you've seen what they do to each other, but at least some of them might think first. Some of them might be reasoned with."

Her mother shook her head, slowly in confusion, while her father appeared to not even be paying attention. Verity scrubbed at her cheeks again, finding salt still clinging there. "It doesn't matter now. Convince the mayor not to chase more monsters through, please?"

"I promise." Her father drew her into another tight hug. The door to the gathering hall opened and Verity stiffened and tried to wrench around to see who it was. Her father rubbed her back soothingly. "It's only your sibling. She wanted to see you too."

Verity was dubious—like most phantom couples, her parents had started trying to conceive her only after her older sibling had moved out, so she had always been closer to the cousins in her age cohort. But maybe she was doing Ztaen a disservice—she'd certainly always been protective, in her own mis-aimed, proto-adult sort of way.

When her father relaxed her hold, Verity turned in her arms to see her sibling. Ztaen wore a female look, for good reason: she was lush with curves and pregnancy. Verity stared, then hiccupped an inappropriate laugh. "I thought you planned to be supporting parent."

"The urge snuck up on me, and my partner didn't mind. She can carry the next one." Ztaen laughed too, and somehow that made things easier than they had been with Verity's parents. Verity disengaged from her father and hugged her sibling carefully. Ztean had a mantie sleeping peacefully, draped across her shoulder, and it startled Verity to see its real appearance, with the sinuous bands of color like tidelines on the beach. She'd gotten used to the invisible state all the mirror creatures took on in the grounded realm.

"Planning on two children already. How domestic of you." The sideways position of their hug put Verity beside Ztean's un-mantie-ed shoulder, and she pressed a kiss to the bare skin between strap and sleeve of her top. As an apology of sorts, perhaps, for teasing at a time like this.

"Can you stay?" Verity's sibling murmured, and Verity squeezed her eyes shut rather than start crying again.

"Not yet." The door to the gathering hall opened again and this time it was Davin who stood in the doorway. Verity jerked away from her sibling, though she wasn't sure why. They'd been speaking in a language he couldn't understand, and what did it matter if he did understand who Verity's sibling was? Wanting to see her family after six years away should make her more sympathetic.

"These are my—" Only as she started to say "mother and father," did Verity check her parents to actually register if they wore male and female looks. Both male. Well, that was not un-heard of for humans, so she changed her choice of word quick-ly. "My parents. And my sister." Ztaen, at least, would stay a sis-ter in human terms for a while. She shouldn't change her look after the first quarter of her pregnancy, and she looked about halfway through the year at the moment.

"Pleased to…meet you." Davin packed a considerable amount of irony into the pause in the middle. "Verity, I told Dakota I'd come check on you." He looked at the ground, as if reluctant, which was rich coming from him.

Her family filed back into the gathering hall, Ztaen leading the way and Verity's father pausing at the last minute to sling an arm across her shoulders for a last side-hug. Then they were gone, the door was shut on the noise beyond—it sounded as if the violence had ceased, at least, if not the shouting about it—and Verity was alone with Davin again.

Davin traced the richly aged wood framing around the door he'd entered through. "If I didn't know better I'd say we were in a completely different building right now."

"That's because we are." The dry cultural discussion with Davin wasn't precisely relaxing, but it felt familiar and almost comfortable by now. Talk about these aspects of the mirror realm, maybe he wouldn't remark on others. "The impressions of one, anyway. Remember what I was talking about with drifting ships? Grounded realm buildings make impressions here, through their reflections, and when they're unmoored by the destruction of their grounded realm counterpart, we draw them in and attach them as is useful."

"So that hall looks just like an old time saloon, albeit one with electric lights—" Davin pointed to the door. "Because it was one?"

"There weren't many strong building impressions in this area until Europeans arrived with large, fine mirrors. So the town was formed around then, and that's where we got the earliest buildings." Verity shrugged. This was dragging out too long. She could see it in Davin's face, the tipping point of going on the offensive.

He moved a step away from the door. "That was impressive in there, how quickly you started that bar fight. I take it they couldn't break your binding?" He nodded to her uncovered wrist.

Verity turned and bent to pick up the leather cuff because otherwise she might have spat in his face. "No. They couldn't. I guess you're happy about that." Without consciously planning to, she stepped right up to him and spoke in a low voice so intense that a few droplets probably reached his chin anyway. It was that or scream at him so loudly they could hear it in the next room and her words would be so distorted as to be incoherent. "Another success to report back."

She rocked back and bent her head over snapping on her cuff. Like anything she said would make a difference to him. When she looked up, though, guilt had splashed across his expression. He started to speak, swallowed, tried again. "I'm sorry, that came out wrong." He rocked a step forward, Verity took one back and then made it two for good measure. "I don't want to get stranded here, but I also want to help you, Verity."

Verity lifted a lip in a silent snarl. "Help me? Why should I believe you?"

"Because when we're back, I'll do something about it." He stepped forward once more and gently closed a hand around the cuff as if securing it, though she'd snapped it already. "I'll have to talk to Dakota, get her to come so we can visit Geneva again. There are a couple people I want to work with the binding, see if it can be removed." He grimaced. "*Not* Archivist Stiles."

Verity didn't answer at first, off-balance. Remove it? As in…set her free? "Why?"

"It's too complicated for me and Siobhan to break. I don't know how." Davin released her wrist and looked up as one of the side doors along the hall opened. Verity didn't bother jerking to look this time because one of the humans had found her already. If it was one of the others, she could always point to Davin as proof she'd been properly babysat.

"Dakota?" Davin's tone was so confused, Verity did twist to see.

And it wasn't Dakota. It was her cousin Pteil wearing a look modeled on her. She had the pleasant, friendly expression right, but Verity could sense her smirking underneath. What the hell did she think she was doing? Did she *want* the humans to find out phantoms could change looks? To think Davin wouldn't notice was absurd. Pteil had missed a subtle mole near Dakota's temple and her hair was an even color with none of the highlights Dakota was always so careful to maintain. She was wearing Dakota's coat, Verity had to give her that. She supposed Pteil had stolen it off the back of a chair. With jeans underneath, at least her clothes didn't give her away.

"Davin." Pteil smiled wider, and more sultry. "I was hoping to finally get a moment in private with you." She strode up to Davin and looked into his face. The height was almost right. Pteil was about an inch shorter than Dakota.

Verity clenched her hands, imprinting her fingernails into her palms. She couldn't call Pteil out without exposing the fact that phantoms could look—somewhat—like existing humans, and she shuddered to think of the kind of fear and paranoia that might engender. Should she play along? Help Pteil pass as Dakota, even? "They'll miss you at the party, Dakota," she said. She hoped her clenched teeth weren't audible.

"Back here is quieter, and more interesting." Her smile for Davin grew warmer and more meaningful. Meanwhile, behind her back she gestured *go, go* at Verity. So this was supposed to be a distraction, then. "That fight in there made me start thinking about my real priorities, Davin…"

Pteil fanned fingers of one hand against Davin's stomach for balance and went to her toes. With no more warning than that, she kissed him, deep and demanding. Verity was supposed to be going, as directed, but she couldn't tear her attention away from the picture of two of them. Did Davin believe it really was Dakota he was kissing? Was he kissing back? He was hardly pulling away. Part of her mind chose that moment to toss up the memory of Davin standing against her back in the kitchen, the feeling of that touch, same as Pteil was experiencing right now. Back in the kitchen, if he'd slid a hand forward, across her stomach, he could have kissed the side of *Verity's* neck, cheek pressed against her skin—

Anger with Pteil started a slow boil somewhere in Verity's chest. How dare she jerk Davin around like that?

Then Davin gently separated them, ending with his hand around Pteil's wrist. He lifted it away from him to hover in the newly created no-man's-land between them. "Where'd that come from?" The words were lightly teasing. Verity couldn't have said why, but she could have sworn that teasing was as false as the gold on a vending machine novelty ring. He tried to catch Pteil's eyes, the way humans she'd watched usually did to flirt, and Pteil tried to avoid a direct gaze, as a phantom would do to flirt. It was so close to absurd that Verity had to bite down on a nervous laugh.

He laughed, also with a false ring. "Sorry, I think your hair got mussed. On your right."

Pteil lifted her hand and stilled, visibly cranking through the series of difficult calculations Verity knew intimately. The moment stretched agonizingly and Verity scrabbled once more for a smooth way to interrupt. She could hardly shout, "Just run your hands over both sides, you moron!"

Davin's expression wiped back to its normal neutrality, though Verity abruptly realized how honest it looked to her now. "That's what I thought. Drop the illusion."

Pteil stared at him, smile slipping sideways into worry. "What?"

"Most humans know their left from their right much faster than that, you dumbass. Go away." Verity pointed to the door Pteil had entered from. An illusion. Perfect. She could run with that idea, working carefully around the truth spell.

Pteil shrugged, apparently philosophical about Verity's failure to take advantage of the distraction. "Thought you might like a chance to jump the queue for the one everyone's clearly interested in. Plus, it's funny." She grinned.

"How old are you, fifteen?" Verity snapped back. She should be grateful Pteil had tried to help and was concealing her real motives now, but she couldn't banish the mental image of that kiss, the two of them so close. "I know damn well you're nearly twice that, since you're my cousin. If you're determined to hang around the humans, at least go bother the others so they don't come back here."

Pteil swapped to her favorite male look and ruffled up her now shorter hair to look either stylish or possibly like a gigantic dork. She blew Davin a kiss and let herself out.

Davin's body language shaded confused. "That…didn't look like an illusion. There's so much magic around here, I couldn't tell before, but when he took it off—" He speared Verity with a tight look. "Was that an illusion?"

Maybe he wanted it to be true. Maybe she could just nudge him in the right direction? Verity didn't have any course left except to try and not shriek with anger at Pteil for doing this to her. Verity had managed to hold onto so few secrets over the years, after all she'd been through, and to lose this one because of her cousin's stupidity— "What else would it be?"

"That's a question, Verity. Not a statement." Davin clenched his jaw. "Try again."

Verity's heart was pounding so hard she had trouble getting words out. What was she supposed to say? She didn't know what to do, she was such a fucking terrible spy and always had been and one of these days the truth spell was going to straight-up strangle her. She wheezed in a couple breaths so she at least didn't pass out. Davin put his hands on the sides of her arms to steady her.

The implied sympathy decided her. Overwhelm him with honesty, and maybe that sympathy would help protect the phantoms. He hadn't reported in about a few other things yet, and he'd said he wanted to help her. "Promise not to tell any-one?" He opened his mouth, and she could already guess his objection. "It's not dangerous to anyone here. Promise. And probably not to any humans ever, but that's too wide a universe of possibilities for me to say anything about."

"I promise not to share if it's not a matter of immediate safety," Davin said solemnly. The silence stretched again. The secret felt stuck in Verity's throat.

"Phantoms...well, we don't have just one look, like humans do."

"So you're shapeshifters." After all that, Davin had the te-merity to sound dubious.

Verity lifted her lip in the beginning of a snarl at him. This was hard enough as it was. "Not shape. Just look. Height, weight, approximate distribution of that weight—that all stays the same. And imitating an existing human close enough to be believable is nearly impossible. I saw you—you noticed something pretty quickly. We still look too symmetrical, and if you've only observed someone briefly, it's hard to get all the details right—" Having found her momentum, the last part came out all in one breath. "So there's no danger of a phantom ever pretending to be someone in any real way..."

Davin looked at the door where Pteil had disappeared, gaze unfocused. "Is that why your sister and cousin look nothing like you?"

Well, that seemed hopeful. More hopeful than a question about if phantoms had ever murdered and replaced a human for nefarious purposes. "In my cousin's case, we're not actually related. Everyone's siblings are generally so separated in age, we grow up with a cohort of children from the town within a year or two of our age. There's not really a better word for that in English than cousin. So she and I played together as kids. And she's my age and should know better."

Davin shook himself and started paying attention to Verity again. "So he's—she's—your cousin is really a woman?"

Verity couldn't take it. Reaction and awkwardness burst forth in laughter. She hunched over for a beat, hands over her face, as she laughed. When she'd gathered herself, she pushed up with hands on knees. "Really a woman? What does that mean?"

When Davin started to look hunted, she waved a hand. "I'm not accusing you of insensitivity about the gender continuum, I'm curious. Pick a definition we can work from."

"Biologically. Secondary sex characteristics from birth. Identifies that way?" Davin's hands still rose a little, palms out defensively.

"That's three," Verity pointed out and held up three fingers. To be honest, she relished the opportunity to explain to a human the sensible way of doing things. "That changes with the look; who knows what look she was born with, toddlers start nudging their look around even if they can't fully change it yet; and I think if she was stuck with one gender while traveling in the grounded realm she might pick male, but who knows. I'm using female pronouns because it's easier to pick one arbitrarily in English and use it where phantoms use a neuter one."

"So…" Davin started, then grimaced as if he needed to figure out what he was going to say before he committed to the sentence. "You could choose to be a man?"

"Not at the moment." Verity held up her wrist. "Can't change looks with the binding even if I wanted to. Which I don't, given it's something the phantoms don't want to be common knowledge. Remember?"

Davin waved away the reminder of his promise as if the greater knowledge of mage-kind was the last thing on his mind. "If you weren't bound, you could, then? Were you born female?"

"I don't remember being born, do you? My parents might remember, they might not." Verity looked down at her body, breasts and hips and every inch familiar after years. What would it be like to wear a male look now? Would it feel unfamiliar? Would any other look feel unfamiliar, for that matter? She supposed she'd have to get free and see. "Get the binding off and I'll show you one of my male looks."

Davin made a noise something like *nnnngh* and strode several steps down the hall. "Maybe we can discuss this more later." The barest hint of his humor returned. "Got to get used to the idea."

"You could always forget about it entirely," Verity suggested hopefully.

He laughed, which seemed to break him out of his thoughts. "Why was your cousin pretending to be Dakota, anyway? Surely not just to make out with a human?"

Verity shrugged while mapping out her phrasing to stay within the truth. Not the only reason, no, but maybe part of it. She hadn't had to *kiss* him to distract him. "Why not? Lure of the unknown. I doubt she was lying when she said she noticed Dakota was the center of attraction."

"Apparently." Davin looked at the ground and scrubbed the side of his wrist over his lips. Probably thinking of the kiss. *Had he been picturing Dakota?*

"If you're that hard up, *I'll* make out with you." The moment the words left Verity's lips was the moment she registered what she was saying. And then she had to follow through, didn't she? She crossed to him and kissed him, closing her eyes. He must have put his back against the wall because the press of his lips in return was light, almost pulling back but not quite, and then suddenly as deep as she could have wished. His hand came up to the nape of her neck, fingers in her hair, and his tight grip on the back of her neck, squeezing the muscles and also holding her in close, was better than anything she'd ever felt in a human's touch before.

And that touch she'd longed for after just a brush on her arms was up and down her body, pressed against his. When Verity moved into the kiss, bringing up her hands to his cheeks, his hair as well, the accidental grind gripped her low in her body and she shoved harder into it.

Davin jerked his head back away from the kiss with a gasp. Verity's eyes popped open and she jerked back herself. What the *hell* was she doing? She didn't trust Davin.

Did she?

Davin held his hands up in front of his chest, like he might have to fend her off while he fought his way verbal. "Was that— just trying to distract me—?"

Verity crossed her arms tight over her chest and turned her back on him. "Hell of an impression you're probably getting of phantoms." Fuck. She needed to laugh it off, like it was just a joke, but she couldn't find the words. Of *course* he'd respond instinctively to someone who felt human, especially when already heated up with thoughts of Dakota, but that didn't mean he wouldn't eventually remember Verity wasn't human. And when he had, he'd pushed her away.

Silence stretched, painful, long enough for her heartrate to slow and curdle instead with embarrassment. Verity wanted this damn trip to be over now. She turned back to Davin. "Why are we standing around? We should look at the damn holes and head home."

Davin held out an arm, apparently having used the lull as well to deeply bury whatever residual embarrassment or annoyance he was feeling. "Lead on."

Verity closed her eyes for a moment to consult her memory, then headed down the hall and selected her door. Hopefully the town hadn't done any extensive remodeling of its public building complex while she was gone.

But the memory of her childhood, her whole life until she was captured, guided her true. Through clinic and library, fountain court and classroom, out to the graveled paths between residential houses. The longer they walked, the more she succeeded in pushing the kiss from her mind as a moment of temporary insanity caused by anxiety over Pteil spilling secrets. That's all it had been.

The sky was filled with the magic of the night, sinuous, sidewinding, curving paths of color dragging into white smears and away into nothing before the next color curled into being. Gravel crunched away into softer dirt, and Davin stopped, mesmerized by the sky. "Aurora. Like the northern lights," he murmured, so quiet as to be reverent. "But the whole sky..."

"They tell the children they're songs," Verity offered. "That we can no longer read. Look, they dance to a rhythm." She traced one with her finger. "Or they're just flares of magic."

"It's so bright out, for being night." Davin tore his eyes away and stared down at the ground. He stuffed his hands into his pockets.

"No more than in the city." Verity continued to look up. "I remember the first time I saw your moon... I'd read about it, obviously, but seeing it, I thought for a moment it was a spotlight in the next city over. On top of a skyscraper."

"No moon...?" Davin looked up, as if to find it despite what she'd said.

"No stars, either." Verity spread her arms as wide as she could. "Vasily was at his cabin in Alaska working on a project for while, and it was just like—" As she had no words for the formless magic, she had no words for that either. Not everything in the grounded realm was grounded. "You could fall all the way up."

Not that she'd trade freedom for stars and the moon. She led the way again, and Davin jogged to catch up after a moment. She traced the gurgle of a branch of the irrigation canal to larger and larger streams, through the silent song of the magic above them.

"Where does the water come from?" Davin asked, human voice brash against the night's tone for all he spoke softly. "You have electricity—is it generated hydroelectrically?"

"Formless magic isn't so different from water, in some respects. It pools, and some of the pools settle into water. Towns are usually founded by lakes." Verity pointed in the direction of this town's lake, though it was hidden by the mist-bank of formless magic at the end of the fields. "The electricity is generated by a turbine powered by the formless magic currents. You need specialized training to build or maintain the system, so I don't really know much more than the theory."

"Phantoms really do eat, sleep, and breathe magic, don't they?" Davin shook his head and lengthened his strides briefly to come even with her rather than trailing. "This place is extraordinary."

"And dangerous. As we go into the formless magic, watch out for creatures." Verity whistled a keep-away tone and put her fingertips to the apparent mist, stirring tiny currents of her own into it like slow smoke. Davin stopped short, and braced his feet when she caught his hand and tugged.

"How do we know humans can even breathe—that?" He gestured jerkily to the formless magic.

"It's not air. You won't be breathing it." Verity cupped her hand and dragged it over the border with their fields. The formless magic refused to come with her, drawing back into itself. "I think I'm allowed this far because you're with me, but I don't think I can leave you here and still 'stay with the group.'"

"All right." Davin slid a hand across her back in a gesture seemed designed more to comfort himself than her, with too much anxiety in it to spark sexual thoughts. Verity didn't comment. A wise phantom was cautious about going even briefly into the formless magic. A wise human had reason to be more than cautious.

Walking into the formless magic was like walking into smoke at first, filled with mirages of color and movement where there was none. The irrigation canal beside their feet remained stark and cast the formless magic into contrast so that it seemed for a moment they stood in a great, gray emptiness but for the water and banks of the canal. Then like an optical illusion, it switched back and they were enveloped by gray substance, no room even to move.

Verity whistled and a group of mantas were startled into sudden movement in the distance, their definition making the magic around them seem like emptiness once more. "They're used to being hunted, around here," she said. At the sound of her voice, Davin gasped in a breath like he'd been holding it for too long. "Please breathe."

"Easy for you to say, phantom," Davin joked weakly. "Are those mantas…rainbow-colored? No, I guess they're patterned like the magic in the sky."

"I suppose they are." Verity hadn't ever made that connection before. "If they were really scared, you might get to see them go invisible even here." She watched the mantas as they dwindled into the distance. From another direction, a bird made a quorking sound.

Davin oriented himself on the sound, though there was nothing to see. "That sounded like a raven."

Verity squinted too, though she had no more luck. "It probably is. Animals slip both directions over the boundary, when things are working normally. We get foxes showing up at the towns, sometimes. Coyotes. Very occasionally housecats."

As they passed, one patch of emptiness rippled with a sense of the presence of unseen material, like a heat shimmer. A sketch of a room's inner corner resolved itself, bleeding in colors like watercolors wicking through paper.

"That looks like a strong impression. Do you mind if we stop by?" Verity wasn't sure why she'd asked the moment after she did—Davin would have no idea why stopping by a strong impression would be useful, and he was already clearly uncomfortable in the formless magic. She might as well state it firmly. They were going over there, because it was a mundane, familiar action she would have performed every week if she was living at home, and she wanted to pretend for a few breaths right now. "It'll take half a minute."

She dragged Davin along by moving fast enough she almost slipped out from under his grip. She counted steps under her breath, always a good habit in the formless magic. At seventeen, her toe sank into a strip of carpet leading to the mirror, like the pattern on the floor created by light shining through a stained glass window. Also impressed were half a nightstand, the tumbled comforter of a bed's corner, and a whole slice of closet. Perfect.

She picked up a paperback book from the nightstand, sighted along the top edge to make sure nothing had been shaved off, and handed it to Davin. One step took her to the closet and she grabbed all the clothes she could see and laid them over her arm in a bundle, hangers and all. They looked like large sizes in modern fabrics, which was useful.

Davin read the cover of the book, then the penny seemed to drop. "That's how phantoms get their stuff. Through reflections?"

"Impressions," Verity said, and bumped into him with her bundle to get him to move out of the way. He rubbed his arm in mock-protest where she knew perfectly well a hangar hadn't actually poked him that hard, because they were all plastic. "We make or alter plenty of things, but we do need the raw material. Things have to stay in place for a couple weeks to get a strong enough impression to use, so that's why I'm grabbing this immediately. People move clothes around or shut them up where they can't reflect."

When she'd herded him out of the impression, she lifted the bundle to indicate their direction. "We'll put these down by the path. Someone should be by to grab them in the morning." Five steps over and Davin placed the book down carefully. Verity let the clothing flump down on top with much less ceremony.

Davin stared off behind her shoulder. "Where did the room—go?"

Verity twisted to follow his gaze. Now she conceived it that way, the formless magic was back to an impenetrable mist. "It's still there. The formless magic isn't really...space, in a way that allows you to see across it consistently. That's why explorers have a heck of a lot of practice before they start trying to anchor new paths through it." She patted the edge of the path with her toe.

"So this leads—?" Davin approached the path as well, maybe planning to test it with a toe, but since there wasn't much to see, except perhaps a hint of solidity like a diffuse shadow cast by a walkway far above them, he overshot and stepped onto it.

"To the next town. There's a whole network." Verity watched Davin with interest as he frowned and shifted his weight, then stepped back off the path. He pulled a face and she laughed. "What?"

"That actually felt like there was ground there to stand on. Everywhere else is so—squishy? No, like walking on air before realizing you've left the edge of a cliff in cartoons." Davin bent to examine what they were walking on more closely. If the formless magic was emptiness, there was apparently more nothing there, of course, and if the formless magic was mist, the mist seemed to go all the way down.

"You might give yourself vertigo," Verity warned. She'd have phrased that more strongly, but at the last moment, her truth spell reminded her that she had no idea how humans would react to any aspect of the formless magic. It just seemed likely, give how often vertigo resulted from other conflicting sources of visual input.

Davin swallowed audibly. "Right. Sorry." Verity held out a hand, and Davin edged up behind her again before they cut across and returned to following the canal.

Eighteen steps, nineteen…at thirty-one, the mist in front of them swam with sudden bursts of color like retinal afterimages after staring straight into a lamp. Davin knuckled his eyes but Verity knew better and rode it out no matter how much hers psychosomatically stung.

The bursts resolved into a long tear, the equivalent in size to what they'd seen in the grounded realm, but there the resemblance ended. It *flamed* with magic, short streamers of it silently crackling from the outside edges of the tear. She had to try twice before she got her thoughts in order sufficiently to speak. "I think this is one of our holes."

Davin grunted in reply, the noise transitioning into a bark of punchy laughter. He leaned over, hands over face, then straightened, fingers running through his hair. "Christ. It's a little obvious, isn't it?" A frown flickered across his face. "I thought the mayor was going to send someone to guard it."

Verity pretended to be distracted by the tear to give herself time to think her way around the truth. Given that the mayor had been the one encouraging people to herd monsters through, she knew perfectly well the chance of one slipping through other times was lower. Verity assembled enough facts to sound good, though. "Hunters can get a sense of creature movements from the fields. And no one wants to stand out in the formless magic for very long. Maybe she was exaggerating to be reassuring."

Davin murmured agreement—she presumed he wouldn't

like to stand around in the formless magic either—and held a hand back to her. "Hold onto me, would you? I'm going to focus on the micro-scale like it's a spell for a minute."

Verity wasn't exactly sure why micro-scale necessitated holding on, as all Davin did was stand there squinting, but she had no objection to holding his hand. Even if maybe she should have. She focused hard on watching for creatures.

"It's actually slowly knitting at the edges on its own…if we bound it from the other side, I bet it would hold well. Especially with all this power for the spell to feed off." Davin shifted his squint further up the tear. She realized the reason for the holding on when he stutter-stepped and pulled on her for balance. Having something small fill his whole view must screw up his orientation.

"It's…" Davin's tone, already distracted, took on a musing note, like a scientist deep in their favorite subject. "It looks like it was literally torn. The edges have snags, like you pulled the hook half of velcro along expensive fabric." Verity searched for any such thing herself. She found a hint of raggedness on the inner edges of the tear, but after too long the brightness made her eyes sting.

Davin drew in a sharp breath. His pull on her hand strengthened, turned into an urgent invitation to come closer instead. "Take the illusion off your binding, would you?"

Verity popped the snap, removed the cuff, and tucked its end into her pocket so it curled to her leg. "What does my binding have to do with…?"

Davin didn't seem to hear her. "Yes! Look." He lifted her bound wrist up in front of the tear.

Verity squinted at it, small magic backlit by the greater, and had no idea what he was talking about. "Did Vasily create the tears as well?" To her, he'd always seemed eager—more than eager—to never visit the mirror realm again. Had that all been an act?

"No, your binding did." Davin twisted his back to the tear and held her wrist in the shadow of his body. "It's like a car accident. Damage from the first car on the second, but don't forget about the paint from the second car on the first. Teleporting through the boundary between realms is wearing on your binding—*because* it's snagging on the boundary. So the boundary tears. The holes must appear near locations you brought a lot of people through at once, or something. I'm not sure."

Verity wrested her wrist away from him finally. His intellectual enthusiasm was getting to her. And automatic denial rose to her lips, but she caught it even before the truth spell could. This wasn't her fault. The humans had bound her, the humans had asked her to teleport, so the humans had made the holes. She had absolutely no reason to feel guilty.

But she did. "You said you can close it, didn't you?"

"Yes." Davin's face sobered by degrees, ending somewhere adjacent to sympathy. "It's your binding, not you—"

"No, you guys did this to yourselves," Verity snapped. "I'm quite aware of that. You'll just have to—" The rest of the sentence played out in her head as she froze from the strength of the realization. *Take off the binding.* Or stop asking her to teleport places, but she doubted anyone would seriously consider that. Dakota and the whole group had gotten used to the convenience and she was sure the Quorum was pleased to have Dakota within a quick hop of Geneva. Why keep Verity around, needing to be fed, if she wasn't earning her keep?

She quickened her steps back along the canal, toward the fields. She wanted to tell Dakota right away. *Tell the Quorum they need to take off the binding.* An easy solution to their problems with the monsters, everyone went home happy. Giddiness bubbled up into her chest, making her laugh.

"Hold on, don't leave me behind." Davin jogged to catch up with her. He didn't share her laughter. "We'd still have to figure out how to break the binding, it's very complex—"

Verity increased her speed to a steady lope. The tug of the grounded town on the grounded parts of herself made going this direction through the formless magic much easier. She didn't care how complex Davin thought the spell was. Convincing people it needed to be removed, that was the hard part. Anything else could follow after. She could be patient. The aurora-colored songs the formless magic tendriled into at the edge of the fields danced with her every footfall. *You'll have to take off the binding.*

15

Verity burst onto the fields and scanned them automatically. A patch of muddy figures had gathered between two fields, and Siobhan lifted an arm in an insistent wave when she spotted them.

Everyone spoke at once, overlapping, as Verity and Davin jogged up. "I told you they'd probably gone to investigate on their own." Siobhan was the most strident, in an apparent final volley in an argument that had stretched longer than her patience.

"But where's Gabe? You also said Gabe was with them." Dakota wasn't that much less strident. "We shouldn't split up, guys." Verity guessed that was why everyone had been dragged out here to look for them, rather than waiting in comfort at the party.

"Of all the possible places to randomly disappear at the worst time—is that him?" Lucy won for most observant. She pointed back toward the massed buildings of the town. Only then did Verity wonder what the mayor thought of the situation. Instead of following Lucy's gesture, she checked the gathering hall and spotted the mayor and a few others lingering in front of it, keeping a pointed eye on the humans. If she was hanging back, she must have believed that Verity and Davin were indeed checking the holes, and now hoped all the humans would leave after discussing their findings.

"Gabe? Who…?" Dakota's confusion finally captured Verity's attention. Gabe was approaching from a completely different direction within the town, and someone else was with him. Verity had been distracted long enough that the two were fairly close by now, and she recognized Pteil. What was her cousin doing?

Gabe strode straight to Dakota. As he put on a last burst of speed, it become clear he had a tight grip on Pteil's upper arm and she wasn't following of her own volition. She still wore a male look, but a different one than the one she'd revealed to Davin. This one was golden-haired again, close enough to Dakota to subtly evoke her face without falling into "long-lost brother."

"I'm sorry I couldn't warn you, but we're going to have to move fast." Gabe stopped squarely in front of Dakota, even more intensely serious than usual, if that was possible. "I've found the culprit and arrested him. We have to get to Geneva immediately."

What had Pteil done? Verity searched her cousin's face, but she looked to be in shock, maybe not even following the conversation in English. Had Pteil tried to hit on Gabe as well? How was that a crime?

"Culprit?" Dakota stared at Gabe, glanced at Pteil, seemed to find nothing more there than Verity had, and switched her attention back to Gabe.

"He created the holes." Gabe tugged Pteil forward a step

or two. "He confessed as much to me. Bragging, once we were alone. He didn't realize that I keep a binding spell on me for emergencies."

Bound? Verity should have noticed that immediately. Here she was listening to the humans, like they were the victims. Except phantoms had driven the monsters through the holes. But that didn't matter right now. "No!" She lunged forward, but Dakota got in her way and she couldn't get more than a glimpse of the prosaic rubber band—which only added insult to injury, somehow—on Pteil's wrist.

"Verity, stay out of this," Dakota said, probably not even thinking about how it was an order. Verity's feet took her back to an observer's distance.

Davin was under no orders, though. He pushed forward to take Verity's place. "Gabe, I've just been to *see* the holes. They were created by Verity's binding—"

"I only know what he was bragging about. Perhaps it was part of a larger plan. Whatever the case, we have to get him to Geneva for questioning." Gabe was never so rude as to interrupt anyone, so when he spoke inexorably right on top of Davin's explanation, even Verity found herself thinking for a moment that she must be wrong, he hadn't interrupted. Gabe was always reasonable. How could this be *happening*? Had Pteil been part of the mayor's plan, perhaps even doing some of the actual herding? But why would she admit that?

Whatever had happened, Verity had to save this *now*. "It must have been a misunderstanding because of the language barrier, I can translate for Pteil, we can figure it out—"

"Dakota." Gabe spoke right over Verity too, as if he was pulling Dakota and himself into some bubble, a completely private conversation no one else could touch. "We have to leave now, before this turns into an incident and someone gets hurt. This way, the Archivists will have the chance to get to the truth."

Verity glanced at the gathering hall. She supposed the phantoms keeping an eye on them only saw the group talking, nothing violent or threatening, and they probably couldn't even recognize Pteil from this distance. She didn't want anyone to get hurt, but maybe this *needed* to be an incident, as soon as possible. She'd wave, get their attention—

"Verity, take us to Geneva." Dakota didn't sound precisely sure, but that didn't matter. The order took hold and Verity extended her arms without conscious thought. Gabe used one hand to touch her wrist, and the other to hold Pteil's hand to her arm farther up. Everyone else arranged themselves quickly enough, except for Davin.

"Dakota, this isn't right—" He seemed to be trying to copy Gabe's utterly reasonable tone, but his volume kept rising.

"Then we'll figure it out somewhere not *here*." Dakota's voice had thinned out, strained.

Davin put his hand on Verity's shoulder, drawing breath like he was planning to continue objecting, but then the order caught Verity up and she yanked them through into the living room at the house and the very next step to Geneva.

She caught one glimpse of the familiar entrance hall before it felt like the blood in her head swooped away and she had to shake everyone off and stagger to the wall that held the mirror. She leaned her temple against it while gray ate in from the edges of her vision. So carrying that many people at once in a double jump—to go straight to Geneva, she'd have had to be in a mirror realm town opposite the city, instead of the one opposite Shoreline—was a bit of a strain. Who knew?

"What time is it here?" Lucy took out the phone and

smacked the side, like that would make it update faster. "Four in the morning? Man, they're not going to be happy with us, even if we have captured the guy who let in all the monsters."

"Verity, are you okay?" Siobhan touched Verity's shoulder and leaned her head into her range of vision to examine her face.

Verity shoved at her. "Go stop him." Gabe was busy texting someone and the more time Verity had to think about it, even with a swimming head, the more wrong this seemed. Why had Gabe had a binding on him? What use would one be on a normal hunt? Siobhan nodded, and strode to join her brother who was already haranguing both Dakota and Gabe.

Pteil pressed herself against the wall facing Verity and plucked at the rubber band uselessly. It must have the standard prohibition against the subject removing it. Verity didn't notice the tears standing in Pteil's eyes until she spoke in their native language, and they sharpened her pitch into something nearly incomprehensible. "Verity, I don't understand, what's going on? Why did they take me?"

"He said you were involved with all the monsters coming through to the grounded realm." Verity finally straightened from the wall and seized Pteil's wrist, but she couldn't get the rubber band off either. "Did you say *anything* to him…?"

Pteil sniffed and bit her lip briefly to try to regain control, perhaps. "No, I put on this look and flirted with him a bit—he seemed interested, we slipped back into the hall, that was all—and he just put the spell on my wrist and I couldn't scream or anything—"

"Interested? You're wearing a male look, Gabe isn't interested in men—" Verity had to close her eyes because her pulse of panic undid all the gains she'd made in staying upright after the teleport. Gabe had *engineered* this.

Then the anger bloomed. Verity's vision was still filtered through some kind of mist and her pulse thudded in her ears, but her body flushed with strength, ready to fight, to *hurt*. Gabe had forced her to betray her own people, and she would not stand by and let him.

"He wanted to capture a phantom! That's all he wanted. My cousin hasn't done anything." Verity stabbed a finger at Gabe as she strode to him. She would—would—*shake* him until he admitted the truth. Punch him, kick him, whatever she needed to do—but Dakota's order to "stay out of this" was still hanging around her and she had to pause and try to rip through it—

"Oh, dear. I see things are getting a bit heated." Archivist Stiles swept in from a hallway. The short, iron-colored strands of her hair were as perfectly in place as if it had been 9 A.M., not 4 A.M. All the humans pressed their palms together in quick, automatic respect, Gabe especially intensely.

Archivist Stiles set a hand on Dakota's shoulder. Though it wasn't wizened, she didn't quite close it completely, leaving Verity with an impression of a claw. "Could we maybe have some quiet from your phantom so we can hear ourselves think?"

"Quiet, Verity," Dakota murmured, eyes glued to Archivist Stiles. Clearly, she still was more than a little intimidated, which Verity might have been too, if she hadn't felt like she was burning up inside from the rage.

Verity fought the order, of course. She fought the binding with everything she had. She'd choke on the spell if that's what it took to make them pay attention to her, to snap Dakota out of her frightened respect for an Archivist and trust of Gabe. As her throat tightened, Verity embraced it, fighting even harder.

And she still couldn't make a sound. Because the order was "quiet," not "don't speak."

Next, Verity slammed against the order to stay out of it, trying to find an edge she could sneak past. She made it a few steps back toward Pteil, but when she tried to place herself protectively in front of the other phantom, her muscles locked up. She couldn't even make it over to Dakota to tug at her sleeve. That wasn't violent! But Verity supposed it was interfering. *Verity, stay out of this.* Stand to the side, quietly. Docilely.

Verity focused on an image of ripping Stiles' hand off Dakota's shoulder, slammed her physical struggle against the binding in that direction. Not that she could do that any more than anything else, but she had to keep trying.

A young woman, her upright stance a creepy echo of Gabe's, entered the main hall from another door and hurried over when Archivist Stiles beckoned. Her footsteps filled the hall briefly, highlighting that they were the only ones in the large space, colors of gilding and paintings muted down to nothing in the dim light and in contrast to the formless magic.

"Make sure this phantom is kept safe until the Quorum can meet tomorrow—this morning," Archivist Stiles directed the young woman. She nodded, and took Pteil's upper arm the way Gabe had in the mirror realm. Verity tried to say something, anything, but she might as well have been shouting at the team on the sidewalk from a window seventy floors above, throwing herself against the plexiglass again and again like this time it would shatter.

"The Archives owe all of you a debt for your efforts," Archivist Stiles said. And then they led Pteil away through the door the young woman had entered through.

Davin growled in frustration under his breath. "At least he won't have to be in custody long. We can come back and present evidence to get him freed to the Quorum itself, if we have to." Apparently he was trying to be reassuring in Verity's direction. She didn't realize that until he'd stopped speaking and was watching her hopefully, because there was no possible reassurance for her at this moment. Like the rest of the Archivists would listen any better than any other human had so far in this clusterfuck.

She flipped Davin off, then turned the gesture on everyone else for good measure. As a gesture of defiance, it was pathetic, but it was the only one she had. She was panting with exertion by now, and the binding was forcing her to keep even that mostly quiet.

Dakota rubbed one palm against the other like she could scrub away some of the awkwardness blanketing them. "We'd… better get home. Come on, Verity." She waited a beat, but Verity wasn't doing a single fucking thing that she wasn't forced into right now, so Dakota had to add a "take us home" before Verity moved.

Back at the house, everyone hovered just as awkwardly in the living room, no one sitting or leaving. Davin rounded on Dakota. "We found out what caused the holes. It had nothing to do with the phantoms."

Lance was the one to voice the scoff that Verity sensed from several directions. "I doubt they had *nothing* to do with it, no matter what you saw in the mirror realm."

"No, what I saw was quite clear." Davin descended into more and more technical terms, as if those would help him convince Dakota. Lucy was the first to notice they were standing in the dark. She shook herself and flicked the lights on.

Verity took up her fight against the binding again, though she felt more like screaming—or sobbing—than summoning a cogent defense of her people at this point. The humans kept talking, a back and forth of barbs without real substance, but she couldn't take any of it in. If she could only get Davin to look at her, maybe he'd recognize she was fighting the binding, but he was focused on his explanation.

Then, a ray of hope sliced into her tangled, knotted mess of frustration and rage: maybe she could make herself pass out.

Dakota liked dramatic gestures—she used them often enough herself—and what was more dramatic than passing out at her feet because of a cruelly tight binding? And that was still staying out of things, it was just being distracting while staying out.

Verity threw herself at the binding with new energy. It flexed tight, preventing movement or speech, and she thrashed purposefully in that tightness. Tighter, tighter, and she wouldn't be able to breathe—but that was like trying to pass out by holding your breath. Whenever she got close, her conscious mind couldn't control the unconscious instinct that made her relax by a single increment enough.

Verity edged closer to Dakota. She could do this. She'd pass out right at Dakota's feet. If she couldn't cut off her own air, Davin had said the binding burned through her energy. She'd burn through it all until there was nothing left. With the way she'd felt in Geneva, that couldn't be far away.

But she hadn't been so close as all that, Verity realized, as one minute of shaking, panting effort stretched into another. She must have needed grounding, not rest, after the time in the mirror realm and the quick transition between. She felt perfectly clear-headed now. It was a long way from grumpiness to passing out. Maybe the binding's energy burn didn't even work that way.

Verity relaxed away from her effort before she could stop herself. Just a breather. She wasn't giving up. Not giving up! She summoned Pteil's face, painted with fear, to her mind's eye. Maybe she was a coward on her own behalf, maybe she'd never really fought hard enough to escape herself, but she would. Not. Abandon. Her. Cousin.

The gray was back, only this time it surged in from the edges and ate her vision in a huge gulp.

16

Someone was holding Verity. Bracing her to sit upright, on the living room carpet. Still night outside the windows, grounded realm night with orange or bluish glows from streetlights, no aurora colors. Davin was crouched facing her, and his expression melted to relief when she tracked on his face. "Drink this," he urged, and she accepted the can of soda he held to her lips.

"What was that? She just—folded up." Lucy's voice, out of Verity's range of vision, was strained, but the fact that she was telling the group what they must have witnessed for themselves mere moments before was even more telling about her emotional state.

"She could have killed herself, she was struggling against the binding so hard. I should have realized—dammit!" Davin's tone vibrated with rage, and Verity felt a stirring of emotion of her own. Waking up had washed her emotionally clean, it seemed, but now a trickle crept in. Not of anger, but of an odd sort of pleasure at anger by proxy. Vindication. "Is that how your morality tells you to treat prisoners, Dakota? Bind them so tightly they die from the struggle?"

"No!" Dakota's voice came shockingly loud. Right against her ear, Verity realized after a moment. Dakota was the one holding her up. "I didn't know she was hurting herself. She should have said something. Her cousin's not going to be hurt, the Archivists won't allow that, we'll just have to talk this out—"

Oh, there was her earlier anger. Verity choked against the soda, and even an order about quiet didn't stop the automatic process of her body doubling up with a paroxysm of coughing.

"Are you all right?" Dakota's voice squeaked.

"She can't answer you." Davin set the soda aside. His voice started low, grew slowly in volume. "Which, if you weren't dumber than a fucking box of hammers, you might have realized given you were the one who *told her to be quiet.*" By the last words he was shouting, into frozen silence as everyone in the room stared at him with shock at the insult. Even his sister.

"How dare you—" Lance rocked forward, but Dakota forestalled him with a raised hand.

"Verity, I rescind every order I've given you," Dakota said, against her hair.

The release of pressure was too much, and humiliating tears dribbled down Verity's cheeks. Maybe she should have jerked away from Dakota, but she was *exhausted*, in mind if not completely in body, and she accepted the support without thinking too hard about who it came from.

She picked up the soda under her own steam, but she had too much to say to waste more time drinking now. "The phantoms didn't make the holes. All right, some people from the town, they tried to herd monsters through them, but they didn't make them. And Pteil wouldn't have even done any herding, she's too young and inexperienced a hunter."

"She? P-who? Who are you talking about?" Lucy's more typical suspicion was back in her voice and she moved to join the group staring down at Verity and Dakota from the front.

Verity stopped, lips parted, trying to think of a way to smooth over her mistake, but nothing came. Fortunately, Davin stepped in. "She means her cousin. The man we just," —his voice turned acidly ironic— "'arrested.' I think it's a translation thing, after her switching back to her native language for a while. She kept screwing up pronouns when we were talking in the mirror realm and didn't seem to notice."

And Davin could cover much better than she, because he could lie. Envy flickered and died without energy to sustain it. She had too many other emotions vying for her attention at the moment.

"And Verity's right. Her binding created the holes." When Davin dived into jargon this time, with that introduction, it appeared to work. Lucy for one looked much struck.

Gabe lowered himself into a chair. "I'm truly sorry. There has been—*I* have made—a terrible mistake." He rubbed his temples. "When he spoke to me, I jumped to conclusions—"

Dakota made a soothing noise, the vibration transmitting to Verity's back. "It's all right."

"Why did you have the binding with you? You were looking for someone you could—" Verity said.

But Gabe spoke right over her. And once again, everyone listened. "I'll speak personally to help clear him when the Quorum meets. We'll fix this, Verity."

For a moment, Verity was so stunned by such blatant manipulation and lies, she couldn't think what to say. A beat later, she thought of asking him to come over so she could spit in his face, but she'd missed her moment and he was talking again.

"We should fix the binding as well." Gabe set his hands, palms up, on his knees. "Tearing holes, almost killing her, that's not right."

Verity couldn't have been stunned a moment before, because she was stunned now. Frozen, in fact. Had she been wrong about Gabe? He'd always seemed reasonable. But no, she hadn't been wrong. He'd had the binding with him, he'd pretended interest in Pteil to get her alone...

Davin sat back on his heels, looking as confused as Verity. "I've been thinking the same thing."

Gabe dipped his head in acknowledgment of Davin. "We should make it a permanent binding. That would be safer for her."

Davin choked on his reply, while Verity finally pushed free of Dakota. She needed not to be lying down for this. Permanent? She had to stand on her feet, defend herself. She didn't make it all the way up, but Dakota rose too and helped her the rest of the way.

Siobhan stepped in where her brother had stumbled. "Do you know what a permanent binding is? Of course you do, Gabe, but do you, Dakota?"

"It...goes under the skin?" Dakota didn't sound sure, and it was Gabe she glanced at for confirmation.

"No, it does not 'go under the skin.' It's not a tattoo. Tattoos can anchor bindings, but they fade with time. A truly permanent binding is anchored to the bone." Siobhan sliced the air, somehow evoking a scalpel and the ooze of blood with how she spat her words. "You carve right down to the bone and you set it here and heal over top so it can't be touched and it's a part of the person for life."

Now Verity knew why Davin had choked. Nausea rose and she gagged, helplessly. If they did that to her, she'd have no hope. No hope of ever being free, of ever going home, of ever being a phantom again. She'd be human, and obedient, and truthful for the rest of her life. That binding, she really would fight it until she died.

"Anything about modern medicine sounds bad when you put it that dramatically. We dose cancer patients with poison, you realize." Gabe's brow furrowed with a disgusting parody of concern.

"Yes, permanent bindings are used in cases like cancer, to bind a tumor so it doesn't regrow, but ethical binding mages don't cut into people for no reason. We set bindings during already-scheduled surgery." Siobhan stalked between Verity and Gabe, and Davin finally mastered his rage enough to join her, shoulder to shoulder.

"This is hardly a usual situation, not with more monsters entering our world all the time." Gabe lifted his hands defensively and rose. "Perhaps it is not the solution we will settle on, but we need to consider it. The Quorum can help with that."

"Over my dead body," Davin said, and lunged. Dakota got a fingernail grip on his shirt, and the sound of fabric starting to tear seemed to bring him back to himself.

"This is—" Dakota's voice wavered. "Getting awfully intense. It's been a hell of a long day. Maybe we should sleep on it, huh? Before we decide anything."

Because, of course, why would Dakota want to take a stand for Verity? She could barely take a stand in her own life, so why would she do it for her pet phantom? Just carve up the pet, that will make it safe.

Davin gave her a disgusted look, but didn't comment further. "Before we sleep, Siobhan and I should go bind closed any holes we can find. Do you promise not to make any decisions or do anything while we're gone?" When Dakota nodded, he strode out, his sister following.

Verity flung out of the room in the other direction, before she could scream. Time for a new plan, one she never would have considered before, but what did suicidal risk matter when the alternative was a life worse than death?

17

Verity bided her time badly. Every moment of the half hour she gave people to disperse, her heart pounded as if she was going to act the very next moment. Finally, she judged it was time, and slipped from her room down to the empty living room.

Under the couch, far back against the wall, one of Lance's smaller knives—though it was still probably a good seven or eight inches—glinted to Verity's cheek-pressed-into-carpet gaze. She'd found it while cleaning a good month back, and kicked it farther under in case of later need. Much safer than keeping it in her own room, and lo and behold, Lance indeed hadn't found it in that time. It took some calculating of angles, but she managed to get her fingertips on it after lying down at the couch's side.

She drew it out and settled her fingers on the grip. Now was when she should feel the pound of adrenaline, but everything in her chest was still filled with a non-stop jangle, so this was no different. She stood, rolled her shoulder with the knife in her hand, testing the weight. All right.

She reversed her grip on the handle to fold the blade up

against her wrist, and lowered her hand to her side. Relaxed. Nonchalant, even if her whole body was jangling now. She had to make sure they didn't notice anything wrong.

She made it to her room without encountering anyone, and began the more difficult wait. She left her door slightly open and listened with every fiber of her being. She wasn't sure how much time had passed when she heard Davin and Siobhan talking as they came up the stairs, but the additional few minutes waiting for them to settle into their room was ten times worse.

She checked that the knife was still minimized, if not invisible, and let her steps take her to their door. Deep breath. She had to look normal. Or as normal as she would usually be in this kind of situation. Which wasn't very, so maybe she'd be all right whatever she did. She tapped with one knuckle. "Come in," Davin said.

His expression tightened a little with concern on seeing her. "Verity. I'm glad you're here. We were just discussing how to present this to the Quorum." He wasn't presently pacing, but he was hovering in front of the blind-covered window with the wound tension of more to come.

Siobhan sat on her bed, on a smoothed island among the rest of the tumbled covers. "And where Gabe gets off talking about fucking permanent bindings. Where the hell did that come from?"

"It's all right." Verity felt vaguely like she should keep talking, but more words refused to come to her. She sat down beside Siobhan, on top of a lump of blanket, but she couldn't spare the hand to smooth it. "It's fine."

"It's not." Davin crossed his arms and stepped forward. Maybe he was only starting to pace again, but Verity couldn't take that chance.

She flipped the knife around and leaned into Siobhan. She slung her arm around the other woman's back to press the edge into her neck. "It will be. Take the binding off." Her voice was mostly steady. Good. Internally, she felt about ready to shake apart. She only had to hold it together a little longer.

Siobhan squeaked. Her hands flew up a few inches, then she got control of herself and lowered them to her knees. "Verity—"

Davin dragged in a breath loud enough Verity suspected he must have stopped breathing for a second. "Put the knife down and we'll talk about it. You don't need to do that, Verity." His face was blank, blank, blank. Verity supposed he was busy revising any trust she'd built with him, but that didn't matter. She didn't care, she had to remind herself of that, as long as she got free. That was all that mattered.

"I absolutely need to do this." No, her hand couldn't start shaking. She wouldn't allow it. She had to stay calm. She had to convince them she'd follow through on the threat or this wouldn't work. "I won't let anyone bind me permanently." Her voice stretched thin, shrill. "Why is this so hard? You're binding mages. This is your specialty, not like Dakota. Just break the fucking binding! I'm not going to go on a rampage, you're not releasing something dangerous into the world. I'm going to get my cousin and go home."

Davin held out his hands, calming, though he didn't come any closer. "We can't. I told you, it's too complicated. We have no idea how."

Under Verity's arm, Siobhan shifted like her muscles were protesting holding one position for too long, then quickly stilled again. Verity bit her lip until she was sure she wouldn't scream at them. She couldn't afford anyone else in the house hearing. "You're lying. You're a fucking liar." She'd heard him, lying so smoothly earlier to the others. He had to be lying now. Had to be.

"He's not." Siobhan spoke softly, like she hoped that would move her throat muscles less. "I'm the one he's been talking it through with on and off for days, trying to work it out. I don't think anyone could break that binding, except Vasily."

"The layers have sort of melted together. So while we could unpick any of the individual parts, they're not individual spells anymore, and they're not shaped the same anymore—" Davin apparently thought she could be buried in jargon, like the others.

Well, she couldn't. "Shut up! I'll kill her. I kill her if you don't break the binding. Is that enough motivation to *work it out?*" She twisted to try to see the knife against Siobhan's skin, rather than just feeling it. She could do it, couldn't she? If she had to? She'd hunted, pulled lifeforce from plenty of creatures.

Siobhan and her brother shared some sort of look. "All right," she said carefully, after a beat. "If you don't say it, Davin, I will." She lifted a hand and Verity jittered the knife tighter. Siobhan froze, bringing her hand no farther up, but she didn't lower it either. "You know he's not lying, and you know you won't hurt me. I think my brother is worried you'll jerk and do something you regret by mistake, but I think you're more in control of yourself than that."

"I will do it!" This was when she had to follow through, but of course if she killed Siobhan, who would craft for Davin? Why hadn't she thought this through? And why would they lie? She should—she needed to—

"You like people, Verity." Davin's voice was very soft, forcing her to focus to hear, focus past the tangled, panicked mess of her circling thoughts. "You like my sister, you even like Lucy. I saw you when she got hurt. Work *with* us, we'll get you free. We'll call Vasily, get him to talk us through the binding, whatever we have to do. I promise. Promise on my life." He set his hand over his heart, deeply serious.

While her brother had been talking, Siobhan's hand had been rising, and she closed it around Verity's wrist now and yanked hand and knife away from her neck.

Verity scrabbled away from her, to at least keep the knife. Promise. Davin could promise all he liked, but why would he help her now she'd broken his trust like this? He'd tell the Quorum she was dangerous for sure and they'd slap a permanent binding on her that much sooner.

Too, too much. All her thwarted action and emotion had to go somewhere, and Verity popped off the leather cuff to cut at the chain with the knife. If she just pressed, sawed hard enough, maybe she could cut it open. She knelt pressed against the head of the bed, laid her wrist across her lap, and focused her whole being on the knife and chain. She'd cut it. Cut it off.

Hands seized her, wrestled the knife away. "Verity!" Or maybe someone had called her name first and then grabbed the knife. Verity tried to refocus on her surroundings. Everything was out of order. Siobhan sounded horrified. Davin had one knee up on the bed beside her. He tossed the knife to skid along the carpet and thud into the base of the opposite wall.

Her wrist and hands were all red. Absurdly red. Splashed with paint. Siobhan clutched them, kneeling in front of her, and Davin subsided to sit on the bed and pull Verity into a sideways embrace. "No," he murmured into her ear. "No, Verity. Please." He sounded so horrified it finally sunk in that maybe Verity should be horrified as well. Horrified about what?

She finally registered the stinging pain of cuts, a few shallow, and one deeper, around the chain on her wrist. Blood. She supposed she didn't react as viscerally as the others because it still looked wrong to her, to have it be red. But her reaction built as well, just slower. "Shit," she said, and finally moved her hand to join Siobhan's over the cuts as the sting shifted into burn. "I wasn't—I wasn't trying to—" Kill herself? Play as big a drama queen as Dakota, to earn herself sympathy? Neither of those things, or anything else. At least consciously.

"Don't worry." Davin was holding her very tightly, but Verity didn't really mind. "Extenuating circumstances."

"Davin, should we…?" Siobhan shifted back to pull up a fold of comforter and wrapped Verity's wrist in that.

"Not under the bigger one. Who knows what it will do to the rest." Davin apparently knew what his sister was talking about, even if Verity didn't. "Binding the cut closed," he clarified after a moment.

"There are butterfly bandages in the first aid kit," Verity offered. "You'll have to wash the comforter quickly or it'll stain."

Davin rumbled a half-hysterical laugh, and kissed her hair. For some reason. "Not your problem."

It wasn't that Verity objected to being fussed over, generally, it was just that it had been so long, the strangeness of it kept catching her unawares. But Davin and Siobhan made her stay where she was, while Siobhan got the supplies to clean and bandage the cut. The butterfly bandages seemed to be doing the job, but Siobhan wrapped her whole wrist in a length of gauze anyway. When she was finished, Verity snapped her cuff on top. The gauze peeked out above and below, but she doubted anyone else in the team was observant enough to notice.

When the bandaging was finished, Davin seemed to come back to himself, and suddenly he was off the bed and no longer touching Verity. He didn't retreat all the way to the other side of the room, but he might as well have. The way he made his sister pause so he could check the side of her neck told Verity where his thoughts had gone.

No, the untrustworthy phantom hadn't hurt her. Verity got up and started pulling the comforter off the bed. "I'm sorry for threatening you," she said, because as inadequate as that was, she didn't have anything better.

Siobhan took the armful of fabric away from her. "Don't do it again." Her tone wobbled on the line between humor and seriousness and she left the room before Verity would decide which way to call it.

So. Her and Davin left now, awkwardly saying nothing. Verity felt adrift, without a direction to throw herself in, so as much as she wanted to find a hole to hide in for the rest of forever, she forced herself to speak. "Were you serious about Vasily?" she asked a patch of carpeted floor. "Can he actually help anything, or were you just saying that?"

"He can't harm anything." Davin shrugged. "It's his spell."

"Yeah, but if he was going to take it off—" Verity wanted to fidget with her bandage, but rubbed her arm above it instead. "I guess the situation's changed a little." And he was a pretty powerful Archivist—or had been, before he exiled himself off to who knew where, somewhere no one could find him. Maybe he could make some calls in turn, and at least get Pteil home. It was a little hard to think straight through her own most visceral fear for herself, but if she couldn't save herself, she needed to at least save her cousin.

"I can probably get hold of him, but it might take longer than we have," Davin offered, diffident.

Verity shook her head. "No, I'll do it. If he won't help, I doubt it'll be because it was me asking." He had, after all, always been kind in the time she'd lived with him. He'd never mentioned permanent bindings.

"Wait." Davin's voice stopped her with her hand on the doorknob. "You have a way to get hold of him? Of Vasily? This minute?"

"Yes?" Verity felt it out, but Vasily's orders about secrets didn't stop her. "If he chooses to answer. I have no idea where he is, or what time zone he's in, but he's as likely to answer at this time of day as any other." Davin was still staring at her, so she added, "I know his videochat account. Dakota isn't supposed to know. Did he not tell anyone else about it?"

Davin started after her, but Verity didn't open the door yet. Once she'd called Vasily, she wanted to wallow in her guilt alone, thank you very much. "This isn't your problem," she pointed out.

She dared a glance at Davin quickly enough to catch him rocking back, more figuratively than literally. "I want to help."

"Why?" Verity rubbed her arm again. "I just threatened your sister. I don't get you."

"I can't say I like the lingering mental image." Davin grimaced, and Verity felt like she was back on firmer ground, though she felt bereft for no good reason. Exactly, don't trust the phantom. "But you've been put in an untenable situation, pushed harder than anyone should be. Who knows what I might find myself doing in the same situation, out of desperation."

Verity didn't know what to say. She knew what she wanted to do, which was accept the help, whatever the motives behind it, because she was awfully tired and she had a lot more fighting to do yet. Despite her every effort to the contrary, she did trust him, she realized with a start. Trusted him not to be working against her at least. And that would have to do for now. "Okay," she said, lamely. She opened the door for them.

"You should have something to eat first," Davin said, and Verity had to laugh, shakily. All right. Maybe that would help chase away a little of the stale adrenaline that was currently making her limbs heavy. They weren't done yet, tonight.

18

Verity nibbled on a last Oreo, staring at her laptop as it made gentle chiming noises. Vasily clearly wasn't at his computer, but the question was whether he'd left it on and somewhere he could hear the chimes. She'd set her laptop on her bed and angled the screen well back so the camera could also catch Davin lurking behind her, but now she fidgeted with it, enlarging the small view of herself to check what impression it gave of the room.

Then the call was answered, and the picture of herself minimized automatically. Vasily looked every inch the hard-drinking, hard-thinking Russian professor, even with his hair combed neatly down rather than standing out in a white bush. Except, of course, that he didn't drink, and no longer taught anyone in his self-imposed exile.

The view of his room revealed nothing about his location. Bookshelves filled the visible wall, and if there was a window elsewhere, it wasn't casting any daylight on the scene. He raised brows that were peppery, not fully white, at her, though of course he'd known who it was when he answered the call. "Veska. It is pleasure to hear from you."

His Russianized nickname for her warmed her unexpectedly, and their usual teasing slipped between the cracks of her current fear. "I see that you've been out there in your fortress of solitude so long your articles gave up and returned home without you." She knew his accent was nowhere near as strong as he sometimes pretended, and his English was perfect. Though she supposed she couldn't blame him from using a bit of his act around a stranger. "This is Davin—"

"Dubois." Vasily's gaze focused over Verity's shoulder and his accent ratcheted down. "You're looking much better." Apparently they did know each other. She supposed that didn't surprise her when she thought about it, though. Given what she assumed were Davin's Quorum ties.

"Archivist." Davin pressed his hands together, and his voice came out like his jaw was a bit clenched. "No need to bring that up."

"Not particularly an Archivist, 'out here in my fortress of solitude.'" He grinned, suddenly. "How apt. I'll have to remember that. What can I do for you, Veska?"

All of Verity's words suddenly dried up. He was kind, yes, but he was the one who'd bound her in the first place. Why would he change his mind now? "My cousin—he needs to be freed. He's innocent—"

"And you," Davin rumbled from behind her.

"Yes, and me. If you could tell Davin how the binding can be broken…"

Vasily's brows rose once more, higher this time. "Why?"

Verity took a deep breath, shoving her various arguments into some kind of order. Blurting them out all at once would make them incomprehensible, not persuasive. Davin leaned over her shoulder to reach for her wrist. "Show him the binding."

Verity growled at him, but she couldn't really fight for her hand back without disturbing the binding. "Stop that. I'm not the drama queen around here, Dakota is."

"She was cutting into her own skin in trying to sever the binding," Davin told the screen, inexorably. Verity smacked his shoulder, not hard, until he let go of her. The tussle at least meant she didn't have to see Vasily's reaction.

"I have control of myself now." Verity focused on the wall, which made things a bit easier. "That's not why. The reason why is that Gabe arrested my cousin on a trumped-up charge, and I need to get him home and now Gabe's talking about a permanent binding for me, and I can't—" Couldn't talk, apparently. This tightness in her chest had nothing to do with any spell. Persuasive, she was persuasive. "My cousin is innocent, but Gabe clearly brought him back to the grounded realm for some other reason, and I'm worried that while the Quorum is making a decision, something else might happen to him—"

"Gabe?" Vasily prompted. Verity still didn't look at him, but she tried to stare a little unfocused in the right direction, so it might look like that was due to camera angles.

"Gabriel Sherman. One of Dakota's boys." Silence fell, and Verity had to look at his face.

He looked old, suddenly, as if he'd aged ten years in a few minutes. "And so our mistakes always do return to us." He shook his head. "My mistakes, Veska. Not yours. I'm sorry."

He touched his temple, as if tired, but before Verity could think of a response, he began. "You must understand, I was unprepared for the mirror realm. I did not really understand what I'd seen, so when I recognized a phantom, I reacted immediately out of fear."

"It's more afraid of you than you are of it," Verity murmured, low, but her mic must have been good, because Vasily smiled, thin.

"As I learned quickly enough once I spoke to you. The point is, I did not plan your binding. I threw it at you without thinking. I do not know how to remove it myself, or believe me, I would have when Margaret's plans became clear."

Verity had to absorb that and concentrate on breathing for a second, so Davin seized the opportunity to step in. "Margaret Stiles? Archivist Stiles? What's her part in this?"

Vasily's fingers beat a tattoo on a hard surface out of the camera's range. "She learned of my visit to the mirror realm, learned of the formless magic there. I gather she conceived of the idea of exploiting it somehow, but first she needed access to the mirror realm."

Verity gasped in air, but it didn't make much difference to her swimming head. Was that—was that why they'd taken Pteil? But Vasily wasn't done yet.

"She asked me to take her there. I knew of no reason not to, so she and several of her best students accompanied me on my next trip. I think she knew even then I'd refuse her the moment I learned of her real motives. So she tried to bind one of the phantoms, to provide her the long-term access she wanted. I caught them at it and dragged them home again, but they managed to smuggle along a bound creature in the chaos. I presume the beast was too wild to be bound to teleport home with mages in tow, because it escaped soon enough."

"The jaguar." Verity grabbed Davin's arm for his attention. "The one that killed Lance's little brother. That's why the jaguar was near the research station, where jaguars didn't usually cross through the boundary." She pressed her hands to her face. "Morons! Of course you can't get a jaguar to take you anywhere. They can't teleport, they just want to rip your face off."

"I think pausing to ask local informants could have prevented a great many problems, throughout human history." Vasily offered her another thin smile. "It should have stopped there. But Margaret has possession of a secret of mine. Without another means of returning to the mirror realm, she put that secret to use as blackmail. I wanted to set you free, so she couldn't use you, before I disappeared so she couldn't use me either, but I couldn't." He scrubbed at his eyes. "I tried. Believe me, I did. But I couldn't break the binding, and while I doubt any in the Quorum would publicly condone Margaret's actions, I know plenty who'd look the other way if she presented them with such a plentiful source of magic, already harnessed.

"In the end, the only course I saw was to transfer you to someone too independent and too naive for Margaret to manipulate, and convince her that she shouldn't let any other binding mage poke at your spell. Verity, believe me, I thought Dakota would treat you well…"

"This isn't Dakota's fault. She's been—" Verity hesitated, not finding the right word. Kind as well, in a bumbling way. Which didn't help, in their current situation. "She has terrible taste in men, we'll say that."

"Gabriel Sherman was taught by Margaret, certainly, but she has had many students over the years, and not all of them entered the circle of her hand-picked protégés. I hadn't realized that she was wise enough to maintain some who appeared to lack strong ties to her…" Vasily growled low in his throat. "You are correct, if he brought a phantom to the grounded realm, it is almost certainly to serve Margaret's purposes. They'll be looking to bind him without free will. Margaret will no doubt have been honing a spell for exactly that purpose, these years."

Verity shoved to her feet. Vasily made a noise of protest, so her movement must have disturbed the laptop and made his view rock. "We have to rescue my cousin. Now. Before they bind him and Stiles gets unrestricted access to the mirror realm."

"I agree. If Dakota needs additional convincing to help you in that endeavor, tell her to call me using the number I gave her." Vasily's gaze through the screen shifted, sharpened. "And perhaps Davin can give you some assistance with the Archivists."

The screen blanked to the neutral gray of the disconnected chat program. Verity twisted back to Davin. "I *knew* it! Are you going to tell me why you're really here, now?"

He looked pained and held up a hand. "Tell you what, in a minute, I'll explain whatever you don't put together yourself." He pulled his phone from his pocket and found the number he wanted, then put it to his ear. After a moment of unfocused gaze while it must have been ringing, his face engaged. "This is Investigator Dubois. I know it's early, but I need to speak to Archivist Khare."

Investigator? What the hell was that, when it came to mages? Verity leaned forward, though she still couldn't hear the other side of the conversation.

Davin waited for about a minute, and then answered some question with a noise of affirmation. "It's about the phantom we brought in a few hours ago, to fulfill the requirement to solve the mirror realm monster problem. We have reason to believe that Gabriel Sherman, who instigated the arrest, might have had ulterior motives, so we wanted to make sure the phantom—"

Davin's expression darkened with surprise. "Yes, a phantom. At the main Archives. Yes—" He repeated a few more pieces of his original information and with each one Verity felt her muscles contract a little more, trying to curl her up into a ball and make it not be true. She knew it without Davin having to tell her. Archivist Stiles had never had any intention of handing Pteil over to the other Archivists. She'd taken her to who knew where, so she could bind her in peace.

"If you do hear anything about another phantom in the grounded—in this realm, would you pass it on? Thank you, Archivist." Davin ended the call, and let his hand with the phone fall. "The Quorum apparently hasn't heard about any of this. We're on our own."

"Something I would have been anyway." Verity shut her laptop. "So. I can only assume you aren't aligned with any of Stiles' supporters, but you do work for the Archivists."

"I do." Davin lifted his phone, made a noise of frustration apparently at not knowing what he had wanted to do with it, and let it fall again. "When questioned, mages have a tendency to tell the Archivists what they think they want to hear. The Archivists, to preserve the quality of their information, thus have a long tradition of sending out more…discreet questioners."

"Spies?" There was very little Verity felt happy about at the moment, but getting to use that word on someone else did give her one brief flare of pleasure.

Davin pulled a face at her, but didn't seem to begrudge her the prodding. "Undercover detectives."

Verity held her arms open. "And why were they worried about the scary phantom now, and not years ago? What did you report? That I just wanted to get home, or that I'm a threat?"

Davin's expression hardened. "Verity. Stop it. I'm on your

side."

Verity shoved to her feet. "No, you're on the side of the people who will ask no questions if someone else takes care of the distasteful parts of plundering my home for resources!"

Davin clasped her arms, grip on the tight side of comfortable. "You know why I'm here? Because Archivist Stiles' pushing reminded them of your situation, and the Quorum had questions about the ethics of keeping a sentient being prisoner. They needed more information to resolve them. So, yes, they're going about it in a typically ass-backwards bureaucratic way, but we are on the same side. And I hope you can guess exactly what answers to their questions I've been planning to report. Very strenuously. All right?"

"All right." That did track with his actions, Verity supposed. She didn't feel like they were done yet, but—she jerked away from him as the thought seized her. How could she waste time indulging her own selfish anger at a time like this? "We need to go make Gabe tell us where they took Pteil."

Davin got to the door first, steps thudding loudly even on carpet as he raced to Gabe's room and pounded on the door. Verity pushed up beside him and tried the knob. Unlocked.

Even in comparison to the others who had only brought enough stuff to crash at the house for a few weeks, Gabe kept his room neat, but now it looked particularly soulless. The overhead light wasn't enough to reach every corner, so Verity strode over to flick on the lamp beside the bed. No possessions anywhere, only the bed made with military precision.

Verity hissed out a series of curses in her own language. Of course Gabe was gone. He wasn't *stupid*, not like they were, in not looking for him before now.

"What's going on?" Dakota spoke from the doorway. Her

tone added an exasperated *what now?* tone.

"We should call everyone together. See if they'll help." Davin was speaking to her, Verity realized after a moment. Was she the one running this show, now? She hadn't expected that.

"We should be so lucky," she muttered, but Davin was right. "Dakota, can you call a team meeting?"

Dakota stared at her. "Um. Okay." She moved out of the doorway, but stood undecided beyond it.

Verity pushed past her and did a quick circuit banging on doors and shouting, "Downstairs! Five minutes!" It wasn't that late yet, and no one was in their pajamas when they emerged, though Dakota's hair clearly had yet to be blow-dried after a shower. The darker, damp color suited her skin better than the brassiness of the usual gold.

Verity clumped downstairs before she could regret taking the lead from Davin. How could she persuade them of the seriousness of the situation, without going overboard and making them dismiss whatever she said as hyperbole? She barely let everyone make it into the living room before she launched into the explanation. She probably didn't have long.

"Gabe was lying to us, about why he arrested my cousin. Vasily says Archivist Stiles has been trying to capture phantoms to gain access to the mirror realm's magic for a long time, and now we've handed one over to her, the rest of the Archivists mysteriously have no knowledge of it—"

"Is that...blood, on your jeans?" Lucy asked, apparently more observant than even Verity herself.

Verity brushed at the brown stain. So strange, how it could turn from such brightness to mud in the end. The stain, of course, couldn't be brushed away. "That doesn't matter." She paced to stand with her back to the mirror, in her usual place.

"We have to find out where Stiles and Gabe took him. Please."
Was that politeness, or begging? She couldn't tell. As long as it
worked, she didn't care.

"Woah, back up." Dakota held up her hands. "Vasily? The
Archivists? What?"

Verity summarized what Vasily had told her as quickly as
she could, leaving out her conclusions about Lance's brother.
Pointing that out in—comparative—public seemed unnecessarily cruel, and also beside the point at the moment. The sub-
sequent call to the Archivists wasn't hers to tell, though, and
she glanced aside to Davin.

He'd come to stand shoulder to shoulder with her. Verity,
with what attention she could spare for such comparatively idle
thoughts, wondered if the symbolic alignment of their stances
was on purpose. His call was much more easily summarized,
and then he waited.

"We're supposed to believe you have an Archivist on speed
dial?" Lance asked.

"I'm an investigator." Judging by the tone of the noises of
surprise, unlike Verity, everyone here was aware what an investigator was.

Dakota sat down on the couch with a thump. "But that
woman only died just before—you had to have left before she
was even in danger—"

"Investigating what?" Lance sat next to Dakota and lounged
back with a pointed lack of caring that also enabled him to sling
his arm over the back of the couch behind Dakota's shoulders.
"You and your sister both?"

Siobhan lifted her hands and backed up a symbolic step. "I
tag along to complete a pair and provide support, but the less I
know about the reasons for why we go anywhere, the happier I

am. Your first question is all him."

"Investigating me," Verity said, lips thinning with the effort of keeping in a laugh of bitter irony. Of course Dakota would assume it would be about her. And of course Verity would assume the same, she supposed, only she'd been the one proved right. "Something about ethics and keeping sentient beings prisoner, wasn't it? But that's beside the point. Now that we know we can trust our sources of information, I need to know if you'll help me find Pteil."

"Why not just turn all this information over to the Quorum?" Lucy nodded to Davin, clearly happy to drop the responsibility of explaining it all to the Quorum on him. "Sorting this kind of shit out is part of the Archivists' jobs, after all."

"Bureaucracy has two speeds, slow and slower," Davin said. At least he admitted it in public, as well as privately to her.

"And Vasily hardly named Stiles' supporters. If he even knew all of them. We don't know what influence they have, so I think it's safer to keep all Archvists well out of it. So it's up to us." Verity looked around at everyone again.

Dakota traded looks with the others, expression torn. Verity was watching her so closely, silently willing her to at least engage, and keep asking questions, that Lance took her by surprise. "This isn't Verity just freaking out about the permanent binding thing, is it?"

Davin growled and launched into an instant repetition of the facts—why would Gabe be mysteriously missing now, if he wasn't up to something? Why wouldn't the Archivists know about the phantom if Stiles' actions were aboveboard?

Verity didn't bother adding her voice to his. A wave of hopelessness rose up in her. Why was she bothering to try to save her home or her cousin? She couldn't even save herself.

She gritted her teeth and rode it out. She'd felt this before. It would pass. She had to believe it would. It would pass, and she would find—something to say. Something. Something to convince them.

Everyone was so loud at the moment, it didn't matter anyway. No one would hear her. "I'd kill myself first." The truth spell didn't even twitch.

Dakota stared at Verity, then put her hand over Lance's mouth. "What did you say?"

And now it would sound pathetically dramatic in the sudden silence. "I said, I'd kill myself before someone put a permanent binding on me, but honestly, I'd rather die to get Pteil home and keep all phantoms safe, if that was an option on the table. Suicide while he's still about to suffer the same fate is useless."

"Truth," Davin murmured, beside her, but Dakota didn't seem to need the reminder. She'd gone white.

She surged to her feet and strode to grasp Verity's upper arms, fear lacing her tone. "Verity, why is there blood on your jeans?"

Verity turned her head away. "Not that." All of this was far too personal to be talking about in front of Lance's sneer—she was sure he was sneering on the inside, even if she couldn't currently see it—and she felt too raw to be touched, but if it would help Pteil and her people, she had to do it.

"But—" Lance started.

Dakota whirled on him. "No." When he opened his mouth again, she got louder. "No! Shut up. I'm serious." Everyone held their breaths for a few seconds, but Lance subsided.

"We need to start making some kind of plan to get Verity's cousin home. Who's in?" Davin turned toward the others.

"First we need to know where this phantom *is*," Lance

pointed out. Verity almost jerked, physically, from suppressing her initial urge to snap at him. This time he was completely correct.

Lucy lifted her hand, diffident. "I have some friends who know her students. Maybe they can find out. She won't be doing a binding on her own, not without a crafter to pair with her, and at that point, why not have your other students help out?"

Verity attempted to gently pry Dakota's hands off her arms, but didn't succeed. She wished she saw a way to say this nicely, but— "After Gabe, why should I trust you, Lucy? Maybe you're working for Stiles too. I know you've never trusted *me*."

Lucy dropped her hand to look at both of hers in her lap. She didn't look offended. "I think I've met Archivist Stiles two or three times in my life. As for why you should trust me saying that…" She glanced at Dakota, and while the other woman didn't say anything, Lucy seemed to draw a little confidence from it. Trying quietly to impress her, perhaps. "I guess because now we've seen your home and your people and they're *weird* people, but still people. And because you passed out and got back up still worried about your people instead of yourself."

Her lips pressed briefly into a wince of sympathy. "And because of the effort you're putting into hiding that bandage over your binding. I think any sane villain would have made a play for sympathy for that and everything else long before now. Which I guess I should have seen much earlier."

Verity shoved that wrist behind her back and stubbornly kept it there, even when Dakota murmured worried half-phrases, asking to see it. Did she want Lucy's sympathy? It was better than her suspicion, at least. "That's still not the important thing here. So Lucy's in. Who else?" Siobhan raised a hand with an air of wanting to be official about it.

"Of course." Dakota squeezed Verity's arms, sounding completely confident, like she'd never felt any other way. That was pure Dakota, all over. "Lucy, go ahead and contact your friends. Then, once were know what we're dealing with, we'll plan in more detail for getting in and out." She finally let Verity go.

Lance seemed to decide that Dakota wasn't sitting back down for the moment, so he abandoned his sprawl and stood. "Well, have fun, you guys. I don't see the point of tangling with Archivist Stiles for kicks."

Dakota's expression clouded. "You just heard about her plans to steal mirror realm magic."

Lance shrugged. "Yeah, she's got big plans. And right now she has one phantom. Maybe. And no mechanism for using this magic even if she can get to it. I'll let the phantoms defend their own realm if they're so worried."

"But that's the problem, they will defend it—" The conclusion spilled out of Verity, leaving room for something like nausea to surge up in its place. "That's the beginnings of a *war* you're talking about."

She clenched her hands. They needed all the help they could get, and if this was cruelty, so be it. "I'm surprised you're not champing at the bit, Lance, to punish Stiles for what she did to your little brother."

Lance snarled and strode for her, trying to make his push into her personal space intimidating. Verity examined the pretty, product-tamed fall of his hair, and refused to move. Davin shifted crankily beside her, but seemed to realize what she was doing enough to stand back and let her do it. Dakota looked from one to the other, shocked into silence, as per usual. "What?" Lance demanded.

"Weren't you *listening*, Lance?" Verity looked him in the eye. He wasn't that much taller than her, no matter how he acted. "Stiles stole a jaguar monster. She must have taken it somewhere to study it. It got free and had to be put down. I wonder where that might have happened. Somewhere like a research base, maybe? Where there was no history of jaguar monsters before this one mysteriously started rampaging around and killing little boys—"

"Shut up!" Lance stabbed a finger into her face. She did. She was honestly surprised she'd gotten as much of that out as she had. He must have been trying to process the idea. "If you think you're going to drag up my brother to *play* me…"

"So call your parents." Davin's voice rumbled over them both, repressive rather than aggressive. "Ask them if Archivist Stiles was in Toronto at the time."

Dakota stroked Lance's arm, and suddenly all the fight went out of him. "Fine. I'm in," he snapped. "And if I'm in, we should do this properly. We don't need to fuck around with Lucy's friends of friends. One of my…contacts. For dead monster research." He caught Verity's eyes challengingly to go along with his touch of irony and she sneered back at him. "He's talked about how he's got a partner who cleans up after Stiles as well. They take monsters from her when she's done with her own research. I bet he knows where she's based when she doesn't want the Quorum looking too closely."

Verity tuned out Dakota's praise of Lance for the idea, and reminded herself they needed this lead desperately. Lance got out his phone and texted something he showed to Dakota and sent after she nodded. Then he slid the phone away as if that was it.

Dakota frowned at him. "Well? Isn't he going to reply? You said they did pick-ups at all hours."

Lance shrugged. "The people doing pick-ups aren't the

ones we need. We need their boss, and I don't know when he'll answer. He's usually busy." Verity could only imagine doing what. "Or asleep. He tends to go flat-out until he falls over. It's no good calling him, you have to wait for him to call you back. Should be within twenty-four hours."

"What if we don't have twenty-four hours?" Verity demanded. No one else had an answer for her, of course.

Lance startled her by leaving Dakota and crossing to her. "You're welcome," he said, matching her earlier sneer with his tone, and strode from the room. His footsteps clomped up the stairs a beat later.

Lucy looked around at them all, wide-eyed. "I'll go—um. Call my friends too, in case we can get something back from them more quickly." Her escape from the charged atmosphere was a little less precipitate.

Verity tried to think past the steady, heavy pulse in her mind of everything that had changed that she needed to assimilate, but couldn't, not right now. They needed to plan how to get Pteil away from Stiles and prevent a war, but how could they possibly do that without knowing where Stiles had her? "So we...wait. For now." But wait with a purpose. Was there anything else she could do? She couldn't think of anything. Except perhaps to find some time to not think, for a while, and guard it carefully. As long as they were waiting.

19

Verity detoured to the kitchen for more food on the way to her room to lie on her bed and stare at the ceiling and not sleep. Sleep would help with whatever plan they might end up forming when Lance's contact got back to them, but she decided to be realistic about her chance of getting any when she knew Lance's phone could ring any minute. Or not for hours. She glanced into the living room as she passed, the rest of the package of Oreos in her hand, and saw Dakota still sitting on the couch.

She wasn't making any noise, but every muscle of her body shouted her distress. She sat hunched over, hands tucked up against her belly where Verity couldn't see them, and stared a hole in the carpet.

Verity could have kept walking but somehow she...didn't. With everything else churning in her mind, she wasn't quite sure why she padded into the room and sat next to Dakota, body oriented toward the woman and away from the mirror over the mantel. It wasn't like she took any pleasure in seeing

Dakota's misery.

"Gabe was just using us," Dakota said at length.

"Yeah." Verity set the cookie package on the floor and extracted an Oreo.

"When I was a little kid, we'd use those as a fortune-telling game." Dakota unhunched enough to free her hands and gestured to the cookie. Verity must have looked dubious, because Dakota laughed. "No, I'm serious." She hovered her hands over the cookie until Verity released it. "One side is Boy One, the other is Boy Two, and Boy Three is the center. Twist the cookie apart, and whichever part gets the most filling is the boy you're going to marry. Or the third one, if it's evenly split." She illustrated, and Boy Two carried the day.

Verity let Dakota keep the losing boy and stole the extra-creamy bite back for herself. "Not all of us have three candidates, you know," she teased as lightly as she could.

"Three crushes out of your entire school class are easier to assemble." Dakota rotated her cookie-half in her fingers rather than eat it. "I think I loved him, Verity—I mean, still love him—I don't know. And now he's betrayed me. Us. I can't believe he used me like that, but I love him."

Verity bit back an "of course you do" and made a noncommittal listening noise instead. Easy to be in love with a man when he was out of the running for an actual commitment. "What about Lance?" Maybe that wasn't completely nice either, but that Verity did feel had to be said, to inject a little realism into this conversation.

"I don't know." Dakota set her cookie on her knee so she could bury her face in her hands. "I love him too, but in a different way—I don't know! It's all so fucked up."

In the pause of Verity not finding any safe answer and taking refuge in silence, she started mentally tallying Dakota's "I don't know"s. Three so far. Or was that four?

Dakota drew in a deep breath and straightened. "I know, it's my fault for not being able to decide..."

Two weeks ago—hell, two days ago—Verity would have continued to make encouraging noises, but now she couldn't sit on her real opinion anymore. "Oh, you've made your decision." She waited for Dakota to focus on her, frowning. "The decision not to decide." She hummed the line from one of Dakota's favorite musicals. When she seemed not to recognize the snatch of tune, Verity sang it. "I've never known someone my entire life who works as *hard* as you at not deciding, Dakota. Anyone else would have drifted one way or the other, through laziness, or unconscious preference, or external constraints, but not you. You always keep then men you love perfectly balanced, and that doesn't happen by chance."

Dakota stared at her, lips parted slightly, but nothing coming out as she grappled with the idea. Finally, she managed: "Oh." She scrubbed at her lips. "It's not on purpose."

Verity offered her a flicker of a thin smile. "I never really thought it was."

"I never knew you could sing." Rather than withdrawing further into her own thoughts, Dakota's attention returned to Verity.

"Not particularly. I mean, I have perfect pitch, which is kind of cheating."

"I didn't know you had perfect pitch either." Dakota laughed in a ragged huff. "I guess I don't know a lot of things about you." She snapped her spine straight suddenly. "Like why you put up with me. Look at me. You're in a terrible situation, and I'm whining about myself again."

Verity tried to muster some righteous indignation to inflict on Dakota, now she'd been handed the engraved invitation for it, but she found she was simply too tired. "It's not really your fault. You're the hero. We're just your team."

"What?" Dakota peered at her.

Verity swiped a thumb across Dakota's forehead. "It's written right here. Great power, great responsibility, terrible love life, lots of guilt and angst. Hero. The story follows you and your quest."

Dakota caught her hand and didn't let it go. "Okay, maybe I have a little angst—a lot of angst—sometimes, but I'm not stupid, and I know I'm not the one with the quest here." Her voice wavered as she tried to find the notes, then strengthened to sing the prompt. "I wish…"

Verity spoke, rather than sang, because her wish wasn't in the song. "To go home." She picked up the rhythm again, loosely. "I wish…more than all the power in all the formless magic in the mirror realm." She grimaced. "My people—and all the mages too, I suppose, if it comes to war—are in danger from Stiles right now, though. I survived the last six years."

With only a deep breath and a flicker of eyes across her face, perhaps checking for hostility, Dakota embraced her. "I'm so sorry, Verity. I should have tried harder to get you free, no matter what Vasily said."

That easy gesture, no hesitation at all, coaxed out a little more cautious honesty from Verity. "I suppose I'm glad you didn't give Stiles an excuse to get involved earlier." She exhaled on a laughing note. "When *I* got charge of *you*, you were only twenty, you might recall. Not known for being the wisest or most politically dexterous age."

"God." Dakota huffed once more in pained humor. She pulled back, but only to drop her forehead against Verity's shoulder, as if in place of hitting it on a hard surface. "I wondered back then if you were a hundred years old or something. You seemed pretty together."

That made Verity laugh in turn. Together? Hardly. Homesick after nine months in the grounded realm and frightened out of her mind at what the change away from Vasily might mean, more like. "You realize I was about twenty-five myself back then, right? You've caught up to that point yourself."

"Ha," Dakota said, lightly self-mocking, and pulled away completely this time. "We'll get your cousin back, keep your people safe, and then do something about your binding, okay?"

Verity shook her head and stood. She didn't want to hope too much based on other people's promises only to land hard once more. She'd focus on small things, the things she could do herself. "One thing at a time. You should get some sleep. If Lance's contact is on anything approaching a sane schedule, the later it gets, the more likely it is he'll fall over first and won't call Lance until morning." And it was going to be a long night, wondering if he wasn't on a sane schedule.

"Only if you do too," Dakota countered, as Verity slipped out of the living room into the hall.

Davin was leaning against the wall at the bottom of the stairs. She raised her brows at him. He fell in behind her, then trailed her all the way to her room. "Why the escort?"

"I wanted to make sure you were okay." Davin stopped in her doorway, but he seemed too tense to prop up the frame with his shoulder this time.

"I'm fine. I plan to stare at the ceiling and not be able to sleep and generally feel pretty miserable, but I think with luck I'll survive until we hear back from Lance's 'contact.'" Verity sat on her bed and put her hands on her lap. Right. Waiting. Processing. Something like that. The humor helped a little.

Davin came inside enough to shut the door and give them privacy, but then he remained right there, back against the door. "We'll solve this, Verity."

"I know. Dakota's hero team, go!" Verity swung her fist sardonically. "Play your cards right, and she'll be so impressed you'll get a real kiss and more from her."

"Christ!" Davin surged away from the door with a growl. "Why is it so hard for everyone to believe that Dakota is not the one I'm interested in?"

"Sorry, I—" Verity's apology died before she'd finished forming it in her head as her unconscious took another listen to what he'd just said and sent up urgent messages. He hadn't said "believe that I'm not interested in Dakota."

She was probably gaping at him, as her mind jumped to a very particular conclusion and she tried to wrestle it back down. She didn't need to be as narcissistic as Dakota. He could be talking about...talking about...who?

Davin flumped onto the bed beside her, and put his head in his hands to avoid looking at her. Which was—a good sign? bad sign? she knew this, for humans of this culture, but not instinctively and she was losing it in the intensity of the moment worse than her left and right. He exhaled on a note that lifted near a laugh. "I figured phantoms wouldn't necessarily be interested in another species, but then your cousin kissed like she meant it—and then with *you*, it was so..."

"Like I meant it too?" Hey, words were back. Kind of. "I'm

not a virgin with humans." Which she might have been able to put more awkwardly, but she couldn't presently imagine how. "Even if I was still at home, it's pretty well accepted that if you're visiting the grounded realm—I mean, attraction cuts across the species and there's no reason not to—consenting adults and all—don't even have to worry about protection—" She stopped herself with a curse in her native language that turned into a laugh. "Trust me, I meant it. Can I just kiss you again now?"

Davin met her halfway in the best kind of reply to that question. The pressure of his lips was cautious at first, and Verity could tell she would need to lead the way. She closed her eyes and deepened it, concentrating on sensation as her fingers came up and mapped the nape of his neck, how the hair dipped and whorled over muscle and tendon. She slid fingertips down to his collarbone, and there she met fabric.

She pulled back, a quick breath, and felt for the hem of his shirt, yanked it up. Davin laughed, and brushed his thumbs across her closed eyelids. "What are you afraid of seeing?"

The building warmth pooling in Verity's body receded in the face of worry as her eyes popped open. She remembered this. For more than a kiss, seeing your partner was a thing. She smiled at Davin without answering as he drew the shirt off himself, muscles pulling with the most exquisite breath of asymmetry as he moved. All right, she did like looking. But she also wanted to *feel*. She traced a muscle, trying to ignore her eyes and focus on touch, but vision was so demanding, always pulling at the attention.

She rejoined the kiss, so at least she could close her eyes then. She pushed into it, lips, tongue, demanding and him happy to give it back and just when she was feeling again, he drew slowly back. She opened her eyes this time, and his smile was wonderful, she had to admit, pleased and eager. She shed her shirt too and Davin beat her to the clasp of her bra.

He caught her lips briefly, teasing, then held her eyes and brought his hands up to cup, to caress, ending with his thumbs along her nipples. Verity tried to focus, tried *hard*, but he was staring at her, and all she could think about was how humans stared to be intimate. So she moaned, borrowing a note from Dakota, one Dakota probably didn't realize Verity had even heard, but what could she expect when she forgot to close her bedroom door in her hurry half the time?

Davin smiled wider. "You like this?" He increased the pressure.

Yes, was the correct answer to that question. If she hadn't been so nervous, Verity might have had the presence of mind to moan again instead. Of course, if she hadn't been so nervous, it might have been true. But it was *almost* true, and Verity made the mistake of trying to tough it out. Just had to get the word out—

Her next breath came in hardly at all, and she had to pull back and wheeze a cough to clear her airway and then Davin was really staring at her and embarrassment swallowed her. Way to screw up human sex *again*. "Were you trying to *lie*?" Hurt seeped into his expression, and he stood up and abruptly away from her.

Verity caught at his wrist. "Davin, no. Please. I was just trying to do it right, okay? I like you, I like the idea of this, but it doesn't seem to come naturally to me. Truth." This was worse than just not feeling right herself. She couldn't bear the thought that he would be hurt.

After a moment of silent consideration, Davin turned his

hand up into hers and slowly sat again. "Who taught you that you had to fake it? I want to kick his ass."

Verity judged that question rhetorical, so she let the silence pool and Davin's scowl slowly dissipate. He lifted her hand to kiss the palm. "Shame on both of us for trying to jump in without talking out the hidden obstacles. How do phantoms make love, then?"

"There's a look you wear—you just feel all over." Maybe bringing up wearing a different look wasn't a good idea either, but even had the truth spell miraculously disappeared the moment before, Verity wanted to be honest with him. "That's not how this mostly human look works for me, but I've got that mostly mapped out on my own, but..." She took a deep breath. If it wouldn't work for him, it wouldn't work for him. They could go their separate ways. "Can't we close our eyes? Someone's look—it doesn't matter. To phantoms, I mean. It's what you're feeling, and seeing is distracting. That's all I was trying to do, but I know it's meaningful to humans. Like I don't want to see you."

"Oh." Davin exhaled in a slow trickle of understanding. "I would like to see *you*. Your face. If you're enjoying it."

"I don't mind that." Verity traced a fingertip path along his side and he shivered with a low laugh. It must have tickled, she realized, and she flattened her palm against the spot.

"I have an idea." Davin rose and crossed the room in two steps and tugged an escaping scarf of Dakota's off the top self. It had a predominately blue pattern, with tiny squares of black and white tumbling in lines up and down its length. He gestured Verity to rise, and when she did, nudged her around and looped it over her eyes. Her world was cast into slightly navy darkness until she closed her eyes as he knotted it at the back of her head.

"Now." He kissed where her shoulder met her neck, so like what Verity had imagined in the mirror realm, she shivered. His hands found her breasts from behind and she tipped her chin up slightly. Just feeling. "Good?"

"Yes." No lie there, no wheeze in her voice. His touch left her and she waited one breath, another, anticipation seeping in and taking her over. She could hear him moving, but his feet were soft enough on the carpet it was hard to pinpoint the direction. When he laced his fingers into her hair, kissed the side of her jaw, she gasped from the electric surprise of it. He continued down the side of her neck, from the front as he had from behind, and she reached and found the muscles of his back and dug her fingers into them.

He'd wanted to see her face, he'd said, so when he leaned back, teasing her with fingertips only, there at her nipple, there at the line of her hips trailing to the button of her jeans, she turned her face up to him. Not knowing where the next touch would fall, every inch of her skin stood in heightened readiness. It was closest to feeling like a phantom she'd been in six years and the joy of it was nearly delirious. She hoped he could see that.

And it only got better. When he was close enough, Verity held him closer and ground herself against him through her jeans and then he'd pull away again, teasing himself as much as her, if what she could feel with her fingers through his jeans was any indication. Grind, pull away, touch, embrace, and grind again, a slow rhythm, but a rhythm nonetheless, and so, so delicious. "Good?" he'd ask, and "Yes," she'd reply, a rhythm too. She was already halfway through her climb and they still weren't completely undressed.

When he popped her jeans button, she wiggled pants and underwear off together. She popped his button in her turn, but her fingers had just enough fumble without sight that he laid his over hers, and then stepped back to remove his jeans himself. The moments without touch again sang across her skin, and she rolled her hips and ground against her hand to the sound of his zipper, the fall of fabric.

This time, he urged her back, until her thighs hit the bed and she boosted to perch on the edge and spread her legs. Now his fingers trailed along her inner thighs, drawing closer to her core. When he caressed, cautious again at this last step, she took his hand in her own, and held it at the right place so she could grind, grind *hard* and climb higher.

At climax, she didn't moan. They'd never been like that for her, because a gasp better suited the way every muscle seemed to clench before release, a wave of buoyant giddiness. She might have worried, might have tried to find some pleased sound to make, but he must have seen just fine, heard it in her gasp, because he cupped the sides of her face to kiss her and she could taste the hum of his delighted laugh lingering on his lips.

"Now you," she urged, and reached and found his hard length, building a picture of it in her mind with touch as he gasped in turn. She couldn't quite guide him in without his help, but when she had her hands free to lean back on the bed, she found the right angle and he slid in so *easy*. She wrapped her legs around his ass and he leaned over and wrapped one arm across her back, fingers and palm splayed into a perfect handprint she could feel against her skin, one smoother point pressing in from his thumb ring. New rhythm now: faster, and increasing, hardly long at all until his fingers dug into her back and he gasped too, then relaxed.

"Good?" she asked, this time, delighted. This kind of sex, with a human, she wanted to do *again*.

He withdrew and leaned against her, cheek along her hair and the side of the scarf, just breathing, apparently not verbal for a beat or two. "Yes," he agreed. "God. Verity."

"Davin," she countered, as they carefully disentangled. She felt she was probably grinning wide enough to look like an idiot, but she didn't care. He deserved such smiles.

20

Verity had never expected to, but when they'd cleaned up and slipped into bed together, apparently she did sleep, or at least doze for maybe half an hour or so. She drifted into full wakefulness pressed tight against his side, clinging to him. She hoped he hadn't found her unconscious, desperate cuddling to be smothering, as his breathing felt like he was still fully awake. Apparently she was still starved for intimate touch.

When she started to disengage, he slung an arm over her hip to keep her from moving completely away. "Hey," he murmured, low and welcoming. He pressed a quick kiss to her lips. "Humans not so bad?"

"Humans not so bad," Verity agreed. The flood of pleasure still hadn't quite faded, and it kept at bay any other thoughts of problems she had with humans, and things she was going to have to deal with soon enough. "Phantoms not so inexplicable?"

"No." Davin laughed. "Though I knew you were a phantom even before I met you, and I was still a goner when I first saw you."

Verity thought back and pulled a face. "Dragging around

manta corpses and trying to keep Dakota together? I can't imagine the naked suspicion was particularly sexy either."

"Alluring and mysterious," Davin teased, and kissed her forehead this time. "That first teleport was a hell of a thing."

"I guess that was the first time you touched me, when I took your hand," Verity murmured, then shook her head at own rambling. "I keep remembering it as being in the kitchen. When you showed me right and left. Because you initiated it, I guess. That's when I started thinking about humans that way again, and then I didn't admit it to myself until the mirror realm. Or even then. I tried to convince myself you were imagining Dakota or some other human while you were kissing me."

"Absolutely not." Davin laughed, low, rumbling in the air between them. "I think your cousin did me a serious favor when she—he—" He frowned over the stumble. "Which should I use?"

"Either." Verity lifted a shoulder in a shrug. "They're both true at some point. Maybe male to avoid tripping in front of the others. I sort of switched of over in my head for that reason."

Davin's attention shifted internal. "I've been thinking about that too, a little."

"Uh-oh?" Verity laughed too, when he lifted his hand to prod her in the hip in protest of her teasing.

"I don't think mages finding out about phantoms changing…looks, or whatever you called it, would be the end of the world. Don't get me wrong, it requires a bit of a mental shift. Took me a while to digest the idea. But I don't think it would mean rampant fear and suspicion. Looking like someone else is perfectly possible for anyone with access to a good illusionist, with all the, I presume, same attendant problems with behavior mistakes making it easier to spot than in the movies."

Davin must not have dozed at all, to have time to come up with that. Verity circled her fingertips around a mole on his hip and took a few beats of silence to think it over herself. "It might all be moot if Stiles pulls us all into—"

Davin cut her off by pulling her in, too close to see his expression, though in exchange she could feel every nuance of his voice through his chest. "Don't, Verity. Stay in this moment with me for a little longer, please?"

"All right," Verity agreed. It wasn't so hard to do, when she tried, with him holding her. She gently pulled back after a moment to make talking easier and picked up the conversational thread. "It's actually fiendishly hard for us not to smooth out even someone we've studied carefully into symmetry."

"Why is that?" Davin's curiosity wakened in his expression. "Maybe that's a stupid question, but I've been wondering. Phantoms looking overly symmetrical when they have one look makes sense—that's just how they're built. But when you can look like anything, why not look more naturally human? You certainly do."

"That's because the binding is holding the look for me." Verity took Davin's arm and brushed her fingers along the skin. He had the lightest pattern of freckles to go with his red hair, only visible when you really looked. Probably fading from the summer. "A look is like—a song you're humming in your head all the time, not really paying attention to it. You need the repetition of the chorus and verses to keep it flowing. A look that appears more human is like—a song with one note different each verse, in a different place each time. You can sing it, but only if that's pretty much the only thing you're thinking about.

If you want to walk around and talk to people too, it's nearly impossible."

She let his arm go and tucked her hand against her belly. "Maybe it's not the end of the world, if other people find out about us changing looks, but I'd still rather you didn't tell them yet. Let it start somewhere else, not with me. I've brought enough trouble as it is—"

"No." Davin touched her lips with the side of his thumb, gently silencing. "Archivist Stiles did." In her own mind, Verity modified that. Vasily had started everything, in a way. And then the phantom elders had continued it, by sending her, and she'd done her part, by being dumb enough to get caught...a whole trail, piece by piece, that led here.

"And there's time enough to worry about that later. I don't know about you, but I'm not done basking yet." A smile slipped around the corner of his mouth. "I have another question for you. Have you ever had sex as a man?"

Verity laughed, before she realized that could be a heavy question as well. "Is there a right and wrong answer to that?" Davin pulled a face at her, and she smacked his arm. "No, I mean it. Is it going to turn you off or something? I know you realize intellectually I can't white lie, but I don't know if you realize it emotionally. I saw your reaction when you found out about my male looks."

"I promise." Davin pressed his hand over his heart, then over hers. "No wrong answer. I won't be turned off unless it's me you're asking to have sex with you as a man. I've had time to go a few rounds with my society-installed gender norms."

"I have," Verity said, and left it there. No need to get detailed. Or add "duh." When you were young and experimenting, why would you not experiment with all the possibilities?

"Honestly, I don't know you'd read my male looks, should I get them back, as very masculine. My trial by fire in learning the nuances of Western human behavior has been exclusively the female set."

"We'll have to see." Davin frowned at her wrist, distracted, and when he lifted it between them, Verity saw that the gauze had a trailing end from where it must be unwrapping itself underneath the cuff. He unsnapped the cuff and carefully pulled it away. "Looks good," he said, examining the butterfly bandages. "Just re-wrap it when you get dressed, maybe, to keep the leather from irritating it." He lifted her wrist and kissed the cut.

For a moment, his frown deepened, then he licked his bottom lip. "That's weird—"

He spasmed, retching. Verity sat up instantly and supported him to the edge of the bed, trying to get him to the bathroom if that's what he wanted. Rather than making it to his feet, he collapsed to his knees, then his hands and knees, on the carpet, still retching. Nothing was coming up, but his whole body spasmed with each attempt and he gasped for air in between. He coughed too, the flat, desperate cough of nausea denied.

"Davin?" She knew there was no way he would be able to tell her what was wrong in his current state, but she didn't— what should she do? Scream for help? Wake the household so Dakota could allow her to teleport him to the healers?

His sister. In a flash, it came to her. Siobhan would know what was wrong with him, what to do. Or if she didn't, they'd know to go to the healers. Verity yanked the first blanket she touched off the bed and wrapped it like a cloak around her shoulders. "Hang on, I'm getting Siobhan," she told him.

At the door of Siobhan and Davin's room, she couldn't help a brief hesitation before knocking. What must she look like to a human of this culture, naked and wearing only a blanket? No time for that. She knocked.

Siobhan answered wearing a tank top and pajama bottoms, like she'd also tried to talk herself into sleeping while they waited on the call from Lance's contact. Her eyes were wide awake, though. Verity didn't give her time to do more than raise her brows at the blanket. "Davin. He's sick, I don't know what's wrong—" She tried to keep her voice low, not sharing the information with the house.

"Aw, hell." Siobhan joined her in the hall, closing the door behind her with a firm click. Her gaze settled heavily on Verity, and the grip on the blanket she kept having to adjust, and she strode for Verity's room without being told.

Davin was still coughing, retching, helpless, when they arrived, but weaker now. More curled into himself in misery, still on hands and knees. Siobhan leaned over him, jerked up one of his hands, and yanked off his thumb ring. He collapsed to sit with the side of his head against the bed, quiet, just breathing again.

Verity felt like she could breathe again too. What the hell had just happened? If it was something to do with the ring, why was he wearing it?

Siobhan brandished the ring at her brother. "Dammit, Davin! If you're going to demand they make your binding impossible to remove yourself, you have to *tell people* about it in case of emergency. People other than me!"

Verity slipped past Siobhan, dumped her blanket on the bed, and helped Davin up. Or planned to help him, at least. Once she got a hand under his armpit, he seemed to take it as a point of pride to stand the rest of the way on his own. He seemed a bit shaky, but otherwise fine. Only then did Verity start thinking about what Siobhan had said. "His binding?" She peered into Siobhan's hand. The glow of magic did shimmer from the inside of the band, though the outside still looked completely mundane.

"I'll be fine in a minute." Davin stood straighter as if to prove it. "I'll get a drink of water or something—" He headed for the bathroom.

"And put on some goddamn pants," his sister called after him.

Which was an excellent idea in Verity's case too. Her pants and underwear were easy, but she had to hunt for her bra, which just drove the embarrassment home. Siobhan didn't say anything, and Verity didn't dare check her expression until she was wearing a shirt again.

Siobhan looked amused. And a little awkward, but amused nonetheless. Certainly not scandalized. "You don't look...surprised," Verity finally ventured, to at least have it out in the open.

"Not particularly." Siobhan grinned, suddenly. "All right, to be fair—and so I don't sound too smug—I was completely aware of my brother's feelings on the subject, but I didn't know you well enough to get a read."

Oh. Well. Verity supposed that wasn't actually completely new information, since Davin had apparently been attracted to her since they met, but that hadn't really sunk in yet. And maybe she didn't quite believe him. He could be unconsciously revising his memories to fill in attraction earlier. She couldn't imagine how she'd actually been alluring at the time, stressed out and suspicious.

Now she was being as bad as Dakota. "Binding," she said, firmly. Discussions of sexual shenanigans later. Or never. "What just happened?"

"It must have malfunctioned." Siobhan glanced at the bathroom door in time for her brother to return and start pulling on his clothes. "How much does she get to know, Mr. Secretive?"

"I'm a recovered Ghost addict," Davin said starkly, then turned his back on them to find his shirt.

Siobhan gaped, like she hadn't expected the admission anywhere near that easily. Verity stepped into the silence. "So you're bound not to use?"

"Not to even want to use. To be physically disgusted by the thought of it." Siobhan nodded to the wet patch on the floor where Davin had vomited a little stomach acid, even if nothing else had made it up. He glowered at it too, and disappeared to the bathroom, probably to find a cloth.

Siobhan eyed the ring on her palm. "He'll have to sensitive for me so I can fix it, though."

"Can I?" Verity held out her wrist. "Maybe I won't see in enough detail, but I can certainly see. We could try." She made herself not glance after Davin. She wanted to do *something* to help him. She empathized with the feeling of having lost a secret you'd tried so very hard to keep.

"Really?" Siobhan took Verity's wrist to find her pulse, and her eyes widened. "No shit. Not as good as a binding sensitive, but certainly better than trying to make do with an explosions sensitive or something." Her frown increased as she examined the ring. "It looks fine from what I can see. Same as always."

Verity lifted her free hand. "Maybe it wasn't malfunctioning. He was—" Come on, Siobhan knew this already. "Kissing my skin. Maybe Lance left a product sample or something around the house and I came in contact with it. Touched it, spilled it. If the binding's supposed to keep him from taking it, then he would have reacted—" She tried to remember any mysterious substances she'd touched lately, but it had been one hell of a day, and it wasn't like even Lance would be dumb enough to scrawl MY DRUGS in marker on the outside of any container. "We should check. To make sure. Before Davin runs into it. There's nothing new in Dakota's bathroom, I know that for sure, but in the kitchen or somewhere else…"

"God, yes." Siobhan turned with her for the door immediately.

Davin returned and frowned at them as he bent to scrub at the carpet. "I need that back, Siobhan."

Siobhan hesitated, looking at the ring. Then she tossed it lightly for him to catch. "Maybe this is a sign that you've gone long enough you don't need it anymore."

Davin settled the ring on his thumb and continued to scrub. "Maybe," he said, in a tone that meant "hell no."

Verity left him to it and thudded down the stairs, Siobhan close behind. The kitchen still seemed the most likely to her, with all the mysterious Tupperwares in the fridge and left out on the counter. But the living room could be cleared quickly, so she might as well do that first. She turned that direction at the bottom of the stairs.

Between the moment she reached for the light switch and the moment the room flooded with light, she heard the moan. Too late to stop her hand and back out of the room, of course. Dakota and Lance were on the couch, Dakota straddling his lap. Apparently their horniness had been so all-consuming they had only removed the bare minimum of clothes, so Dakota was still wearing her shirt. She twisted to discover the source of the sudden light, squeaked, and pressed herself against Lance's chest, though her breasts weren't what she was currently exposing to them.

This wasn't the first time this had happened, of course. When Verity first arrived, Dakota had been living alone for long enough, they'd had to agree on some rules about staying in the bedroom very quickly. And it wouldn't be the last time, undoubtedly, unless she really did get free of her binding. Verity had learned quickly that the best strategy was to appear so unconcerned that Dakota felt doubly embarrassed on her behalf.

"You *have* a room, Dakota. I know, I've seen it," Verity said. "And his phone damn well better be in earshot." When Dakota, wide-eyed with embarrassment, pointed to the phone on the end table, Verity forced herself to walk right past them on the way across to the entrance to the kitchen. When she was free, she'd never have to walk in on Dakota, ever again. She could hold onto that thought.

Siobhan seemed to take it all in her amused stride and wolf-whistled before following Verity. Verity assumed the tastelessness was her own coping mechanism for not giving in to embarrassment.

A low-voiced argument started up behind them. Given what she knew of both Lance and Dakota, Verity suspected it was over whether to re-clothe and stick around to apologize, or adjourn upstairs and pick up where they'd left off.

She and Siobhan went through the whole kitchen and Siobhan sniffed every unlabeled substance they found, but she said she didn't catch even a whiff of whatever Ghost smelled like. It didn't take as long as Verity had expected, so a contrite Dakota and a cranky Lance were still sitting awkwardly on the couch when they returned to check the living room properly.

Davin arrived in the other doorway and looked like he wanted to tell them to give up the search, but he must have seen something in his sister's expression, because he bowed his head and didn't say anything.

This time, Dakota seemed to notice Verity's hurry. "What's going on? More bad news?"

Davin's secret wasn't hers to tell, so Verity tried to reveal as little of it as possible. "Davin's sick. I guess he reacts badly to Ghost, so we're trying to make sure there isn't a source in the house he came into contact with inadvertently..." She looked pointedly at Lance.

Lance snorted, and looked pointedly at her wrist in return. She realized it was uncovered now, cut and butterfly bandages exposed to everyone, and clutched it against her chest. "Did you bleed on him or something?"

Verity loosened her clutch in surprise. "What?" Davin's similar exclamation didn't make it to quite such a coherent form.

"Ghost. It's phantom—" A flicker of a sneer to his lip. "Sorry, mirror realm monster blood. Much diluted, but that's what it's made of." When everyone had stared at him for too long, he added, "I thought every mage knew that."

And Davin had kissed her cut. Her blood may have been human-red at the moment, but apparently it was still enough like Ghost to set off his binding. Her stomach dropped away.

Maybe it was only her dislike of Lance, but when he said everyone knew, she immediately assumed that was a lie and wondered why he knew when no one else did. And that made her thoughts race even faster. "I can't believe you not only killed my pet, you sold it to some fucking mage-run meth lab!"

It was Dakota's turn to voice the thought, this time. "What?"

Verity turned to her. She was the one Verity needed to convince. "You've seen him, he has cash. A lot of cash. And he takes care of all the dead monsters, sells them to his mage friends for 'research.' Where the hell else would someone get monster blood to manufacture designer drugs?"

Davin was suddenly in front of Lance, hoisting the man to his feet, hands balled in the fabric of his shirt. "You—I can't believe it—no, I can—you pathetic excuse for a human being, you fucking waste of magic—" His words tumbled into each other as he shouted. He freed one hand and drew it back to punch. Lance's face twisted into a scowl and his hands came up as well.

"Davin, don't—" Verity refused to be one of those fluttery women in the movies who stood near fighting men and breathlessly begged them to stop, but now she was in the situation, she was very aware of friendly fire. If she got in too close, she could very well get an elbow to the face without Davin probably even realizing it.

"Davin." Siobhan's voice sliced across her brother's, probably with the ease of years of practice. "Like it or not, we need Lance to talk to his contact so the guy will tell us where Stiles is. Then we'll want both of you in the fight for the phantoms. For Verity. If you injure each other, you'll be fucking useless. Got it?"

Davin scoffed, but he did let go of Lance's shirt. For a frozen second, it seemed like Lance would be the one to rejoin the fight. But when Dakota looked wide-eyed at Verity—maybe asking for advice, maybe not, but Verity offered it anyway—Verity set the back of her hand to her forehead, evoking the fainting heroine.

And she had to give Dakota this, she ran with it. She grabbed Lance's arm and leaned against him like one of those fluttering women, tangling any attack he might have launched. "Please, Lance. We're all on edge."

He grunted in protest, maybe so Davin wouldn't have the last word in manly, derisive sounds, snatched up his phone, then allowed Dakota to steer him toward the stairs.

That left the three of them in painful silence. Verity smoothed her hands on the thighs of her jeans, which made her remember her wrist. Her dangerously blood-leaking wrist. She held it against her chest again, even though it was as scabbed over as it had been when she walked down here. The silence was getting unbearable. "I think I'll wait down here for a while, so I don't have to hear them if they're continuing up there. Great minds think alike, I guess. And ours do too."

That got the lack of laughter it deserved. Verity couldn't stop herself from babbling, though. "I'm serious, though. No reason you guys have to stick around."

Davin abruptly collapsed onto the couch and stared unseeingly at a point on the floor, hands tucked between his knees. "You deserve a better explanation."

Verity perched on a chair arm. What was the right answer to that? Thank God, I was dying of curiosity? Oh, no, you don't have to do that? "Okay," she said, diffidently.

Siobhan came over and set her hand on his shoulder, but he tried to roll it off, so she gave up and went to hover by the mantel.

"When I was in college, I got engaged to a non-mage woman. We were into the party scene. She'd take E sometimes, it never did much for me. But we weren't letting the partying take over our lives, or anything, our grades were still good—" Davin finally focused on Verity, like he wanted…what? Absolution? Forgiveness? Judgment? Maybe he didn't know himself.

"And then people started getting into Ghost. Jen tried it, but she just rambled on and on for hours. She said it was too weird for her. No fun. But I was curious, and when I took it, it was so—" He let out a shuddering breath. "Well. You know how that story goes. Same thing every addict goes through, only it was so much *stronger* for me. Looking back, after that first time, I was already fully hooked. If I wasn't the only reason the Archivists put out the warning, I was at least one of them. I guess we know why it's extra addictive for mages, now. The mirror realm magic."

He went back to staring at the floor. "And it started taking over my life, and I was trying to hide it…" For a moment, he looked like Verity sometimes felt, fighting the truth spell, but fighting his shame to make the confession that followed. "Jen got worried. She was trying to help me, but I didn't want help. I found a crafter who was young and kind of naive, and convinced him that Jen had found out something she shouldn't about mages. So we bound her, only it was to not notice anything wrong with me. I could do anything I wanted, and she wouldn't even see it. Not consciously."

Verity sensed that where this story was going, Davin was going to come to more harm from that binding than Jen, but reading his defeated body language and Siobhan's flinch, they clearly considered the fact that he'd bound her at all to be harm enough.

Davin stalled out for a few seconds. "The next part is really Siobhan's to tell. I was pretty out of it at the time."

"You think it's *easier* for me to tell it?" Siobhan was crying, Verity realized with a little shock. She'd been so quiet about it, Verity hadn't noticed in her focus on Davin. But she scrubbed the tears away and continued on, her voice just as strong. "He overdosed. If I hadn't happened to visit, that evening…and there he was passed out on the couch, with hardly a pulse, and Jen was walking around, making dinner, like he was just watching TV. I got him help, but—" She smeared at renewed trails of tears. "We removed the binding from Jen, but we couldn't explain what had happened. All she knew was that her fiancé had been dying in front of her and she hadn't done a thing about it. The guilt *destroyed* her. And him, for destroying her. There wasn't a way for the relationship to come back from it."

Davin twisted his fingers together until the knuckles went white. "Siobhan, I'm sorry—"

Siobhan rounded on him. "No. Don't start with the apologies. We've done that. Now we're moving on with our lives. I still love you, I love the different man you've made yourself. I wish I could see a time when your self-imposed penance will end, even if it's years from now. You can't punish yourself forever."

Davin sighed, and released his hands. "It's not penance." The words had a well-worn quality. One of those arguments, between couples or family members, that would never quite die. "It's paying back a debt." His gaze flicked to Verity and he lifted the hand with the thumb ring briefly. "This was not a simple spell. Vasily helped design it, as well as several other Archivists, with the illusion so it can't been seen, and the binding not only to prevent me from using, but make sure I won't *want* to. I investigate for them to pay them back for what they did for me."

Siobhan crossed her arms and declined to continue the argument, and Verity realized now was when she had to say something. How did she say something when she wasn't sure how she felt herself? To wear a binding, perhaps forever, seemed enough of a penance in and of itself. For what crime?

That single, initial taste of Ghost? For being a partier? For being young and curious? For using his magic to harm someone by harming himself? "If I'm ever to earn parole for my mistakes, I think you deserve it too," she said.

Davin just shook his head. Siobhan looked at her sharply. Probably wondering about what exactly those mistakes were, that Verity would rank them against Davin's. Verity would enlighten them both once she was free, she promised herself. She couldn't yet.

Silence ensnared them once more until Davin pushed to his feet and headed upstairs. Siobhan followed him, with one last look at Verity. Finally, Verity found herself where she'd intended to be at the beginning of the evening: alone, thinking.

She was fairly certain the scale of the things she had to think about had surpassed her ability to process them, however.

21

In the wee hours of the morning, Verity finally convinced herself that even if Lance was an asshole, there was no way Dakota wouldn't wake her up when the call came in, and went to bed. She slept badly, and late, so she arrived at the tail end of breakfast hours to eat her cereal when most everyone else had already stacked their dishes in the dishwasher. Or sink, if they were lazy and their name started with "L" and ended with "ance." She wasn't alone, though. Davin drank coffee morosely at the opposite end of the table and Siobhan and Lucy sat together along the side, discussing something on Lucy's laptop with rather strained brightness.

Verity tuned in briefly, to catch a snatch of, "so rather than layering the two different spells, they tried using two crafters and one sensitive—" and then tuned back out again. That experiment was a long-standing interest of Lucy's, nothing to do with their current situation.

Bass-heavy dance music filtered in from the hall and footsteps clomped closer. Lance looked in, ringing phone in his hand. "Dakota?" Not finding her, he turned away.

Verity and Davin shoved to their feet at the same moment. In Verity's case it was because she was going to cling to Lance like a leech until he found Dakota and answered the damn phone. She didn't realize what Davin's motives were until he made a swipe for the phone and Lance jerked it out of his reach.

The ring's section of music ceased, then began again, the lull revealing how charged the air between the men was once more becoming. "What, you think you're going to get his name so you can report him to the Archivists after he tells us what we need?" Lance let his hand with the phone fall as he paced forward into Davin's personal space. Davin didn't yield, and they stood chest to chest. "Fuck you."

They'd *done* this already, last night, and any minute Lance's contact would hang up. Verity slipped up beside Lance, tugged the ignored phone out of his hand, and retreated to the other side of the room. *Vlad the Impala*, the screen said. She wasn't sure why one merely tasteless blood-related joke in the sea of true immorality that was Lance's involvement in the Ghost trade made her burn with renewed rage, but she pushed past it.

"Lance's phone," she answered sweetly, spinning out a couple non-lies in her mind, ready.

"Who is this?" The male voice was undistinguished enough, through a mediocre connection. Lance and Davin scuffled briefly, maybe Davin restraining Lance from trying to retrieve his phone, or Lance preventing Davin from calling out the same question in return.

As long as they mutually kept each other from interfering, Verity didn't care. "Did Lance ever mention his, um, friend, Dakota?" She lifted her voice a little, striving for Dakota's speech patterns as well as her phobia of the word "girlfriend."

"Oh, Dakota." The contact's voice settled with understanding. Verity had thought Lance would have talked about her. His

act was so badass and uncaring, there was no way he didn't
moon over the woman he was in love with in private, maybe even at length. "What's this about Archivist Stiles? Where's
Lance?"

All right. Verity had truth sketched out for this, but now
she'd have to start talking and hope she didn't paint herself into
a corner as she went. "We figured out that Archivist Stiles was
responsible for the jaguar that escaped. You know the one, with
his little brother—? Anyway, if I can spare him some of the bad
memories by dealing with this myself…" She'd consider it a
necessary evil.

"Shit, man," the contact said. "I know about his brother.
What can I do to help?"

"She's got another mirror realm creature, we think she's trying something even more dangerous this time." Dangerous to
phantoms, not little brothers. Verity felt like she was dancing
through an action movie booby-trap, requiring split-second
timing to stop just in time. "Do you have any idea where she's
taken it?"

Verity switched to speakerphone and held the phone out
for everyone to hear. She waited for Lance to call out, or grab
the phone away from her, but he was apparently enough invest-
ed in stopping Stiles that he was willing to accept the information if it was gained without threatening his contact.

The contact made a thinking noise. "Well, when we do
pick-ups for her, they're always at her student workshop. You
know the one about an hour away from the Archivist base in
Toronto?" Verity didn't, but when she looked around at the
others listening, Lucy nodded emphatically.

"Thank you, that's what we needed," Verity told him.

"Good luck," he said, and sounded like he meant it. Her
stomach twisted as she ended the call. Was that luck tainted if

it was wished by a magical meth cooker? She decided she didn't care, if they had what they needed.

She handed the phone back to Lance. A heavy pause tightened the air between them, and Verity wondered if he was considering an objection to what she'd just done: *I'm going to tell Dakota what you did.* She could imagine how juvenile that would sound out loud, and she'd bet Lance could too, if that was really what was passing through his mind. In any case, he gave her an all-purpose sneer and stayed silent.

Lance turned and mockingly showed Davin the screen and the alias there. Verity stepped over to Lucy, anxious to keep things moving if the two men started fighting again. "You know the place?"

"One of my friends was dating a guy who worked with Archivist Stiles. We came by to pick him up before a conference and stayed the night once." Lucy sketched a rough floorplan in the air with her hands. "It's this old private college dorm building. Workrooms on the first floor, bedrooms on the second, so people can stay for a month or two, if they want. There's a basement, too. I'm pretty sure it was just used for storage when I was there, but I imagine if you wanted to lock someone up, it would work pretty well."

Lucy bounced in her chair with excitement. "And! Later, my friend's boyfriend was telling this story about someone sneaking out in the evenings when they were supposed to be spending every waking moment on Archivist Stiles' latest project. The students maintain a back entrance. I guess the basement is built like an old root cellar, so it has those doors set into the ground at the back. They're supposed to be boarded over, but it's too useful a route not to use."

Lucy's rising volume in her excitement must have caught Dakota's attention in the hall, because she looked in and then joined them when she saw everyone's expressions. Verity tuned out and thought furiously as Lucy repeated everything, and had the outline of a plan ready when she wound down. It was simple—too simple?—but she didn't see how complicating things would help in this situation. "So we go up to the front of the building noisily, as a distraction, and only one or two people go in the back to get into the basement and let Pteil out..."

Dakota lifted her hands, voice stretching thin with worry. "Hold up. Are we seriously talking here about staging some kind of assault on a bunch of students in an Archivist facility? We could get in serious trouble with the Quorum—"

Verity could hardly believe it. What had Dakota expected, that they'd be knocking politely on the door of Stiles' vacation cabin? "We wouldn't be assaulting them. And I can't see that the Quorum is going to be *happy* with us no matter what we do. We don't know how much support Stiles has, so we need to get this done and then ask forgiveness instead of permission." Dakota wasn't afraid of a fight, why was she getting cold feet now?

"Yeah, but I hadn't realized we'd be trying to force our way into one of the student research centers." Frustration tightened Dakota's expression, finally giving Verity the key to what was going on. She'd always suspected Dakota resented the Archives and the hierarchy of students she'd never been able to fit into, at the same time they loomed larger than life in her mind as the ones who controlled the salary currently providing her livelihood. The thought of directly going up against a bastion of that hierarchy must be smashing the two emotions against each other.

Fine, let Dakota wring her hands over that dissonance later. Right now, Verity didn't care, except that now she had a better idea how to aim her arguments. "Davin can help with the arguing for forgiveness part, right?"

Davin straightened in surprise from where he'd settled in a weary lean against the doorway to the living room. He didn't look haggard, precisely, but the bland expression he'd adopted after the flare-up with Lance was heavier than it had been since he first arrived, without the spark of humor beneath. He grimaced. "That…depends. If we start hurting students…"

Lance scoffed loudly. He sidled up to try to slide his arm around Dakota's waist, but she fended him off. He shoved his hands into his pockets. "They're *research students*, for Christ's sake. What kind of resistance are they going to put up, throwing their laptops at us?"

It was Lucy's turn to scoff. She did it with enough feeling that even Lance was momentarily silenced. She closed her laptop with a snap and fanned her fingers on top of it. "I'd be worried, if I were you. Not about what we're going to get in trouble for doing to them, but about what they could do to *us*. Archivist Stiles works her personal protégés *hard*, everyone at the Archives knows that. That's a hell of a lot of practical experience with each of their specialty's spells, and you know every class of spells ever invented has offensive applications."

Siobhan tried to break in, but Lucy apparently wasn't done yet. Her tone took on enough of an edge Verity could finally detect the real fear in it. "And they *believe* in her. That's the thing I don't know if any of you guys can properly understand. Maybe that's part of why I failed as a student, I didn't believe enough, but whatever Archivist Stiles has told them about what they're doing, they really believe it's the most important piece of re-search in the whole world. And they'll defend that."

Now Lucy was done. She slumped a little, and didn't object when Siobhan set a hand comfortingly on top of one of hers. "It did sound to me like Verity's plan involved significantly more sneaking than attacking of students, however dangerous," Siobhan said.

At least Siobhan had been listening. "Exactly. If we create a *distraction*—" Verity drew out the word, to make sure everyone processed it.

Lance snorted and flopped into a seat to demonstrate his nonchalance. "How about you leave the plan to Dakota?"

Dakota seated herself on the side of the table opposite him, perhaps continuing to keep her distance out of residual em-barrassment from last night, but he jerked so she must have kicked him under the table. "Verity has seen us all fight plenty of times, except for Davin and Siobhan, and it's not like I have any more perspective on that than she does. I'm curious where she'd put people."

Verity wondered about her own qualifications, once every-one's eyes settled heavily on her, but she pushed on. "We'll want the illusion pair out front, to look splashy while engaging as little as possible. Then Dakota and I are the ones to sneak in the back, say, since Dakota can work alone, and I'll need to be along to convince Pteil to come with us. So Davin and Siobhan can join the group at the front."

"Will we be much help if we're not engaging?" Siobhan folded her hands on the table in front of her. "Usually the point of putting the binding pair behind the illusion pair is to sneak close enough to touch people and actually use our spells. If we're just creating a distraction and then legging it when Pteil's out, won't we be staying out of reach?"

Which was a fair point. Verity grimaced. "More people at the back just increases the risk of being noticed. You guys could take some of the monster paintball guns, couldn't you?"

"Do those do anything to humans?" Siobhan asked. "Other than be an annoyance?"

Lucy drew a deep breath and straightened a little. Maybe the concept of "engage as little as possible" had penetrated. She formed her fingers into a gun and "shot" her opposite palm. "It stings pretty bad. Without two points to run a current between, it won't stop someone's heart, but you probably won't want to shoot anyone in the head. Who knows what it would do to the brain. And you could get eye damage, same as with regular paintballs. So basically, it probably would be a decent distraction."

Dakota leaned forward, getting more into it as the plan got fleshed out. That was the hunter Verity knew. Part of her must have forgotten they were talking about Archivist students. "So you guys keep everyone's attention up front by making illusions of an attack and shooting at them from a safe distance. Once they see through the illusion, take off. Verity and I can teleport out once we have her cousin, then come back for you guys—"

Verity hated to rain on her enthusiasm, but this was a problem she could already spot coming. "I doubt Stiles will have left any reflective surfaces in the whole building, if she can possibly help it. They won't want Pteil using one to get away on her—his—own."

Davin ducked into the living room. "Verity can bring her own. We went out and got this, this morning." He returned a beat later with a tube. He brought it to the table and rolled it out, revealing it to be mylar, attached to a thin, flexible sheet of black plastic to give it some rigidity.

Verity turned her head instantly, avoiding the reflection, then forced herself to look back. The mylar was attached completely smooth, without wrinkles, which helped. She could feel—no—yes—she could feel flickers of the mirror realm that came and went as Davin shifted his weight on the hands holding the tube open. With residual curl from the plastic backing, the reflection distorted away from something travelable. "Not if it's not flat." She stood and added her two hands at the other two corners of the two-and-a-half- or three-foot square. That put her close to Davin, but not intimate. Odd, how awkwardness could sap the intimacy out of nearly anything, now Davin had discovered she was dangerous to him.

Everyone else added hands to the edges, and the mylar finally settled flat. Verity shivered. There. She could teleport through that right now, if Dakota was with her. She lifted her hands and turned away again. "How are we going to walk through if we need to hold it open at the same time?"

"Duct tape," Siobhan said, with great solemnity. A laugh flickered across to at least Dakota and Lucy, and the tension dropped a little.

"Fair enough." Verity tugged away the plastic and rolled it tightly. She eyeballed the length lying across her hands. It would stick out of the top of a backpack, but she could zip up to it on either side. It would be visible from the back, but the point of this was to get in and out without being seen at all.

Lucy touched her phone's screen with a fingertip, some automatic check she didn't seem to notice until after she'd done it. Resistance seeped back into her expression. "Wait a second. I know we closed the holes here, but if we teleport around, won't we make new ones in Ontario?" She must have been checking for monster reports, and that had reminded her.

Davin shrugged. "The holes here weren't hard to close. We can check for any in Ontario before we leave, now we know what to look for."

"We won't have travel time, too, remember," Verity said, trying to keep the frustration out of her voice. "If sneaking up to the building and grabbing someone from inside takes more than an hour, we're probably already pretty fucked. No non-magical humans are going to get chomped because of any holes we missed around here in that time."

Lucy fidgeted, checking for monster reports yet again. "But—"

Verity clenched her hands from the sheer visceral need to slam them down on the table to make all this stop. They knew where they were going, she wanted to *leave*. "The more time we waste chewing over this, the more time Stiles has to finish the binding on my cousin. Then she can start going after the form-less magic and provoking a war at any time. So if you think it's a bad plan, by all means, amend it, but otherwise—"

Dakota shifted, apparently not sure whether to chastise Verity or agree with her, but Lucy nodded convulsively and held up a hand to forestall her. "It's a good plan. I'm still in. Sorry." She scrolled on her phone, acting like that was all she'd wanted it for in the first place. "No snow there right now, any-way. Temps in the forties. Bring your coats."

She rose, leading the way for a general dispersal. Dakota moved too quickly for Lance to catch her for a private word. He subsided at the table for a moment before digging in his pocket for a receipt and a pen. He scribbled something on the back.

Davin caught Verity's eye and lingered and so Verity did too, joining him and his sister. She assumed this was the "thanks for last night, but it's never going to happen again" talk. Before Davin could say what he wanted, though, Lance approached them.

"Look." He held up the paper and spoke to Davin. "Promise you'll make sure Bryce gets credit for the help he just gave us, and I'll give you this. These are the guys I sell to. Give it to your bosses, or whatever."

"I promise," Davin said, in shock. And Lance did hand it over. He dipped his head, making the apology clear, though still unvoiced, and caught up to Dakota in the hallway. She must have been lingering to see what he was up to, even having just snubbed him.

Davin clutched the receipt as if he expected the words to be written in special ink that would disappear the moment he tried to read it. Then he jerked out his phone, already scrolling to a contact. He paused, casting an apologetic look at both Siobhan and Verity.

"Go," Verity prompted. She was just as happy not having the awkward conversation she'd feared. She could imagine it all in her head perfectly well. He nodded, offered her a smile that disappeared like the words hadn't, and strode out of the room as he lifted the phone to his ear.

"Huh," Siobhan remarked. "I guess Lance isn't all bad."

Verity sighed. Abruptly, she found herself wishing she could believe the kinder interpretation. "You saw Dakota standing right there. He was doing it to impress her. Nothing to do with Davin." She slid her hands into her pockets, but that didn't end up making her hover any less awkward.

"Sometimes trying to impress someone makes you a better person." Siobhan pulled a teasing face at Verity. "Don't you believe in the transformative power of love?"

It was Verity's turn to make a face—a disgusted one. "If he ever gets her to commit to him, he'll stop trying nearly so hard, trust me. It's only the competition that does it."

"Harsh," Siobhan declared. "What is this, sour grapes on everyone else's relationships? What's wrong with the one you've got?"

That allusion was just oblique enough that Verity had to search to come up with the meaning. "I'm not envious. And that's not a relationship. That was—" What was the word? It didn't seem like humans always had an easy time choosing the right one either. "Not serious. We're not even the same species." As the danger of her blood had so amply illustrated. It had been a wonderful, pleasurable encounter, but she wasn't stupid. She could tell it would have to stay an isolated encounter.

"Said the Cro-Magnon to the Neanderthal." Siobhan smirked, making it clear that was some kind of joke, and slipped out.

Verity stared after her. Well, she supposed looking that up would occupy her mind and keep the fluttering mixture of fear and excitement from taking over her body before they even made it to Ontario.

22

Walking in to the former campus ended up burning a lot of the flutter out of Verity as well. Department stores were her go-to for teleporting when she didn't have a private building on the other end. They had plenty of mirrors, and reasons for people to be wandering in and out. Her other favorite, public bathrooms, was out with the mixed-gender group. On the map, taking the three-quarters of an hour to walk from store to former campus rather than screwing around at the car rental office and driving across town had seemed the most efficient path, but that didn't make the walking more fun.

Lance and Lucy walked in the center of their knot, hand over wrist, holding an illusion of no one there. For the last stretch, they walked along the highway. They were clearly at the edge of town but not yet at a wild space; the view stretched off toward the horizon across farmland or as-yet undeveloped lots—not flat, certainly, with a green line of hills to meet the blue—but uninterrupted by buildings or any of the trees that seemed only to cluster around those buildings or roads.

The former campus had the solid, red brick buildings set in apparent acres of lawns of a modern campus, but lacked the extensive parking lots. Even if they hadn't known which of the three clustered buildings everyone was staying in, the haphazard accumulation of vehicles on a much browner and haggard patch of grass next to the most sprawling one gave a clue.

Dakota stopped before they left the sidewalk at the edge of the campus property to strike out across grass. Everyone stopped with her and watched as she rolled her shoulders and loosened her stance as if readying for a sparring match right there, instead of several hundred more yards across a very docile lawn before sneaking in a back door. Lance twitched his free hand toward his shoulder and then glowered, probably thinking of the knives Dakota had made him leave behind. Lucy, in contrast, seemed calmer and only flexed her free hand once. Perhaps she'd made some headway on the walk in convincing herself they really wouldn't have to engage the students.

"Everyone ready? Clear on the plan?" Dakota asked. The answer was obvious enough she got only mumbles in response. Of course everyone was clear on the plan. It hadn't been that long since they hashed it out at home and they'd gone over it again outside the department store in Ontario. Everyone was very clear on it.

And according to that plan, now was the moment when Dakota would put up an illusion for herself and Verity so they could split from the main group. Only Dakota was hesitating, who knew why. Probably something to do with her lack of self-confidence about her magic again. Verity fidgeted with her backpack, resetting the straps over her shoulders. The mylar tube was long and light, the roll of duct tape was small and heavy, and the two didn't balance well inside a bag otherwise empty except for an extra paintball gun in its holster, just in case. "I can keep quiet if you want to just do a visual one," she offered, to get things moving at least.

The strategy worked, and Dakota shot her an annoyed look and gestured her in close. "Sing at the top of your lungs if you want." When Verity sidestepped over, an illusion snapped up around them. From the inside it looked fine to her, but the inside wasn't the problem. And she couldn't see spells at a resolution to know any different, anyway.

They split from the group, padding across the grass. Verity declined to sing. They angled for the back of the building, while the others swung more widely for the front. They'd wait behind an illusion for their moment, so they wouldn't want to stand somewhere they'd get bumped into.

The bushes around the base of the building had gone wild, over decades perhaps, with little effort made besides chopping them off in a buzz-cut line so they didn't block the windows. On the first time past the cellar doors they missed them completely. When they reached the end of the building, they turned back and tried again. This time Verity ran her hand along the branches, bending them to see through.

The double doors, set at a slight angle to the ground, were weathered to the same shade as the building's window frames, gray that had once been white. The bushes seemed to have embraced them so thoroughly Verity wondered how anyone could possibly get in and out, but then by chance she jostled a branch that had been hooked into one of the next bush over, and the two sprang apart. Not enough to leave a hole, but certainly enough to push through by bending back a few light, whippy tendrils rather than snapping mature trunks.

"If anything has 'haunted house hinge screech' written all over them, it's these things." Verity pointed and kept her voice low despite the illusion. It wasn't that she didn't trust Dakota, her instincts simply wouldn't let her speak any louder when she was standing right outside the window of her enemy. "Can you make sure the illusion covers them before we try to open them?"

"Got it." Dakota pushed through the bushes to stand beside the doors. Once past the bush barrier, the ground was fairly trampled. She took her out her phone and texted the others. A beat later, a door slammed open on the other side of the building and voices shouted indistinctly. The others were being distracting. Now they just had to get inside before the others had to pull back, and search while they were hopefully being chased off.

Dakota reached for one of the two handles, but Verity stopped her. "You be ready with a spell in case someone's on the other side, and I'll open them. They look heavy, but I'm sure one person can manage. I doubt students are always able to sneak out in pairs." And there was the slightest depression in the dust before the center of the doors, where one person would scuff their feet as they opened them alone. Verity grabbed one handle and threw the door open quickly to allow Dakota a view of the steps revealed inside. It didn't haunted house screech, but it did creak slightly in the manner of flexing wood. A pause, a breath, and no thrown spells, so Verity opened the next and let Dakota precede her down.

She closed the doors carefully before catching up to Dakota at the floor level of the basement. It wasn't unusually damp, or unusually dark, but concrete foundation walls and sparse fluorescent light bars didn't really allow a light and airy atmosphere either. Verity was most struck by how enclosed they were. They'd come down into a hallway space, the doors set into a concrete wall at their back, and brick walls on either side stretching away to a T-intersection, a few yards down. The brick construction looked sturdy enough, but seemed to have been built without any thought for appearance, so the brick surface and mortar were ragged and uneven.

Dakota strode away to the first intersection and chose the northeast path without hesitation. Verity glanced down the other way and saw no threat, but plenty of doors. "My cousin could be in any of these rooms. We need to check—" But Dakota and the illusioned space around her were getting away from Verity, so she jogged to catch up.

She caught Dakota's wrist. "Wait, I'm going to look in the rooms."

"We should clear the basement first. Otherwise, we're vulnerable while we're looking inside and our backs are to the hall." Dakota tugged a few steps farther.

"It's a freaking maze down here. That'll take forever to clear, and more people can always come down anyway. Better to look as we go, and then we might find my cousin and be out of here before too long. You can watch the hall, I'll check the rooms." Verity yanked Dakota toward the nearest door, and this time the woman gave in.

After all the fuss, of course, the odd little rhombus shape of a room held only dusty metal folding chairs, banquet-style tables, and a couple fat computer monitors and other equipment in an ugly gray shade of plastic that Verity had seen in old movies but hadn't really believed anyone actually used. The next room held breaker boxes and loops of slightly worryingly exposed wires that vanished up into the ceiling at various points.

They turned a corner onto an obvious dead end with only one door leading off the southwest side of it. Dakota braced herself at the mouth of the dead end and Verity continued on without her.

Of course, that was when a tall young man turned into sight down the hall, carrying a flashlight. "Hey!" He started forward at a jog. He'd obviously seen Verity, but whether he'd seen Dakota wasn't clear—

Dakota braced herself, confidence settling over her shoulders like a cloak, and tossed a spell. It exploded beside the man's head with a silent concussion that made Verity's ears pop even from where she stood. He gasped in pain, staggered, and only remained upright by hanging onto the wall while he retched, balance apparently shot to hell.

He swiped the air with his flashlight, a heavy metal one, but Dakota stepped into him, avoiding it gracefully, and touched his shoulder. "Sit down here and be silent and don't try to warn anyone," she said and bent down after him as he slumped. The binding spell glow settled into a patch at his shoulder and he didn't even seem to fight it, just let his head fall against the brick.

The whole fight had taken perhaps ten seconds, and now Dakota's opponent was on the ground, going nowhere. Verity couldn't help but feel a little impressed. Some things, Dakota was very, very good at.

Before Dakota could tell her to hurry up, she opened the single door and glanced into the dim room inside. The fractured-glass colors of a mirror realm creature made her heart leap but her brain squashed that hope before it could pass beyond her quickening pulse. It wasn't her cousin in invisible form, it was a manta. An oddly still manta. It rippled the edges of its wings slightly, so it was alive, but it should have either fled or attacked. Instead, it just lay there.

Verity edged closer. It had a harness of some kind making

an X across its back, attached to a chain on a ring set into the floor. The nylon strap glowed with a binding spell. Easier to bind the creature not to remove the harness than to bind it not to attack and stay in the room, Verity presumed. That matched what she'd heard mages say before, about how the more exceptions a binding would need—the manta could leave the room if someone escorted it, etc.—the harder it was to cast.

The manta looked…emaciated, was the word Verity found herself reaching for. She'd never seen a mirror realm creature that had starved to death before, because any that did would be in the formless magic and broken down by it, but its weakness and the tight look to its skin seemed to point to nothing else.

They must have been feeding it only with food, Verity realized abruptly. Mantas weren't designed for that—they could eat food, but they were inefficient about processing it, so it took a hell of a lot to keep them alive, compared to a phantom or a jaguar, or even a wolf-type. It wasn't like Stiles and her students would have had to sacrifice humans to it. A few larger dogs or pigs would have been fine. But she supposed they were too squeamish to give it live animals to pull lifeforce from.

A footstep at the door made Verity start and she whirled. It was Dakota, of course, but it provided a strong reminder that she needed to stop getting distracted. "Five seconds," she promised in a low voice and dug out the paintball gun from her backpack. She couldn't miss from this distance, and the electricity crackled across the manta's back. It curled a wing for a last time, then flopped completely flat.

"Another failed experiment," she said to Dakota's confused look as she pushed out of the room, stuffing the gun back into its holster and swinging her backpack into place. "Come on."

The next door they encountered was locked, as was the one

after. Dakota didn't want to stop and try to explode the locks and Verity wasn't sure if they should either. They could simply be empty rooms, as the locks were the original, historic ones below the knobs, not anything new or obviously more secure. The maze of a basement had a lot of rooms, and already two were locked. Pteil couldn't be in both of them.

As she hesitated over the second, it was Dakota's turn to jerk on Verity's arm. "Come on. We can come back if we need to. There's so much dust, no one's in there."

Verity scuffed her shoe across the floor. Of course, both of them had walked up to the door before thinking to check for footprints. "All right," she agreed, though the ticking of an imaginary clock felt like it was winding the muscles in her shoulders tighter with each second. This wasn't a video game, where the boss wouldn't spawn until they started up the stairs, and they had hours available to open every single locked chest down here.

Dakota bypassed the next door, jogging ahead to check down the next corner. Verity examined floor and knob carefully for dust this time, and so lost sight of Dakota. No dust that she could see, but every surface down here was dirty, so even now it wasn't as useful as she'd imagined at the last door. This one was locked too, but—there. A flash of a binding spell. Keeping the door shut, she'd bet. It had to be this one!

"Pteil?" she called through the door, quiet, then a bit louder. Nothing, no reply, no sound of movement. Was she wrong? Was this another jaguar or Stiles' expensive wine collection, or was Pteil unconscious? "Pteil?"

And then she heard it, straining with her ear near the ancient keyhole. Someone panting, straining to breathe. Fighting a binding.

Verity whirled from the door. This was the one they needed to explode. "Dakota," she called down the hall as she sprinted for the corner, trying to be soft but carrying.

Dakota must have been keeping her illusion up without thinking, because the only part of the presumable fight Verity heard was a thud, almost simultaneous with her rounding the corner and seeing Dakota on the ground, unconscious. Too late to run, because Stiles and her students had seen her.

Stiles was holding the wrist of a young woman, who gave the impression of being even tinier than Lucy, though measured against the rest of the students in the cluster, she wasn't that short. Verity tried to make herself count the other students, but fear prevented her from expanding her focus and it didn't really matter anyway. She couldn't throw even one spell at them.

"How delightful. They did bring the other phantom to us." Stiles smiled at Verity, which only made her expression sharper. That "us" was laughable. Stiles was the only important one here, her students were simply supporting her.

Dakota groaned, a sound more suited to being forced to get up before eight in the morning than a fight with a corrupt Archivist for the fate of a whole people. But if she was rousing, then maybe Verity could get them out of here. She had the mylar in her pack, if she could make it over to Dakota and spread it out quickly, before they realized what she was doing—she could use Dakota's body to hold open one side, even—she'd need to pull Dakota to her knees at least, so she could "step" forward—

But everyone was staring at her right now. She needed to distract them, to play more frightened than she was—all right, she was pretty frightened, but she could play more unthinking—so that they took her motions as fidgeting, not purposeful. "The Archivists know that you have a prisoner you didn't turn over to them. They'll know to find you here." She made sure to look behind the students, as if expecting reinforcements.

"Oh, is this a story in which I have gone rogue, and the forces of authority will arrive to rescue you as soon as you have sufficient 'proof'?" Stiles walked over to Dakota, prodded her with the toe of her boot, then retreated to her more impressive-looking position at the head of her group of students. "I'm afraid that's not the story we're in. The Quorum is pragmatic enough to take advantage of access to plentiful resources when it's offered, and large enough to mire itself in discussion if individual members have reservations. And, given that as a member I am far more familiar with all the mages' many treaties and laws than you, I can assure you that nothing I am doing is against the rules. Your realm simply has too much magic not to use it, Verity."

She glanced behind her, making the movement mocking. "Are your friends supposed to be coming to your rescue?"

Verity swallowed against panic clawing at her chest, and despite her instincts, let Stiles see it. No, the others were supposed to be well clear, drawing students off, not fighting their way in. The numbers didn't support that. But if they weren't clear—or if Stiles was just trying to psych her out—

"What did you do to Dakota?" Verity moved to her. She could go to her knees beside her, appear to check for injuries. Then she'd just have to get the mylar out.

Resistance. Something at her back jerked her to a stop and Verity pulled out of the backpack straps but then the grip fell on her wrist, tightening to the edge of pain. She twisted to find a burlier student examining the pack, holding it up with one hand while he held her with the other. He tossed it to Stiles, and Verity thought maybe while he was distracted she could kick her way free. Her first kick had no apparent effect when it thudded against his leg. She tried again immediately, aiming better this time, but he twisted her arm up behind her back and *kept* twisting until her elbow screamed and the pain flashed up and down her arm in both directions and she couldn't move because that made it worse.

Stiles drew the tube out of the pack and unrolled it with interest. "Ah, a portable reflective surface. A relatively smart move." She picked at a corner of the mylar, pulling it from the more rigid plastic, and ripped her hand down the center of the square, tearing and crumpling in equal measure. She tossed it aside and the nearest student kicked it the rest of the way up against the wall.

Verity hadn't gotten even a flash of reflection from it, it wasn't like an open connection to the mirror realm had been taken from her, but it felt the same. The old need to run, which had sprung into being when Vasily had first bound her, hadn't ever really lessened, she realized now. It had been buried, but it had been growing beneath the surface of her mind all that time and now it was choking her. She needed to get *free* of Stiles, but she could hardly move. When the burly student behind her marched her forward after Stiles she had to go.

"We'll put them in the other cell," Stiles said, finally releasing her binding crafter, or at least that's what Verity assumed the young woman was. If she wasn't, Verity couldn't think further over the rising tide of panic. She couldn't get free by running. She wouldn't, she needed to stay calm enough to think, but she couldn't.

Verity couldn't turn to see, but someone grunted like they'd picked up a heavy weight, so apparently Dakota was being carried wherever they were going. Stiles opened a door farther down the hall, but when the burly student would have shoved Verity through, Stiles held up a hand. "Verity and I need to have a private talk."

The pressure on Verity's arm eased slightly, enough that she gathered herself to respond, but then her cheek was mashed into the wall and the student leaned his weight against her instead. She faced the doorway, so she got a truncated slice of view as Dakota was carried inside.

Then more noise, approaching footsteps blended with grunts and curses and scuffling. Verity spared a second for a desperate hope that it wouldn't be—

A couple students—spattered with little blotches of color, Verity noticed with a pinprick of satisfaction—shoved Lance through first. He went as quietly as Lucy, just behind him, only hissing curses under his breath, which made Verity sure that he must have been bound not to fight back. Siobhan was limping, Verity couldn't see why in her slice of view, but she could see Davin was taking most of her weight with her arm around his shoulders. Siobhan saw her, gasped out the beginning of some question, but Davin was facing the wrong way and then the door slammed shut. Stiles gestured her crafter back and they set a binding on the door, the same as had been on the door Verity had found. So that room *had* held her cousin. Much good knowing that did her now.

"That's all of them." Stiles touched her iron hair absently, but of course it hadn't dared to become disarranged and she dropped her hand again.

"What did they do with Ken?" The student who'd spoken up looked like he was now fifty-percent sure it had been a terrible idea, but he didn't shrink under Stiles' gaze. Verity supposed at least he had that much conviction, to stand up for someone. On his own side, of course.

Stiles didn't bother answering directly—her manner made it clear without words that if he would only have *waited* for *five seconds* he would have gotten his answer. Whether that was true or not. Instead, Stiles divided the students up, pointing at about half one by one. "Check the rest of the basement, see what they've gotten into down here. I presume Molsberry is sitting bound somewhere. The rest of you, sweep around the building upstairs."

Everyone trooped off, leaving Verity with Stiles, her crafter, and the burly student holding her. She rolled her shoulders, testing the weight on her, but he leaned in harder and she gave up again. Her talents had always lain with talking, not punching her way free. "So you have your own little loyal army? And the other Archivists allow that? Or maybe they just don't know about it."

"Army?" Stiles laughed. Far from being the cackle she deserved, it was a rich sound that suited a mature yet still stunning woman. "A dozen students is hardly an army, Verity. Hardly overwhelming odds, as such things go, either. Too bad your battle plans were so predictable."

She stepped close enough to block much of Verity's view and drew her bound wrist out from between her belly and the wall. She discarded the leather cuff as she had the mylar, dropping it like a piece of trash to the floor.

Whatever she planned to do, Verity could only hope talking would make it more difficult to concentrate. "Predictable?" Keep talking, please keep talking.

"You think I was not completely aware of the illicit back entrance? Please. I have been teaching for decades. If you don't give students an obvious way to circumvent the rules, they'll only hurt themselves trying to create a new one. Of course you'd try to use this entrance. I only had to wait. Now." She switched to a lecturing tone. "This is quite a well-made binding, so it's more efficient not to break it. We can simply switch the ownership to myself, as Vasily did to Dakota. You can study it in detail later, see if that helps you replicate it." The lecture turned acid on the last sentence.

She was talking to her crafter, Verity realized. She couldn't see anything different about the spell as they worked, but then she wouldn't. "So you were hoping to draw me in all the time? Is making a new binding for my cousin not working out quite yet?" she asked, but Stiles ignored her completely.

Minutes ticked by and Stiles' scowl grew. Finally, she hissed something under her breath, probably some kind of imprecation against Vasily. "Fine. We'll have to remove it to see how it's built, then start again. Don't lose hold of her when the spell starts to crack."

And at the bottom of it all, what did Verity have left? Useless humor. "You sure you can even understand one of Vasily's spells, never mind replicate it? He's not hobbled by having to train up a new spell partner all the time. How long do you get out of them before they learn to think for themselves, and you have to find a different one, dewy-eyed at the honor?"

"That old fraud is the one hiding from *me*. No, *crack* it open," she spat at her student. "It's the simplest thing in the world. Why can't you do it right?"

Verity couldn't see the young woman, but her voice trembled. "I can't get—a grip on it. I don't know. That's just what I'm seeing through you. What it feels like to me is that I'm sliding off. It doesn't matter how hard I tear at it."

"Won't share your toys, you old bastard?" Stiles said, apparently to herself. "So be it." She returned her attention to her crafter. "Go join the others. I don't need you anymore. There are other ways to break a beast to useful work than spells." Her tone had passed acid and gone to a glittering, frightening place, so it was no surprise when the crafter's footsteps disappeared at a run.

"Let her up, I want to see her face." Stiles' expression blanked to match her glittering tone as she examined Verity. Verity let her gaze go unfocused so she wouldn't have to see that expression and lose her nerve. "I'm curious, Verity. I may not have found the way to switch ownership—without murder, of course, though I suppose you'd love to believe me capable of that—but I found the most interesting little exception in that spell. Tell me your original purpose for coming to this world."

Verity gritted her teeth. She didn't know what Stiles could see in the spell, but if Verity didn't say anything, Stiles couldn't see anything. She was concentrating so much on maintaining blankness in her body language as well, she didn't see Stiles' backhand before it connected, smashing pain across the side of her face and those gritted teeth.

She stumbled and the burly student let her go, either out of surprise or at some gesture. The next blow carried her into the wall, temple scraping against the rough brick. Time skipped over the moment she spent stunned and then the kick to her stomach folded her up and her next awareness was of her hands and knees hitting the floor, her face on fire. "Are you a spy, Verity?" Stiles demanded, massaging her hand like Verity's face had made it hurt.

Verity wasn't going to answer, she was determined not to give Stiles the satisfaction. But the kicks kept coming, hard little smashing points of agony from the toe of Stiles' boot and she curled up to try to protect her face as best she could, catching them on her forearms, her shins. "No!" she shouted. The blows finally paused and she couldn't stop herself from babbling, trying to maintain that pause. "No, I was just a dumb kid, exploring. Not a spy. Not."

"Ah." Stiles sighed with satisfaction. "Get her up." The world was washed with sticky red and by the time Verity realized that blood from the cut on her temple was streaming into one eye, her head had cleared a little and Stiles had the door open. Not like paint, a part of her mind noted with hysterical clarity. Like jam.

"I'm sure the Quorum will be delighted to lend all their strength to rebinding a *spy* so she can give us information about her real purpose," Stiles sneered as Verity was shoved through the door. "And perhaps they'd see the sense of sending someone of our own to the mirror realm immediately to ensure an attack is not imminent." Then the door slammed and Verity stood swaying a little, trying to get her eye clear enough to see properly. She swiped at it, but the blood just kept flowing.

"Verity!" Dakota was suddenly there, throwing an arm over her shoulder that Verity immediately shrugged off so she could pull off her fleece. Dakota seemed to figure out what she was doing without explanation, for once, and helped her with the sleeves so she could bundle and hold it against her forehead so she could see properly. The more she moved her arms, the more they ached. She assumed bruises would be blooming soon.

"Come sit down," Dakota urged. "Why would she do that to you?" She led Verity to the wall, fortunately with the bricks thickly painted on this side so the surface was smoother, and helped her sit down against it.

Siobhan wasn't far down the wall, one leg stretched out in front of her. When she tried to scoot down, she hissed in pain and examined Verity from where she was. "Seriously. Fuck, Verity. They fucked up my knee, but only when we were fighting. Once we were all bound not to, they stopped."

Verity searched out Davin, finding him on the other side of the room, arrested as if in mid-pace. She reached out to him, suddenly desperately wanting him to join her. Wanting him to sit down at her side and hold her and let his touch pull her into a moment, however brief, where she wouldn't have to think of any of this.

His face went stark with—what? Disgust? Fear? He didn't move and after a painfully awkward breath, another, Verity lowered her hand. She finally noticed it was covered with stupid red-jam blood as well the stickiness she could feel down her cheek and neck. Anger flared, all the hotter for being contrary to what she knew was only sensible. He was right not to get near her when she was bleeding like this. They'd only had an encounter, fueled by curiosity and lust. But it wasn't *fair*, either. He didn't have to *kiss* her. He wasn't in real danger.

Verity didn't have the strength to sustain the anger for long and it left her hollow when it burned out. Whatever she may have come to feel about Davin, if she'd had time to get used to the idea, didn't matter. So be it.

"Stiles was angry with me because she couldn't subvert the binding," she said when her mind limped slowly back around to the unanswered question. Dakota sat down beside her and gave her a sideways hug, which Verity didn't throw off, because…well, maybe it helped a little. A very little. "And I think she hasn't managed to make a spell that works to make Pteil teleport, either. So we should have at least a little time while she figures out her next approach on my binding. Time to…" She'd meant to say escape, but that seemed foolish now. Not when

Siobhan could hardly walk.

Dakota followed Verity's gaze to the door. "We all tried the lock the moment she closed the door the first time. She's more than good enough to make a binding spell to hold it closed that can't be broken from the inside." Verity didn't bother to nod. That was only to be expected.

"So the spy thing was because she can't get rid of your binding herself? She wants the Archivists' help? But weren't you cleared of that long ago? Because of the truth spell?" Lucy had her knees to her chest, hugging them.

"Sounded to me like Archivist Stiles knew different," Lance rumbled from the corner. He was also seated, knees up, but he had his wrists resting on them in perhaps the most stereotypically brooding posture possible without a background of a burning, apocalyptic wasteland. "*Are* you a spy?"

"Of course I'm a fucking spy!" Verity didn't realize she was screaming until she heard her own voice, or crying until she felt the liquid trickling over her sticky skin. "An untrained, useless fucking spy." Her volume lowered, but not her anger. How she hated herself right now. The others, they wouldn't be hurt further, she was sure of that. They'd walk free with a little argument, and she'd be bound to Stiles and used to plunder the formless magic and that would mean war, and it was all because of *her.*

"Why else would I come to this damn realm and hang around? Vasily was the first human to make it into the mirror realm and we needed to know if there would be others. Because if it's one thing humans can't stand not having, it's someone else's land."

"It's not like anyone's planning a damn invasion," Lance growled.

"Oh, and outsiders exploiting resources and then pulling

out *always* ends well for the natives," Verity snapped back. "And how long until someone decides the exploitation would be much more efficient with the realm directly under your control?"

She didn't know if any of them were planning to voice the objection, but she didn't need them to, she could hear it in her head just fine. "And no, not all humans are like that, and maybe phantoms were planning an invasion of here first, you don't know, but there are *more of you than us*. Do you understand what that means? It means that all it takes is one of a certain kind of human coming to power, and organizing others to follow them, and then you're invading our realm, and with seven billion of you, the probabilities are not on the phantoms' side. That seven billion holds hundreds, thousands, I don't know, of that kind of human, and all that needs to happen is for them to take power and Stiles *has...*"

"Verity." Dakota repeated the name like this wasn't the first time she'd tried to break in. "Shhh. Sweetie." She tried to tighten her hug but Verity broke free to hunch over in her own patch of misery.

She could imagine Lance's next objection as well, so she answered it before he made it. "Vasily understood that. He said he was creating the exception to the truth spell because he didn't want any of his own secrets to come out under questioning, but really he didn't trust Stiles, or probably a lot of other people either."

Dakota stroked her hair, and Verity watched a drip of blood that had escaped from under the fleece splat onto the concrete floor. "Maybe we need more travel, not less. If more humans see the formless magic, maybe you'd all understand how dangerous it really is..."

Another drop joined the first, making a puddle that was

more dark than red in the dim light. A puddle…

An idea lit up and took Verity over between one breath and the next, like wildfire. She looked up. "Davin!" He started and shied away from where he'd been standing, staring at her, but he could damn well put his fear of her blood aside for five minutes if it would get them out of here. She was certain he could manage to avoid licking his fingers, even if he smudged his hands by accident. "I know you and Siobhan can't break the binding, but could you—stretch it in a specific area? I need my blood to be the right color."

Davin looked at her like she was speaking her native language rather than English. "The right…color?"

"Phantom blood isn't red." Verity suddenly felt so close to getting out of here, she begrudged him every word of explanation, and they tripped over each other as she tried to get them out in half the time. "It's silver. Like the creatures. You've seen it." She twisted to Dakota. Maybe she'd understand quicker, having seen more monsters. "Phantoms can teleport through a pool of their own blood. It's self-defense. In an emergency, you can at least get *out*. The binding keeps me too human for my blood to be reflective, but if you can stretch it just for that one thing—"

Davin's expression crumpled. "No, you can't!"

Verity felt like he'd ripped away anything else she might have said. No? What was that supposed to mean? If he and Siobhan couldn't stretch the binding, that was one thing, but who was he to say what she could and couldn't do? When she and her people were the ones at risk, and he was the Archivists' pet investigator and probably the least at risk of anyone here.

"You can't kill yourself for us!" Dakota said, tone very similar to Davin's, once Verity really listened.

Oh. "It doesn't have to be *fatal*," she said, and laughter with an edge of hysteria at the confusion seized her for a breath, until she inhaled raggedly and stopped it. "Look, this floor is flat enough, a thin layer would be all that it would take." She fanned out her fingers above the two drops of red blood.

"Good enough for me." Siobhan held out a preemptory hand for her brother. "Get your ass over here so we can escape."

Verity switched hands holding her jacket to her forehead so she could extend the bound wrist to Siobhan, since she assumed Davin wouldn't want to touch it. There was some jostling and hissing in renewed pain from Siobhan but finally everyone was sorted out, Davin kneeling in front of them both. Verity closed her eyes so she wouldn't accidentally catch his as he worked.

"Ha!" Siobhan said a few minutes later, sounding quite pleased. Verity retrieved her hand and touched the fingertips to her cheek. The new blood leaking from under the fleece shimmered against her skin, metallic.

Verity ripped the fleece away, the better to remove what scab had formed. It hurt, of course. When she leaned on her hands, head down, to drip straight down to the floor, her arms hurt much, much worse. The heavy raincloud gray of the bruises was already clear.

"Jesus," a woman muttered, though low enough under her breath, Verity couldn't tell which one it had been. The puddle oozed viscously larger with each drop, reflecting her haggard face back up at her. Too slow. She pressed at the wound despite the pain, until it streamed like it had before.

And then the puddle was big enough and Verity's connection to the mirror realm snapped into focus, almost bringing on fresh tears, of relief this time. She held them back because she didn't want to disturb the surface.

"Come on. We need to get everyone standing," she said, and struggled to her feet herself. There was no way to take Pteil with them, but at least this much freedom got them closer to saving Pteil as well and took both Verity and the template of her binding away from Stiles.

23

Verity took them straight to their usual healing mage clinic near home. Dakota's home, that was. They came out through the mirror the mages left by arrangement in the basement storage room of the residential home that had been adapted into a clinic, among the linens and toilet paper. Not that the healers took regular human clients, but even most mages would be somewhat disturbed by people appearing at random.

In the fuss and chaos of getting everyone seen to, Verity hung back, conscious of how strange her silvery blood must look. The healer couple were made of sterner stuff than that, however. Once they transported Siobhan to a bed and presumably healed her, they worked their way through checking over and treating everyone else, all the way down to Verity. One examined the bruises on her arms and legs, then had her take off her shirt to allow him to check her ribs. Then, silvery blood or not, he cleaned her face and attached a couple of butterfly bandages without any comment. Verity expected that to be all, given that the cut had already stopped bleeding, but they joined hands ready for magic as she swallowed the pain pills they'd given her.

The first healer gave her a thin smile. "You'll be hating life if we don't do something about those bruises before the adrenaline wears off, trust me." As the spell settled over her, the pain eased off to sheer relief, like a constant buzzing noise you had forced yourself to stop noticing until blessed silence returned. She still ached, especially along her ribs, but she'd take it. Siobhan was undoubtedly worse off.

When the healers left to return to Siobhan, Verity wandered out of the treatment room to the waiting room to curl up on the sleek couch worthy of any non-mage doctor's office.

She must have dozed, because when Dakota touched her shoulder, it brought her out of a morass of directionless worry that refused to form itself into a new rescue plan. "We're convening in Siobhan's room to figure out what we're doing next," she said.

The room's beginnings as a plain old bedroom made it softer, warmer than the hospital rooms on TV. Little equipment was needed, anyway—generally either a healing spell would work, or it wouldn't, and the healing mages passed their patient on to the mundane medical system. The light peach color of the sheets complemented the pinstripes separating dark green in the curtains, better decorating than any of the rooms in Dakota's house managed.

Siobhan sat up against the headboard, leg out in front of her with a pillow to hold the knee slightly bent. "So the word is they have to call in another pair before they can heal it," Siobhan told Dakota as they entered. "Usually for a broken bone, you bind it together in the right position, then heal it. But with all the—" She wavered her fingers above her knee, and laughed.

"Bitty bits of broken cartilage or whatever the fuck, they need an expert to get them all into place before they do anything."

"Besides give her drugs," Davin remarked, deadpan. There wasn't enough room for him to sit on the bed, so he had to hover from a distance, not that that seemed to be cramping his hovering style any.

"Yeah, I'm on the good stuff." Siobhan laughed again. "But I told them I had to be at least clear-headed enough to listen to your awesome plan to get back in there and kick Stiles' ass."

Verity drew her finger along the ledge on top of the wood footboard. She was singularly lacking in awesome plans right now, whether or not a little retributive ass-kicking was included with the rescuing. Dakota jumped in to think out loud before Verity could even organize her thoughts. "Well, we shouldn't divide our strength this time, that's for sure. Why not fight them properly?"

"Numbers," Davin said simply.

"And they'll all be full pairs, and we've lost Gabe and now Siobhan so we won't have explosions or bindings." Lance was brooding upright this time, shoulder against the wall and arms folded over his chest, but at least he was speaking sense instead of assholery. "And really, if we know it's a serious fight we're getting into, Lucy should keep out of it."

"I—" Lucy pushed away from the wall and rolled her fingers down into fists. "I'm coming along. You guys need me, and this is something worth fighting for."

"Phantoms?" Verity asked. She couldn't help herself. She didn't understand what had changed for Lucy, so she couldn't trust it. She believed research-oriented Lucy could find something important enough to take her into a straight-up fight, sure, but this something?

"No, helping a friend of a friend," Lucy said, and smiled thinly. "And not letting Stiles manipulate the Quorum into starting a war no one wants."

"Lucy should be able to come if she wants to. I can craft for Davin," Dakota added, to address Lance's other objection. "And I'm *good* at explosions."

"But you're only one person, Dakota," Verity said. There was…almost an idea, at the tip of her mind. If only she could capture it. "I'll admit, you're a badass in a fight, but they'll overwhelm you within a minute." Now she had the floor, she'd better use it if she wanted thinking-out-loud time for herself. "I suppose we could try to get an Archivist we trust to prod the Quorum into action, or wait until Siobhan's on her feet, but while we delay Stiles could finish the spell on Pteil and jump to the mirror realm immediately."

Lucy made a frustrated noise under her breath. "Prod them?"

Verity assessed her remaining store of diplomacy for the space of a breath, then softened the words that had originally sprung to her mind. "Stiles said nothing she was doing was against the rules, and I don't think she had any reason to lie about that."

Lucy hung her head, which surprised Verity. She wouldn't have expected the old Lucy to be embarrassed on behalf of the Archivists for anything. "She'll hide the other phantom before the Quorum catches her with him, of course. That's sketchy, treaty-wise. But other than that, she's right about not breaking any rules. I mean, she hurt Siobhan, but we kind of attacked first."

Dakota's lips thinned. "Verity, hold up your arms, would you?"

Verity took the opportunity to check the bruises there herself, too. They protested vehemently when she twisted her wrists too far in trying to see. After the healing, the gray was closer to a thunderstorm than rain, but there wasn't much swelling left.

"So that's okay, then?" Dakota asked Lucy.

Lucy hunched farther in on herself. "We don't have rules about phantoms. Except the treaty. You know that. We have basic morality, sure, but that's the kind of the thing that takes time to discuss and rule on. And if she does have others on the Quorum arguing her side..."

None of that was surprising to Verity, so she listened with half her attention. She still had that seed of an idea, struggling to break free through her emotional exhaustion. Based on...

"Gabe." Verity interrupted Lucy, because she had to let the idea tumble free, catch it before it was gone. "He'd be the perfect distraction. They trust him, he could walk right up to the building and they'd let him in, and if we were covered with an illusion behind him..."

"But why would he help us?" Hurt took over Dakota's expression as if she thought Verity was bringing up her traitorous lover specifically to needle her.

"Because we can geas him." Davin's voice was heavy with resolution, when Verity would have expected reluctance.

Siobhan slapped her thigh on her good side with delight. "Yes! Poetic justice."

Davin's face fell. "You're in no shape to be crafting, drugs or no drugs, Siobhan."

"Dakota can craft for you." Lance had straightened from the wall, apparently somewhat enamored of the idea as well.

Verity didn't give Dakota time to object. If she gave Dakota time to think about it, they'd be back to "love" and "I don't know" and she couldn't take that shit right now. She needed to pull Dakota along in the momentum of the fight. "What would we even be making him do? Walk into a building without looking suspicious. That's not going to hurt him."

"And it won't be anything permanent, remember," Davin added. "Even if they were allowed without permission, permanent geasa are far beyond my skill."

Dakota's face crumpled. "I don't—"

"How do we get close enough to bind him?" To Verity's surprise, it was Lucy who cut Dakota off this time.

Verity didn't even have to think about that one. "Dakota can call him. Tell him that I turned on her and so did everyone else, and she's on his side now, phantoms should be locked up, can he come and help her?"

Lance whistled in appreciation. Verity didn't particularly want his appreciation, and he immediately went on to illustrate why. "You're a manipulative little—"

"Lance," Dakota snapped. "Why would he believe that any of you would turn on me? I mean, he should know better than that about Verity, but I get that his thinking's probably clouded by the fact that she's a phantom."

Verity started counting off on her fingers. "Well, Siobhan's out of the picture. You can tell him that and it'll match whatever Stiles might have told him. And Davin's got to stay and hover protectively over her, and besides, Gabe doesn't know him well. He'd probably believe that Davin would look at his injured sister and say, 'screw you, this isn't our fight, we're out.'"

"I won't," Davin said, low.

Verity dared a quick glance at him, then away again. "I know." Of course, that was the same level of loyalty he'd have given any of the team, she was sure. Nothing special being offered to her. "Anyway. Lucy's not trained to be out in the field fighting, so she could believably be standing back, and that only leaves Lance." Who did exactly what Dakota told him. That was more of a problem.

Inspiration dawned. "Tell him you found out I slept with Lance and when confronted, Lance picked me over you."

Various choking noises reached her from around the room, except Siobhan who tried to look pained, but couldn't hide her delight. After a beat, Verity realized that must have made things worse, because Siobhan so obviously knew what she was talking about. And Davin too, a beat later. She'd told him she'd had a human lover, after all, if not his name. She felt a sudden absurd need to justify herself to him, but when she caught his gaze, he grimaced in sympathetic humor, not anger. She relaxed without realizing she'd been tense.

Dakota took a while to put things together enough to speak, probably out of willful denial. "Verity..." She grabbed Verity's shoulder to turn her to face her. "*Did you sleep with Lance?*"

She looked so *hurt*. Verity swallowed. She hadn't meant to hurt her that badly. Dakota slept with other men, was Lance not supposed to sleep with other women? "If it helps, I didn't enjoy it much?"

"Hey!" Lance packed an amazing amount of injured masculine pride into one syllable.

"No, it doesn't help!" Dakota laughed on a note that made it sound like she could either do that or scream. "When was this?"

Verity had a good answer to that, at least. "After you first slept with Gabe, and you and Lance had that big fight. You guys were taking a break, weren't you? I mean, I assumed..." She trailed off when Dakota's expression made it clear that wasn't a good answer either.

Dakota pressed her hands to her face. "God. Verity." She fumbled out her phone. "All right. Fine. Let's do this."

Dakota managed to convince Gabe to meet them at home without a hitch. She sounded more than believably pissed with both Lance and Verity. For some reason. At home, she waited for him at the front door, Verity waited for them both in the shadows down the hall, and Davin waited for the rest of them next to a chair, pulled away from the table in the dining room.

When the door finally opened to Gabe's key, he swept her up into a hug instantly, expression hard to read in the evening light against his dark skin, but easy enough to guess. "Dakota! I'm so sorry. I'm here for you."

To her credit, Dakota dropped a binding over him without hesitation, the glow settling over the back of his neck, like she might have thrown a necklace as she put her arms around him. "Come into the dining room, Gabe."

And he came quietly. Verity couldn't understand, until she realized that as a crafter, he couldn't see the spell, and he couldn't feel it unless he was fighting it. He didn't want to fight it yet.

She slipped into the dining room from the kitchen entrance, arriving as Gabe did start to fight, his eyes on Davin. Davin, who should not have been there, according to the story. "What—?"

"Sit down," Dakota said, then turned away and hugged herself.

Gabe sat, but there must have been nothing in the binding to keep him quiet. His voice rose. "What are you doing, Dakota? I love you. I'm here to help you."

"Why are you trying to hurt my friend, then?" Dakota turned back, and Verity looked at the floor. Friend. Was that true, or was Dakota acting? Dakota was terrible at acting.

Where anyone else might have laughed, or scoffed, Gabe grew only more earnest. "Dakota, phantoms—they're just magic, wearing a face. That's all. Humans are programmed to respond to things with faces, but that doesn't make pulling the stuffing out of a teddy bear murder. Magic is made to be used. You're like someone destroying a dam because they don't think the birds perching on it want the water used for generating electricity."

"There's this concept called sentience, Gabe." Verity couldn't hold herself back. Every human that had ever ignored her, sneered at her, here was one sitting in front of her who actually had to *listen* to her. "Have you ever heard of it? It sort of opens one up to the idea that humans aren't the center of the fucking universe, and there might be other self-aware, thinking, feeling, creating *beings*."

She was close enough now to spit in his face, and she was getting ready to do it, too, before Dakota pulled her back. "Verity," she said, slowly, over and over until Verity was forced to calm down enough to look at her. When Dakota saw her eyes, she let her go. Verity still felt the anger trying to shake her apart, though.

Davin came forward, but Dakota gestured him back. "I don't think I can do this. Shouldn't we be better than they are?"

"We're making him walk into a building, that's all," Davin said, but Verity's earlier argument didn't seem to do any more good coming from him.

"I still love him, Davin." Dakota spoke the words like she

was pleading for something, tears standing out in her eyes. Verity could *hear* the soundtrack music swell around them all.

Fine. Dakota wanted to make a scene, Verity would make a scene too. "You do not love him," she ground out between gritted teeth, then repeated it louder to make sure Dakota had heard. "You love the *idea* of being in love. You love the feeling of—" English didn't have the word she wanted, so she translated as best she could from her native language. "Flush love. Not partner love. Not the kind of love where you *work* together with someone, to live together. Flush love, where you don't need to work, because it comes easily, and then it *fades*."

"Limerence," Davin contributed. Verity didn't know the word, but she nodded anyway, trusting him to know what he was talking about.

Dakota gaped at her, without words for several seconds. "Verity...how can you say that?"

"Because friends tell each other truths," Davin said.

"Sweetheart." Gabe had never been one to interrupt, but he seemed to see his moment now, painfully earnest as ever. "Don't listen to her. She's just trying hurt you enough to get you to do what she wants. I love you."

Dakota's mouth firmed into a line, and strength slipped visibly into her backbone. "Verity can't lie, though. You can."

Verity didn't think Gabe was lying, about loving Dakota. But if Dakota needed to believe that, to make a clean break, to heal from Gabe's betrayal, Verity would say not a word.

"I would never lie to you—"

Dakota dropped another binding onto Gabe's shoulder. Silence, this time. His mouth continued to work but nothing came out. She offered her hand to Davin.

"Wait." Verity stepped up to Gabe's face again. He closed his mouth and regarded her serenely, clearly ready to accept whatever she wanted to throw at him. That was fine. He probably wouldn't listen, but it would help her to say it. "Pay attention, Gabe. You're about to find out what it's like to be bound. How it *feels*." At the last moment, she found she did want him to acknowledge her. She spat in his face, and saw a brief flicker of disgust cross his features as it dripped down his cheek. She'd take it.

Then she stepped back to watch, as the others laid the geas.

24

Outside the Ontario rental car office they'd teleported to, Dakota removed the silence binding so Gabe could call Stiles. They huddled beside the rented minivan under a wan floodlight as Davin ordered Gabe to be believable. For simplicity, they'd included the whole team in the ranks of people who could give him orders and Verity was glad they didn't have to talk Dakota into each new order.

Gabe was believably, typically terse. He was bored of sitting around being useless in Shoreline now he was thoroughly burned with Dakota, he said, so he'd hopped a plane to see if there was anything for him to do where the action was. He didn't look at Dakota, or any of them, as he said it.

Dakota didn't renew the silence binding, but Gabe didn't say a word for the entire drive to Stiles' base anyway. Verity watched him in the row of seats behind her in the minivan, illuminated by the uneven light of passing streetlights. If being bound bothered him, he didn't show it, not even deep in his eyes. Watching him tag along with the group, one might be forgiven for thinking he must not mind being bound very much.

That thought made her shiver, a movement that didn't warm her and left nausea behind in the pit of her stomach. Was she looking at herself from the outside? Verity pressed her fingertips against her corners of her eyes, letting the chill from her hands ground her. She wasn't trying to deny Gabe was a sentient being. And she wasn't suggesting he be bound for the rest of his life.

She touched the cut at her temple as well, reassuring herself that the bandage was holding for perhaps the fiftieth time just on the drive. Dakota pulled off onto a side street and hesitated, biting her lip, for a moment before jumping out and leaving the driver's door open. "Go ahead and drive us up, Gabe. Without doing anything out of character or suspicious."

Gabe slid out and walked around to the driver's seat without comment. Verity shifted her new backpack to her lap to check the contents again obsessively only to have the dome light go out after Gabe's door shut. She continued her check by feel while her eyes adjusted. Duct tape, a new mylar insta-mirror, check. It hadn't worked before, but that didn't make it a bad idea. They still might need to get the hell out quickly.

Since they were almost there, she zipped up her new, borrowed fleece. It was black, which made her feel like she'd be a bit less exposed out there in the night, but of course if the illusion failed with them right behind Gabe, no amount of camouflaged clothing would help them.

And then they were there. Gabe parked up by the building like he had every right to be there. Lucy and Lance created the illusion in the car, and once everyone climbed out they jostled for a few moments to pack as close as they could and still walk. For once Verity didn't have to have everyone's sweaty hands all over her body, so she snagged a spot on the outside of the cluster.

"Nothing out of character or suspicious," Dakota reiterated unnecessarily to Gabe, and then he was striding across the lawn, to the front door. Verity realized she hadn't seen it yet. It was fairly impressive, especially when lit up at night. Concrete blocks molded with swirls flanked the arch, and there were three or four steps up to what might be the original, heavy wood door.

Gabe pushed a slightly incongruously modern doorbell to the side and waited on the top step. Their knot of people oozed up the stairs, with Dakota two down from Gabe at the front and Verity on ground level at the back. Stiles' pet crafter opened it, and on seeing Gabe, dipped her head in immediate apology and disappeared. "Archivist!" could be heard from inside.

Stiles herself arrived promptly. Regardless of the hour or situation, her expression and posture were as unyielding as ever. "The plan wasn't for you to show our hand so soon to Dakota, you realize," she said without preamble. "They even showed up here. The phantom pulled them out through a mirror made of her blood before she could be useful. You're only lucky they can't safely take any of this to the rest of the Quorum."

Gabe shrugged. "I underestimated how much she was attached to her pet and pushed too hard. If she had a more realistic view of phantoms, it wouldn't have been showing anything like our hand."

Stiles hmphed, but certainly didn't seem suspicious. Verity found herself trying not to breathe, like that would pause her heart so Stiles wouldn't hear that pounding noise either. Which was silly because with Lucy's delicate, practiced touch guiding her illusion with Lance, their sounds were fully shielded as a matter of course.

"Well, come in. I've got to get back to working on the binding. We don't want any mistakes this time." Stiles' tone hardened and Verity could imagine the pet crafter flinching behind her.

"Like the jaguar?" Gabe asked blandly.

"Exactly. A bunch of parents weeping over their dead children is *just* what we need right now to truly derail the project." Stiles' voice turned acid.

Lance's growl rumbled from the center of the group and Lucy squeaked. "No! Steady power or it's going to flicker—"

And Stiles' gaze sharpened. Aimed at them. "What—"

She swept Gabe to the side of the front step with one arm, then rocked back to drag a pair of students forward. "Someone followed him. There!"

Verity dove without thinking, pressing herself low into the space between bush and concrete steps. Dakota thudded into her shoulder and the night behind them crackled with a quickly expanding burst of electricity, dendritic tendrils imprinted against her eyes in an afterimage even after the lightning flash faded. Explosion spells were supposed to be a bear to aim, when you weren't Dakota, but their effects were big enough, it usually didn't matter.

No one screamed or fell, so Verity could only hope that the others had ducked to the other side of the steps. The illusion lingered without them behind it, drawing another burst of electricity and then a concussive explosion that made Verity crouch lower, hands to her ears.

Gabe stood patiently at the far edge of the top step. Verity supposed he was unable to run—suspicious—or join the combatants, as no fighting on the side of Stiles and her students had been one of their first orders to him.

Any minute, someone inside would come into the doorway and get the right angle to see them, and then it would be all over. Verity gritted her teeth against another blast. They'd be running, Stiles would have the high ground, and her numbers would crush them into paste.

They had to go, now, while it was still a surprise, try to slam through into the building, make this into a close fight where bindings could be laid and the hallway would constrict the students' numbers and create the chance of friendly fire.

Verity shoved at Dakota. "Go!"

That was the only suggestion Dakota needed. She surged up the steps, tossing concussion spells as fast as one of the paintball guns, twice as fast as the pair attacking the abandoned illusion had managed.

And as Verity had hoped, the rest of the team pressed in behind her, the last charge of the hero too much of an archetype for them not to get caught up in it. The pounding-heart sizzle she felt as she joined them might have been a bit of a thrill of her own. Or it might have been paralyzing fear barely conquered by sheer stubbornness.

And Gabe was still standing there. Without conscious planning, Verity sheltered with him as a shield for the space of a breath while a concussion spell sailed past. "Throw a flash back at them," she snapped at him. "Blind them."

And he did. A flick of the hand to toss it as soon as it was formed, because without a sensitive, he couldn't set it off at a delay. The team was facing away from him, fighting their way into the building, so it seemed not to affect them much. It did leave another wash of retinal afterimage color over Verity's vision because she hadn't quite believed he'd really do it, and didn't close her eyes fast enough.

She clenched her fingers around a handful of fabric at the back of his shirt. "You brought up the jaguar on purpose, didn't you?" she hissed.

Gabe didn't answer, didn't grandstand, but she could *feel* his smirk in his entire body. She shoved him into the doorway. "Go where I push you," she said, hearing in her own tone the shaking need she had to turn her fingers to claw runnels in his back, if she couldn't reach to scratch the smirk off his lips.

Inside the building was chaos. Dakota's fire had paused because Davin had one of her hands, and they were lunging at students who came too close, snaring them with binding spells. A few stood like statues between the door and the team's current position, fouling everyone's aim and the reach needed for bindings. An illusion spell bisected the room, held up by Lance and Lucy crouched together against one wall. It glowed bright, screaming that it was hiding something behind it, but it was large enough that it didn't help the students pinpoint them. Verity would bet the illusion showed even worse chaos, overwhelming visual input of friend and foe and incoming spells flickering around each other.

Verity searched the crowd as best she could, peering over Gabe's shoulder, and found Stiles and her pet crafter had retreated to the back of the entranceway, where it narrowed to a hall. Like hell Verity was going to give her the opportunity to escape, grab Pteil, and vanish who knew where. "Another flash!" She closed her eyes and shoved Gabe forward in the split second after the flash while everyone in the room flinched. He knocked into someone but she kept going.

Another few steps and her vision was clear again, and Stiles was right there—everyone had noticed them by now of course, but the students already had opponents they were focusing on. Someone grunted in protest at another binding from Dakota and Davin, and that stopped anyone else from worrying about Gabe. She'd bet that he also was still enough one of them that deciding to target him would take time to think that they didn't have.

And she was a phantom, without any spells to throw of her own. "Body-check her crafter," she told Gabe, and gave him a shove to help him on his way. She couldn't have moved a braced, full-grown male an inch, but he wasn't braced. He and the crafter slammed into the corner of the hallway doorframe and went down in a tangle, both stunned.

Stiles bared her teeth at Verity. "Violent animals need to be put down." She launched herself at Verity. Without spells, apparently she was still more than ready to beat Verity into a pulp with her hands and the hard toes of her boots once more.

"Gabe, biggest concussion you have!" Verity dropped, hands clasped behind her head to mash her arms against her ears. Stiles was on top of her, but then the whole world *whomphed* and even Verity felt dizzy. Stiles, having been upright and moving, didn't stay that way for long. She collapsed against Verity and was still.

Verity gathered all her stability and shoved the woman off, opened her eyes to try to respond to the next attack. But Stiles was unconscious and as Verity watched, a small drop of red paint or jam traced a line—like lipstick—from the inside of her ear down her cheek in its quest for the floor.

Gabe and the pet crafter weren't moving either. Verity started to shake. She wasn't out of danger yet, she needed—needed to pull herself together—but already the noise around her was decreasing. She crouched down again to hold herself together.

Dakota stepped into her range of vision and bent to press a binding to Stiles' chest. Verity's hyperfocus made her start when Dakota's hands were next on her shoulders, because she'd been staring at Stiles, waiting for her to wake up and start fighting the binding. What kind was it? To keep her still? To keep her silent? Would Dakota have thought of the fact that Stiles could still rally her remaining students even if she couldn't move herself?

"Verity, it's over." Dakota's tone was gentle. Not patronizing, but Verity thought about bristling. She wasn't a sobbing wreck. She was just—shaking. A little. A lot. But Dakota really was the expert on fights. Verity was big enough to admit that. So she let herself be guided over to the side of the room. It was over. The fighting part. They still needed to do so many other things.

Things she'd remember in a minute. They had a little breathing space. Things could wait.

25

Verity stayed with Lucy, who was assigned to guard everyone currently bound asleep, while everyone else swept the basement for remaining students. On their way to the upper floors, they paused to assure Lucy the back entrance was bound shut, so the empty basement would stay that way. Seeing as she felt steady on her feet and was almost thinking straight, Verity set off to find her cousin. Maybe she should have taken someone with her, but she didn't want to wait that long.

The stairway to the basement took some opening of doors to find, but she knew exactly the room she wanted. Tracing her way to it from the other direction didn't even take that long.

She shoved at the door, but it was still bound locked, of course. "Pteil?" She kicked at the heavy wood, but of course that didn't help anything. "It's Verity. We're going to get you out very soon, I promise." So much for not waiting. But at least she was here to reassure Pteil.

That "soon" stretched, and stretched, until Verity could barely stand it. Where were the others? Rescuing Pteil was the point of everything, why were they screwing around upstairs?

Footsteps thudded up, Dakota's running tread. Her after-battle glow hadn't faded, leaving her with a sharp grin. "Davin called Archivist Khare—he says we can trust him—and he's going to bring some other Archivists who are on our side to investigate." Her delight bubbled up into laughter. "And probably arrest Stiles. And Gabe. At the very least. We just need to show them the phantom they had locked up."

Verity's stubborn grip on the doorknob must have dawned on Dakota, because she toned the glow down a little. "Is this where—?"

"Yes, so break the binding already." Verity kicked the door again even though she knew it made her look childish.

Dakota pressed her palms together, uncomfortable. "The Archivists should be the ones to break the locking spell, so that it's unimpeachable proof..." She attempted a reassuring smile. "They're going to be on the first flight out..."

"Fuck that noise." Verity slung the backpack she'd forgotten about off her shoulder and pulled out the mylar. "We'll go get them." She tore off a length of duct tape with a very satisfying rip and affixed one side of the mylar to the floor at their feet. "If it tears a hole in Geneva, there are plenty of binding mages there to take care of it. And another one here will get fixed with any others we've made already."

"Oh!" Dakota stared at her for a beat, and then her grin snapped back into being. "Good plan."

It took an effort of more will than Verity really had to hold back as the two Archivists entered the cell, but she borrowed a little against the next day's and stayed out in the hall. From the way they exclaimed not when they first opened the door, but when their footsteps had crossed the room, she suspected that Pteil did not look physically ill-treated, but on closer examination, the binding spell around her was a cruel one.

They exclaimed, they discussed in low tones, Pteil finally gasped as the binding on her must have been removed, and Verity slipped in when the discussion moved to the doorway and then farther into the basement, probably in search of privacy. Verity caught a snatch of "…if Margaret's students didn't realize…" as they hurried off.

Pteil was sitting on a metal folding chair, perhaps drawn from the very cache of them Verity had seen elsewhere in the basement. Her head was down, and she was breathing with a bit of a hitch like she was holding back tears. "Is the binding completely gone?" Verity asked in their native language. "If you can still feel anything, I'll go and drag them back to get rid of it—"

Pteil rose with a jerk, and a sob escaped when she saw Verity. Verity closed the remaining distance in two steps to embrace her. "I'm sorry," Pteil said over and over, nearly incomprehensible through the tears.

"No, Pteil. It's my fault. It's all right, fleck. You can go home. I have a mirror out here in the hall." Verity tried to guide her cousin in that direction, but she clung to Verity tighter and didn't move.

Pteil drew in a shuddering breath. "I don't think I can, yet. I feel so shaky, and I've only gone mirror to grounded realm and back once or twice."

Which Verity hadn't even considered. Which was a sign of how her time in the grounded realm had changed her. Every time she teleported was a hop at least partially from grounded to mirror realm, and she'd certainly done enough of that. She wasn't sure if it was good or bad, but she didn't like the fact that she hadn't realized it until now.

"That's fine," Verity said, pushing her thoughts aside. "I'll go get Dakota, and I'll take you home. Around here, we'll probably end up in the formless magic, but we can put you on a path to the nearest town."

Pteil nodded, head still very low, and Verity suppressed an unexpected flicker of frustration. A binding wasn't *that* shattering. You should come out of one fighting, running, taking your escape, not waiting for people to give it to you. But that wasn't fair. For one thing, Pteil could hardly have slept since she was taken. Verity needed to get Pteil home. She looped her arm around Pteil's waist.

Upstairs, one of the Archivists was now on his own, questioning Dakota. His skin tone was very similar to Verity's, but where her features were boringly even, his were long, sharp, and filled with character. "And so we knew that we needed to get in and guard the cell until you guys arrived, so Stiles couldn't disappear the proof of what she'd done," Dakota was saying.

"Mm," the Archivist agreed without pressing her for details, so maybe this was the second time through this story. Verity was sure that the hero would get to relate her triumph often enough as she encountered various mages over the next few months. The man turned when they reached the top of the stairs. No surprise, as they were making quite a lot of noise because Pteil wanted to cling to Verity and not let go. Verity wished she wouldn't. She kept putting pressure on Verity's bruises.

"Ah, good. I'm Archivist Khare." He pressed his hands together before his chest as Verity had seen mages do to Archivists before, but never the other way around. Not that she'd encountered many Archivists. Was he being pointed about her not making the gesture? She didn't have the hands for it at the moment. She struggled to rearrange Pteil and then abandoned the effort. If she offended him, so be it.

Davin stepped into the hallway from one of the rooms and approached. He seemed to be planning to speak to Dakota at first, but then he noticed Verity. Complex emotions twisted through his expression, and he completely ignored the other two humans to stride right for her. "Verity!"

Verity dodged as best she could so he wouldn't touch her. "Watch it in front of your boss," she murmured. She didn't want him to lose his job because someone misread the hug that he'd probably intended to give her out of kindness. She doubted the Archivists would be sanguine if they learned how entangled he'd gotten with the target of his investigation. She might not have gotten the chance to know him very well, but she would bet that he wouldn't do very well if he lost that particular job. And if she was honest with herself, she didn't want any touch from him right now if it had to be only kindness.

Davin rocked back on his heels, and Verity did her best to ignore him. "Dakota, can we take my cousin home, please?" She realized belatedly that probably wasn't Dakota's call to make. "Archivist?"

"By all means," Archivist Khare said. "We owe you greatly for this, Verity. We hope you'll agree to testify at the trials of Archivist Stiles and the others. And we will of course also be considering your case as soon as possible."

Verity almost asked if the Quorum planned to discuss it at length, but she knew it would come out rudely, so she clenched her teeth and only nodded. Give it another few months, and maybe something would come of that.

"Why don't we take everyone and continue on home to Shoreline from there?" Dakota suggested, coming to support Pteil's other side. Pteil flinched from her, and Dakota rocked back looking hurt.

Verity considered explaining that to get home from the point in the mirror realm corresponding to their current location, they'd have to drop back into the grounded realm, and only then teleport across. But she was tired, and it didn't really matter. It would feel the same to her passengers, just a few more steps in the journey. "Fine," she said, and waited with Pteil while Dakota went and rousted people out. As they arrived, they accreted around Verity.

One step, another into formless magic. Verity stumbled, but the press of people around her kept her upright and the damn bruises complained again. She couldn't move without jostling them against something. That transition had been unexpectedly hard, but who knew why. The there/not there colors of the formless magic made her stomach flip over, then back.

But she could see the ribbon of flat gray that definitively, stably, without roiling colors, marked a path in the distance. "Stay here," she directed the humans, and peeled herself and Pteil out of the knot. They seemed to hardly hear her, they were clinging so tightly to each other. Only Davin had been inside the formless magic for more than a few steps before, she remembered, and Lance's voice followed her as she led Pteil away. "How...how am I seeing this? Without a sensitive?"

Something smooth and chill slithered against Verity's free palm and she caught it instinctively. She lifted her hand as they walked. Not…rain. Not here. Not water or liquid at all, she realized. The binding chain.

Had broken.

The world seemed to pause for a breath while Verity caught up, her excitement only swelling after her mind had had time to encompass it. The spell had *broken*. She was *free*. All of the teleporting, Stiles hammering at it, Siobhan and Davin stretching it, all of that had taken its toll, and now it was broken.

Pteil finally increased her pace now the path was clear in front of them. She pulled away from Verity when Verity stopped to stare at the metal links across her fingers. That was when one of the humans screamed.

Verity whirled. If it was Lucy, it was a scream, if it was Dakota, it was an urgent call to battle instead, she supposed. A pack of wolf-type creatures was streaming around the humans, circling for now. They snapped teeth at the humans, gradually tightening in. It wouldn't be long now before they attacked.

Was that Verity's problem?

She was free. She could walk out of here on that path beside Pteil, never enter the grounded realm again as long as she lived. Go back and spoil her sibling's child and live a normal life.

But. Davin. And Dakota. And even Lucy, and what was she doing, even considering consigning humans to death? Her… friends, to death. She was running before she finished the thought. "Pteil! Run to the town!" she called, without looking back.

Lance drew his knives from the sheaths at his back, though it wasn't like the wolves were going to award points for style. Dakota grasped desperately at where her guns currently weren't. "Verity! What do we do?"

"Back to back, facing outward!" Verity judged her distance, slowed down. Wolves hunted only the formless magic, so she knew little about their tactics. Explorers who'd been surrounded this way sometimes escaped to tell the tale, but they were always alone. What would a pack do when choosing between a cluster of targets, and a single one? "Lance, throw me one of your knives!"

Lance snarled, but one knife flew to embed its point in the ground, several feet to Verity's side. She snatched it up. "The wolves can jump much higher than you think they can. Protect your throats!"

"Bipedal wolves?" Lance's voice stretched thin enough to nearly snap. "They may have fur, but they look like fucking velociraptors to me!" He kicked one in the head and a second buried its teeth in his lower leg. He shrieked and slashed off its head. Everyone else drew in tighter, not kicking.

Verity braced her feet and whirled the borrowed knife to feel out its balance. Longer than the ones she'd last used six years ago. She whistled piercingly to draw the pack's attention. "Come and get me, I'm all alone," she taunted in her native language. Whether they understood her or not, it felt right.

The wolves whistled among themselves for a few seconds, and then the pack peeled away and pounded toward her, fleet on two feet. She waited, held her nerve until the first had circled behind, keeping track of it through her peripheral vision. Then she whirled, touched, pulled its lifeforce. Phantoms were the top predators because they could pull it *fast*, and the wolf dropped immediately.

Oh, it was glorious. After six years with only food, the energy burst into her like flavor after years of eating only ashes, or water after hours of baking under the sun, or maybe even a little bit like an orgasm.

When the wolf collapsed the next pushed forward to take its place. It snapped at her and caught her wrist but she pulled its lifeforce anyway and didn't let pulling from one distract her from those behind it this time. She sliced at one leaping from the side, blinding it on one side by carving a line down its muzzle, and it didn't try to bite her when she pulled its lifeforce to finish it off.

But she couldn't guard her back completely, that was the point of the pack. One reached her shoulder and bit in hard. She couldn't reach it with the knife, and she couldn't throw it off, but she was so full of lifeforce, full to giddiness with it. Another found her ankle, got its teeth caught in the heavy denim of her jeans and she decapitated it as neatly as Lance had. She pulled the lifeforce from the head.

Now pain was seeping in from her shoulder, from her back as the attached wolf raked her skin with its back claws. She was having trouble standing with its weight and shimmering, metallic liquid of her blood and the wolves' blood was spattered everywhere as dark little dots and splashes in the formless magic around their feet. She slashed, and whirled, and slashed, and that kept them dancing back, but she couldn't hit any of them, get them down to pull from.

"Verity, listen to me!" The sharp command of Dakota's tone got through to her even when the order no longer carried the weight of magic. "Get ready to go!"

And Lance was carving a path through the wolves to her and those that couldn't escape were caught between them and she pulled from the ones he'd slashed and she was overfull of lifeforce now. Like it would spill up and over like vomiting after gorging on food, though lifeforce didn't work that way. A bite on her calf, from behind, and Verity twisted, dispatched that wolf. It was getting hard to move now, her vision wasn't working right. The formless magic wasn't this gray.

Someone tore the wolf from her shoulder and its jaw was clamped so tight that her shoulder must have shredded as it left, because it hurt so *much* and she needed to sit down, sit down *right now*, but there was nowhere to sit and someone was shouting at her. "Go! Go!"

Go. Go home. Right. Three steps. One in the grounded realm in one place, a second between, and a third in a second grounded realm place, the one so familiar to her.

One—

26

Verity fought out of dreams only reluctantly, unable to ignore the urgent press of her bladder. She didn't want to get up. She wanted to stay curled up here in the warm where it didn't hurt. But now she was this far awake, she might as well climb the rest of the way.

She shifted, pushed away the lump of blankets she'd been hugging so tightly. She didn't actually hurt that much. But her wrist—she felt—

Verity jerked her eyes open. There was a new chain on her wrist.

Of course there was. She subsided back into the blankets. She should have thought of that before she bravely saved the humans. Of course they'd bind her again. She'd had a moment of freedom and chosen to give it up for less than nothing. She wanted to feel angry. She wanted to feel rage, to use that rage to push herself up and out of bed and into the faces of whatever mages it took to get the binding removed again.

But instead, she felt hollow. She reached for emotional energy and came away with nothing, like dropping a pebble into a well with no splash.

"Verity!" Davin's voice. And there was her rage. How could he? How *could* he? Was he the one who'd made the new binding? Heat built and seeped and filled up the hollowness.

Davin was still speaking, sounding oddly near tears. "It comes off. It comes off."

It took her several seconds to process his words, and by that time, he was fumbling with her wrist. The simple hook clasp parted, and the bracelet fell away onto the sheets.

Verity looked from the chain to him and back. "Then why was I wearing it?" she demanded.

Davin seemed to realize he didn't have much time for an explanation before she punched him, because he stumbled over his words in his rush. "We had to hold you to human form, you were bleeding so badly, and the healers didn't know what healing spells made for a human would do to a phantom. Siobhan and I told everyone that we recreated Vasily's spell wholesale, but it's only a binding to human form, that's all. Nothing else. You can take it off yourself anytime you please, but you should probably leave it long enough for the healing spells to—"

Verity clenched her hand over the chain to throw it in his face, but he retreated quickly, arm raised. "But if you're awake the spells are probably close enough to finished anyway. I'm sorry, Verity, please. You were *dying*."

Maybe the explanation had been working at the back of her mind, trickling in and neutralizing her anger gradually, but Verity suddenly felt more tired than angry. She dropped the chain back on the sheets and propped herself on her hands to stare down at it. Unbound.

And she felt—right. Like a phantom. "I'm a unicorn named

Sparkles," she said, and the lie just tumbled right out and it was such a silly lie to choose, she started laughing, laughed hard enough that her throat protested and it turned into coughing.

She focused on Davin. As he tentatively lowered his shielding arm, he looked terrible, haggard shadows smeared across his face and pooling under his eyes. "I should still have taken it off earlier, I'm sorry." His voice sounded like guilt was tearing at his gut.

Verity didn't have a good answer to that, so in silence she pushed her legs off the side of the bed and only then realized that it wasn't her bed. "Why am I in Dakota's bed?" A semi-hysterical laugh slipped out. "Did you change the sheets?"

"It's bigger. And easier to have people in here to keep an eye on you without feeling like sardines. You've been sleeping for about a day and a half." Davin edged closer, like his fear of her punching him was easing. "The healer did all the bleeding wounds, but they said they couldn't do the remaining bruises until you'd rested and eaten and it was lucky you'd eaten so well just before you were hurt, because they had a little extra energy to play with."

Verity had started to check her bruises—the raincloud turning a bit ashy-white now—but she looked up at Davin when he implied he knew she'd been pulling lifeforce. But he hadn't put the prohibition back into the chain. Or so he said. There weren't any creatures around to practice on.

One thing she wanted to check immediately, though. "Mirror," she said, the effort needed to stand making her terse, but Davin seemed to understand her.

"Here." He got a good grip around her waist and supported her to the bathroom. The mirror had been cleared of the streaks she'd left on it, and the mirror realm called to her. She braced both her hands on the tile counter and drank in the feeling. She could go there, if she wanted. Go *home*.

Davin remained with her, hands on her hips, body pressed against her back. "Before you go, please, there's something I want to say to you."

"Okay." Verity closed her eyes. She was awfully weak, and hurting after even such a short walk, and she did like him there. Holding her. Liked it far too much for her own good, maybe.

"I'm sorry for something else too." He gulped, continued after a pause. "In the cell, when I saw the blood, I froze up—I shouldn't have treated you like that. I don't want to let Ghost ruin every good thing in my life and I just—I just wanted to apologize."

Verity shook her head. No, she was too emotionally tender to stand sudden hope, in addition to all her healing physical wounds. "Treated me like what? You don't owe me anything."

"But I'd like to. If you could ever forgive me."

Verity's eyes popped open and he was smiling at her in the mirror, thin and twisted. Who was she kidding, she'd already made her decision when she leaned back into his touch instead of leaving through the mirror. She turned in his grip so she could set her cheek against his shoulder and rest for a minute that way. "I'm still going to be dangerous to you. That's not going to change. Are you really sure? Because I can't..." She couldn't tell herself she should never hope for something between a human and a phantom, and believe it again.

"The vast majority of people who aren't into bloodplay manage to avoid that problem," Davin said, his laugh a rumble against her skin and his clasp of arms across her back tight and maybe a little desperate. "Really sure. Promise."

"I'm too weak to travel home at the moment anyway." Verity would have liked to stay in her current position longer, but she had bruises and also— "I really need to pee," she admitted with extra plaintiveness, which won her a great laugh, better than it deserved.

Davin stepped out while she took care of that, and after washing her hands, she stared into the mirror and tried to change her look.

It was *hard*. Frustratingly so. Verity managed to lengthen her hair a little, lift her cheekbones, but when she let go, she fell right back into her old face, if a more symmetrical version of it. The next time, she managed a different eye color. So maybe it was like an atrophied muscle. She was about to leave it for the moment, when Davin came up behind her again. She pulled her look into something with hyperfeminized facial features, well out of the average. "There. Beautiful," she told him.

Davin shook his head. "Not a hundredth as *attractive*," he said. "As just you."

"They're both me," Verity said, but fell back to her usual face again. Until she'd built up her metaphorical muscles, she supposed he was actually right. And because an answer that good deserved a reward, she turned, closed her eyes, and kissed him.

And then he had to catch her because she was getting light-headed. "Damn, I didn't know I was *that* good a kisser," he teased. "Come on, Ms. Bloodloss. Bed. And I'll come back with something for you to eat."

In the bed, Verity hooked the binding on, then off again to prove she could, then left it on. Davin was probably right about the healing spells. And it would make humans outside Dakota's posse much more comfortable, and also make it easier for her to walk around among regular humans without her face looking off. That done, she caught Davin's arm and scooted over so she could drag him down on the bed with her.

"You don't look great yourself. Come on. Meal can wait until after a nap." She scuffled around in the blankets until she had one of the extra pillows dragged between them for her to hold. "So I don't strangle you in my sleep."

"'Ware the kraken," Davin intoned somberly and then kissed her forehead. "All right. Short nap." He put his head down, and almost that fast, he was asleep.

Verity watched him for a while, hearing again the note in his voice when he'd said she was dying. She wasn't sure if she was ready for the responsibility of causing such pain. She wasn't sure when things had got serious enough between them for her to have such thoughts. But hunger triumphed and she slipped carefully out of the bed on the other side. If she stood up very slowly, she could walk around on her own without falling over, she discovered.

She looked down at the tank top and pajama bottoms someone had put her into, and decided they were good enough. She padded toward Dakota's door, only to meet Siobhan coming in. She was using a basic cane to ease some weight off her knee, but she didn't seem to be in any particular pain. When she saw Verity was up, she smiled, but it was when she searched the room to find her brother fast asleep that her face really lit.

"Thank God," she whispered, and gestured Verity to follow her into the hall.

With Verity taking care that she didn't get lightheaded, their speeds about matched. When Siobhan had gently shut the door behind them, she turned to Verity, grin spreading. "Thank you for making him sleep. I hardly dared calculate it, but I'm pretty sure he was at something crazy like forty-plus hours without more than a doze."

Verity twisted back, though of course the door was in the way now and she couldn't reevaluate his appearance in that light. No wonder he'd looked haggard. "Why? What's been happening here? I thought it was all over but the shouting when we left Ontario."

"He was determined that someone should be there to tell you about the new binding," Siobhan nodded to Verity's wrist. "When you woke up. And I guess he was afraid the shock of seeing you wake would make me forget everything I ever knew about the spell *I helped make* if I spelled him for a shift or two." Her tone turned what could have been acid annoyance into exasperated humor.

"Come on, you must be hungry." She led the way downstairs, starting the conversation back up again when they were on the ground floor and she wasn't wrangling her cane and the stairs. "Honestly, I think the guilt of not helping you in the cell was eating him alive. So he set his own penance again."

Verity stopped halfway between the pantry and the fridge. Cereal? She wanted something more substantial than that. But she wasn't sure she dared brave whatever leftovers might be oozing around in the back of the fridge. And thinking hard about food meant that her chest didn't tighten around guilt of her own about how she'd treated him on waking. But she thought they'd both forgiven each other, maybe—she hoped—and she probably should make some kind of response to Siobhan. "It all right," she said, lamely.

Siobhan pulled out a chair for her, with an extremely dubious look. She let the conversational thread drop, though. "We cooked a big batch of Texas chili last night, you don't have to worry about food." She lifted the soup pot from the fridge to the stove and then spooned out a bowl to heat in the microwave.

Verity accepted the chair. Now she'd been reminded of the events in the cell, her mind started examining those memories with the perspective of a little rest and calm. She felt like her own remembered words had slapped her in the face. Had she really confessed to being a spy? In front of the entire team? "Are...the Archivists planning to show up again now that I'm awake? To talk to me?"

"I think you're supposed to go Geneva to testify in Stiles' trial, but we haven't heard anything about when that will be yet." Siobhan set the warmed bowl in front of Verity, then remembered to go back for a spoon. A few seconds ago, Verity might have swiped up a fingerful, but worry had dulled her appetite.

"Has anyone told them about—about—" Verity stirred her spoon around. Should she be direct? Or had Siobhan dismissed it as something that had slipped by under the truth spell's hyperbole exception?

"You being a spy?" Siobhan selected a chair of her own and arranged her bad leg when she'd eased into it. "I'll admit, I'm curious. Do you consider yourself to *still* be a spy, or did that stop being true sometime in the last six years?"

"No. I stopped being a spy in my own mind perhaps five years and eleven months ago. Even if I did want to run home and tell them everything, I don't know what good it would do. What did I learn in my years here that's useful? Dakota's favorite musical is *Into the Woods*? I missed Stiles completely, and they're already pretty damn aware of that situation now without me." The smell of the chili was too much for her, whatever her mental state, so Verity dug in. "But you don't know I'm not lying."

"There's this thing called 'trust' that even binding mages tend to rely on." Siobhan leaned back, getting comfortable. "No one told the Archivists. Who would, anyway? After all, Davin's in love—"

She seemed ready to continue on, listing everyone's motives, but Verity clattered her spoon a bit too loud against the side of the bowl at the unexpected word. She corrected her aim and lifted it to her mouth to give herself an excuse not to respond right away. Love? That was a heavy word, in English. After her pretty little speech to Dakota, which type where they talking about?

Siobhan laughed, simple and bright. "Don't look so shocked. You must have had an inkling, or you wouldn't still be in the grounded realm."

"I'm too weak to travel safely at the moment," Verity said, trying for nonchalance.

Siobhan subsided into an impishly quirked smile. "Don't worry. Even if Lance felt like shooting his mouth off, Davin told the Archivists that he thought maybe Stiles had layered on a geas to make you appear to incriminate yourself to get the Quorum on her side later, and the stress of the opposing compulsions was what made you rant. And I agreed that's what it had looked like."

Verity ate another spoonful. Another kindness, stronger than she had expected. "Thank you."

Siobhan looked down and massaged her knee, seriousness creeping in. "*Are* you going to stay in the grounded realm?"

Verity stilled her spoon. "I'm…thinking about how best to work that, yes." She offered Siobhan a lopsided smile. "I do have friends here, you know." Here she finally got the truth spell off, and she still went around surprising herself with what her truth ended up being.

Siobhan huffed something that sounded like embarrassed pleasure, and went to ladle herself some chili as well. "Speaking of the clowns around here, Dakota tore a strip or two off Lance while you were out. About his choice in lovers."

Verity didn't have to care anymore, she reminded herself. She was no longer tied to Dakota. But her curiosity didn't listen, and swelled up anyway. Verity gave in. "Yeah? What did she say?"

27

Two weeks later, the setting of Stiles' trial reminded Verity of a strange cross between the courtrooms and celebrity weddings she'd seen on TV. The ranks of chairs facing a dais fit a rather informal courtroom, but the rich, gilded atmosphere of the Archives' modest ballroom—modest on the scale of royalty, and probably smaller than several other rooms filled with shelves elsewhere in the building—evoked the wedding. In both cases, ritual was a bit less regimented, but no less present, and very few of those who might be interested had actually been allowed to attend.

As Stiles and Gabe were led away, the audience of Archivists rose unhurriedly to help themselves to coffee and tea from a sideboard. Verity, Dakota, and Davin, as the only non-Archivists in the room now Gabe was gone, also rose but lingered uncomfortably on their own beside a corner of the dais. Dakota finally wandered off to peer at a painting like she was trying to download culture through her eyeballs and Davin shifted to stand beside Verity's shoulder. "Don't they…sentence them, now they've been found guilty?" Verity asked him.

"There's only one sentence. Gabe gets to choose whether to be bound to never commit that crime again, or be imprisoned. For life, or until he changes his mind about being bound. Stiles would normally get the same choice, but she's such a powerful binding mage, I suspect they won't give her the chance to be bound and then break or wiggle out of it. Or be free to go around talking to her supporters, either. She'd probably try to manipulate the Quorum into pardoning her."

"Good." Verity leaned into Davin's touch as he caressed a hand over the back of her neck, then remembered where they were. She tipped her head to check his expression, but he looked resolved, in a way. "Are you being pointed?"

Davin started slightly, then smiled at her with an edge of sheepishness. "I suppose I am. Is that all right with you?"

Verity thought about Davin losing his job, and also about Siobhan's opinion that he needed to let that particular penance go someday. "If we do it right, it is. Bring it, Archivists' Pet." She pivoted to face him and caught him in a truly wolf-whistle-worthy kiss. He was tense at first, but then he got into the humor of it and even grabbed her ass.

Dakota laughed uncomfortably and edged back into conversational distance. "Guys, the Archivists are looking."

"And thus, they have fallen prey to our cunning plan," Verity said, and Davin muffled his laugh into the curve of her neck. She disengaged enough to walk again, but kept hold of his hand. "Come on, I want to talk to them."

Verity towed Davin over near the coffee, where she planned to wait politely for Archivist Khare to finish his conversation, but he broke off as they approached and was waiting for *them* by the time they arrived. "I have a proposal for the Quorum," she said, before she lost her nerve. She glanced back at the dais. Should she wait for people to collect themselves and return there? Or would they want to reschedule for another day?

Khare inclined his head to her, and most of the other Archivists drifted into easy earshot behind him. "And we're quite interested to hear it. I gather that the other planned discussion is no longer needed." He gestured to her new binding, and she would have hidden it with her opposite hand if she hadn't been holding onto Davin. Of course they could see what was and wasn't in the new spell.

Deep breath. "I suspect you'll agree that the treaty between mages and phantoms is in need of some updating and expansion. For that, though, you'd need a steady means of communication. Perhaps you could even hire someone for the position." She paused a beat for effect, then the rest of her planned words tumbled out. "I, for instance, wouldn't be averse to a steady income. I'm no diplomat, but I could certainly carry messages. Ferry real diplomats in, if things go well. Hell, I'd be willing to play taxi and teleport people in and out of Geneva if you pay me enough." Davin's hand spasmed on hers, and when she checked his expression, he was grinning. "I could team with your investigator so you have one who can jump on problems right as they appear."

Khare's brows rose, and Verity got the sense that he wasn't often caught that much by surprise. He recovered himself quickly and smoothly, though. "What of the holes between realms that were caused by your earlier teleportation? Has that problem been solved?"

Verity freed her hand from Davin's, and unhooked her binding. She let her hand hang open so the Archivists could see the links draped across her fingers before she curled the chain into her hand, unseen. "It was the active binding spell that tore the boundary. Inactive spell, no tears. I'll take it off before I teleport anywhere."

Khare dipped his chin in a nod, and his tone grew slightly weightier. "And you would be conveying information back to the phantoms as well?"

Verity reminded herself that she had little to lose now that she was unbound, and hooked the bracelet back on to stall while she made sure she had just the words she wanted laid out in her mind. Faint heart never won. "Of course I will. I have family there. I'm not going to go searching for secrets while I'm here, but I'm not going to not talk to my family while I'm there either. Don't use me to teleport anyone on secret mage business."

Khare's next nod was sharper, like he approved, though there was a low shush of murmuring behind him. "That is fair."

Verity held up her hands. This was going much better than she'd expected. She hadn't had time to get all her disclaimers in yet. "I can't make any promises about anyone at home being in a mood to deal at the moment, of course."

"Certainly. We will bear that in mind in our discussion of your proposal." Khare bowed over his hands to her, and she returned the gesture this time. In this situation, she presumed it was a dismissal.

She hooked her arm into Davin's and went to hook onto Dakota on the other side. Dakota allowed it, but leaned across her to frown at Davin. "Did you know about this plan?"

"Nope," Davin said. He slid Verity a sideways look, blankness hiding some worry. "Are you only staying because you want to seek out Archivist Stiles' supporters?"

"I'll keep an ear to the ground, certainly. But that's not the only reason I'm staying." Verity wasn't sure if she could make herself say it out loud, but it seemed Davin needed to hear it, so she'd try. "I mean, a big reason's you. This—us—it could be something serious, right? Just don't ask me to use the L-word yet, okay?"

Dakota grumbled under her breath, but didn't seem angry. Davin laughed and drew Verity in closer, though she was still attached at the elbow on the other side. "It's a deal. And I notice Quorum hasn't fired me yet for consorting with a phantom."

"Give them time. They still have to discuss," Verity told them, but her voice skimmed across the surface of laughter she was holding in. She towed the two along with her toward the exit and the nearest mirror in the hallway. Maybe this would all work out, though. Eventually, after the Quorum had had enough "at length" for their discussion.

28

In fact, Verity was hired after only a week. There were a lot of details to work out yet, but they'd named a number, and she'd negotiated them upward. And then she'd gone shopping. In the bathroom she shared with Dakota, she was trying on the fruits of her spree now. She settled her military-style jacket, dark blue with gold braid and buttons, over her red tank top, and smoothed her fingertips over the couple areas of hand-sewn red where the epaulets had been. She was a bit rusty at alteration as well. She pulled on the red satin gloves she'd made fingerless, and then picked up the hair clip with a feather and beads on the ends of two leather thongs. Still pretty restrained by the standards of home, but she liked it.

Dakota slipped in from her room while Verity was experimenting with setting the clip different heights above her ear. "Woah," she said, and gestured for Verity to face her. Verity snapped in the clip and then complied. "You—that's a big change."

"I felt in the mood for one." Verity wasn't completely sure what had motivated her—when she first arrived in the grounded realm, she'd dressed as boring as possible to blend in. And then somehow that had turned into…maybe dressing as boring as possible so as not to draw attention to the fact she was a phantom, or maybe being too stressed out with being in captivity to care? She wasn't sure.

"You look like a phantom," Dakota said, then dipped her head in embarrassment at the obviousness of the comment.

"I'll tell you a secret." Verity leaned in to her ear to whisper. "I *am* a phantom." When Dakota protested, she waved her off, laughing. "No, I know what you meant. Now that you've visited the mirror realm."

Dakota huffed in response, a little bit of a laugh, a little bit of continuing embarrassment. She watched Verity as she checked her clothes one more time in the mirror. "You laugh so much more when you're comfortable."

"What?" Verity turned back to her with a slight frown. That could well be true, but she had no idea where it had come from.

"I mean, you're always funny, but I guess I got used to you being too serious to join in the laughter." Dakota rubbed a hand along the thigh of her jeans, uncomfortable herself. "You were…funny to make people pay attention to you, weren't you? It struck me, when Davin and Siobhan got here and he was talking to *you* all the time, and it made me realize people hadn't really, before."

"I didn't really think about it myself, either. Maybe you're getting observant in your old age." And Verity should probably stop thinking her of as being twenty years old, as well, with the corresponding maturity. Verity leaned the other way to see through the open door into her room. "Davin's going to be here in a minute, then we'll be heading off."

"Have you—" Dakota looked at her hands. "Thought about where you're going to live?"

"I'm not moving back to the mirror realm, we're just visiting." Verity touched her hair. And she was getting a little nervous about that visit now, if she was honest. "I dropped off a note for my parents that I'm alive, after what they must have heard from Pteil, but I do owe them a proper visit. Then I'll come back here and take up being a messenger and teleporting for the Quorum."

"No, here, I mean." Dakota edged closer, then braced her feet as if giving a speech. "Since you can be based anywhere in the grounded realm and still teleport wherever. And I wondered—but of course, you probably don't want to stay here. I mean, with bad memories of being bound. And there's no particular reason you should. But if you wanted to. You wouldn't have to pay rent..."

Verity's nervousness smoothed out as she focused on Dakota and suppressed any hint of a laugh. "Are you trying to convince me to stay, or to leave, Dakota?"

"I thought maybe you might want to stay." Dakota got softer and looked at the floor. "I know I've taken you for granted..."

Verity considered saying, "yes, you have," but that seemed unnecessarily snarky. She let silence be her agreement instead.

"But I would like you to stay." Saying the words lent Dakota a little confidence, and she looked up. "Maybe we could start over. Pretend like we just met, the teleporter and the hunter, and get to know each other properly. You're so good with people—"

Verity winced. "Better at manipulating people, some would say."

"Well. Two sides of the same coin." Dakota shrugged and smiled lopsidedly.

Verity's impulse to agree was nearly immediate, but she hesitated, thinking it over to be absolutely sure. She'd told Siobhan she had friends, and maybe she should also admit Dakota was one of them, as annoying as she sometimes was. And it wasn't like she was ready to run a human life in the grounded realm completely on her own, even with her years of experience. "Okay. Thank you."

Dakota stared at her for a second like she thought she hadn't heard right. "Really?" When Verity nodded, she grinned. "And needing to ask that question will take a little getting used to."

"What do you mean?" Verity asked, startled. Was it that obvious how far down Davin had stripped the binding? She'd rather hoped that most people other than the Quorum would assume it was mostly the same, with a few modifications to avoid tearing holes. Had Dakota seen it in the spell herself?

Dakota shook her head, and reached out to touch Verity's bracelet. "No, I can't really tell that level of detail about the new spell. But you obviously can remove the binding and teleport without me, and don't have to follow my orders anymore. I'm not completely dumb as a box of hammers. Like hell Davin would have put the truth spell back in. I'm not quite sure what the binding is even for anymore, to be honest."

Verity figured she owed the other woman a little honesty in return. She unhooked the bracelet and let her features settle back into a phantom's symmetry long enough for Dakota to see. "To keep me looking normal so as to not freak out the regular humans. And the mages too, for that matter."

"That's probably a side benefit of staying here." Dakota watched with interest as Verity put the binding back on, nodded, then turned to go. "People will assume the binding spell hasn't changed much either, and not worry about you." She lifted her fingertips as she reached the door into her own room. "Have a good trip."

Dakota made an excellent point, which bothered Verity for some reason, and then bothered her that she was bothered. She clearly needed to start over getting to know Dakota as well.

She heard the door to her room open, and Davin joined her a moment later. She held out her hand to him. "Ready?" When he nodded, she still found herself hesitating. "Dakota just asked me to live here when I take up the new duties for the Quorum, and I think I agreed. Is that okay with you?"

Davin was surprised into a laugh as he took her hand. "Do you think she'll drive you completely crazy?"

"Probably not *completely*." Verity pulled a face at him, and he kissed her in lieu of agreeing explicitly to the living arrangements. She tugged him to face the mirror. That was all right then. But first, they had a visit to make. Three steps to home.

One…

ACKNOWLEDGMENTS

This book was truly born of my love of urban fantasy, so I think this section should begin with those authors whose books I devoured, sinking into the world of ordinary people caught up by magic: Tanya Huff, Patty Briggs, Jim Butcher, Ilona Andrews, and Rachel Caine were some of the very earliest for me. I'm sure there were others, swallowed by the march of time and decay of memory, but all those books were in my hands when it started. It started, in fact, when I was in undergrad and graduate school for archaeology, meaning I looked at not only the urban fantasy heroine, but her team, the creatures and monsters among them. What about those creatures? What about their *culture*?

My astoundingly amazing critique group, Corry L. Lee, Erin M. Evans, Kate Marshall, Monte Cook, Shanna Germain, and Susan Morris, offered keen suggestions on not just the manuscript but the outline and even the cover copy, as well as wise advice in general. Django Wexler and my agent, Cameron McClure, also helped shape the original manuscript with their feedback. Shannon Page provided copy editing, and Kate Marshall cover design and formatting. Duane Wilkins at the University Bookstore and Peter Honigstock at Powell's have generously supported me and many other Pacific Northwest authors over the years.

Other supporters are, as ever, too numerous to name, among my family and the local communities of speculative fiction writers, archaeologists, and choristers. Thank you all!

Get a sneak peak of a new novella
in the SILVER series

Mistaken Captives

Faith's cheek was smashed against something unyielding and chill. She was lying on something hard. That much came to her in a half-awake haze, and then adrenaline burst through her body. Her heart pounded as her eyes snapped open. Those men. They'd killed Laurence and kidnapped her.

She was lying on industrial tile and staring at an industrial table leg bolted to the floor. Beyond it, there were floor-level cabinets under a counter at the edge of the room. Everything was lit with the slightly harsh wash of cheap fluorescent light banks, though with a hole of dimness in the center of the room like a single bank had burned out. Faith sat up, swiping at her mouth and nose, though of course there was nothing there now, and the weird lingering chemical-y scent in every breath was just her imagination.

Everything was silent, but she peered into every corner anyway. Nothing moved, no sign of the kidnappers, though there was a person-sized lump on the floor on the other side of the table. Faith's pounding heart made her peer into every corner a second time, before she moved. God, if that was Laurence's body she'd probably puke or something, but she absolutely had to know.

He still had a cloth over his mouth and nose, slid slightly off center, so maybe the chemical smell wasn't her imagination after all. Faith yanked it off and tossed it as far as she could. He was breathing. She could see that even before she took his pulse. It felt strong enough, but she didn't have much basis for comparison, especially since her hands were shaking so hard she wasn't sure she had her fingers placed exactly right on his neck. He was flat on his back, though his arms were flopped, one on his chest, one up near his head, like someone had dragged him in by the ankles and not worried about how his arms knocked around.

His shirt was completely soaked with blood from chest to hem, the fabric bunched up around the jagged tear crossing it. The top of his jeans was black and damp, though it looked like the denim hadn't wicked as far. Reminded of the splatter, she looked down at her own shirt, but the brown dots there seemed so polite in comparison.

Faith groped for her first-aid training, but her thoughts felt like they were shaking at the same frequency as her hands. Put pressure on the wound to stop the bleeding, but the blood she could see was browning, drying. So the bleeding had already stopped. You weren't supposed to ever remove the compress, just keep up the pressure until help arrived, but when were they going to get help? She knew she should leave it alone, but she couldn't help herself. She needed to know how bad it was. She took one side of the shirt between thumb and forefinger and lifted it away, wincing at the blood sticking it down.

Nothing. Bloody skin, yes, but it looked smooth. Faith moved around to kneel at Laurence's side, and carefully rolled the shirt fabric as high as possible over his chest. She couldn't see even a scratch. But that couldn't be right. It had to be under there somewhere. She reached out to wipe at the blood, but stopped herself. She was in enough danger from disease as it was. She pushed to her feet. Maybe there was something around here to wipe with, before she went so far as sacrificing her shirt. She didn't think kidnappers usually left paper towels lying around in their basement prisons, but basement prisons didn't usually have sturdy tables and cabinets.

When she surveyed the room again in the patchy light, she suddenly realized what it reminded her of: Chem 101. It was like an abandoned classroom, or maybe a low-level industrial lab. Something with a lot of workspace and supplies, but no facilities for really heavy chemicals.

There were three doors. One behind them, which Faith set aside for the moment. Laurence's head was pointed in that direction, so whoever had dragged him in had probably left the same way and locked it behind themselves. That left one door at the back of the room, and one at the side. She went around the other side of the huge central table to avoid stepping on Laurence, and arrived at the back door first. As she got closer, she saw it even had an official exit sign above, but smashed so it no longer illuminated. She tried the handle, and it turned like it wasn't locked, but the door wouldn't move a millimeter. Blocked. Faith kicked it experimentally, and it thudded dully. No give. Her brain caught up a second later, and she stopped breathing for a second. What if the kidnappers heard the noise and came running?

She forced herself to take a breath. Come running to see what? That their kidnappees were banging around, trying to get out? That couldn't be unexpected. If they didn't trust all the doors to hold, they would have tied them up.

If the kidnappers had meant to let them go, they would have hidden their faces. Faith braced herself on the door handle again as the thought bubbled up. The light-headedness was probably left over from the chloroform or whatever had been used to knock her out, she told herself. Where did she know that from? Somewhere real, or a mystery novel? Or worse, her far-too-extensive *CSI* viewing habits? She knew better than to accept those as the full truth.

Anyway, it didn't matter. She could still scout their prison. And help Laurence.

The second door had no handle, but when she hooked her fingers into the hole where the entire assembly had been removed, it opened onto a tiny, windowless bathroom. The room had a toilet, a mirror, and a sink with an eye-wash attachment bolted onto the side. And a stack of one-ply institutional-looking toilet paper rolls in the corner. Faith grabbed one, ripped off the outer wrapper, and wrapped herself a nice wad around her hand before dampening it at the sink.

When she returned to Laurence, the blood resisted her, too sticky to wipe without so much pressure that the toilet paper wore away. But she managed to remove enough to be sure.

He had no injury. Whatsoever.

Faith sat back on her heels and shucked the bloody mass of paper off her hand. A voice at the back of her head lectured about washing her hands immediately, but she ignored it. Had this been *staged*? Was Laurence working with the kidnappers? They'd slashed some fake blood pouch and then—dumped him in here with her? Why? He could be off showering and then giggling with his compatriots over a hot meal while she assumed he was dead.

Faith pinched the inside of Laurence's forearm, digging her fingernails in. He had better not be faking unconsciousness. He moaned and weakly pulled that arm away, ending with it only flopped a little closer to his body.

"What the *fuck*." Saying it out loud helped Faith focus a little. She had some questions for Laurence, so maybe it was time to help him wake up. She stood and returned to the bathroom to wash her hands thoroughly. She drank straight from the faucet, and then cupped her hands underneath for lack of anything better to carry water in.

Most of it leaked out before she made it to Laurence, but enough remained to spatter his face when she opened her hands. On the second trip, she had more success, and opened her hands fast enough the water fell all at once and made a satisfying splat noise.

Laurence sputtered, coughed, and dragged his forearm over his face to clear the worst of the water before he opened his eyes. "Lady."

Faith presumed he meant her. She stepped back a little, to be out of range if he sat up and reached for her. "What? I needed you awake. You have some explaining to do. What was all that with the fake blood? Are you with those guys?"

Instead of sitting up, Laurence fanned fingertips over the side of his face like his head was killing him. "Fake—?" His other hand went to this stomach, and slid over the damp, smooth skin. "No, they definitely got me—small cuts can still bleed—" His excuse stumbled over itself, like he was trying to remember a script through a hangover.

Locks clunked on the other side of the door Faith had picked as their entry point, and she ignored Laurence to retreat to the end of the table farthest from that door. She had nowhere to go if the kidnappers did come after her—the bathroom door swung outward, so she could hardly barricade herself in there—

but she felt at least a little better with the table between her and them. She gritted her teeth, and told herself that if they'd wanted her dead, she would be dead. Or raped. Or maybe they'd wanted her to wake up first—fuck. Faith clenched her fists. Just let them try.

The dark-skinned man entered alone, a huge dog at his heels. It was whitish gray and lean like it was a wolf cross. The dog growled, a low, warning sound rather than something that sounded like a prelude to an attack. In contrast, the man held his hands open, pretending he was nonthreatening. "You're awake. Good." He nodded to Laurence, who struggled into a sitting position, panting as if in great pain. "Sorry you got dragged along, but you were in the way. Don't worry, though. When the Roanokes ransom Susan, we'll throw you in for free." He laughed. "Think of it like a vacation."

Faith tried to measure the man's distance from the open door behind him from the corner of her eye, but the dog looked at her and paced over to stand more directly in her path. It was like he'd sensed she was thinking of making a run for it. She focused her attention on the man again. He didn't sound like a kidnapper. He sounded like a frat boy assuring a school administrator that the beer he'd just dumped on his head would wash out, barely able to hold in his snickers long enough to get the words out.

It took her longer than it should have to process that, because it made no sense. "Susan? What the fuck are you talking about? I'm not Susan." Did she even look like Susan? She hadn't seen her own doppelganger in the crowd, but she hadn't had long to look. There had been other women with Asian features, but Faith's had been diluted since her Thai grandmother. She'd have thought she could never be mistaken for white or Thai.

Laurence got a good grip on the table and hauled himself up. He growled, sounding remarkably canine himself. Once there, he swayed, deathly pale, and failed to launch himself at the kidnapper in a whirlwind of violence, as had clearly been his intention.

The kidnapper chuckled. "I'd heal up for a bit before you try anything, if I were you. We had to keep adding chloroform for longer than we'd intended. You probably lost some brain cells." He paused, and Faith's words finally seemed to catch up with him. He frowned at her, seeming to see her properly for the first time. "Oh, please. The only human at the Were wedding? You think we're stupid?"

"Shut. Up." Laurence got paler, if that was possible. "She's not Susan. She's some—waitress."

The kidnapper rounded on the dog. "You said it was her, Amak!"

Faith drew in a deep breath. Insane. At least one of their kidnappers was stark fucking nuts, blaming his pet when things went wrong. Maybe that was good? Maybe it meant he'd make more mistakes? Her heart was beating so fast she could hardly breathe, though. She had a terrible feeling that insanity in her captors would make her situation even worse.

And then the dog sort of—stretched and twisted and then there was a naked man straightening to his feet, and Faith backed up until she hit the counter behind her. In the movies, reality blipped like that and you didn't even blink, but she was looking at this with her eyes, and deep in her mind she *knew* that and so her brain ground to a stop. It couldn't—the dog hadn't—

"You saw her too," the naked man said. He had black hair, like the second kidnapper. He was the second kidnapper.

"Talking to her son." He tipped his nose up, inhaled deeply. "It's not like you can mistake the scent."

"But what if she's the *wrong* human?" The dark-skinned man whined.

Amak crossed his arms. He seemed to be answering his friend, but he looked at Faith as he spoke. "If she is, we'll have to find somewhere to dump the body. She just saw me shift, after all." He shook his head with simulated frustration. "What a pain in the tail."

Clarity snatched Faith up and held her above the situation for a breath, two. If she wasn't Susan, these men would kill her. Right now he was just threatening her to make her drop what he thought was an act, but something told her they really would carry out that threat if they became convinced of the truth. Laurence was in no shape to do anything, and she couldn't take the kidnappers on unarmed, two to one. Ergo, she needed to be Susan.

Two to one when one of the men had been a dog. Or a wolf.

Faith ruthlessly pushed that aside. She could think about special effects or hallucinations after anesthesia later. Right now, she needed to be Susan, and stay alive. "All right, fine. We can stop the act, Laurence. It's clear they're not going to let me go." She curved her lips up in an expression that was nothing like a smile at Amak. "Can't blame a girl for trying, can you?"